DEADLY ANGELS

Ricki Thomas

A Wild Wolf Publication

Published by Wild Wolf Publishing in 2015

Copyright © 2015 Ricki Thomas

First print

ISBN: 978-1-907954-44-3

Also available as an e-book

www.wildwolfpublishing.com

Further titles from the author

Hope's Vengeance (2009)
Unlikely Killer (2010)
Bloody Mary (2011)
Holiday of the Dead (2011, contributor)
Bonfire Night (2013)
Wild Wolf's Twisted Tails (2013, contributor)
Black Park (2013)
Rings of Death (2014)

Dedication

Roxan Couch and Lesley Willis, that New Year's Eve was unforgettable ... Take a dire situation and throw in three crazy chicks and a failing hospital ... I haven't laughed so hard since. Sharing some of the darkest days of my life with you two amazing women gave me the strength to get through. I can never thank you both enough for being by my side, then and now.

And not forgetting Lady Anouska Semp, of course, whose wonderful eccentricity has kept me laughing since. Those dark days are history now, and I'm so happy we came through them with this friendship.

Finally, to the staff at Weston Park, Sheffield, and Barnsley General, thank you a million times – I'm still here because of you guys.

Chapter 1
Notes from the Dead

'Bitch hounds going to kill me. This is all I can do. She's coming. Swallow this now.'

"It was lodged in his oesophagus."

"How did he die?"

"Inconclusive."

Thirsk squinted as the dazzling headlights of another car blinded him and he gripped the steering wheel hard, annoyed. He glanced at the clear bag on the passenger seat containing the extraordinary evidence recovered during the routine post-mortem of a man dead before his time – a handwritten message he had swallowed, one that made no sense but was mysterious enough to warrant Hugh Smythe to call him. What could it mean? He would have to deal with it, but not now, the meeting he had been dreading with the Superintendent was looming.

His mobile buzzed and for once the intrusion was welcome. He answered abruptly, "What?"

"Are you driving, guv?"

"What do you want, Toni?"

"Pull over and I'll tell you. Can't have you breaking the law, can we?"

Sighing dramatically, he pulled into a lay-by, leaving the engine running for warmth. "What?"

"I called the hospital for that next-of-kin you wanted me to find, I've got her name and address here."

"You made me stop my car for that? I'm in a hurry, you know." Thirsk watched the ring-road traffic over his shoulder and accelerated into a gap.

"I just figured you could see her while you're out, rather than come back here and all that messing about."

"No can do, I don't have time tonight and I haven't got time for this call either."

He was about to hang up but Toni's enthusiastic voice persevered. "Twelve Astbury Cottages, and the village is only a couple of miles from your apartment. Night, boss."

Thirsk bristled as he realised she had put the phone down, somehow always able to get the better of him no matter what. Whippersnapper! He glanced at the clock on the dashboard. He had forty minutes to get to the restaurant and still needed to change into a smarter outfit, but the enigmatic note was persuasive. Passing a sign for Astbury, he indicated left. He may as well call in.

Minutes later, Thirsk parked beside the tiny cottage that had been built for a farmhand and his family alongside twenty more in the village of Astbury, and he rapped at the roadside door, pushing the dangling ivy aside. Although a light glimmered through a gap in the curtains, nobody appeared and he tapped again, louder. "Can I help you?"

The voice had come from behind and Thirsk was startled as he turned. "I'm looking for... damn," Toni had not given a name for the address, "the occupier."

"I'm her mother and I can tell you she won't want to see you, so would you mind coming back some other time." The woman who was roughly his age dragged a key from her pocket and fed it into the cast-iron lock.

"It's about Tobias Sutherland," he showed his badge, "I'm Detective Chief Inspector Thirsk."

Rhea Parkins frowned. "I see. Kate's inside." She turned the key and followed him in. They found Kate curled into the end of a sofa, the barely-there lighting silhouetting her into the sombre figure she was. The wetness on her cheeks glistened as she glanced at them dolefully, intruders to her cavern of doom. "Kate, this is a police inspector. He's here about Toby."

"It doesn't matter what you say to me. He's gone and nothing will bring him back." Somehow she curled into a tinier ball and Thirsk considered she may slip through the cushions and never be seen again.

"I've just come from the hospital after the pathologist called me about a matter found during the post-mortem." Kate winced at the words, the harsh reminder that her husband no longer felt or cared, and her face crumpled. Thirsk had never understood women, their illogically heightened emotions and embarrassing tears. "Oh, and I'm sorry for your loss."

Rhea sauntered to the corner and fished for the lamp switch, and instantly a pleasant, homely glow flooded the quaint room. "Why would the pathologist involve... unless..." She laid a hand protectively on her daughter's head. "Did something bad happen to Toby?"

"Kate, would bitch hounds mean anything to you?"

She regarded him, curious. "*The baying of hounds at the grim gate of death ring out to herald me to the underworld.*" Noticing the officer's confusion she elaborated, "He said that before he died, he was in a right state. You see, Toby is – he was – an historian and his speciality was Greek mythology. The goddess Hecate's ghostly dogs would howl to indicate her presence, sometimes a prelude to death, so when a female annoyed or upset him, he'd call her a bitch hound. It was just his little quirk. One of the many." The tears that had flowed during her recollection spilled from her jaw to her arm and she tried impossibly to choke them into control. "Maybe he was trying to tell me they were coming after him but I didn't understand."

"Right. Thanks." Thirsk was desperate to escape the heavy atmosphere, not one to understand outpouring grief, and he ducked under the low frame in his hurry to leave the room, eager to dispel the cloud of darkness with fresh air.

Rhea approached from behind as he fidgeted with the front door. "That's it? You come in here out of the blue, tell us something happened during the post-mortem, ask a ridiculously bizarre question and just leave without even giving us a modicum of a reason? I don't bloody think so."

Like a prisoner caught escaping the camp, Thirsk mumbled to the woman, "How well did you know Tobias?"

"He was my son-in-law, what do you think?"

"Not at all, then. Thanks for your help, Mrs – um – Kate's mum."

Another attempt at freedom was thwarted as she stood between him and the door. "Do I have to chain you up to keep you long enough for some answers?" She saw the tempered smile and her cheeks reddened slightly as she fiddled with her wedding ring, an ongoing habit despite her husband's death three years previously. "Inspector, just tell me what's going on. That's my daughter in there and she's heartbroken. At least let me give her some kind of reason in all this madness."

With a reluctant sigh, Thirsk released the door handle. "I don't know myself, that's why I need to ask questions and I doubt you'll know enough about the ins and outs of Tobias's life to give me the answers. Until Kate's ready to talk, I may as well bang my head against the wall."

"Try me. Take me for a drink, somewhere you can be frank without upsetting my girl. I'll do my damnedest to fill in the gaps."

Everybody and their dogs assumed Hugh and Marcus were lovers because they flat-shared, but the truth was banal in comparison. Having met at medical school, they had both started their careers as newlyweds and subsequently lost their wives to one drama or another, leaving them both in need of a roof over their heads and a good laugh. It had seemed obvious the pair should rent together. However, neither bothered to dispel the rumours, they were of little matter. Hugh had finished work hours earlier than his friend, an anaesthetist on a regular late shift, and normally he would have taken a book to bed by now, but the post-mortem earlier that day had unsettled him.

Marcus blustered in alongside the delicious, greasy smell of back-street takeaway. "Oh, I would have bought two kebabs if I'd known you were still awake."

"I'll swap you a third for two cans of beer."

Flinging his jacket over the back of his chair, Marcus slumped into the cushions that had shaped to fit his body over the years. "Deal." He grasped the beer that Hugh had cracked open and divided the pitta bread and chilli-laden meat. "What's keeping you up?"

"I found a handwritten note inside one of my bodies today."

Marcus snorted as he took a bite. "What, *'Boo – I can see you'*, or something like that?"

"It was as if he was predicting his death. His murder. I called the police."

"And?"

Hugh shrugged. "That's it. He put the note in a bag and took it with him. Virtually not a word. Mind you, it was Thirsk and you never know what to expect with him."

"I have yet to meet him. So is he going to let you know what it's all about?"

"No idea." Hugh fished into his trouser pocket and pulled out a folded sheet of paper, straightening it before setting it on the table. "I probably shouldn't have, but I photocopied it before he arrived."

"Pretty cloak and dagger, eh? What's the story on the patient?"

"He was a young bloke in his twenties, Tobias Sutherland…"

"Had a hernia op a week or so ago?"

"That's right."

"I was the anaesthetist. I hadn't heard he'd died – nothing to do with my work, I hope. No, I would have heard about it if it was."

"That's the thing, I can't really find a reason for his death. He was healthy before he went in, breezed through the op and was due to go home the next day, but his liver began to fail. They took him to the SHDU and by the next evening he was dead. I found nothing during the PM that could explain what happened to him."

"Intriguing. I guess you've sent samples to toxicology."

"Of course."

Although a quiet man, Marcus was popular, mainly for his talent of listening. "I'll keep my ear to the ground for what the gossips are saying."

Superintendent Fitzpatrick bristled as he ordered a second glass of wine from the waiter. "Been stood up, sir?"

"What business is it of yours?"

"Sorry, sir, I didn't mean to offend you. It's just we have other guests waiting and it's an hour past your booking."

Fitzpatrick angrily retrieved his mobile from his pocket and found Thirsk's number. "If he doesn't answer this time I'll be out of your hair. Thirsk, where the hell are you?"

The line hung silent for a few seconds and Fitzpatrick imagined he could hear cogs of lies whirring in the detective's mind. "Sir, I'm sorry. I was called in to the hospital today about an inconclusive post-mortem and I started some minor investigations. Dinner totally slipped my mind."

"Utter bollocks and you know it. You've been fighting off promotion for so long I'm beginning to wonder if it's really what you want."

"You know I want it, it's just..."

"You're petrified to take the next step. You're stuck in a rut in every area of your life and you're too damned scared to do anything about it. I'm tempted to wash my bloody hands of you."

"Sir, no. Look, forget promotion, forget everything else. Stay there. I'm just down the road, I'll be there in five. I'm bringing a lady to see you so don't go anywhere. In fact, order a bottle of wine and some fiddly finger foods, that'll give you something to do."

"Are you keeping the table, sir?" The waiter watched as Fitzpatrick slammed the mobile onto the serviette.

"Get me the wine menu. And some canapés."

By the time Thirsk arrived, Rhea in tow, the starters and chardonnay were on the table, and using his impeccable manners to hide his irritation, Fitzpatrick welcomed them both warmly. "It's lovely to meet you, Mrs Parkins – may I call you Rhea? Do you mind me asking why we're meeting?"

"Inspector Thirsk thinks my son-in-law was murdered."

"May have been." Thirsk brought the evidence bag from his pocket and explained the situation to his superior, and Fitzpatrick listened with interest as he filled himself with vol-au-vents and petit-fours, too hungry to wait for the main course. "So I brought Rhea with me to tell you about Tobias's allegations in the hours leading to his death. Go on, Rhea."

She took a sip of Dutch courage as she prepared herself. "I thought it was just the liver failure making him go mad, you know, toxins swamping his body and all that. Toby was very ill.

He was so agitated, as if in utter panic. Whether his problem was real or imaginary, there's no doubt that Toby was terrified.

"He'd been on the waiting list for a stupidly long time, so by the time he went for the operation, Toby was actually looking forward to going under the knife. That was last Tuesday. It was a routine procedure and everything went to plan. Toby was improving well and on Thursday afternoon the doctors told him he'd be able to go home on Friday. Then in the early hours of Friday morning, Kate got a call saying that his condition has worsened and that he was being moved to high dependency, or SHDU, or whatever they call it nowadays. She rang me and I took her straight there. Kate can't drive, you see."

Thirsk snatched a glance at Fitzpatrick, hoping the intrigue would keep his attention to the end and he refilled Rhea's glass. She sipped, grateful. "I went in with her. We were expecting him to be unconscious – when you see people in intensive care on the telly they always are – but Toby was very much awake and something had scared him greatly. I mentioned this to the nurse and she told me it was because his brain hadn't been getting enough oxygen. She said that could make people go crazy. But she wasn't concerned, so nor was I. I settled Kate with him and went home to bed."

Fitzpatrick was tiring of the unfortunate story. "I can understand this has troubled you, Rhea, but..."

"Sir, shut up and keep listening." Affronted, Fitzpatrick glared at Thirsk, who said, "Carry on, Rhea."

"I slept until noon. I wouldn't have woken then, I was so tired, but Kate called me in a panic. She said Toby's condition was getting worse, that he was completely yellow. Like a stale banana, she said. I drove straight there and was shocked to see Toby completely delirious. He kept saying things like the bitch hound had drugged him, or the bitch hounds were killing him."

"That's the bit that drew my attention here, sir, the flipping between the two. Like he's talking about different people."

"Or he is simply delusional through illness, of course." Fitzpatrick waved to the waiter who dutifully stepped forward with his notepad and pen. "I'm sure neither of you will mind if I order for all of us, but I can't wait any longer, I'm starving. Three steak au poivre flambé au cognac, medium rare with seasonal vegetables. You're not a vegetarian are you, Rhea?"

"Well, no, but I'd rather have the fish."

"Seared swordfish with onion, lemon and rosemary coulis, madam," the waiter suggested and she nodded. He added, "And the vegetable?"

"I'll just have steak, thanks. Well done." Thirsk wanted to laugh at his joke, but the subject of the occasion was too sombre. He poured more wine into Rhea's glass. "So, Tobias was aggravated, accusing either a woman, or several women of trying to kill him."

"Poppycock."

"Sir, just listen. Go on, Rhea."

"Well, we listened to what the doctors told us, that his brain was firing off due to lack of oxygen, that they were treating his liver failure and that they had no reason to believe he wouldn't get better. Eventually they sedated him and both Kate and I were pleased they had. It was horrid to see him upset when he was so ill."

Disgruntled with Thirsk's disrespect, Fitzpatrick glowered. "So let me guess: the man died and you're suspicious because of the things he said when his brain was firing off erratically."

Thirsk prodded the evidence bag. "I'm suspicious because of this. If a man is dying he may write a note, I accept that, but I don't accept he'd swallow it unless he really believed there was a threat."

"In your little scenario who are you accusing?" Fitzpatrick glared at Thirsk, whose eyes met the tablecloth, avoiding his boss. He hadn't thought that far ahead. "Rhea?"

She shrugged. "Toby had no enemies, he was an all-round good guy."

"We've got a full caseload already, so if you're attempting to make me authorise an investigation into Kendrick Hospital, you can bloody well think again. I apologise for my language, Rhea."

"Sir, there's something there, I can feel it." Thirsk was not one to beg and his plea jolted Fitzpatrick. "Just me. Well, just me and Toni Fowler. She's only a rookie so her time won't you cost much."

"I have friends very high up in that hospital, Thirsk. If I hear of you treading on even a single toe, you'll have hell to pay. Now, what about your promotion?"

"I'm sure that can wait until we haven't got company."

Chapter 2
Old People Die

"Hey you, whatever your name is, come here. There's something wrong with Nellie." Angela used a stage whisper to avoid disturbing the other patients in the bay and she tapped the elderly woman on the hand to rouse her, checking the line to the cannula simultaneously. Nellie made no response.

Irritated at the slight, Halina strolled from the nursing station to assist her superior. "What's up?"

"Nellie's not responding." Angela shook the woman's frail shoulders gently. "Go and get an obs machine. Quick."

The patient in the next bed lay watching the drama, the most exciting thing to have happened during her lengthy stay of tedious days and disturbed, sleepless nights. "She was gurgling a while ago, sort of grunting and moving around."

"Yeah, thanks Pat." Angela dragged the curtain around the bed for privacy as Halina brought the equipment through, and she scrabbled in the tray, clipping the pulse monitor to Nellie's finger. There was no output and the two nurses glanced at each other. "Go and bleep the on-call doctor. Do you know how to do that?"

Disgruntled, she scowled at Angela. "Of course I do."

Angela usually relished the graveyard shift, which she did four weeks out of eight. Most of the patients would sleep through without a problem and demanding doctors or indignant relatives were an infrequent burden. Long and quiet hours, interrupted only by the drug rounds and regular observations – so easy nowadays with the automatic machinery that monitored the heart, blood pressure, breathing rate and oxygen levels at the press of a button.

As a result of budget cuts within the National Health Service, only a few staff worked nights, but this gave her the freedom to put her feet up and read the gripping novels she adored without concern of her slackness being reported.

16

Nellie Gleeson dying unexpectedly had not been part of the plan and she was annoyed. Doctor Nelson, world-weary and sleep deprived, approached the desk and propped himself against it. "Can you let a relative know I've pronounced the death?"

Halina was hovering nearby, hands behind her back, aware her presence was unwelcome – Angela's offhand dismissal when she had arrived on the ward had broadcast that loud and clear. "She was fine when I changed her drip earlier."

He sighed as he patted her shoulder. "She was ninety, old people die."

Halina smiled and took a vacant seat, grateful for his reassurance. "Was it the infection, do you think?"

"It shouldn't be, not with the medication she was on, but I doubt they'll do a post-mortem on somebody her age." He stroked his beard, youthfully wispy, into place. "It'll be natural causes."

Angela found the number she had been searching for and grasped the receiver, dialling an outside line. "Is that Nicholas Gleeson? I'm calling from the hospital. It's about your mother."

John sat straight, fully awake now. "What do you mean, she's dead? She can't be. She was fine when I visited her earlier. She can't be."

Beside her husband, Fran shifted up the pillows, propping herself on her arm as she listened to one side of the conversation, the subject obvious. She rubbed his shoulder gently, willing emotional support as he slammed the phone down. "That was Nicholas. Mum's died."

"I gathered. Are you okay?"

He shook his head and swung his feet over the side of the bed. "You know what this means, don't you? It means we don't inherit a bloody penny. She was going to change her will when she got out of hospital, she promised me."

"I know, but if it's too late, it's too late. We're used to having no money anyway."

He stood, feeding his feet into slippers that warmed instantly. "It's the bloody principle, damn it. Mum and dad had two sons and dad would have wanted me to have my fair share, you know that." Collecting his tartan dressing gown from a hook on the door, he shrugged angrily into the folds. "Now Nicholas and that godforsaken wife of his get everything. All that bloody time and effort I wasted trying to get on her good side and here I am, stuffed up the Khyber by her," his tone was contemptuous, "unfortunate natural death." He screwed the tie around his waist with a flourish. "I wouldn't put it past my bloody brother to have killed her, I swear."

Fran had seated herself against the pillows during his tirade, any thoughts of sleep abandoned and she tutted. "Don't be silly, John. What a preposterous idea."

He stepped to the window, pushing the curtains aside to reveal the darkness of the cloudy sky. "I'm going to fight this, just watch me, and you'd better be on my side. Half of that inheritance is rightfully mine and that is what I intend to get."

"Whatever." There was no point talking to John when he was in one of his moods and Fran slumped down the bed, hugging the covers over her shoulders against the wintry cold.

Nicholas gazed at his mother, still warm in death, and marvelled at how she could easily be mistaken for being asleep. He laid a hand on the sheet that covered her night-gowned body as tears slipped along the lines of his face, set by a laughter that was not apparent now. They had always been close in a way that nobody around them understood, each knowing the other's thoughts without having to ask. He had always known he was the favourite child, seemingly from birth. The baby of the family.

In the sixty-four years they'd had together, she his rock and protector, he the cherub of unabated joy, he had considered this moment – her death – on many an occasion. Nellie had been sickly for as long as he could remember with one infection after another, having numerous hospital visits or stays and antibiotics of every kind available. But somehow her fragile body had been robust against the suffering that life had battered her with, emotionally and physically. She had been a fighter on both counts.

And now she lay, her spirit departed, cooling on the trolley in the morgue, a small pile of medical notes strewn at her feet.

18

Adele put her arm around her husband and hugged him close. "I told you not to come and see her, I knew it would upset you."

"It's no surprise I'm upset, my mum's just died, but I knew it was on the cards. Ninety's a grand old age to reach, all said and done."

"Have they told you what she died of?"

"Not as such, just that her ticker gave up, that it's one of those things."

The morgue attendant shifted his position to remind the sad couple of his presence and Nicholas asked, "What happens now?"

"We give you the death certificate, you arrange a funeral director and they'll help you with everything you need to do."

"So there's no need for tests or anything like that?"

"I doubt it at her age. I can't imagine there's anything suspicious about her death."

Halina closed the door quietly to avoid waking her housemates and she threw her bag on the table, clean but ugly and old. She filled the kettle and set it to boil, throwing a teabag and sugar into a mug, and sat on one of the four wooden seats to wait for movement in the house. The last-minute one-night placement had been a disaster with the patient dying on her shift, but the woman had not been kindly, with her blatant racism and aloof dismissal, wielded wickedly as if it was acceptable to be rude once you reached the twilight years, and her carping and patronising had been a bitter pill to take. Halina had become used to the treatment, she was at the brunt of it wherever she went, but that didn't stop it hurting. She was Polish by birth and proud to be, and she was excellent at her job.

A skittish puppy, Marek bounded into the room, cheerful as he always was, and he fetched another mug from the cupboard to join Halina's. "Good night at work?"

"It was a nightmare, a patient died and the charge nurse was a right cow. I hope I don't have to work with her again."

"So you were only doing one night at the Padway?" The kettle clicked and Marek poured water into the mugs.

"Yes, I'll give the agencies a call after I've had some sleep, see if there's anything a bit longer term available. Anyway, what are you doing up so early, it's not like you?"

The tips of Marek's fingers slipped into the pockets of his jeans and he raised his shoulders, chuffed. "After eleven months and five days of living in the UK – not that I was counting – I've finally got a proper job."

"That's brilliant, tell me more."

He stirred the teas, disposing the teabags into the bin, and brought them to the table, setting them on the scarred, unvarnished oak. "It's at Randall's Biotech in Uxbridge, I'll be working in the labs. I start Monday."

Halina was a morose person by nature, with a permanent sadness in her eyes, and this smile was a rarity. Marek enjoyed the way her eyes twinkled, blue and watery, and his heart thudded in his chest. She covered his hand with hers, genuine. "I'm so pleased for you. At least immigration can get off your back now."

"Halina…" The words were sticking in his throat, a simple sentence he had wanted to say forever but had never had the courage. "Now I've got a job, now I'm earning, I was wondering if, well, you know…"

"Go out some time?" The smile reappeared and he melted with relief. "Of course I will, I've been waiting nearly a year for you to ask."

Nicholas and Adele had been in the hospital canteen for hours, nursing coffee after coffee as they digested the news that he was now an orphan, albeit an aging one. He had repeated endlessly how ridiculous he felt his reaction was, knowing how gravely ill his mother had been during the past few months, the unrelenting bronchitis and pneumonia, but the fingers of reality still tore at him. Despite having drawn a comfortable private pension for the past four years, he still felt abandoned and lost without the security his mother's presence had steeped him in.

Adele had lost her own parents years before and although the grief had been agonising, she'd never had the bond with them that her husband had shared with his mother. She hated to see him so hopeless. "Do you want another coffee?"

Nicholas pushed his cup aside. "No," he glanced at his watch, "I can't believe John doesn't even want to see her body."

She shrugged, peeved herself at his older brother's behaviour but always the peacemaker. "Everybody deals with death in different ways. Maybe he's in denial and seeing her would make everything too real."

"You know our John, though, he's a mercenary bastard."

"Come on, love, you're tired. It's been a long night."

"I'm not being unreasonable, Adele, I think it's really cruel. After all, she gave him life."

"Let's go home. You can get a bit of sleep and then deal with things later."

Pushing his chair aside, Nicholas stood, resolved. "No, I'm going to go and see him, give him a piece of my mind."

Fran had prepared a tray laden with a selection of biscuits and four earthenware mugs of tea and she brought it into the lounge, instantly hit by the frosty atmosphere that matched the February weather. Upright and uncomfortable, Adele was seated on the worn sofa, John standing by the patio doors surveying the unkempt garden and Nicholas beside the gas fire, leaning on the mantel above. Using the tray, she pushed magazines and junk mail from the coffee table to clear it and put her hands on her hips. "Don't you think we should be doing something practical, organising the funeral or something, rather than bickering like children?"

The men remained stern, facing away from each other, but Adele smiled gratefully. "I agree, poor Nellie only died this morning and she'd have hated to think you two would be at loggerheads."

John turned to face the others. "Yes, but we all know what the real issue is, that I've been left out of the will and all because of a stupid disagreement fifteen year ago. You know as well as I do that she'd agreed to rewrite it to include me once she got out of hospital."

Nicholas was equally angry, but due to his brother's lack of compassion, not finances. "See, that's it, it's the money. That's all you care about, money, money, money. What about the fact she gave birth to you and raised you. And loved you. What about the person who's just died, without whom you wouldn't even be on this planet?"

"That's an easy thing to say when you know you've got a million plus coming your way."

"Then I'll give you half. It's only bloody money, after all."

John snarled. "No, you won't. You say that here in front of the women but when it comes to signing that cheque you know damned well you won't be doing it." He strutted across the carpet towards his brother, fuming. "I'll tell you the truth and I'm going to bloody prove it if it kills me, but I think you did something to kill her just to stop me getting my hands on my share of the money."

Three jaws dropped, stunned eyes widened. Nicholas's lips wavered, tongue churning in his mouth, trying to seek a fitting response to the outburst. Eventually, "I can't believe you just said that."

Adele was equally horrified. "Nor can I."

John was now the lead speaker, at his podium within the comfort of his home. "I'm going to insist they do a post-mortem because I want to find out exactly what killed my mother."

Chapter 3
The Butch and the Lapdog

Marcus stepped from his bedroom, more nervous of his visitor than he should be. As an anaesthetist any dealings he had with people were usually whilst they were asleep and he was not keen on meeting anybody new at the best of times. But a week of listening to gossip had shown up one coincidence too many and he believed that contacting Hugh's friend was the most responsible course of action. Hugh was bustling away in the kitchen and a huge, older man filled the chair he had vacated. "You're Detective Thirsk?"

Thirsk stood and leaned forward to shake hands, his long arms covering the distance between them easily. "And you must be Marcus Coetzer. Hugh tells me you have some suspicions about what happened to Tobias Sutherland."

Marcus took two beers from Hugh, passing one to Thirsk, and sat in his own chair. "Not him specifically, no. But I'm concerned about the unit he was on when he died."

"In what way?" Thirsk swigged his beer, wincing at the tangy metallic taste of the can.

"The SHDU – Surgical High Dependency Unit. It's located on Ward 34. Hugh told me last week that he'd called you about Tobias's post-mortem, about the note in his oesophagus. I said I'd keep my ear to the ground and listen out for the gossip. Thing is, there are two nurses who regularly work weekday nights in the SHDU and the more gossip I hear, the more concerned I'm getting. Hell, they even call them the Dodo's – as in, go on the ward and you're dead as a dodo. At least that's what I surmised."

"What are their names?"

"Rebecca Burke and Theresa Heinrich."

Thirsk scribbled the names down, unsure about his spelling. "Go on."

"There are all these rumours that they like to play games with their patients. Shit like giving them drugs to make them urinate or soil themselves, things that humiliate the people in their care."

"Brings another possibility for the nickname, eh: go in there and end up doing dodos."

Marcus was uncomfortable, eyes darting awkwardly in any direction but at Thirsk, however Hugh was laughing as he brought a tray of bacon butties through, setting them on the table. "And now you know why he annoys me so much."

"What? I'm just saying." Thirsk took a sandwich, savouring the saltiness. "So where are you going with this, Marcus? You think Tweedle Dum and Tweedle Dee may have killed Tobias?"

"I don't know. Even if they didn't, surely someone should look into allegations as serious as these."

"But there are no allegations, just rumours."

"Can't you put someone in the hospital, some kind of spy? I would offer myself, but I'm an anaesthetist so I'm in the basement most of the time. And Hugh here's stuck in the path lab."

"Angela Crabtree would do it, I swear she went into the wrong career, she's so nosy."

"Whoa, you two. Grown men behaving like five-year olds. This isn't a game. I can't just shove somebody extra on a ward without good reason. If you can find me some kind of firm evidence that shows these two women have been mistreating their patients then I will investigate at the drop of a hat, but a bit of he said, she said? No way. Thanks for wasting my time, Hugh."

Thirsk made no attempt to leave, munching his food, swilling it down with beer and Hugh chuckled, "You have beer and bacon butties, that's never a waste of time."

"Look, the NHS is renowned for its cover-ups, just look at how long it took for the alarm to be raised on Beverley Allitt."

"Who?" The younger men both raised the same question.

Once again feeling his age, the brief interlude into Hugh and Marcus's world of thirty-something-singledom dashed, Thirsk grumbled as he chewed, "Google it."

"At least let me go through the records at work and see if anything turns up." Hugh's curiosity interested Thirsk. They had known each other a while through their jobs and he had always been level headed, so his willingness to believe something may be untoward tugged at Thirsk's suspicions.

"What you do at work is your concern, you don't need my permission."

"No, but I do need you to listen if I – if we – uncover anything. Is it a deal?"

Thirsk pushed the last piece of bread into his mouth, dusting his hands over the carpet. "Can't hurt. Anyway, what's going on with the tox report? Have you heard anything yet?"

"For Tobias? No, nothing yet. These things can take weeks."

"Get them to speed it up a bit, tell them it's a suspected murder case. Put them on to me if there are any problems."

As soon as Marcus led Thirsk from the room to see him out, Hugh took his worn address book from the desk and dialled a number. "Angela, it's Hugh."

"Hugh?"

He laughed, "Come on, Angela, it's not been that long since you left Kendrick. Hugh Smythe. We used to date each other, remember?"

She tittered nervously. "Yeah, sorry Hugh, I just wasn't expecting to hear from you. What's up?"

"Do you have any holiday coming up? No, scrub that, do you fancy going for a drink tomorrow? I've got, well, an exciting possibility for you."

"If it's anything that involves cockroaches and formaldehyde again, then you can forget it."

"No, it's about catching a potential killer."

"I'm hooked! My place, seven-thirty tomorrow. Smart casual, you're taking me to dinner."

Work was buzzing, but Thirsk could not shrug off the unease surrounding Tobias's death. He had briefed Toni the week before on the note found in the deceased man's throat, of the angst he had hallucinated before his death, and like the excitable person she was no matter what, she had bounced off the walls with a grin the size of Wales. She always managed to annoy Thirsk whatever she did, her enthusiasm abundant and unrelenting, but he had spotted a top detective right from the start and she never failed to disappoint, despite her tender years and lack of experience.

And today she had come up trumps again, not that Thirsk intended to feed her glory. "My mum was telling me about a friend's friend who stayed in the SHDU a year ago and was really distressed about the way another patient was treated during her stay. I went to see her."

"Go on."

"Her name's Sandra Miller. She was quite ill after an operation and they'd transferred her to the SHDU. She said that she didn't remember anything that clearly, either she was sedated or the painkillers kept her asleep most of the time, but she said that when she was coherent she could hear another patient screaming a lot and there was always laughter alongside."

"What? The patient was laughing and screaming?"

"No, the patient was screaming. She assumed the laughter was from nurses, or maybe doctors. She said she still gets unsettled about it now."

"So in that case we need the patient or his/her family to make a complaint, not someone who's a friend of a friend. And even then the complaint would be addressed to the hospital, not the police."

"You're dismissing this?"

"I'd be laughed off the force if I even considered taking it seriously. Your mum's friend of a friend was ill, doped up to the eyeballs. She's not remotely witness material."

"You make me want to spit sometimes. Sir." Thirsk rolled his eyes at her impudence, withholding a smile. "So why did you ask me to look into it then? You clearly never intended to investigate."

"You know the rules, Toni. We're the police, we investigate when there's a crime, not a supposition." She flung herself in front of her computer screen, not intending to speak to him ever again and he considered he may have been too hard on her. "Look, as it happens I've got a gut feeling about this one, but I know Fitzpatrick would never give me the go ahead on the scant information we currently have. I want you to go and see Kate

Sutherland, Tobias's wife. She's refused to talk to me so far, but maybe you, a young girl, more sympathetic and all that."

And she loved him again. "You're the tops, boss."

It was over a week since her husband had died, and each day had brought a little more acceptance of the fact he would never be coming back. However, her life remained non-existent, a tedium of nothing, of nobody. Her mum had been wonderful, trying her best to perk her up and, at least, make sure she ate every day. But she wasn't Toby, and Toby was all she wanted. The knock on the door stirred her but she didn't move, uninterested. Only the caller was persistent and seconds later stood before her, a wide smile and gangly arms. "The door was on the latch, I hope you don't mind."

"Go away."

"I can only imagine how much you're hurting, Mrs Sutherland, but I'm here to help."

"Can you bring Toby back? No. Therefore you can't help me. Shove off."

"I'm PC Fowler, and I was wondering if you could tell me about the time Tobias was in the high dependency unit. Your mum told us he was quite distressed."

"Of course he was distressed, the hospital bungled his operation and he was dying. Wouldn't you be upset?"

"Why do you say bungled? Do you think there was medical neglect?"

Kate regarded her caller or the first time, a petite whippet with blonde hair tied in a bun beneath her cap and she realised how scruffy she must be. It had been a week since she'd bathed and she wore the same pyjamas she had slipped into on her return from hospital following Toby's death. Toni took advantage of the lull and slipped onto an armchair. "I don't know. All I know is it was a routine operation and now he's dead. Surely something had to have gone wrong. He was only twenty-eight."

"Do you recall the names of the night staff on the SHDU?"

"No, I was totally focussed on Toby. Hold on though," she grasped her forehead as she searched her memory, "actually one of them was called Rebecca, I remember now."

"Did she say or do anything that you felt was unprofessional?"

"No. No, I don't think so. The other one, though, hard-faced crone she was. She was rude to the patients. Not Toby, but two of the others."

"How many were on the unit?"

"It has four beds, they were full."

"Tell me about the things you felt were wrong."

"Just little things. You know, one after the other, things that add up into one big thing. She'd be rude to the patients – quietly, always quietly – when they had no visitors. Maybe that was why she wasn't untoward with Toby, because I was there so much. Let's put it this way, I wouldn't fancy her looking after me."

"Has anybody told you about the note they recovered from Toby's gullet?"

Kate nodded, stretching her legs forward, days of disuse making them tingle. "Mum told me. It's just the kind of thing Toby would do."

"So it doesn't concern you?"

"It damned well does concern me. Toby was dramatic and suggestible but only where and when it was deserved. If he felt the need to write that someone was coming to get him, especially with how ill he was, then he was scared."

"But you've been ignoring the fact we want to investigate."

Kate's green eyes met Toni's blue, a stern finality that made her shudder. "It won't bring him back, will it?"

Hugh was more nervous than he cared to admit about seeing Angela Crabtree for the first time in over two years. Many times during their six months together he had considered she may be 'the one', but she'd nipped that idea in the bud when she had gained not only a new job miles from where he lived, but a new fella too. At the time, he had hated her as passionately as he'd loved her, but time had healed and now, as she opened the door, he felt nothing but a hug coming on for a good old friend. "Angela, you look amazing."

"Thank you," she tripped through the door on kitten heels, ginger curls cascading over her shoulders. "Did I tell you where you were taking me?" Hugh held the door of his Toyota wide and she clambered inside. "Fredrico's in town. That's not over budget, is it?"

"Of course not."

"So what's this all about then? You mentioned a killer."

They drove, parked, ate quesadillas with guacamole followed by sizzling chicken fajitas and finally came up with a plan: Angela would take her remaining two weeks holiday and blag her way onto the nursing staff at Kendrick – unofficially, of course. It had been two years since she'd left so most of the new faces wouldn't recognise her and if anyone did, Hugh would say she was working for him. It was an unusual way of spending her time off but she couldn't afford to go abroad anyway.

Angela waved the waitress over. "I'll have sweet tamales and chocolate, please. Oh, and coffee. Strong."

"Just ice-cream for me, please."

"You know, I remember seeing Rebecca and Theresa. They always seemed a bit weird. Thick as thieves."

"I only know them by sight. Bloody frightful pair, if you ask me."

"They were the kind of people who shouldn't have been allowed to work together, far too cosy and shadowy with it. I didn't like them then and I doubt I'll like them now."

"Do you think they'll remember you, though? I'm not sure the plan will work if they do."

Angela twisted her corkscrews into a bunch, holding them against her head neatly and removed her glasses. The transformation was enough to set Hugh's mind at rest.

All four beds in the room were occupied but none of the patients were troublesome, asleep for most of the time, and a sedative took them back there swiftly if they woke. Rebecca and Theresa sat nursing coffees by the desk, attending to paperwork. Thirsk opened the door slowly. He had never been to intensive care and didn't know what to expect, yet the thought of gasping ill people on the brink of death turned his stomach. "No unauthorised visitors in here." Theresa marched sternly towards him.

He flashed his card and smiled. "Detective Chief Inspector Thirsk, I want to ask you a few questions about a patient who died on your unit a couple of weeks back." He noticed the worried glance shared by the two nurses. "It won't take long."

Theresa headed back to the desk, returning to the warm seat she had just left. "Who and why?"

"His name was Tobias Sutherland and he died on the sixth. The cause of death is so far inconclusive, we're waiting on tox reports, but we do have reason to believe that the circumstances surrounding his death may not be straightforward."

"Do you remember him, Rebecca?"

Theresa glowered over the rim of her glasses in a way Thirsk surmised as threatening but Rebecca was unperturbed. "I vaguely recall the name, nothing more."

"I see. You lose so many patients every fortnight I can imagine it must be hard to recall each one."

"Unfair, Mr Thirsk. We have a high rehabilitation success rate." Theresa folded her arms, indignant.

"That's right."

So if Rebecca was the yes man, that made Theresa the butch, the dominant leader. This investigation was *so* happening. Thirsk smiled affably, his curiosity in the pair rising by the second. "I'll give your memories a quick boost." He brought a small snapshot of Tobias from his pocket. "This was twenty-eight year old Tobias Sutherland. He came in electively for an operation on an inguinal hernia on the third of February and was recovering well, but shortly before he was due to go home, expected to be the next day, his condition worsened. On the fifth, his liver began, inexplicably so far, to fail. He came to your care in the early hours of the sixth and died later that day."

"I remember him now."

"Me too." Both nurses set sympathetic smiles.

Of course you do, he thought sarcastically. "His family tell me that he was concerned about the care he was receiving on your unit."

"He had no reason for any concern. We're professionals and we treated him accordingly."

"That doesn't change the fact that just before he died he swallowed a note claiming he was about to be killed."

Rebecca gasped but Theresa was ice-cold. "He was under the influence of drugs, powerful sedatives and, if I remember correctly, he'd had little oxygen in his blood so he'd probably become somewhat unbalanced."

"Or he was genuinely concerned and saw the desperate action as the only way to tell the world that he was being disposed of."

Theresa stood, rod straight and incensed. "Are you accusing us of something, Mr Thirsk?"

"Not at all, what would make you think that?"

Rebecca's mouth was forming and un-forming words and she looked to her colleague for guidance. Theresa was less disconcerted. "Do the management know you're here?"

"I've only come to ask a few questions."

"Rebecca, call security." The lapdog followed her orders and Theresa pointed to the door. "I think you've upset my patients enough this evening, Mr Thirsk. Would you mind leaving?"

As he walked from the room, nonplussed, Thirsk reiterated to himself that the investigation was most definitely on.

Chapter 4
Projecting

Hugh had enjoyed catching up with Angela on the Friday night. They had stepped straight back into the shoes they'd been wearing when they were together and the years apart drifted as if they had never happened. He was pleased to be her friend again, although he could not deny the attraction was still there. For him, anyway. She seemed more confident than before, a glow to her skin that came from within, and she appeared to be genuinely happy. He'd wanted to ask if she was dating but it was none of his business. Maybe they would reach that conversation soon.

The beginning of the week had passed in a blur of routine post-mortems, the highlighting factor of the day a call from Angela to confirm she would be officially on vacation from Friday night for two weeks. He scanned his to-do list and the first post-mortem due was an elderly woman who had died four days before. On autopilot, he deftly cut a Y into her chest and abdomen.

He had been working at her body for a while, weighing the organs, inspecting the heart and blood vessels, hosing the mess, when the door swung open and Angela strutted in. He plopped the kidneys into a dish and stood straight. "What are you doing here?"

"I swapped shifts with a friend because I need a uniform for next week and I thought I'd better get that sorted. It stinks in here."

"Not as much as the wards, what with all the BO, farting and belching. I thought you had a friend who was lending you her spare uniform."

"She went cold. I think she's had an argument with her boyfriend. Anyway, I remember where everything is so I'll get hold of something."

"You know, if you don't want to do the journey to and from Oxford every day while you're here next week I'm quite happy to sleep on the sofa so you can have my bed."

"You're so gallant. But I might take you up on it. Well, I'll have the sofa if Marcus doesn't mind, I don't want to put you out of your own bed."

The silence was uncomfortable and Hugh felt it would be the most natural thing in the world to hold her close, never let her go. But he was in bloodied gloves and apron. Hardly romantic. He busied himself in Mrs Peters' abdomen. "Right then, good. I'll, er, leave you to it."

Thirsk stood before Fitzpatrick's desk and he was outraged. "I have given you evidence that warrants an investigation. Why are you black-walling me? This abuse of patients could go back for years and somebody needs to look into it." Fitzpatrick opened his mouth to reply but Thirsk's tirade continued. "Imagine it was your mother being looked after by those two witches, or bitch hounds. But, oh no, you can't do that, what with your fancy private medical care and all that."

"Thirsk, that's enough." Fitzpatrick's face had reddened and he shouted, "My personal life is an absolute no-no, do you understand that? I hear what you're saying and I understand your frustration, but in this case things are being dealt with in a different manner. I've been in touch with the hospital and they're carrying out an internal investigation. If any concerns are raised from that, they'll be in touch."

"They're doing a cover-up?"

"They're investigating, but without the furore that having you involved would create."

"You mean you actually trust these bastards?"

"We all have to trust somebody and I have some very good friends…"

"That," Thirsk silenced his superior with the word, "explains everything. Bloody trousers rolled to the knees and stupid bloody dances with frog entrails on your heads. You make me puke." He slammed the door behind him and stomped to the lift, jabbing the button.

Reaching the ground floor, he stormed through the reception area to the car park, intent on wasting the rest of the day with beer and whisky, and Toni's voice was an irritation.

33

"Guv, I've just heard from Kate Sutherland, she's remembered something."

"Not now." He flung the door of his Audi open, heaving his huge frame inside, and started the engine, reversing swiftly and skidding through the gates.

He accelerated away.

"Is now a good time?"

Thirsk slammed the brakes on, the car behind nearly nipping his bumper as it swerved. "What the fuck are you doing in here?"

"I climbed in when you did. I need to talk to you about Kate."

His immediate thought was to chuck her out, send her back to the station with her tail between her legs, but the truth was he needed to talk too. He drove a mile from the town centre, a quieter pub that served good ale and better food, and parked up. "Before you tell me anything about Kate I want to talk to you about something, and you're to keep it strictly between the two of us."

She followed him to the bar, nodding when he asked if she wanted soda water as usual. "The Super has told me we have to drop the case. The hospital is carrying out an internal investigation."

"You've got to be kidding."

"Did you really expect anything different?"

"But I was reading about the Beverley Allitt case and..."

"You're about five years old, how have you even heard of that?"

"I read a lot. They held an internal investigation and the case was delayed forever. Allitt even managed to continue working as a nurse, despite the fact she was under suspicion for murder. Multiple murders. They'll just find those two bitches guilty and sweep it under the carpet with a rap on the knuckles to keep the hospital looking good."

"I know that." Thirsk paid for the drinks and took them to a table, along with a menu. "But what can we do?" His mobile began to ring and he planned to ignore it but relented when Toni sat back, waiting for him to answer. "What?"

Soon into the call, Thirsk indicated for Toni to drink up and he swigged his own pint, small streams dribbling over his unshaven chin. "Thanks, Hugh, I'll be there as soon as possible." Within minutes they were back in the car and on their way to the hospital.

Hugh awaited them, now busy on another body, and he grinned widely when Thirsk arrived with a constable in tow, enjoying the pallor of the older man's face from the thick stench of death in the room. "I didn't really think that what I had to say would warrant a special trip here, it was just a routine matter. You had to get away from the office, didn't you?"

"The powers-that-be at the hospital have put the kybosh on my investigation. I've been told in no uncertain terms to leave it."

"Oh, then it's lucky I got Angela in then, isn't it? Who's your friend?"

Toni stepped forward to shake the proffered hand but pulled her own back on seeing the blood and gore. "Toni Fowler. Who's Angela?"

Normally Hugh meddling with his case would have annoyed Thirsk, but he reminded himself it wasn't his anymore. In fact, he was, now the strings had been pulled, quite impressed they were about to have a stooge in place. "Give me the details of who's involved in this now so I can keep up to date."

"There's me and Marcus, he's just concentrating on sifting through the gossip, and Angela. That's it on our side."

"And until I find concrete evidence that will demand a police investigation, it's just me and Toni. She's agreed to work unpaid overtime as much as is necessary."

"No way, have I! I do have a life outside work, you know."

"All that pumping iron and running marathons can wait a couple of weeks, you obviously don't use enough energy during the day so a little extra work will do you good."

"I can't imagine we'll need you much anyway, Toni. It's Angela who'll be doing most of the work. It'll probably all be innocent and blow over soon, I reckon, I can't see we'll ever prove Tobias was murdered."

"No tox screen yet, then?"

"Yes, now you mention it. He had a high level of paracetamol, morphine and propofol in his blood, but that is consistent with the medication he was given during his time here. The build up of paracetamol is likely to be the cause of death."

"Then he was killed. It's not as if he took an overdose himself."

"Some people have weak livers. His was marginally smaller than average and he was a slight man anyway, he probably just couldn't safely tolerate as much. The family will see the report and if they choose to do something about it, I'm sure an inquiry will follow. But either way, it's out of your hands."

"You called me all the way over here to tell me exactly what my Super's told me already."

"No, I gave you a courtesy call to tell you to expect a letter about," he leant to another trolley and uncovered the head, "Mrs Peters. I'm referring her to the coroner for an inquiry. It was just a routine call, then you got uppity and drove over here. I didn't ask you."

Toni felt bad for her boss, his day was collapsing into a hopeless heap, but she had to hold a chuckle back over Hugh's impertinence. "Why don't you call it a day, guv, start afresh tomorrow?"

Thirsk paced the room, muttering, eager to save face. "What about Mrs Peters? Was she on the SHDU too?"

"No, ward thirty-four."

"She looks about eighty, surely it was old age?"

"She was, and it probably was."

"So why the inquest."

"She died from an air embolism, a large one and it's not consistent with her illness or lifestyle."

Thirsk strutted back to his car, ashamed of being shown up and angry at the world, and Toni trotted behind him, struggling to keep up. "Guv, I still need to talk to you about Kate."

"The case isn't happening so it's irrelevant."

Thirsk snatched his keys from his pocket and dangled them from his hand, tempted to make her walk home. In a swift, unforeseen movement she had the keys and ran to the other side of the car. "You know, I'd never have put you down as a quitter,

36

but thinking about it now, you'd never have bothered to find out who the baby was on the Baby Jane case if I hadn't joined the force. You were a quitter twelve years ago and you still are now."

"Kick me when I'm down, why don't you. Give me the bloody keys and stop messing about."

Toni hung the fob in the air, the car between them. "Kate."

"Fuck you. Well, you'll just have to tell me at the pub. In fact, you can drive, then I can do what I do best and get hammered."

"Such a role model." She unlocked the car and slid into the driver's seat, adjusting it from one extreme to the other to accommodate her shorter legs. She waited until he was inside and belted and started the engine, not brave enough to inform him that she had never driven such a powerful car before. "Kate told me she remembered something."

"Go on."

"On the Friday morning when Tobias was in the SHDU, he told her that the night staff had been playing games with a patient. He said he couldn't see what they were doing, but could just hear the patient – a woman – crying while they taunted her about having soiled the bed. Kate said that Toby had an odd imagination at the best of times so she didn't think anything of it."

"Did she tell you his exact words?"

"Not really, she's a little confused by everything that's happened."

"Then there is no further evidence, is there?"

She steered the car through an entrance and parked next to the pub they had vacated an hour before. Turning the engine off, she stared at Thirsk. "You're determined not to be a part of this, aren't you?"

"I'm not interested in wasting valuable drinking time assessing a case that isn't authorised. And be careful of that Kate, it sounds to me like she found any excuse to call you and if I'm right that means she's lonely."

"Maybe she is. Her husband's just died and she's human after all. Unlike some."

She caught his eye but he chuckled sardonically. "She's projecting onto you. You're a link to her husband and she needs someone to talk to. She'll keep calling you now until either she gets over him, or you put a stop to it."

Toni held the door open and Thirsk stepped into the real-fire warmth of the traditionally decorated bar. "You're so cynical."

Toni opened her eyes, the moonlight through the un-curtained window shedding a blue-tinged blanket over the room that was her haven. The phone continued to ring by the bed and she glanced at the clock. Two a.m. Annoyed, yet concerned something may have happened to her family, she grasped the receiver. "Hello."

"Toni, I'm sorry to bother you so late, I didn't think you'd mind."

The memory of Thirsk's warning hours earlier jumped into her mind and Toni sighed. "Kate. I don't mind this time, but don't do it again, eh?"

"Thanks, it's just I had a dream about Toby, I thought it may be important."

Chapter 5
Paranoia

The dismal winter days passed slowly, grey skies rarely clearing of cloud, sometimes spewing rain, sometimes snow – a miserable anti-climax after the heart-warming bustle of Christmas. Both the Gleeson brothers had consulted solicitors, neither speaking to one another now the feud had been cemented, but no action could be taken on either side until the overworked pathologist at the Padway Hospital could find a slot for the non-urgent post-mortem of their mother's body.

Brown, official envelopes, sent first-class, arrived at both households on the same morning.

Nicholas trotted down the stairs when he heard the postman close the gate and he scooped up the mail to read at the breakfast table where Adele was eating her muesli. He flicked through the pile. "Junk. Junk. Junk, and... junk. Oh," he tore at the paper, "this one looks interesting. It's from the hospital; it's the post-mortem report. Where's the... It says mum died of a pulmonary embolism."

"Isn't that a blood clot? I thought you said it was her heart that gave out."

Nicholas slumped onto a seat, resting his head on his hand as he scrutinised the letter carefully. "It was, love, the embolism caused a cardiac arrest. It says there was a rupture to the right ventricle, and... It says referred to coroner, what does that mean?"

"Doesn't the coroner certify death or something?"

Their bewilderment and lack of knowledge held the silence for a moment, until the phone on the side began ringing. Adele answered, "Hello – John, this is a nice surp... yes, the postman's just been – he's got it in his hand. What do you mean?" She held the phone out, regarding it, shocked. "He's just hung up. He says he's going to the police to tell them you murdered Nellie."

Halina was in her second week of unemployment, a travesty in her mind due to the number of car accidents and broken bones being caused by the recent adverse spell of harsh weather, so when she saw the incoming call to her mobile was from one of the employment agencies she was registered with a rare smile brightened her face. "Hello. Hold on a minute, can you repeat that? That was ages ago, weeks." She knew the date they were talking about exactly, the date she last saw a dead body; how could she forget that? "She was just an old woman, I can't see what the fuss is about, but thanks for telling me anyway."

As an aside before hanging up, she asked, "I don't suppose there are any jobs going, are there? I don't care what, I just need some money, the rent's due – oh, okay." She cut the call and set her mobile on the table beside the remnants of the meal she had prepared for herself and Marek.

"You don't have to worry about the rent, you know. My job is secure and my salary is regular, I can cover your share."

"I don't want to rely on you financially, I make my own way in life." She paused before remembering, "Oh, but thanks for the offer. I'll be fine, something will come up."

He wanted to support her, to make her happy. They had known each other almost exactly a year, and although they had only been a couple for a few blissful weeks, he knew she was the woman he'd been seeking, his personal Miss Right. But he could also see how fiercely independent she was, how the scandal – whatever it was, Halina refused to elaborate – that had rocked her world in their home country had given her a tough and impenetrable exterior. "What was that about an old woman? Trouble?"

"It's all a ridiculous waste of time. There was a ninety year old woman on the ward on my stint at the Padway Hospital, the last time I worked there. She died and now they're making a big fuss about it. The agency was just letting me know what's going on before the letter arrived."

"What letter?"

"There's going to be an inquest into her death and I have to give evidence. Nothing to worry about, I'll just give my story and they'll be done with me."

"That's stupid, a ninety year old. Obviously she'll have died from natural causes at that age."

"I know. It'll all boil down to money, that'll be involved somehow. It always is."

Angela had spent the weekend at home in Oxford, tidying and organising, enjoying the airy studio and she was dreading the next two weeks of man-smell and mess in Hugh and Marcus's apartment. The idea of returning to her ex-employer as a spy sounded so much fun, but after a desperately overworked week she was exhausted and wished she had paid for a ticket to Ibiza after all.

After her final shift at the Padway Hospital on Friday, Angela had travelled to Kendrick after work and brazened a visit to the SHDU, wearing her stolen uniform and a borrowed party wig, the pretence being she was following up on a patient she had particularly liked, but the atmosphere had been hostile, her presence clearly unwanted. An uncomfortable episode, but at least she had seen the layout and regime.

Now it was Monday morning, and she was about to head back to Kendrick when the postman called with a buff envelope that was as mysterious as it was worrying. She tore it open and read that there was to be an inquest regarding a deceased patient she could barely remember.

She racked her brains trying to put a face to the name and eventually Nellie Gleeson and her cutting, insensitive remarks returned. Angela shook her head with distaste. She'd not been upset when the crabby woman had died and was miffed that she would have to waste at least a day attending an inquest into the old biddy's death. She shoved the letter inside her handbag and grabbed her rucksack from the floor by the door. After a courtesy text to Hugh to tell him she was on her way, she left.

Twenty miles of stop-start traffic later, she pulled into Kendrick Hospital, making her way straight to the pathology lab, and Hugh offered a broad smile on seeing her. "It feels like you've been gone forever."

"I'll bet neither of you have done the dishes since I did them Friday night."

"I'll have you know that I did them last night. I wasn't expecting you until this evening."

41

"I know, but I got bored. I thought I'd start off early, spend some time with the day staff on the SHDU and, if I can get away with it, still be there for when Rebecca and Theresa turn up tonight. I'm sure I can swing it." Angela tossed her rucksack by the door and sat on a viewing chair. "You've been to an inquest, haven't you?"

"Quite a few. Why?" Hugh took the heart from the cadaver he was working on and examined it carefully.

"I've got to attend one. I've never been to one before and I'm a bit worried."

"Worried? Why?" He slopped the heart into a dish and took it to the scales.

"The woman was on my ward when she died unexpectedly. What if they try and pin the blame on me?"

"Are you to blame?"

"No, of course not."

"Then you have nothing to worry about. I'm guessing the PM was inconclusive for it to be going to inquest. Who did it?"

"I don't know, to be honest. After she died I thought no more of it. It's come as a surprise. She was ninety years old, I think. Really old, anyway. I thought it would just be from natural causes."

"I had one of those last week only she was eighty. She died from an air embolism that was inconsistent with her state of health and lifestyle. I had to refer that one to the coroner too."

"I'll tell you what, I hope nobody ever performs a PM on me, the thought of it makes me sick."

"All you are is a carcass once you're dead, a chunky slab of meat. Who cares what happens to your body."

"Hugh Smythe, you can be pretty morbid sometimes. Anyway, I'll see you later, I'm outta here. Wish me luck."

Angela took the lift to the second floor, unsure how she was going to find a feasible excuse to spend time on the SHDU, but confidently hopeful she would wing it all the same. She decided to have coffee and lunch in the canteen, see if she knew anybody there while she formed a plan. As she carried the laden tray to an empty table a waving caught her eye and she was pleased to see an old friend and colleague. "Hey, Luce, I'll join you."

They wasted the next ten minutes, Angela's food rapidly cooling, catching up with the basic gossip of their lives – who was with whom, how their jobs were, their home lives and hobbies. "So what are you doing here then? I thought you worked at the Padway now."

Angela almost spilled the truth but she stopped herself. "Thing is, I've left. I came back here to see if there are any jobs going."

Lucy drummed her fingers against her lips as she thought. "I know there are two temporary jobs going on my ward. Well, not so much my ward, but the SHDU, it's part of the ward. One's twelve hour nights, the other days. I don't think I'm supposed to know but you know how word gets round."

Angela, who had attempted her first mouthful of cold cottage pie, dropped the fork. "Really? I want that job. How do I get it?"

"Sister Kennedy's interviewing after lunch, that's all I know."

"It's lunchtime now." Angela had already forgotten her unappetising meal and was scrabbling her rucksack, coat, gloves and hat together.

"Yeah, there were two girls waiting when I came down here."

"What ward?"

"Thirty-four."

Halina had been grateful to take the call from Nursing Angels.Work had been scarce and money was increasingly tight. Marek had been as good as his word and had contributed to her rent, but not without expecting, or at least suggesting, payback. He wanted them to leave their house-share, move somewhere they could be alone together. A place to call their own. She could not deny that she was enamoured with him, he ticked all the boxes, with kindness and attentiveness in abundance, a steady career with excellent chances of promotion and a sweet nature that would make him a wonderful father one day. But they had only been dating weeks, and even after six years she wasn't sure she was ready after the disastrous and harrowing finality of her marriage. She hadn't told Marek the dark secrets of her past, it had never seemed the right time.

She sat as directed on the hard, plastic chair and eyed the two women before her. Sister Kennedy, forty-something and kindly, was clearly harassed and wanted the interviews over so she could bustle back to work. Erika Gomez was dressed in a suit, neat and starched, nipped at the waist to emphasise her curves. She began by explaining that the SHDU was under review and they needed two staff, one days, one nights, to complete a time and motion study over a period of four weeks. Hence, the job was temporary, but would be looked upon favourably should the successful applicant wish to work at the hospital in the future. "You have a glowing résumé, Halina."

"Thank you."

"What do you think you could offer to the role?"

"As it shows on my CV, I'm fast, efficient and I get the job done. Have you seen the references?"

Sister Kennedy already disliked Halina, finding her obnoxious, arrogant and egotistical. "Yes, they're impressive but we're a close knit ward and…"

"From what I've been told about the position, I won't be interacting with anybody but the staff on the SHDU, so my interpersonal skills are irrelevant, however I have always managed to successfully fit into whichever team I've worked for as my reference from the agency states."

An hour later, Angela, a CV and two fake references hurriedly bashed out in Hugh's office, sat in front of the two women, both weary from the endless questioning. "I don't remember seeing your name on the list the agency sent to us." This time it was Erika who disliked the applicant on sight.

"Really? Well, I wouldn't have known about the job if they hadn't sent me here, so maybe they got my name wrong or something."

Erika bristled but Sister Kennedy was smiling warmly. "Your CV is good and I see you've worked for us in the past."

"Yes, up until two years ago. I've been working at the Padway Hospital ever since."

"It says here you finished there last month, could you tell me how your job came to be terminated?" Bad cop Erika was determined to catch her out.

"They're reducing staff, last in, first out. I don't think anyone's job is safe there, not in the current climate."

"It's always difficult to contemplate redundancies, I know first hand." Over the ten years Kennedy had been in her job her staff had reduced by half, leaving control of the ward a constant nightmare. She could see her colleague was unimpressed with the candidate, but Erika had raved about the Polish woman and insinuated the job was hers, despite Kennedy's objections. The others hadn't been nearly as qualified as Halina and Angela and their only solution was a compromise. Later that day both women heard they would be employed by Kendrick Hospital through the agency, Halina on days, Angela nights.

Hugh was thrilled for Angela but she wasn't kicking her heels with joy. Her wish to spend four weeks working nights with the notorious nurses, Rebecca and Theresa, had been granted, but now the reality that, after her vacation finished, she would spend a fortnight working days at the Padway and nights at Kendrick was worrying. "I'm going to be knackered, I won't get any sleep."

"Why not take another two weeks off?"

"I've used up all my leave already."

"What about pulling a sickie?"

"Hah, sod it, I'll come up with something nearer the time. Anyway, I start tonight, so if it's okay with you I'll nip back to yours and have a bath before I come back."

"No problem," he fished in his trouser pocket, "I brought the spare key for you." The room was quiet, neither knowing what to say, if to speak at all. Eventually, Hugh managed, "Angela."

"If you're going to say something awkward I think we'd better stop there."

"Why not, though? We were good together. Weren't we?"

"You think I didn't have a reason to leave you?" She knew the only problem they'd had was her reluctance to commit. Now, she'd already accepted she liked him more than she wished to, but was scared.

Hugh bowed his head, fidgeting with the scalpel in his hand. "I'd better get on with some work. What time do you start tonight?"

"Eight. Can't wait."

Hugh reluctantly watched her stride through the door and his heart sank. Maybe she was right, maybe they worked best as friends.

Clean and fresh, Angela excitedly donned the uniform she had been supplied with and twisted her hair into a neat chignon before replacing her glasses with contact lenses. The shaving mirror in the bathroom was small and awkwardly placed, but with a bit of stretching and squirming she managed to check her appearance and was comfortable it was acceptable. She grabbed her bag and was about to leave when Marcus bumbled from the bedroom, not quite awake. She posed in various positions with a wide grin. "How do I look?"

"Different. Hugh told me you'd got a proper job there. I bet you're relieved not to have to skulk around hoping nobody will catch you out."

"You bet, and with the added bonus that I'll be right where I need to be on the SHDU."

"Playing detective, no less." He grinned, walking to the kitchen to wake himself with coffee. "Just one thing," he turned back as she opened the front door, "be careful, won't you. With Rebecca and Theresa. I don't trust them."

She skipped through the door. "Don't worry, I can handle them."

After driving the short distance, she happily made her way to the SHDU, keen to get started. Theresa and Rebecca had already arrived, both catching up with the patients' charts and Theresa peered over the top of her glasses. "What are you doing here?"

"I'm Angela, the new girl."

46

"I recognise you, I've seen you before somewhere." She rested against the back of the seat, studying her.

"You must be mistaking me for someone else." Angela's appearance had been transformed since she had popped into the unit on Friday night, and it was two years since she had worked for the hospital. And even then she had barely seen the women. Did Theresa have the memory of an elephant? "Or maybe you saw me earlier when I was here for the interview."

"I was home asleep at lunchtime."

Angela wished the woman would drop it. So what if she had seen her before. "Well, maybe I just look familiar, it's not as if I'm the kind to stand out in a crowd. There are probably thousands of girls who resemble me." Theresa leant towards Rebecca and whispered, and Angela felt a creepy tingle along her spine. She forced a smile and changed the subject, "Where do you want me to start?"

Theresa stood, arms crossed and intimidating, and she approached Angela, towering over her. "I know why you're here. That time and motion study is bollocks and we're not stupid. The police think we had something to do with a patient's death and our work is being monitored to try and catch us out. Well, I can tell you that we're both strictly professional and you won't find a single fault with any of our practices. I don't trust you, so stay away from me and I'll leave you alone. Cross me, though…"

The threat was loud and clear, but Angela felt like laughing at the playground bullying. "I've never heard anything so ridiculous. It was the hospital that hired me and there wasn't a single word said about watching either of you. I think you're paranoid. Now, if you can pass me the patient notes I'll get on with my job."

Chapter 6
A Dose of Morphine

The atmosphere in the SHDU over the first few nights had been uncomfortable, but Angela had settled in once Theresa had become accustomed to her presence. However, she found the lack of variety in the department tiresome, the relentless concentration on just four beds if the unit was full, and she had no time for the two nurses she had been working alongside. On a superficial level, Rebecca came across as warm and caring, but scratching the surface showed an organised and ruthless persona with no emotional connection to her patients.

They had completed the handover from the day staff and Angela had brought coffee to keep them caffeinated and bushy-tailed. She lounged back in the comfortable chair, crossing her legs. "You never get attached to the patients, how come?"

"They're having intensive care, they're seriously ill. Some die and if you had feelings for them it would drive you crazy."

"I suppose." It made sense, but Rebecca's detachment was unnerving. "What about you, Theresa?"

Theresa was the opposite of her colleague, she didn't appear capable of warmth and her stern, businesslike manner bordered on unsavoury. "It's a job. Why care about people you don't know, people you'll never see again. I do the work I have to do to keep them alive and comfortable and I go home. If they die, they die." She pushed herself from her chair and strolled to the nearest patient, fifty-five year old James Cameron, checking his outputs and marking the results in his medical file. "This one, he won't make it through the night."

Angela spat her coffee back into the mug. "Sister Kennedy said he was doing well."

Theresa shook her head. "What would she know? She's too busy faffing around and moaning about how busy she is." She tapped the file with her pen. "His blood pressure has been steadily dropping throughout the day and the sats are in the low nineties, despite oxygen therapy. He's probably suffering from cell damage by now and," she held up the urine drainage bag, "as you can see from the colour of this, his kidneys are failing."

"Yeah, but there are things we can do to help him."

Theresa briskly moved to the next patient. "Call it experience. I've been working here twenty-seven years, there isn't a single thing I haven't seen. I just hope he doesn't die on our shift, it wouldn't look good on us, would it. Not with you investigating us."

"We're back to that, are we? I'd hardly call a time and motion study an investigation."

Theresa assessed the young woman in bed two who'd had surgery to repair her ruptured spleen after falling from a horse. "You may have made yourself comfortable in here but I haven't forgotten why they employed you. All of this rubbish simply because one bloke croaked. As if we'd be dumb enough to go around murdering patients. But the bigwigs think we did it, regardless of our glowing rehab record."

"Did you?" Angela bit her lip, wishing she would stop thinking out loud.

"No, it's more than my job's worth. Anyway, even if we were misbehaving, we'd hardly do it with you looking over our shoulder, so nothing's going to come of this anyway. Pointless, if you ask me." She moved to the third patient, the fourth bed unoccupied.

"Well, if you're right and that's why I'm here, you'll be pleased to know I've seen nothing but professionalism from both of you. You won't be getting a bad report from me if they make me write one." Her statement was true, she had seen nothing untoward in the five nights she'd been working there, but she still had suspicions all the same. The two nurses were a menacing double act, a sinister pair of shadows who lived and breathed together, casting their evil to those in their care. It was not what was said and done that disturbed Angela, more what passed between the two by eye contact.All the things left unsaid. Angela trusted neither woman and hoped that if she were ever to fall ill enough to need special care, she wouldn't arrive on their bay.

The night continued without drama, the three women chatting sporadically between jobs, and in the early hours

Rebecca unlocked the drugs cabinet and took out one of the brown glass bottles, filling a syringe with a colourless liquid. She took it to Mr Cameron and fed it into his intravenous cannula. "Morphine, before you get suspicious. It's prescribed."

Angela sighed wearily. "What is it with you two? I'm on your side."

Her words were drowned as the machine attached to Mr Cameron began to wail and the threesome stared at him, unnerved, before Rebecca came to her senses. "He's arresting, call the crash team."

Toni's week had been stressful, if mundane. Once more, she had been working under the lecherous Andy Feldman and she detested him as much as she had done when she had joined the force nearly three years before. On Friday night her colleagues, grateful to be free of work for the weekend, had invited her to their weekly binge-drinking session at The Cat and Mouse, but she refused as she was training for a half-marathon two weeks ahead. Instead, she had gone running, cross-country, relishing the beauty of the rolling hills on the outskirts of the city.

She was exhausted when she returned to her delightfully gothic flat on the top floor of an old monastery, and after a quick, nutritious salad, she tumbled into bed. An hour later the phone rang, waking her and she rolled her eyes when she noted Kate Sutherland's number on the display. She turned over and pulled a pillow over her head. After seven rings the answer phone clicked on and Toni waited for Kate's voice, but the caller hung up and dialled again. After the third time, Toni answered. "Kate, you can't keep ringing me like this. I understand you need someone to talk to, but that person isn't me."

A sob came over the line. "I know it's late but they told me today that Toby was overdosed with paracetamol. I need to know that you're still investigating his death."

Toni dragged herself up the bed, hoping the correct posture would make her voice more commanding. "We have nothing to investigate. As far as I understand, the hospital is completing an internal inquiry and if you're unhappy with the care he received it's them you need to go to." She had not heard about the results of the toxicology tests but assumed Thirsk had.

"But Toby was murdered, surely that's a matter for the police."

"I don't understand the ins and outs of it all, but if my boss doesn't think there's anything untoward about his death, then neither do I."

"Your boss is an idiot. Toby swallowed a note saying he was being killed and then he died. What more proof is there?"

"His liver and kidneys failed, he…"

She shouted with frustration, "His liver and kidneys were poisoned with paracetamol. Somebody gave him that paracetamol. Somebody has to account for this."

"Kate, don't make me have to change my phone number."

"Wouldn't you do the same? If it was your husband who'd been killed in his prime of life, wouldn't you kick up a fuss?"

Toni knew she would do exactly the same and she felt sorry for Kate, but she also felt sorry for her sleepless self. She cut the call and pulled the wire from the telephone socket, killing her phone for the night. Thank god she hadn't given Kate her mobile number. Only, an hour later, having finally drifted back to sleep, she was woken by the intercom buzzing and once more she dragged a pillow over her head, groaning, "Piss off."

Her mobile began to ring and Toni gave up. Whoever was at the door didn't intend to go away. She dragged her dressing gown across her shoulders and took the call. It was Thirsk.

"There's been another death on the SHDU and I want to know everything about it."

"Guv, this could have waited until tomorrow. I was asleep."

"Lucky you, I wasn't. Can't. Been having problems for a week now. Let me in."

Exasperated, Toni stepped to the hallway and pressed the door-release button. "Just because you can't sleep doesn't mean the rest of us have to suffer. You can have five minutes, then I'm going back to bed."

Presently, Thirsk loomed up the narrow staircase and through her low front door, the old floorboards creaking under his weight. "Make us a coffee, will you, I can hardly keep my eyes open."

"You're a bloody hypocrite and a pain in the arse."

"And you should remember I'm your boss before you speak to me like that." She glared at him as she filled the kettle. "You remember that girl Hugh said about, Angela Crabtree. Well, somehow she managed to get a temporary position working on the SHDU. She's been there all week. Anyway, she rang Hugh and told him a fifty-five year old man had died following a routine appendectomy. She said that one of the staff, Theresa Heinrich, had predicted the death, even though he'd been reported as stable when they came on shift. The other nurse, Rebecca, had just given him what she said was morphine before he went into cardiac arrest."

"And I'm still wondering why this couldn't wait until tomorrow. Or, better still, Monday."

"Because I'm up for promotion and I need to score some brownie points. Plus if you want to train as a detective, which I believe you do, it'll help to have a recommendation from me."

In her tiredness Toni wanted to throw the coffee over him, rather than pass it nicely. "That's bribery. Here, I haven't put sugar in it as I don't have any. You can have honey if you must use a sweetener."

"No way. Well?"

Toni dribbled some cold water from the tap onto her chamomile tea. "What did Hugh say about it?"

"He only knows what Angela said, but he's going in later today to do the PM as he's keen to see if there are any signs of foul play."

"Then until he's looked at the body, there's nothing we can do."

"Get dressed, we're going to the hospital. I want to speak to the two bitch hounds myself."

"Guv, you'll get in trouble, the Super told you to leave this one alone."

"I'm always in trouble, and the Super saying that just makes it more intriguing for me. Clothes, woman. Now."

Marcus had been covering for a colleague on the night shift – he'd had nothing better to do on a Friday night and the money would be useful now he was saving for a deposit to step onto the property ladder. As an anaesthetist, his job was to keep his patients asleep and painless during their surgery, which usually went smoothly, but the emergency operation on a young man's failing heart after a road accident had been harrowing. He glanced at the clock through the window of the theatre and imagined he could see the sun rising outside as dawn unfolded. They had been working on the youth for three hours and although he was now stable, they'd had to resuscitate him several times. He was seriously ill but no beds were available on the intensive care unit, so the next port of call was the SHDU. Luckily they had a spare bed.

Marcus liked Angela and had enjoyed her presence over the past week. During her stay the flat had been tidier, the air fresher and the laughter more abundant. He knew his best friend idolised her and wished they could sort things out. They would make a great couple, if only they would unbury their heads from the sand. He hurried alongside the trolley as the patient was transported to his new home.

When they reached Ward 34, Marcus could hear a commotion coming from inside the SHDU and he slowed the porter outside, listening intently. "Mr Thirsk, I have already told you your presence is not welcome in our unit. Do I have to call security this time?"

Thirsk's voice was clouded with incomprehension. "I'm only here to ask a few questions, what on earth is your problem with that?"

"Police involvement can only mean that you're suspicious about Mr Cameron's death and we've done nothing wrong. You picked the wrong two nurses to bully."

Tentatively, Marcus opened the door, almost apologetic for his presence. "I believe you're expecting Jacob Middleton, just come from theatre."

Rebecca sauntered to the patient, industriously helping the anaesthetist and porter to move him from the trolley to the bed, transferring his drip and laying a gown onto him, tying the shoulders deftly. Theresa hadn't finished with Thirsk. "Are you going to leave voluntarily or shall I have you removed."

Angela hated confrontation and she couldn't bear any more silliness. "Come on, Theresa, if you've done nothing wrong there's nothing to worry about."

With relief that someone was prepared to stop the preposterousness of the situation, Thirsk smiled at the woman he knew to be Hugh's friend, and their conveniently placed stooge. "Thank you, Angela, at least somebody around here has some common sense."

"Angela. You called her Angela. You know her." Theresa was gobsmacked and Rebecca had ceased all activities. "I knew we were being investigated but I thought it was by the hospital. Is she a policewoman?"

"No, I'm here to do a time and motion..."

"Get out. All of you. Including you, Angela. We did nothing to cause James Cameron's death and you can't prove otherwise, the post-mortem will show that. Leave us to deal with our new patient and get the fuck out of here. I can't work effectively in these conditions." Theresa took the notes from the trolley Jacob had been laid on. "Rebecca, he's written up for morphine, twenty milligrams. Sort that, will you? Why are you lot still here?"

"Ms Heinrich, I am conducting a police investigation into the deaths of two of your patients and I need to speak to you. We can either do it informally here or I can drag you back to the station."

"What, arrest me? You have no grounds for that so I don't give a toss what you threaten me with."

"Theresa Heinrich, I'm arresting you for..."

"Guv, you'll have hell to pay." Toni had been watching from the sidelines, stifling every yawn that threatened.

"Nurse, it hurts." Rebecca raced to the new patient, a syringe in her hand, and administered the opiate.

Thirsk continued with his caution without concern for the lashing he would undoubtedly receive from Fitzpatrick later and steered Theresa from the room. There was something deeply disconcerting about the so-called angel and he was determined to find out exactly what made her tick. Toni shrugged at the two remaining nurses, the bewildered anaesthetist and hapless porter, embarrassed, and followed.

Head down to avoid becoming involved in the scene, Rebecca fitted sticky electrodes to Jacob's body to monitor his heart and the wailing from the machine shocked her. "I don't believe this. He's arresting. Get the crash team."

Angela immediately sent the message, while Marcus assisted Rebecca to keep Jacob alive until help arrived. Toni heard the fuss from the corridor and she ran back to see what was happening. Angela grasped her arm. "That's what happened with Mr Cameron. She injected him supposedly with morphine and he crashed and died. We were all here when she did the same to Jacob. She's a killer."

Rebecca was astride Jacob's body, pushing on his chest rhythmically and she gritted her teeth. "I'm not a killer, I'm trying to save his bloody life."

Toni had no idea what to do next. Did she haul the nurse from the man and hope someone took over effectively while she arrested the woman? Did she leave her to do her job and ask Thirsk about it when they got back to the station? What would he do? It took seconds for her to come to her senses, clearly recalling the nurse pumping a drug into the patient. "Rebecca Burke, I'm arresting you on suspicion of causing death by injection, what you say…"

The crash team came, stabilised the young man and drizzled off to wherever they had come from, leaving Marcus and Angela alone. "Oh." It was all he could manage, wondering quite what had happened during the past quarter of an hour.

"Oh." Angela was equally stunned. "I guess I'm in charge."

"Thirsk." The thunderous roar came from the corridor and Thirsk glanced at Toni. "My office. Now."

He shoved the last of his bacon roll into his mouth, moistening it with the dregs of yet another coffee, and stood, having rehearsed the anticipated bollocking in his mind ever since he had arrested Theresa Heinrich. He sauntered the short distance to Fitzpatrick's office and entered without knocking. "You wanted to see me, sir."

"What the hell do you think you're playing at? Not just one, but two bloody nurses."

"Well, strictly it wasn't me who brought Rebecca Burke in, but yes, I believe they may have been involved in the death of a patient last night."

"I told you to keep your nose out. The general secretary's been on the phone and he's livid. Not only did you leave an intensive care ward without any properly qualified staff, you arrested those women on a hunch rather than evidence."

"Have you met Theresa Heinrich?"

"No, as it happens, but that's irrelevant."

"No, it's not. She's the coldest bitch I've ever known and she's definitely covering something up."

"Let the pair of them go and then come back to my office where we'll discuss this. And your future on the force."

"No, sir. I won't." Thirsk watched his superior's face redden further and waited for the bang as his head exploded. "Sit in on the interview with Theresa. After that, if you still feel she's innocent then I'll happily send her home."

"It's the bloody weekend and I'm supposed to be playing golf in Henley this afternoon. My wife is already furious that I had to come out this morning because of your cock up." Thirsk said nothing, knowing his boss was mulling the rational suggestion. "When are you interviewing her?" Fitzpatrick sighed.

"Hugh Smythe went in early this morning to do the post-mortem. As soon as I've heard from him I'll take the results in with me."

"If this is all a waste of my time, Thirsk, I swear I'll swing for you."

"Sir, it won't be. She's guilty as hell."

With impeccable timing a knock on the door halted the exchange. Toni opened it a crack and peeped through. "Sorry to disturb you but I thought this may be important. It's a fax from the hospital."

Thirsk snatched the paper from her, scanning it swiftly. "It's from Hugh. He's only done the preliminaries, but says he's already ninety-nine percent sure the patient died of an insulin overdose due to the smell on the body. He's opening him up now."

"Isn't that something to do with diabetes?"

Thirsk looked to Toni, who shrugged her reply. "I think so, but if Hugh's making contact before the post-mortem is done, then it has to mean something bad."

Fitzpatrick stood, shaking his head slowly. "The powers that be at Kendrick Hospital are in uproar about those two nurses being here. If we're going to hold them for any length of time I need more than that."

Thirsk picked up the phone. "I'll give him a call and ask him. When I'm ready to see Theresa I'll let you know."

Hugh knew as soon as the phone rang that it would be Thirsk on the other end of the line. He tugged his bloodied gloves off and took the call. "I knew you wouldn't know what insulin was."

"I do. People inject it when they have diabetes." Thirsk was proud of himself for remembering at the last moment.

"I'm still working on Mr Cameron, but unofficially I'm sure he died of hypoglycaemia. This is most commonly caused by an overdose of insulin, but I've looked in his notes and there's no record of him having diabetes. In my opinion, and strictly off record, Mr Cameron was injected with a large quantity of insulin and that's what caused his death."

"When will you know for sure?"

"That'll depend on how long toxicology take to process his tissue samples, and even then they may be negative as insulin degrades rapidly."

"Well, mark them as urgent."

"I will, I only contacted you early as Angela told me your sidekick seemed concerned when you arrested Theresa, so I thought this might help you keep them locked up while you looked into things."

"Thanks for that, the Super's spitting bricks at the moment. Off the record, Hugh, what's your take on all this? Do you think there's something unsavoury going on?"

"Marcus did a bit of background work on the SHDU and the amount of times the crash team is called to the department is higher than average. I hate that I think so, but I think your suspicions are qualified."

"I've heard you. Hugh, get those results as quickly as you can, I want to throw the book at these women."

"Women? I thought you'd picked up Theresa, who's the other?"

"Nobody's told you? Toni arrested the other nurse as another patient crashed while we were there, just after Rebecca had injected him."

"You think he may have been given insulin too?"

"You're the medic, surely you can test his blood or something."

"Did he die?"

"No, not that I know of."

"Like I said, insulin doesn't last long in the body. If he didn't have blood taken soon after injection it'll be unlikely to show up now, but I can arrange for testing anyway if you want, that's if someone else hasn't already."

Hugh ended the call and rang the SHDU to arrange for a blood sample from the young man he had known nothing of, and after finishing his forgotten cold tea he pulled on a fresh pair of latex gloves. The cavity of James Cameron's chest was exposed and waiting for him, the fruity smell from the body now familiar. He used his scalpel to slice through the anterior and inferior vena cava, the pulmonary vein and artery and the aorta, and removed the heart from where it had given its final beat. It seemed perfectly healthy, considering the deceased's age, with cholesterol deposits minimal. He took each internal organ and found them to be the same. James Cameron had come to hospital with a ruptured appendix, he'd received emergency surgery and had been recovering well; his death was certainly questionable.

Hugh prepared the samples to send to toxicology and made a mental note to call in a favour requesting their speedy processing. He wished he didn't, but he strongly suspected James Cameron had been murdered, and that saddened him.

Halina had taken the call from the pathologist and she reported it to Sister Kennedy. "The thing is, I know something's going on here and obviously I'm as concerned about being involved as anybody is. I'd rather you took his blood. Or someone else. Anyone but me."

Kennedy ran both hands through her greying hair, stressed to the brim. "Halina, I haven't got time for this. The reason we're both in doing overtime is because two of the weekend staff are off with colds, and I've a million and one things to do. Just take the sample and send it off. It's no big deal."

"What is going on, anyway?"

Kennedy had been briefed and was in utter shock that fingers were pointing at members of her team, but she wasn't at liberty to spread gossip. "I don't know."

Halina opened a plastic drawer and selected the equipment she would need to take the specimen. "I heard the night staff had been arrested."

"Rumours spread like wildfire here, just ignore it. Every member of my staff is competent. This is all just silliness." Her dismissal was final and she scuttled hurriedly from the room.

Halina noticed Jacob was awake and strolled across. "I just need to take some blood. How are you feeling, any pain?"

Jacob's breathing was shallow, sweat on his brow. "A little."

She plugged the syringe into his cannula and began to draw vials of blood from his arm. "I'll see if you can have any more pain relief in a minute. You look a bit jittery, a bit hot."

Halina put the blood samples on a nearby table and dragged the obs machine over, taking the thermometer and pushing the disposable nozzle in his ear. "I feel weird, like my heart's going a zillion miles an hour."

"I'll see what we can do. I'll be back soon." She patted his hand tenderly, reassuring him, and was soon with Sister Kennedy once more. "I'm worried about Jacob. His heart's going at over a hundred and his temperature's thirty-eight seven. Also, his breathing's shallow and he's slurring his words. I think we should call the doctor."

Kennedy wondered if anybody was capable of doing their job without involving her. "If you think he needs a doctor then get a doctor, for heaven's sake." She sneaked a cigarette and lighter from her bag; she needed a break, even if it was only five minutes.

Halina bleeped the doctor and tagged her colleague, Stephen, on the arm. "Jacob needs some morphine, would you mind doing it while I go and get us some coffees?"

"Sounds fair to me." Stephen checked the dosage on Jacob's chart and unlocked the cupboard, taking a brown bottle and preparing to give him the twenty milligrams he was written up for. Accidentally, he overfilled the syringe and without thinking, he discharged the extra, but an odd smell of plasters prompted him to squeeze out some more onto a surgical pad, sniffing carefully. Sister Kennedy was nowhere to be seen and Halina was in the kitchen, so he tagged a doctor when he entered the room. "Does this smell like insulin to you?"

Thirsk was tired of Theresa and her correctness, the way she always had a smarmy answer to everything he said. She had insisted on her right to have a solicitor present at the interview and that had wasted valuable hours of the twenty-four he was allowed to keep her without the further authorisation he knew he wouldn't get. Fitzpatrick had been no help either, indicating he thought the whole business was a waste of time. They took a break and Thirsk took the opportunity to try and cement his case. "You can see why I think she's up to something, surely?"

"She's not a very nice person at all, but that doesn't make her a murderer. I imagine working in a job like that you need a great deal of resilience."

"Are you on their payroll or something?"

The door opened and Toni entered, excitable and annoying once more. "We've just heard from the hospital. The morphine bottle on the SHDU had insulin in it. Rebecca must have thought she was administering morphine last night, but it was insulin."

"I got that the first time you said it. How did the bottle get full of the wrong drug?"

Fitzpatrick was already on his way up the stairs. "It was an accident. Let those two women go and find something else to waste your time on. This case is over and I don't want to hear a smidgeon about it ever again. Understood? Oh, and while you're at it, you can tell the coroner he can go ahead with the inquest on Tobias Sutherland, that we've completed our investigation and found nothing untoward."

"We didn't investigate anything."

"We don't need to. I want those nurses released and you getting on with some real crimes instead of whatever personal vendetta you're waging against the hospital. It's an order, Thirsk, do as you're told."

Thirsk had no choice this time, he had played his trump card and lost. He wanted to know who had switched the medication but knew it was futile looking for answers.Banging heads with the National Health Service was clearly not the done thing. "You tell the bitch hounds, Toni. I wash my fucking hands of this conspiratorial brick wall." He stormed up the stairs, huffing and livid. "That fucking woman's a murderer and nobody seems to give a shit."

Chapter 7
The Inquest into Mrs Gleeson's Death

John hated courts with a passion and did his utmost to avoid them – the air of authority, of crime and punishment, and strict, unworldly judges setting fines and convictions, changing lives – but his accusation towards his brother meant that attendance was a necessity. Since he had demanded the post-mortem on his mother's body, a small struggle worth ultimately half a million pounds of his rightful inheritance, he had spent hours on the internet searching for answers and he was confident he would be heard when his time came to speak. He rounded into a small slot in the crowded car park and killed the engine.

To his dismay he noticed Nicholas having a cigarette, leaning against his car, and he kept his head down to avoid being noticed as he climbed out, but Nicholas had been waiting for him and he trotted over breathlessly, discarding the butt onto the ground. "I've got nothing to say, except what I'm going to say in there."

"You're not still harping on about me killing her, are you? You and I both know that this is about money, not how mum died."

"You killed her because she was going to change her will, and if she'd done so, your inheritance would have dropped to five hundred thousand. It's simple, it's obvious, and the police are listening to me."

"Don't be so ridiculous, they'll be laughing behind your back at your paranoia. This is all a waste of time and they'll see right through your motives. Anyway, aren't you even a little concerned that the pathologist involved the coroner? I know I am, because that means they suspect foul play, and if they're right, that means somebody killed mum."

"Yes, you. My point exactly. I'm done with you." John marched towards the entrance, haughty, and Fran tried to catch him up, issuing a sympathetic glance to Adele, who was equally perplexed.

"I didn't do anything to harm mum, you know I never would, and your slurs and slander are going to land you in trouble." Shouting – he was always one to have the last word – Nicholas grasped his wife's hand for support.

Oxford Coroner's Court is a unique building, a miniature stone castle set on a relatively busy street, odd amongst the high-rise buildings that surround it. Today it was unusually busy, with colourful people of all ethnicities bustling importantly here to there, most in suits, bar the few don't-give-a-damns in jeans and sweatshirts. A plaque on the wall showed a puzzling maze of rooms and departments and John chose, despite the embarrassment of needing direction, to ask for assistance rather than attempt to negotiate it. More similar to his brother than either would ever acknowledge, Nicholas held his wife at a distance to follow his older sibling to the correct place. He would not walk with them, but would be able to see where they were going.

Expecting a grand room with panelled walls and sumptuous furniture as television shows depicted, John was surprised to find a more functional office with neutral decor and a barely-there desk. The Coroner, Mr Huntingswood, was unexpectedly friendly, welcoming his guests as they seated themselves and the two brothers relaxed into the informal setting.

The pathologist who had reported the death, Dr Ismail Berker, was the first to be called and he walked to the front with an air of calm confidence. When asked why he had been suspicious of the circumstances behind Nellie Gleeson's death, he explained that routine biopsies taken from the area of the heart, the right ventricle, where the pulmonary embolism had caused myocardial infarction – a heart attack, he explained for the laymen in the room – had an abnormal quantity of both platelets and lymphocytes, which would suggest an air embolism.

"Whereas these are not rare, I felt that in Mrs Gleeson's case it was irregular as she hadn't had surgery, which is sometimes the cause of an air embolism, and didn't lead the kind of lifestyle that put her at risk of developing one. Despite her years and the repeated chest infections she was hospitalised for,

63

she was a relatively healthy woman and her blood vessels, importantly those leading to and from her heart, were surprisingly clear for a person of her age.

"Prior to her fatal cardiac arrest, she'd not had any heart problems – angina, irregularity, high blood pressure – that could lead to such a development. Her illness, the reason for her incarceration in the Padway Hospital, was purely infection related and fully under control by the medication she was receiving intravenously."

"For the benefit of those present who possess little or no medical knowledge, could you please tell us how you know the infection was not a factor in her death?"

"Of course, sir, we routinely sample the blood during a PM – post-mortem – and although tests showed infection levels, they weren't severe, certainly not enough to kill a person. Analysis of the tissues surrounding the embolism showed it had been a large interruption, which doesn't correspond with either the health of the subject, or her medical and physical history."

Nicholas listened to Dr Berker and the summary of his mother's body with a surreal, revolted interest. Had his mother actually been murdered? Who on earth would have wanted to hurt her? She had been a harmless old lady. Yes, she'd had a sharp tongue and when somebody rattled her, she'd always stood her ground, but that hadn't happened often and even when it had it'd always blown over in days. It was slowly dawning that of all the people in the room he was the only person with a reasonable motive to want her dead, and he discreetly flicked through the contacts on his mobile to find the number of the solicitor he had tentatively instructed; he suspected he was going to need him.

Once the Coroner had heard all the evidence from Ismail Berker, he called Robert Nelson, the doctor who had pronounced the death, who explained that there had been no chance of resuscitating Mrs Gleeson by the time he arrived on the ward as she had been deprived of oxygen for too long. Mr Huntingswood interjected, "How do you know? I mean, surely you'd have tried something? She was in hospital, how did she have a fatal heart attack without somebody noticing?"

"I can't answer that, sir. As soon as my bleeper alerted me I made my way straight to the ward. On reaching her bed I checked her pulse, aspiration and optic dilation. Her body was warm to the touch, but her temperature low at thirty-five point two, suggesting she'd been dead a while. With her age and condition I felt any attempt to resuscitate would be futile."

Angela Crabtree, exhausted from another moonlighting nightshift at Kendrick Hospital, passed Dr Nelson as he returned to his seat, and settled onto the chair he had just vacated. She had never attended an inquest into a death before and was more excited than concerned now that Hugh had allayed her fear of the unknown. From the questions the doctors had been asked, she guessed which direction her own inquisition would follow and she was more than happy to drop the temporary nurse who had shared care of the ward that night in trouble. The Coroner finished the standard preliminaries and got to work on the real concerns. "How did you not notice a woman in your care having a heart attack?"

She was prepared. "Due to expenditure cuts within the NHS, the staffing levels at the hospital have dropped dramatically, which means we can't oversee every patient all of the time."

"How long have you worked at the Padway Hospital?"

"Two years, just gone. A year ago, night staff was reduced to a small team of doctors to oversee five wards and two qualified nurses per ward. The level of staffing is not adequate if there are any emergencies during the night. On the night in question, my colleague had called in sick and the agency sent us a temporary nurse. I showed her around, and having worked at the hospital before she was familiar with the routine.

"I was confident in her abilities, so when the drugs round was due at ten, we split the task fifty-fifty. She reported back that there had been no problems with any of the patients and I had no reason to disbelieve her." Perfectly done, she thought to herself. Laying the blame, but nicely.

She smiled at Mr Huntingswood as he asked her what happed next. "The replacement nurse and I were carrying out observations on the patients..."

"What time was this?"

"Just gone midnight. Mrs Gleeson was written up for two-hourly checks. I noticed that something was wrong with her, she'd gone a blue-ish colour. I asked the other nurse to bring an obs machine and as soon as I saw that she had no pulse, we contacted Doctor Nelson, who arrived within five minutes."

"So you believe Mrs Gleeson was already dead when you attended her?" Her positive answer was enough to satisfy Huntingswood, who called Halina to the front. Angela was surprised; she'd suspected she'd seen Halina's face somewhere before when she'd met her during shift handovers, but hadn't realised she was the woman who had temped on the night of Mrs Gleeson's death. She looked different somehow. The Polish woman's appearance and manner on that night had been meek and shy. Now, with her wiry, uncontrollable hair, slightly greying at the temples and without style, she seemed stern and the absence of a smile left her austere. Her use of English was good, however, and her directness a blessing to the Coroner, who had heard far too much rambling in his time.

After a few basic questions he steered into the heart of the inquest. "You were the last person to attend to Mrs Gleeson before her death. Could you please tell me what happened?"

"It was all routine stuff. She was due for her intravenous antibiotics, Amoxicillin-clavulanate, at ten p.m. and I hooked up the bag and fitted the tube to the cannula. I checked the flow, which is standard practice, and moved to the next patient."

"Were you aware of any air bubbles in the tube that could have inadvertently made their way into her bloodstream?"

"Also standard practice, I should have said. There may have been one or two tiny ones, as happens with most IV drips, but none that would have caused harm."

"So you had no concerns about Mrs Gleeson? Was she awake?"

"No concerns. She was awake."

"So, tell me about what happened next, when your colleague raised the alarm two hours later."

"I had been dealing with a patient in another bay and when Angela shouted I came straight through. From the doorway I could see that Mrs Gleeson didn't look right."

"In what way?"

"Her skin was grey and sallow and I could see no movement from the chest area to indicate she was breathing. Angela asked me to fetch the obs machine. When she put the clip on Mrs Gleeson's finger there was no pulse. I called Dr Nelson immediately."

"But when you'd recorded her heart rate, etcetera – done your obs, as you'd say – at," he glanced at his notes on the desk in front of him, "ten o'clock the evening before, the readings were normal?"

"Yes, there was nothing out of the ordinary."

"Nothing to suggest she was about to have a massive coronary and die?" It was rhetoric and Halina, a woman of few words, remained silent. Mr Huntingswood finished his questions to the medical team, moving on to the two feuding brothers and their wives.

He called John Gleeson to the front, intrigued as to why he'd asked for a post-mortem to be carried out on his mother's body. "It is my belief that my brother killed my mother before she had a chance to change her will."

"Your brother, for the record, is Nicholas Gleeson?"

"Yes, sir."

"But the proceedings here today have shown that your mother was alive and well hours after your brother left the hospital. Has this reassured your suspicions?"

"She's dead, he's got a million pounds, of which I should have half, and the pathologist has stated his concerns regarding the cause of the heart attack. What do you think?"

"Mr Gleeson, this isn't a place for pettiness and I ask the questions. I've heard enough. Can Nicholas Gleeson please step to the front?"

Irritated by John's behaviour, Huntingswood felt sorry for the man before him, a gentle manner and softly spoken. "I offered to give him a cheque for five hundred thousand pounds once I received the estate funds, but he rejected it. I also put it in writing that I'd give him the money but he tore it up. I never wanted this inquest."

Huntingswood sighed audibly and sat back in his seat, playing with his fingers. The aim of the inquest was to decide whether Nellie Gleeson had died naturally or her death had been aided, not to establish blame, but a peaceful resolution with every party happy seemed impossible because, although Nicholas and Adele had kept their decorum, John, and to a lesser extent, Fran, bubbled with anger and righteousness.

John stood, aware of how badly his behaviour was coming across. "It's not as temperamental as Nicholas suggests, I was in no doubt that the cheque would not be honoured should I cash it."

"Sit down, Mr Gleeson, you've had your say already."

Nicholas's voice remained calm and mature. "It would have been honoured, sir, I can assure you."

"Would have?" Huntingswood was now interested.

"We couldn't guarantee that now as we've used the money for the charity we run with our two sons. The money is essentially spoken for. We could possibly manage a smaller amount. A much smaller amount."

"Yes, I remember now, I've seen the accounts you've supplied. Very commendable, but it does seem a little underhand to spend the funds when you know that there is a dispute regarding the recipient." Huntingswood was bored with the tittle tattle. Yes, the argument was over a substantial amount, but if the amiable brother had offered the money and the volatile sibling had refused it, then John Gleeson had brought the whole sorry mess on himself by being childish.

"It really wasn't underhand. You see, my wife and both sons suffer from Crohn's disease and we used the money to expand our services by setting up an online help group that sufferers could refer to, it's something we've had planned for years. We formed the charity when I retired four years ago and it's been very successful to date. More so now, with the new group. However, with the recession, it's taken a lot more funding than we initially accounted for."

John stood, unable to contain himself any longer, and Huntingswood demanded he sit immediately. "I can't keep listening to this. We all know that mum was going to change her will, so in effect, Nicholas has taken my inheritance without my permission. That money is rightly mine, everybody in the room knows that."

Huntingswood was fuming. "Mr Gleeson, that is enough. Can I remind you that you are in a court of law? Any more behaviour like that and I'll hold you in contempt of court. I'm adjourning the hearing for lunch, and I want everybody back at one this afternoon." He lowered his glasses on his nose and glared at John over the top. "And behaving like adults."

As he strutted from the court, he felt as if he were back in nursery and he was eager for the afternoon session to be over. John Gleeson, angry and accusing towards his brother, adamant that Nicholas had 'done something' to his mother to protect his inheritance, and then Nicholas, who came across as a gentle and generous man, meek in his speech and manner. It was easy for Huntingswood to dismiss John's issues as a case of sour grapes. The observations taken from the victim after the man had visited his mother had been acceptable and he resolved that they wouldn't have been if Nicholas Gleeson had done anything untoward.

The room was soon empty and Fran grasped John's arm, partly for his reassurance, partly to keep up as he strode away, simmering. "John, you've got to keep calm, you're only getting yourself in trouble, acting like that."

"It's just so wrong, just like him killing her in the first place was wrong."

Clutching his jacket with her hand to catch up and puffing with exertion, she remained two steps behind him. "I know the money would change our lives beyond belief but you can't keep stressing like this, you'll give yourself a coronary. What Nicholas has done is wrong, I know that, but he didn't kill Nellie, the whole idea is preposterous. He adored her."

"He adores his fancy lifestyle and holidays too. Hard up, my arse. Hard up enough to plough my inheritance into that stupid charity that he concocted to polish his halo, yet he still manages to go abroad three times a year."

"You're being ridiculous. The third was in Cornwall and he was staying with his son."

John had stopped outside the small café they lunched in on their rare shopping trips together; it was non-descript but the food was always palatable and cheap. He opened the door and relished the warmth as he dragged his wife to a table. "You know what I mean," he had calmed himself now they were surrounded by diners, "they have no idea what being hard-up is like. Not like us, we've always had to struggle."

Fran squeezed onto the fixed seat and grabbed the menu, scanning it with irritation. "I know that but I wish you'd stop harping on about it. It's only money and I'm getting sick of hearing about it day in, day out. What are you going to do when they rule that Nellie died naturally? And I can assure you Mr Huntingswood didn't look too impressed that you'd turned the money down when Nicholas offered."

John was about to jump into another argument, the same hash they'd locked horns over for the past few weeks, but a business card on the notice board above the table caught his eye and he reached forward to unpin it. His brow furrowed as he flicked the card over. "Why the hell didn't I think of this before?"

Fran crossed her arms. "What?"

"It's a private investigator. I'm going to go and see this bloke," he turned the card again to view the name, "Peter Benson. Maybe he can prove that Nicholas killed mum."

"No," she laid her hands on the greasy table, at the end of her tether. "That's enough. Your mum died of natural causes. Your brother's spent the inheritance, and we're looking forward to years of paying off the debts we've incurred for this farce. You're not going to give any more of our money away, especially to some jobless jerk who calls himself a private investigator."

He slipped the card in his pocket, defiant. "I'll do what I want."

Fran was about to object but a waitress was hovering by the table, scratching the eczema on her elbow. "Sausage, chips and beans. Twice."

"Would you like drinks with that?" The girl attempted a smile that was more a grimace.

Fran's eyes still silenced her husband, lips twisted and scorning. "Tea. Two teas." She waited until the girl had gone. "Pin that card back up."

"Or what?"

"Or else." Fran had thought about leaving John time and again over the dull, struggling years of their marriage, but she had always come to the conclusion she was better off where she was. She had nowhere else to go, theirs being a childless union, and she had no money to leave with, but her husband had become so contemptuous – more so now than ever – and the only subject that aired in their home was Nicholas and his downfalls. She'd had enough this time. "Or else I'll leave you."

As John took the card from his pocket he memorised the number – he would go to the gents and scribble it on something from his pocket before their food arrived – and he reattached the card to the cork. "There," it was uttered with a flourish, "happy now? I'm going to the loo, is that okay with you?"

It seemed as if no time had passed since the morning session had ended and the issue of how the air embolism had been present in Mrs Gleeson's body remained unanswered. Dr Berker returned to the front to give his professional opinion when asked. "In this case, I cannot explain the findings. During the post-mortem, when I discovered how expansive the damage from the air pocket in her heart was, I rechecked the body for any injuries, cuts in the blood vessels and suchlike, that may have allowed a large amount of air into her bloodstream, but could find nothing."

"So how did the air get there?"

"This type of embolism is usually seen as a result of a sudden change of air pressure, deep sea diving lends itself to what is known as 'the bends' if a suitable amount of time isn't spent in decompression units, and flying when at risk is also another presenting factor. To my knowledge, Mrs Gleeson had never flown, nor been a diver."

"Is it possible the air was put there by foul means?"

71

"Yes, it would have been possible through the cannula that was in her arm."

"Had such an act taken place, would the effects have been immediate?"

"In that volume, probably."

"Now, you have put in your report that she had been dead for about an hour before Dr Nelson attended her, which would make the actual time of death eleven p.m. When Miss Kostuch attached the new medication to the cannula at ten p.m. Mrs Gleeson seemed well. So somehow during that hour, air accumulated in her veins to such an extent that she died as a result. Could that have happened naturally with no intervention?"

"Her lungs were compromised because of the infection, but I saw no damage to them that would indicate a possibility of air being absorbed."

"Can you answer my question, please?"

Reluctantly, Ismail conceded, "It would be extremely irregular, but yes."

Chapter 8
Brothers at War

It had been a tiring day for Halina, but she was relieved with the verdict that Nellie Gleeson had died of natural causes. If the findings had been different her world could have been destroyed. She opened the front door and stepped into the kitchen, setting a carrier bag on the table. Marek tripped across the room in his unique, loveable way and threw his arms around her shoulders, but she wasn't in the mood to be affectionate and pulled away. "I bought some, well, not Champagne, but sparkling wine. You know I don't have much money."

"I'm guessing the inquest went well." He pulled the bottle from the bag, pleased to find it already chilled.

"I never expected it not to. She was an old woman who died. The whole process was a silly waste of time and money."

The cork popped and Marek poured into two tumblers, handing one to his girlfriend, who was now sitting at the table, shoes discarded and toes wriggling with freedom. "So, I got paid today, do you fancy a takeaway?"

Halina surveyed the bottle, the glass, the bubbling liquid, while she considered the idea. "You know, I think I'll just take my drink to bed, maybe read for a while or something. It's been a long day." Moments later she was gone and Marek wasn't sure exactly what had just happened. He sipped the cheap wine as he scanned the menu that had been posted through the door earlier.

In the room they now shared, which had freed Marek's room to advertise for another lodger to bring more money in, Halina wasted no time in donning her pyjamas and settling under the covers. As she closed her eyes the memory of the dead woman surfaced and that irritated her. Nellie Gleeson had been a dreadful pensioner, a racist, a small-minded bigot. "You look foreign to me, I don't like foreigners. I want somebody else, someone who can speak English."

Halina had bristled – who wouldn't – but she was used to such treatment, especially amongst the elderly. She had brought the obs machine with her and fed the cuff around Nellie's arm to take her blood pressure. "I'm more than capable of doing my job, Mrs Gleeson." She had attached the clip to the woman's finger to monitor her pulse and clicked a new sheath onto the tympanic thermometer, poking it gently into her ear.

"You come over here, stealing our jobs and housing, living off our benefits. What are you? Polak, Czech, Romanian? Bloody immigrants, you should all bugger off back where you belong."

Halina had remained calm and copied the readings onto Nellie's notes, initialling the entry. "I'm a British resident, where I originate from is no business of yours."

"Yes it is, it's good men like my sons, like my late husband, that pay the taxes for all the things you lot get. It's all wrong."

"I pay my taxes too. I'm working, can't you see?"

"Yeah, in a job that my great-grandson could have. Four years in uni and what does he get? Nothing, that's what. Not even a job at McDonalds. And it's scum like you lot who take the jobs our youths should be entitled to."

Halina had heard the opinion so many times it didn't even register any more and she was about to move to the next patient when, "Kids, that's what you'll be doing next. Getting yourself pregnant so you can live off the state as a single mother, probably claiming disability too. Kids. You'll be up the duff in no time, mark my words."

Until now, Halina had forgotten that part of the exchange and unwelcome tears moistened her eyes. A baby. How could she ever try and replace her beloved Karol, dead – and so cruelly – before his time. The poor little mite. So fragile, so vulnerable. Her mind drifted back to the heady days when she had been in love, the days when everything had been perfect… The days when Borys and Karol had been part of her life, not her history.

The unwanted tears brimmed and spilled and Halina rubbed them brusquely aside, forcing the sadness back into a mental box to compartmentalise it in protection of herself. Her jaw stern, she switched off the light and downed the contents of the tumbler.

Angela had returned to Hugh and Marcus's apartment after her appearance at the inquest in Oxford, and had tucked herself into her sleeping bag on the sofa to catch up with some sleep before her nightshift at Kendrick Hospital started. She had slept like a baby, two full, unbroken hours, when her two friends arrived home together from work. Noticing her, they went to the kitchen and closed the door to avoid disturbing her, but it was too late, she was wide awake. She ran her fingers through her hair to control the mess and trotted to the kitchen, feeding a cardigan over her crumpled blouse and trousers.

"We tried not to wake you, sorry."

"I know, don't worry about it. Is anyone making tea?"

Hugh took the kettle to the sink and filled it, switching it on. "I am now. How did the inquest go?"

"Okay. You know, I thought I'd seen the woman who's got the opposite shift to me on the SHDU before. She was temping at the Padway the night Nellie Gleeson died."

"Halina Kostuch?" Marcus had met her a couple of times since she had started at the hospital and had been unimpressed.

"That's her, yeah. Anyway, we're both in the clear."

"Did you expect anything else?" Hugh removed a ready meal from the freezer and stabbed the cellophane a few times before setting it in the microwave.

"No, she was ninety, well past it. Of course she didn't die unlawfully." Angela had spotted the time and was going to have to hurry.

"So the verdict was natural causes?"

"It was, after a bitch-fight between the woman's sons. It was all about money in the end."

"Just out of interest, how did she die?"

"It was a massive air-embolism in the heart, caused her to arrest."

Frowning, Hugh put the spoon on the side and passed Angela her tea. "I had one of those in an eighty year old a few weeks back. I referred her death to the coroner. Do you know when the transcript of the inquest will be made public?"

"I don't know, you know more about things like that than I do."

"Who did the PM?"

"I think his name was Dr Barker, Berker, something like that. He seemed very professional."

Nicholas and Adele darted through the front door in a playful race for the phone and he reached it first, snatching the handset as he carefully placed the bag containing a chilled bottle of Moët & Chandon on the carpet. "I win. That's twice in one day. You go and pour the plonk, I'll call the boys and let them know."

Adele took the bag to the kitchen, smiling. The past few weeks had been tedious and often heart breaking. Her husband and his brother had never been close, mainly due to John's envy of Nicholas's success throughout his life.

Whereas John had flunked school and wasted the years he could have been carving a career in one dead-end job after another, Nicholas had gone to university, which had given him a solid enough grounding to step into an affluent position with a leading firm of surveyors. In time, he had become a partner and the financial rewards and esteem had given him a comfortable life to share with his now-grown family.

John had been jealous but hadn't tried to better himself, always taking the role of the martyr, the hard-done-by loser who had nothing but bad luck. Fran had tried her best to gee him, but when they discovered that she couldn't give him a family, she had joined him in the role of the downtrodden. She'd become depressed – not that they called it that in those days, she had simply been told to keep a stiff upper lip and get on with it – and as she ate more and more, she left the house less.

It hadn't taken long for the overeating to show and she hopelessly watched what had once been an attractive figure become rolls of wobbling fat that she detested, but with her esteem so low and any hope forgotten, she mastered the art of keeping the house presentable with minimum effort while she soaked up one television program after another.

John had bumbled from one job to the next, being sacked far too often for the snidey comments he was so good at, until he became unemployable due to problems with his back. They had lived on disability benefits since, nearly nineteen years now.

Adele and Nicholas, in contrast, were both fit and healthy, active and cheerful. They'd had their two sons in quick succession in their late twenties. Adele had stayed at home until they were at school and then taken a part-time position in her profession, and their joint salaries had afforded them a lifestyle that, although not grand, was privileged. Nicholas had suggested on many occasions that he could lend his brother money but John always rebuked them, saying he would not take handouts.

No doubt the fact that his inheritance had been spent on funding a charity had, Adele suspected, left him bitter. She hated to see the family battle over something as superficial as money, but she also knew that Nicholas had tried his best to be fair.

Adele took a pair of crystal flutes from the cupboard and polished them with a glass cloth, and she placed them on a tray alongside the Champagne. Peckish, she surveyed the contents of the fridge and decided the smoked salmon parcels she had bought the day before would accompany the bubbly perfectly. She slid them onto a plate, arranging them neatly and garnishing with a sprig of fresh parsley from the plant on the windowsill, and carried the tray to the lounge.

Nicholas was saying farewell to their eldest son on the phone. "Yes, it's great news, in fact your mum's just bought our celebratory Moët through so I'll raise a toast to you all." He cut the call and took the bottle from the tray, removing the foil and loosening the cork. "They're both pleased as punch for us."

Adele tittered as she sat next to her husband, leaning against his shoulder as he silently popped the cork into his palm. "Of course they are, they'll all be coming to Greece with us next month."

He knew she was joking but rebuked her regardless, "Our boys aren't money-grabbers, not like that idiot brother of mine."

John led Fran into the small terrace they had called home for quarter of a century and they both slumped on the worn sofa, their overweight dogs squirming with disgust at the disturbance. "That's that then." He was furious.

Fran reached over the side of the seat for the multi-pack of crisps she had left there the previous night and pulled out a bag of cheese and onion, opening it hungrily. "It's not so bad surely. Wouldn't it be worse if he'd ruled that Nicholas was a murderer? The coroner was so close to going the other way that, in my opinion, we should just be grateful that wasn't the case."

"Be grateful, my arse. We haven't got two pennies to rub together and I'm supposed to be happy about it. I still think he killed her and I can't see why everyone else doesn't; it's obvious to me. "

Fran shoved the dregs of the packet of crisps into her mouth and reached for another bag. "For God's sake, all you ever do is moan, harping on about sodding money all the sodding time. We've always had to struggle and we'll always have to, so we'll just have to get on with it."

John stood and shook his trouser pocket, checking for change. "I'm going for a pint, I don't know when I'll be back."

He stormed out, leaving Fran basking in the light breeze his departure had created, puzzled, and moments later she heard the front door slam. Stuffing the second portion of crisps into her mouth, she knew John had to be up to no good as he rarely went to the pub if they hadn't argued. Suspecting it was something to do with the private investigator, she realised she'd had enough. Of John, of his whining, of her life and their money being wasted. If he wasn't back for dinner she was going to take action.

John waited until he had reached the gate to check he hadn't lost the number he'd written down in the toilets of the café, and pushed it back into his pocket firmly. The pub was on the corner and it took less than a minute to get there. He ordered a pint of bitter and took it to the porch, propping it on the windowsill, and drew a cigarette from the packet, lighting it. After inhaling deeply and coughing, he took his mobile phone from his coat and re-found the scrap of paper, dialling the number.

The 'jobless jerk' his wife had referred to was in fact an ex-police detective who had retired early on medical grounds. He was polite, informative and reassuring, and John felt confident that he had chosen the right man. "The thing is, my wife doesn't know about this, she'd go ballistic if she did."

"That's no problem, we can meet on your terms and, from what you've said, I can't see a reason to inform her. When would you like to meet to discuss it?"

"I'm out right now, she never comes down the pub."

Peter Benson hesitated, debating the clash between the program he had planned to watch and the possibility of an income for once, and he chose the latter. "I'll just feed the cat and I'll drive straight over. Get a beer in for me," he laughed, and John's shoulders relaxed. Somehow, he knew he was doing the right thing.

John was on his second pint by the time Peter arrived and the two men shook hands, before John led the younger man to a discreet table by a frosted-glass window. They sat and supped for a few moments and the investigator took the lead. "So, tell me, why do you think your brother killed your mum?"

Fran hated to admit it, but the only place she could think to go to was Nicholas and Adele's. Her parents were dead, she had no siblings or children and her only friends were somewhere in cyberspace. She hadn't bothered to call them prior to arriving, scared they would reject her if she tried, so her appearance on their doorstep with two bulging suitcases was a complete surprise.

Adele composed herself quickly, moving aside for Fran to pass. "Come in, come in. Just leave your bags there. You look like you need a drink."

Fran followed her sister-in-law to the lounge and collapsed into a chair, grateful she hadn't been bundled away with the rubbish. "I'm sorry I came, I know you owe me nothing."

Adele pushed a glass of brandy into the distraught woman's hand. "Don't be silly. I know things are fraught between Nicholas and John, but that doesn't mean we can't be friends. Now, tell me," she slipped neatly onto the settee, "what's happened?"

Nicholas had been watching the commotion from his chair, whilst completing the newspaper crossword. He had always got on with Fran, although he wished she would tidy herself up, and had no qualms about her staying with them temporarily. He was about to leave and give them some privacy when Fran said something that startled him. "Did you say private investigator?"

"Yes, that's how ridiculous it's got. Well, I made him put the card back, but it was a struggle."

"But a private investigator? Investigating what? The coroner was satisfied that mum died naturally, that I didn't do anything wrong." He poured himself another drink, this time to control his angst.

"He's still harping on that you killed Nellie. He's been going on about it for so sodding long I feel like hitting him every time he says it now." Fran dragged a clutch of tissues from the box Adele held towards her and dabbed her nose, sobbing. "I told him today that if he didn't stop it with the stupid ideas I was going to leave him. Well, I had my suspicions he wasn't going to leave it there, so when he didn't turn up for his dinner I nipped down to the pub and he was sitting with a bloke who was writing notes on a pad. I didn't see his face, but I didn't have to guess who it was, so here I am. I left him. Are you sure you don't mind me staying?"

"Of course we don't, love." Adele patted Fran's hand, reassuring.

"What I mind is these accusations he's spouting. Things like that could really damage my reputation." Nicholas wearily thumped the arm of his chair. "How can I stop him?"

Adele shrugged. "Police?"

"I can't say they'd be bothered. It's not like he's threatened to kill you or anything." Fran had a far greater experience of law enforcement than the other two, knowledge gained from the rough area she lived in.

"So you think he's gone along with this nonsense of a private investigator. In fact, I'll tell you what, I hope he has, because I intend to call his bluff. I'll let myself be followed. I've got nothing to hide, nothing to be ashamed about. And once I've let him harass me enough, then I'll take it to the police."

Peter Benson had realised early into the conversation that John Gleeson was a fatuous man who believed that the world owed him a living, and he had mentally mocked most of their conversation. However, John was also possibly a beneficiary of a decent sum and if he wanted to give that away to follow a theory based in doolally-land, that was his prerogative. Peter took the job. " I'll start with the nurses who were on duty the night your mother died. And I'll find out the names of the other patients who were in the bay that night."

"Really? You know, I'd never have thought of that. Looks like I was right to call you." John finished his beer, signalling to the landlord for another.

"Who you gonna call... Pete Benson!" He continued briefly with the Ghostbusters theme, while the couple at the next table gaped at him, both alarmed and amused. John could see the joviality but not the shallowness of the man he had employed and he chuckled. Finishing his show, Pete continued, "Well, do you have any idea of their names?"

"No," John thought hard, wondering why he had to. Wasn't that the detective's job? "I didn't go to see mum much, couldn't bear to see her in such pain. It was awful. There were two nurses at the inquest but neither seemed to have much to say about it all, just that they'd followed procedure every step of the way. Like they would, covering their own arses."

"Can you remember their names?" Pete was always up for an easy life, the more he could get from John the better.

"No, but isn't that what I'm paying you to do, find them? Not that I know how they could help, unless they saw Nicholas doing something strange, and my brother's way too astute to have a witness."

"What ward was she on?"

John produced the letter he had received from the coroner's office, which detailed the doctors involved and various other titbits. "If it's not on this letter then I don't know offhand. If you struggle I could probably take you there. I'd probably remember by sight."

With a modicum of seriousness – for once – Pete leaned back as the landlord placed two pints on the table between the two men. "I need to know, Mr Gleeson..."

"John."

"What exactly do you want out of this, out of my investigation?"

"Justice."

"Really? Your mother was ninety and the coroner pronounced her death was of natural causes. I don't care either way, I don't give a shit if you're after money, or revenge on your brother, or whatever. As far as I'm concerned, you're paying me to do a job and I'll do it, but I have to know what outcome you're hoping for."

John rested against the back of his chair, mirroring the investigator, and took a gulp of his drink. "I believe Nicholas somehow killed her, and if you can prove me right, I could appeal against the coroner's ruling today and perhaps get his decision revoked. Best outcome of all would be to see that bastard brother of mine sent down for murder. Whatever, it's all important: revenge, yes; money, yes. Seeing that crud of a brother of mine behind bars; the cream of the crop."

"Fair enough and thanks for your honesty. I'll need three hundred upfront. I can give you a receipt and obviously I'll detail my expenses."

John stammered for a moment, but once they had finished their beers the two men walked the short distance to a cash-point and John withdrew the best part of his lifetime savings, passing them reluctantly to Pete, who had already scribbled a receipt on a beer mat in the pub. Pete waited for him to retrace his steps before doing a happy dance on the pavement. Finally he could get up to date with the rent.

Pete glanced at his watch. It was nearly nine in the evening, too late to do much tonight, so he stepped into the warmth of a shop, wringing his freezing hands as he collected a packet of chocolate digestives, a pint of milk and a half-bottle of dark rum. He purchased a scratchcard as he paid and took the items home

82

to assist him as he structured a rough idea of how, and what he would need, to investigate.

It was the final shift of the second week into Angela's moonlighting temporary job at Kendrick Hospital and for the first time since their arrests, both Rebecca and Theresa were working, reducing Sister Kennedy's headache of finding nursing staff to cover for them. Angela came through the doors and Theresa gasped. "What the fuck are you doing here? I told you to leave my ward and I meant it."

"I'm here for another two weeks, like it or lump it."

Theresa's fury rose, her face and neck flushing. "You're a copper and I don't want you on my ward."

"I'm not a copper and I never have been. I'm an SRN and I'm completing a time and motion study on this department."

"Get off my unit."

Sister Kennedy had had enough. "Shut up, Theresa, Angela's staying. Get over it. Can we please get on with the transfer, I haven't much time." Kennedy waited for the muttering to die down and began listing the conditions of the four patients to be left in Theresa and Rebecca's care for the night. "May I just add that nobody has died on the ward since you two have been on leave?"

Rebecca swallowed hard. "You think we're guilty of something, don't you?"

"Somebody filled a morphine bottle with insulin leading to two patients being poisoned, one fatally. Luckily Jacob Middleton has recovered well, although now we have the added burden that he intends to sue the hospital for malpractice. I will find out who was responsible and I won't protect anyone once I know the results. To be honest, I'm disgusted, and yes, I think you two were involved somehow."

"But..." Rebecca was determined to prove her innocence.

"Don't bother, Rebecca. Mud sticks. We were arrested and everyone will believe we're guilty regardless. The fuss will die down and they'll see we had nothing to do with it in the end.

Probably when they catch the person who really was responsible."

Angela followed Sister Kennedy from the first and second beds to the third, listening as she detailed the patients, all new to the room since the previous night. Each one was critically ill, but all of them stable and the nightshift would hopefully pass without drama. She was looking forward to going back to her home in Oxford the next morning; as much as she loved her two friends, their man-habits grated on her and she missed the freshness and freedom of her own place. She suspected that Hugh had fallen for her all over again and there wasn't a lot she could do about it. She had to admit he was still attractive to her, but a relationship would have to be serious and she wasn't ready for that yet, even though her thirty-second birthday was approaching.

"Right, if you haven't got any more questions, I'll be out of here." Angela jumped to the present as Sister Kennedy said her goodbyes. "And when I return on Monday morning, there will be hell to pay if any more patients have died. Is that clear?"

Chapter 9
Malpractice or Murder

Pete, although an insincere man, had a great many friends, all of whom loved him for his colourful and charismatic ways, and luckily one of them worked in the administration department of the Padway Hospital. Lorna had once been his lover, back in his days on the police force, but they had mutually agreed that friendship was a better option for them both.

She knew that having his career severed early had all but destroyed him. He had wanted to make a difference, make the community care once more, but what should have been an everyday tussle with a suspect had led to back problems, initially leaving him unable to move without pain. His recovery had been slow and the pressure of the herniated disc on the sciatic nerve was untreatable without a risky operation that he refused to have.

It had been Lorna's suggestion that he become a private investigator, issued as a joke on a drunken evening at her house, but she'd been proud to support him when he relished the idea and turned it into reality. Just as she was supporting him now. "Pete, it's me, sorry it's taken so long, but I've finally had the time to look into that question you asked me." Despite being alone in the office, she was wary of being overheard and kept details to a minimum.

"Gee, thanks, Lor, I thought you'd forgotten."

"As if I'd dare. I'll text you the stuff, okay."

"Walls have eyes and ears, gotcha. Just give me a simple yes or no, but is the person involved still at the Padway?"

"Yes. Look, if you're coming here anyway, do you fancy meeting up for a drink in the canteen later? It's been a while since we caught up."

"That sounds like a plan. I'll send you a text when I've finished talking to him or her."

"Her. I'll send a text now, and I'll see you later." She finished the call and punched the details she had located into her mobile: 'Angela Crabtree, W29. Also Dr Robert Nelson. Other nurse was a temp.'

By the time Pete received the text from his friend, he had reached his car and turned the engine. This investigation was the only one currently on his books and work had been scarce for a while. Most of the jobs he took were from disgruntled partners who suspected their other halves of having affairs, nothing gritty or appealing, but he wasn't hugely enthralled by the current case either.

He lived just over two miles from the Padway in the busy suburb of Wexmarsh, but despite the short distance, the heavy traffic made the journey tedious. He finally arrived an hour later, forcing himself to appear cheerful regardless that he felt anything but. At least he had Lorna to look forward to, he loved their humour-filled chats. He made his way to Ward 29 and pushed the door wide.

"Can I help you?" The pretty nurse and her cute manner made him blush involuntarily.

"I'm looking for Angela…" Try as he might, he could not remember her surname, but didn't dare check his mobile in front of the smiling beauty before him.

Luckily, "Angela Crabtree?"

"Yes, is she here?"

"No, she's on leave until next week. Can I help you?"

It hadn't occurred to Pete that Angela wouldn't be there and he kicked himself for not checking her hours with Lorna. "No, it's Angela I specifically need to talk to, but thanks all the same. Look," he knew the girl wouldn't give an answer but tried anyway, "I don't suppose you know where I can find her, I'm," he flashed his credit card wallet open briefly, a trick that had worked many times before, "Detective Benson. I need to speak to her urgently."

The attractive smile waned and her features hardened. "I don't know anything about her, except she's not here. Sorry."

Pete grinned affably, the only way he knew, and he thanked her as he brought his mobile from his pocket to instigate the planned meeting with Lorna. He left the ward and summonsed the lift, leaning against the wall as he waited.

"I heard you're looking for Angela Crabtree." Pete hadn't noticed the cleaner approach and jumped. "I know that she lives on site, residential block G, if that helps."

"Yes. Yes it does. Thank you."

"I don't know what you coppers want with her, but she's a nasty cow so I hope she's in shit-loads of trouble." As quickly as she had appeared, the cleaner was gone and with a new spring in his step, Pete hopped into the lift, saved the text he was writing to Lorna and returned his mobile to his pocket.

Within ten minutes Pete had located residential block G and was waiting outside the communal doors. Most of the doorbells didn't have names beside them, but 'A. Crabtree' was clearly labelled in black ink for Flat 7 and he pushed it, waiting. Eventually, on the third buzz, the intercom clicked. "If you're ringing any bell to get an answer then piss off."

"Is that Angela Crabtree?"

"Depends who's calling."

Always one to see the good in people, Pete smiled to let it show in his voice. "My name's Pete Benson, I need to ask you a few questions. Can you let me in?"

"No, I've been up all night and I'm tired. Piss off."

"Miss Crabtree, my name is Detective Benson and I need to speak to you urgently."

He heard a sigh, followed by a click and he pushed the door open, scanning the numbers on the four doors. Climbing up the stairs he did the same on the first floor, and number seven was towards the back. As he approached the door opened a crack, a safety chain in place. "Show me your badge, or whatever it is you policemen carry."

Pete had no choice but to admit his deceit and he pushed a calling card through the gap. "I didn't say I was a policeman, I'm a private detective. Please, Miss Crabtree, I'm here now and it won't take long."

On the other side of the door Angela withheld a smile at the visitor's cheek – he had known she would assume he was from the police – and she smoothed her unkempt curls, tightening her dressing gown at the waist. Unable to sleep anyway she was curious. "Five minutes, okay." She unhooked the catch and opened the door, leaving him to walk in alone as she trudged to the kitchenette, yawning, to prepare a mug of tea.

Pete closed the door behind him and followed her into the impeccably tidy studio flat. "I really appreciate this; I know you nurses work long hours. You must be exhausted." Consideration was one of his endearing qualities and he was well aware that it often opened opportunities for his enquiries.

"I am. I've just come off my fifth twelve hour shift in a row."

"Hold on a mo, I was told you were on leave."

She glared at him. "Moonlighting, okay, and don't let that go any further." He mimicked zipping his mouth and she tried not to smile. "Now, seeing as I'm making one anyway, do you want a tea? Coffee?"

"That's kind of you, thanks. Tea, white, no sugar – I'm sweet enough already."

Angela yawned again, wishing she had been this tired whilst lying redundantly in bed trying to sleep, and she threw teabags into two mugs. "So, what's so urgent it couldn't wait until I was awake?"

"Do you remember a patient named Nellie Gleeson? She was…"

"Oh, for fuck's sake, not that old cherry again. The inquest was yesterday, go and read about it at the court."

"Ah, you do, then."

Again, his demeanour tempted a smile and she concealed it by keeping her head down as she prepared the drinks. "It was all over money, two brothers fighting like kids. The coroner ruled that she died of natural causes, which is what we all expected. Let me guess, it's one of the brothers who's employed you."

Pete took his tea and followed her to the sofa, sitting comfortably while she took an easy chair. "Correct, it's John. He reckons…"

"That the other brother, can't remember his name, killed his mum for financial gain. Why on earth are you bothering…oh, money, of course, he'll be paying you for this."

Pete winked at her. "So you think there's no truth in it all. What about the air embolism, though? Don't you think that was strange?"

"Funny things happen in old bodies, the woman was ninety, for heaven's sake."

"In that case – may I call you Angela? – just humour me and tell me your version of events, then I can tick you off the list."

She tugged her dressing gown tightly around her shoulders and curled her toes underneath her, nursing the hot drink close to her lips. "If you insist. I was doing my rounds and noticed Mrs Gleeson didn't look right, so I got the other nurse to bring…"

"Who was the other nurse?"

"Helena something, I think, a foreign woman the agency had sent. She was at the inquest too."

"Can you try and remember her surname?"

"No. I told you, I've been up all night. Anyway, the old woman was already dead, so we bleeped the doctor on call and he pronounced her…"

"Dr Nelson?"

"Yep. Then we called a porter to take her to the mortuary, standard stuff. The end."

"What about the other patients on the ward, did any of them say anything, or do anything?"

She thought for a moment. "Actually, yes. There was a woman who's been in a couple of times, Pat something or other, she was in the bed next to Mrs Gleeson and she said something about her, I don't know, gurgling or something. I'm sorry I'm being vague, I'm just so tired."

Pete reached across and patted her arm, the action of a woman in a man's body. "That's okay, I understand. What if I were to come back later when you've had some shut-eye?"

"I don't think I'd be able to tell you much more than that, it was a long time ago and we have so many patients coming through the wards."

Pete groped in his pocket for the card he had shown Angela when he'd arrived and passed it to her. "Look, keep this and if you remember anything more just give me a call, or text me and I'll call you back."

Angela showed her guest out and Pete padded across the courtyard and through a busy car park to re-enter the hospital, and once he was in the warm again, he found the draft message to Lorna, heading for the canteen after he had sent the text. They shared a hurried brunch, while he begged her to find the patient named Pat that Angela had mentioned. Hesitant at first, but unable to resist his pleading eyes, she agreed to bring up the admission notes when she returned to her desk, and an hour later he was on his way to Berinsfield to the address Lorna had given.

He rapped on the door, hugging his anorak against the piercing wind, shoulders hunched. Presently the door opened and he noticed the walking stick before the woman, a gnarled body underneath a shock of dyed-black curls. Once Pat Bond had heard the reason for his visit she welcomed him in and they sat in the lounge. "I would offer you a drink but I struggle to get about the kitchen, what with being a cripple and all that."

Instantly, Pete was standing. "Let me make you one. And you're not a cripple. That's a horrible thing to say."

She waved him to sit. "No, honestly, I'm alright. Unless you want one, that is."

"Thanks but no, I just had brunch at the hospital. Huge, it was. So, you stayed at the Padway between the tenth and thirteenth of February this year, and during your stay the woman in the bed next to you died. Does this ring any bells?"

"I've been in and out of hospital since last year, the car accident was in August and I've had all sorts of problems, so I've met a lot of people. What was her name?"

"Nellie Gleeson. She was ninety."

Pat laughed, "I remember now, now you've told me her age. Yes, she was a right character, teasing the nurses with her quick one-liners. You wouldn't believe the things that came out of her mouth. Yeah, what was it in the end?"

"A heart attack. Apparently you mentioned that she'd been gurgling to the nurse who found her."

"Did I? Well, yes, she looked like she was having a sort of fit, not a big one like an epilepsy one, just sort of shuddering a little, gasping and, yes, gurgling. It was maybe an hour before the nurses found her. Maybe more."

"Were you not concerned enough to press the alarm to get the nurses before that?" Pete was genuinely surprised.

"I did and one of the nurses came over and switched the alarm light off, she had a quick check on Nellie and said she was fine, said she was sleeping."

For the first time – a chill running along his spine – Pete realised that there might be something unusual about Mrs Gleeson's death. Surely a nurse would know that a patient was having a heart attack? Or at least check her vitals if told she'd had a fit? "What nurse?"

"It wasn't the ginger one, she was the one who alerted the doctor later, it was some other woman, I'd not seen her on the ward before and I've never seen her since. I think she wasn't English, but I can't be sure. She didn't say much, anyhow."

"Maybe a temp?"

"Probably. She was grumpy, just did what she had to do without raising a smile."

Malpractice? Should this nurse have realised Mrs Gleeson was dying, maybe even dead? Pete's interest in the case had magnified a hundredfold. "Do you remember Mrs Gleeson – Nellie's – sons at all?"

Again, Pat chuckled. "The dark-haired one, yeah, he was a good looking chap, probably a bit old for me, but he had such a sweet face, you know, the type of guy you just want to hug. I vaguely recall another bloke, but dark-hair was there twice a day."

"That evening, did either visit her before she died?"

"Yeah, they both did. The other wasn't for long, but dark-hair sat with her for a while. I don't have no-one to visit me when I go in, I'm all on my own, you see, so I always listen to everyone else's conversations. Bit nosy, like that, me. Anyway, she had him in stitches with the tales she was telling. Thing is, she seemed to find the funny side of everything and she had a quick wit. I had a few giggles myself, to be honest."

"And when he left, what then? How was she? Was she asleep, or…"

"No, she was wide awake, I guess that's why her dying was such a shock. She'd been in such high spirits and she was laughing as dark-hair left. She picked up her knitting and just carried on like before."

"How long after Nicholas – dark-hair – went did she start to fit?"

"Oh, a good few hours. She was sat up for ages, then said she was tired at, let me think a moment… I'll tell you what, I know exactly when she turned her telly off and lay down, because we was both watching the same channel; we're both fans of Newsnight. She was looking forward to it, but when it came on it was all about that Nigel Farage and she made some joke about how shit the rest of the news was anyway, and she said she'd rather go to sleep. It usually starts at ten-thirty so she would have settled down about then."

"You're sure about that?"

"Yes, because they'd have recently done the drug rounds, that's right. That other nurse, not ginger hair but the foreign one, she'd given the other two girls on the bay and me our tablets, then she changed Nellie's drip. I think she was on antibiotics. Anyway, once she'd done it I told Nellie she was just in time for Newsnight. I told her it was all about that Farage bloke and she said it was shit, then she said she'd go to sleep instead, said she was tired anyway."

"And how long after until she started fitting?"

"Maybe an hour or so, maybe less, I'm not sure. I got bored of the program pretty soon, I wasn't so keen on the subject either, so I turned my telly off, lay down and fell asleep, but the noises she was making woke me up and I opened my eyes to see what was happening."

"And you called for assistance?"

"Yeah, and the same nurse came back and said she was okay."

It was imperative for Pete to find out who the second nurse was – if, indeed, she was a nurse and not a deranged impostor – because in his growing opinion, something was very wrong about Nellie's death.

As soon as he left the house, he called Lorna and told her his suspicions. "Oh no you don't, Pete, have you any idea how much work an investigation like that would place on my shoulders? Just let it go. Tell the angry brother that the nice brother did nothing wrong, and that mummy-dear died of natural causes."

Pete reached his car and snuggled into the driver's seat, turning the engine in order to heat the inside. "I can't believe you said that, Lor. Okay, the old girl was ninety, but that doesn't make it right that she was murdered."

"She probably wasn't. The patient was probably just mistaken about timings and when the bank nurse checked her."

"You don't think it is suspicious at all, or you don't like the idea of hard work."

"Both, actually. Just leave it, Pete, you're seeing something that isn't there."

He heard the dial tone and realised Lorna had ended the call, and he was angry that she had been so dismissive because of the victim's age. He needed to find out who the other nurse was before the Coroner's Court opened on Monday, but without Lorna's help how could he? Angela was the only solution he could think of and he headed back to the hospital, hoping she'd had enough sleep now. But this time she refused to see him, regardless of the charm he ladled thickly. She had heard Nellie Gleeson's name once too often and after the glowering reception she had received from the two hostile nurses on the SHDU the previous night, she'd had enough for the week.

But Pete had other ideas. "I'm taking you for dinner whether you like it or not. I'll pick you up at seven."

Chapter 10
In the Shadows

Halina had gone straight to bed when she'd arrived home the previous evening, and the stress of the inquest and having to return straight to work after had knocked her out until gone seven in the morning. She heard Marek's key in the lock and hoisted herself up the bed a little, surmising he'd have been for his regular early run and picked up the papers on the way home. He entered the room with his usual beaming grin. "Hey gorgeous."

"Alright."

"Are you okay? You seem a bit down."

"I'm exhausted, feel like I've not slept a wink."

"Oh dear." She was always tired now and he hoped it wasn't of him. "Sorry I've got to work today, it's not leaving us with much time together, is it?"

"That's okay."

"Good." It was obviously not okay as she had turned her back on him, but he didn't know what to do. Maybe it was her time of the month. Marek opened the door, realising that whatever he did, he would be in the wrong. "I'll go and make breakfast then."

"Okay." Halina watched him leave, closing the door behind him, and she buried her head in the pillow, fighting to control the tears that were threatening. She couldn't understand why she was behaving the way she was, the same behaviour that had led to the demise of her first and only marriage. Marek had tried to have a conversation and she'd spurned him, yet his incessant chatter was the first thing she'd been attracted to, his vibrant and excitable view of life, his optimism and childlike joy in everyone and everything.

The past couple of weeks had covered so much ground she felt her feet were floating, airborne, caught in a whirlwind. They'd been attracted to each other since they had met, the brunt of an 'are they, aren't they' quandary for their housemates, yet once he asked her out, life had gone crazy, what with him moving into her room, sharing their bed and meals, their private thoughts and dreams. And now he wanted them to move out to a place on their own. It was all too quick, but she loved him nonetheless.

Before they began dating, Halina had visited the doctor because of the unending depression that had followed her from one country to the next, a shrouding blanket of grey, and he had given her medication. Although it had been effective enough to take the edge from her misery, smiling didn't come naturally, let alone unabated laughter, and she was aware that her sadness brought the people around her down too.

She explained early on – giving him the chance to back away, she assumed – that her husband and child had died in tragic circumstances and the love that burned for them would never leave. Essentially, she had made Marek understand that he would always be third on her list and she wondered now if should try to put him first. Bury the past.

She hadn't always been depressed, but had often been miserable as a child – no more than any other of her contemporaries, however. Nobody in the village she had grown up in had money, everyone scrimped here and scratched there to survive, but Halina had had the pressure of being a sickly child too.

Often she had felt full of life with plenty of energy, but her mother would reprimand her for getting out of bed, telling her they would have to visit the doctor with her sore throat, or temperature, or rash, and very often she would be sent to hospital for tests that never seemed to give results. On dark days when she felt sorry for herself, she would wonder if her mother imagined the illnesses because of the sympathy it brought her, but on good days she had enjoyed the stays; the nurses always tried to make the children on the wards happy.

When Karol was born, Halina had finally understood her mother's deep anguish and worry. Having a child who cried too much, or seemed hot and bothered, or wouldn't eat, or would eat and vomit, she had soon restarted the cycle, taking the baby to the doctor frequently with the desperate fear that he was ailing. That he may die.

95

On that final day – the day her life stopped – he did die, and the guilt she felt was overwhelming because she knew that had it not been for her he would still be alive. And it had all been down to her ridiculous jealousy, because she'd been convinced that Borys – dear, handsome, hardworking Borys – was having an affair. Stupid, reckless envy. She knew now she had been wrong, so very wrong, and her punishment was a lifetime of regret, but if there was any good at all to come from it, it was that she had learned not to make the same mistake twice.

Yet here she was, pushing Marek away. She knew she loved him, that he loved her, yet her subconscious was doing everything it could to destroy what could be a wonderful relationship. How could she stop it happening all over again?

Halina threw the cover aside and traipsed down the stairs, intent on rectifying the damage she had done. There was no way she wanted to lose another good man. Jozef and Julita were in the kitchen so Halina stopped by the door. "Marek, I want to tell you something special, have you got a minute? In private."

He turned the gas off under the pan, the scrambled eggs all but done, and followed her to the hallway, away from prying ears. "You know I love you, right?" Marek remained silent but nodded. "It's just, with all this tiredness, I think I may be pregnant. Would you want me if I was?"

"I think the question's the other way round, don't you? Since we got together you've never let me in. I know you lost Borys and Karol and that it nearly destroyed you, but I've pretty much come to the conclusion that I'll never be enough for you."

"Is that why you've been so quiet lately?"

Marek nodded again and Halina held her arms out for a cuddle. "You're enough for me and I really hope I am expecting. Maybe it's time for me to start moving forward at last."

Crushed into the bosom of the woman he loved, Marek could feel his joie-de-vivre returning. "You really think you might be having our baby?"

She kissed his cheek, his forehead, his lips. "Tired and sick, that's how it was with Karol. I really think it's a yes."

Hugh phoned the Padway Hospital and finally found someone willing to give him the email address of Dr Berker's secretary. He tapped a simple message to introduce himself, but gave no detail as to why he was making contact. He pressed send, resolving to forget about the mysterious deaths and enjoy the weekend. But with no plans – with no Angela – it seemed impossible. "She makes a difference here, doesn't she?"

"What?" Marcus continued reading the newspaper and munching his cheese sandwich, snug amongst the cushions and relishing the laziness of the weekend.

"Angela, it's not the same without her."

"You really like her, don't you?"

Hugh stood and stretched, hiding his blushes from his friend. "Guess so."

"So ask her out."

"It didn't work out the first time, why would it be any different now?"

"You won't know unless you try. Call her."

Hugh didn't take much persuading. His mind had been buzzing all day, debating whether he should or shouldn't, and the only thing that had stopped him so far was the fact she had worked through the night and must need her sleep. "Angela?"

"For god's sake, what is with you people trying to stop me sleep? The phone's been going all day. Well, twice."

"I was wondering if I could take you out to dinner tonight."

"Oh." She liked Hugh. Liked him a lot. But she quite liked amiable Pete Benson too. "I've got plans tonight, sorry."

"Oh, okay. I shouldn't have asked."

Angela felt mean, she could hear the disappointment in his voice. "Look, I don't know how I'm going to manage the next two weeks, working eight-hour days at the Padway and twelve-hour nights at Kendrick. I'll be some kind of zombie by the time it's all over."

"Can't you drop the Kendrick job now? Surely after the furore over Rebecca and Theresa's arrests there's nothing more to find. I mean, you haven't seen them do anything untoward, have you?

"No, they've been completely professional. Nasty women, but they do their jobs."

"Has anyone said about the morphine being swapped for insulin?"

"I thought it would have been mentioned a bit more. We've been questioned, all the staff on the ward, but that's all."

"Who by, police or hospital?"

"Some woman called Erika Gomez, she's high up in admin, but I'm not sure what her title is."

"She's the General Secretary's PA so the investigation's coming from the top dogs. So what are you going to do about work?"

"I don't know. Try, I suppose, and if it gets too much I'll have to give the Kendrick job the push. Anyway, I'd best go and have a shower, I feel rank and I'm being picked up in an hour."

Hugh cut the call, full of embarrassment that he had asked her out, and jealously swimming with hatred for the lucky man who had snared her first. The truth was she had made no moves towards him, not a single inclination in his direction and she'd probably had a boyfriend all along. Stupid. Why hadn't he seen that? "She's blown me out."

"I'll bet it's not as dramatic as that."

Hugh snorted, downtrodden now. "Fancy going for a beer?"

Marcus grinned. "Now you're talking."

Marek had been working at Randall's Biotech for five weeks and had fitted into the laboratory team with ease. He was an astute and clever man and he learned quickly, but his enthusiasm for the groundbreaking drug they were developing was what caught his superior's attention the most. Weekend working was supposedly frowned upon, the modern company stressing the importance of a life outside the office, but Marek was beginning to find this a hypocritical statement. A new facet to the drug had been noted and to analyse it required all hands on deck – expected, not asked. He had agreed to work Sunday too; with a baby on the way, they needed the money.

The baby. The most precious thing to happen to him in his whole life, the creation of a child, and with the woman he had loved for longer than he'd been dating her. He stepped off the bus, conveniently close to their home, and trotted to the door, letting himself in. In seconds he was back at the door, waiting for an ambulance to arrive. Halina had locked herself in the bathroom, distraught. "It's just come round the corner, are you ready?"

"They'll need to see me up here first, they don't take you to hospital unless it's necessary." Halina checked her sanitary pad, washed her hands and traipsed back to the bedroom, where she lay back against the pillows, legs on the covers.

Marek waved at the ambulance as it pulled up the kerb and he trotted up the stairs. "Are you still bleeding?"

Halina nodded sadly. "I've just changed the towel, but I can already feel it's soaked. I don't know what I would do if I lost this baby, I couldn't bear it."

He hugged her close, devastated himself. "Don't think like that. You've got to be positive. Everything will be fine."

Two paramedics came up the stairs and completed a general examination of their patient whilst getting the details of why she had called for help. "I'm twelve weeks pregnant and have heavy bleeding, so I'll need to be admitted. I'm a nurse, I know these things." Marek's jaw clenched and he gazed through the window, confused as he mentally calculated dates. It was a blow that she had conceived before they'd got together, but he reasoned that she had never told him the baby was his.He had just assumed. However, that could be dealt with another time, because right now she needed his support.

The paramedic laid a hand on Halina's shoulder, gently pushing her back against the pillows. "That's for me to decide, my love. We'll take a few details and if I feel you need to be seen in hospital, that's where you'll go."

Halina had been right, and half an hour later she was in the back of the ambulance on her way to Boxton Park Hospital. The wait in the cubicle in Accident and Emergency was tiresome, but eventually she was admitted for monitoring, with a scan planned for the next day.

Marek waited until midnight, desperately trying to be strong for his girlfriend, before kissing her goodnight. "I've got to go, I have to be up for work tomorrow morning – well, today now."

Halina's eyes watered, tears threatening to spill. "You mean you won't be coming back tomorrow morning?"

"I can't take time off at the moment, you know that."

"Marek, this is your baby. Aren't you at all concerned?"

"It can't be and you know that."

Her mouth hung open. "What do you mean?"

Marek was pained. He wanted to trust Halina with every bone in his body, but she had lied. "If you're twelve weeks pregnant then it can't be mine."

Halina smiled coyly, embarrassed. "If I'd told them I was five weeks they wouldn't have taken it seriously, they don't until you're past the first trimester. They would have left me there to miscarry without trying anything to save the baby."

"Really? My God, Halina, I'm so sorry I doubted you. I should have realised."

Once more he smothered her face, her eyes – tears – with kisses, tender and loving, and she pulled away, laughing. "So will you come first thing tomorrow?"

He chuckled. "Look, I'll try and get away for my lunch hour, come and see you, and I'll come by straight after work."

She couldn't help herself, it was her instinctive reaction. "Don't bother." Halina slid down the bed, pulling the covers over her face. "This baby clearly means nothing to you and nor do I. Go to your stupid work, just forget about us and have a good time."

"Don't be like that, Halina."

"Just go away."

"I can't win with you." Marek gave up and strutted from the ward, guilty of abandonment, and he realised he would have to take a taxi home which annoyed him further, the money better spent elsewhere.

Having had her attempts to sleep destroyed so many times over the day, Angela had still been tired when Pete knocked on her door, but she had scrubbed up well, showered and fresh, wearing a woollen dress and heels. Not one to bother usually, she had attempted some make-up to accentuate her features; it mattered to her what Pete Benson thought.

Nearing thirty-two, Angela had never been married, never really had a long-term relationship. In fact the six months with Hugh had probably been the most intense of her life. She enjoyed the single status, the freedom to do as she pleased, when she pleased, but she couldn't deny the loneliness. Pete was a bit older, not too awful to look at, and he had a quirky, sweet personality – at least what she had seen of him during their brief encounter in the morning had given her that impression. And she loved his perseverance, that he had not given her a chance to rebuke his offer of a meal.

McDonalds, though? She could think of far more romantic places to dine than the quick-fix burger bar and she felt massively overdressed. But it was a start and she sat at the table, hair coiffed and make-up thick, dress too tight and the sexy, revealing neckline uncomfortable. Pete waved from the queue as he ordered and presently brought the fat-laden food across. "I hope you're hungry, I went large."

They unwrapped their meals and tucked in. Pausing with a handful of fries by her mouth, Angela asked, "So what's happened then, why did you want to see me?"

Pete took a serviette and dabbed at the sauce that dripped from his lip. "You know you said another nurse was working that night, a temp from the agency, do you know which agency?"

She shrugged. "No, I've no idea which ones they use nowadays. I've been there for two years now so I don't use them. Why?"

His food forgotten now, Pete launched into Pat Bond's recollection of the day Nellie Gleeson died and Angela listened keenly to the new perspective. "The way she tells it does sound a bit dodgy, but I'm sure it was all innocent. I mean, what would she gain by killing a ninety year old?"

"I don't know, that's what I need to find out but I can't do it alone, well, without help from someone in the hospital. I was

101

kind of hoping that you..." He ended with widened eyes, his eyebrows high and imploring.

Waving her hand with a girlish giggle that surprised him, Angela blushed. "It's more than my job's worth. So I suppose you'll be telling grumpy brother that kind brother didn't do it, then?"

"Shit, I never thought of that. If I tell John what I know he won't need my services any more. I suspect he'd just find another way of getting at Nicholas, but then if Nicholas knew... Trouble is I've never met him."

"We've had the police investigating a death at Kendrick Hospital, why don't I find out the detective's name and pass it to you. I could text my mate now, he's a friend of the bloke." Pete caught up with his cooling food while Angela tapped a short sentence to Hugh, and moments later he replied. "There you go, his name's Thirsk."

"In that case I won't be telling them anything. I used to work on his team and he's a dickhead."

"Alright then." She mulled as she took another bite of her Big Mac. "How about playing the brothers against one another. You know, tell John – I assume he's the grumpy one – you're still investigating, but tell Nicholas you believe she was murdered and you need the expenses to look into it."

"That's blackmail! Anyway, he'd go to the police, I'm sure."

"What about telling Nicholas what John's up to and ask him if he wants you to prove his innocence. From what I gathered at the inquest, Nicholas – kind brother – was pretty loaded, and I know from what was said that her estate was running at over a million pounds. If he's just inherited that...Has he?"

"Near as damn it."

Angela picked up another chip in readiness, dangling it beside her blood-red lips. "Worth a try then, why not just go and meet him, play it by ear? I mean, you must need the money if we're having our first date over a McDonalds."

"Date?" Now Pete understood why she was dressed so tartily and the hairs on the nape of his neck stood on end. The idea hadn't been anywhere remotely near him. He stuffed the burger into his mouth to stop himself saying something he would regret as she continued to chuckle at her lame joke. He chewed, sipping his drink. Eventually, "I will go and see him, but I'll have to wing it once I'm there."

"Nice one, can I come? It'd be nice to do something exciting for a change."

"No." Pete hadn't meant to be so forceful, but if Angela had designs on him he needed to quell them quickly. "No, I think what I'll do is check their house out first, see if they need any obvious work done. You know, gardening, painting, whatever. I can tailor-make a business card or flyer of a tradesman, that way their suspicions won't be raised."

"Oh. Okay." She was crestfallen and he felt guilty.

"But I do need to know the name of the nurse, the temp."

"Her first name's Helena. No, Halina. That's all I can remember." It would have been easy to find out at work, but she wasn't about to start adding to her things-to-do list and do his job for him; she'd not missed his reaction. "It'll be on the coroner's report, why don't you wait for that."

"Er, yes, that's what I was about to say, that it would be far easier to look at the report when it comes out. Yes." He shoved the burger back in his mouth to silence himself.

Pete managed to get away from Angela soon after the meal using research on Nicholas as an excuse and he purchased a four-pack of lager on the way home. Relaxing in his pyjamas with the beers, he booted his computer up, eager to find information about the more popular and widely known brother. He typed in Nicholas Gleeson and the results were plentiful.

Pete redirected to images and scanned the many photos, deep-brown smiling eyes, crinkled at the edges, a handsome jaw with a beaming smile, all taken at various charity events. He read a couple of news articles, each one showering the man and his dedication with praise. Pete had no doubt that Nicholas Gleeson would make the Queen's Honours List before turning seventy.

Cracking open his second beer, he tried John Gleeson's name. This time there was only one result that was definitely his employer and that was simply his name in an article about

Nicholas. No wonder John had issues regarding his brother, he must have been in his shadow all his life.

It was half-past midnight by the time Marek arrived home and he snatched a couple of slices of bread from the fridge, too tired to bother buttering them, and stumbled up to bed. In the darkness, the tasteless bread filling a hole, he willed himself to sleep, but thoughts of Halina and her temperamental ways unsettled him. He remembered the first day they had met. He had just come from Poland and been allocated his room in their house by the Polish community in Slough, who also assisted him with paperwork and documentation.

He liked her almost from the first moment. It wasn't her looks – she wasn't the prettiest, or the slimmest, or the most fashionable – it was the sadness in her eyes that made him yearn to protect her, a haunting blue that held a tale of hardship and loss. And then, on a knife-edge, she would laugh outrageously, an infectious tinkle that would go on and on until she cried.

One evening, over a bottle of wine after their housemates had gone to bed, Halina mentioned the loss of her husband and son, of the pain she felt every day and how it never left her. He fell for her so hard that day, knowing that underneath the tough exterior she projected was a vulnerable, timid child.

He began to woo her without making it obvious, nurturing her self-confidence with his caring manner and brick by brick he broke through the walls she had built around herself – behind them was a smart mind and a sweet and caring personality. He loved her so much and couldn't understand why she had turned on him, rebuilding the barriers and withdrawing into herself.

Still unable to sleep, his mind whirring non-stop, Marek gave up and went downstairs to make a hot, milky drink, and he was surprised to find Julita sitting by the table nursing her own. She and Jozef were a wonderful couple, their relationship solid and unbreakable, and Marek explained what was keeping him awake, how Halina had gone from loving and hot to freezing cold. "I know she's worried about losing the baby, but if that happens we can try again, we've got all the time in the world."

"That's just it, though, Halina can't see that. As far as her mind sees it, she was in love with her husband and child and they left her. She lives in utter dread that everyone she loves is going to leave her and the threatened miscarriage confirms just that. She needs security and it will take a long time for her to learn that you aren't going to love her and die."

"Do you mean I should marry her?"

"Your words not mine, but yes, I think it would help. I know you're both hard up at the moment, but it doesn't have to be an expensive wedding, all that matters is that you're both there."

"I suppose it's the right thing to do anyway, with a baby on the way. A least we could be a proper family."

"She told me you want to move out of here, get a place on your own."

He nodded. "I'll have to save up first. That's why I didn't object to the overtime, only even that's annoyed her."

"Her first son died, she's scared she's losing this child; give her some space and reassurance. And if you need any help choosing a ring, I know just the place."

Marek laughed as he stood, clasping his mug and going to the door. "Anyone would think you're on commission. Anyway, let's take one step at a time, eh, I haven't even asked her yet."

Back in bed, the covers pulled tight to his chin, he missed the feeling of Halina's body next to his, the sound of her breathing, and he realised Julita was right. He didn't know how, or where, or what with, but sometime soon he intended to propose and he would find the best ring, something unique and special. Something that matched his wonderful lady.

Chapter 11
A Life Barely Started

As soon as his alarm went off at six in the morning, Marek rang the hospital to see how Halina was and they told him she'd had a comfortable night with no problems. They didn't yet know when her scan was due, suggesting he call back later in the morning. He dressed and breakfasted and left for the twelve mile commute to Uxbridge.

Randall's Biotech was a huge building, modern and shiny, and immaculately presented and Marek never ceased to wonder how he had managed to get his dream job with such an esteemed employer. The company had been established thirty years before to research diseases and possible cures and Marek, having gained the highest grade – a 5.0 – at the University of Warsaw in each of the three sciences he had studied, was a valued addition to their team.

The department he worked for was assessing and testing the possibilities of using tetrodotoxin – the poison found in some sea species, including a variety of puffer fish – as an anaesthetic, and his work in the laboratory had so far been well received. They were due to start trialling the new drug, Tetranaesthia, on rabbits soon, having successfully completed their tests on mice and rats. If the drug continued to be a success, they hoped to start subjecting it to humans in twelve to fifteen years.

However, working for such a prestigious company had its downfalls and timekeeping was one of them. Days off, both sickness and holiday, were frowned upon and, although they would never admit it, overtime – not necessarily paid – was expected. Marek couldn't take time away, knowing that pleading for compassionate leave would fall on deaf ears. But Halina needed him.

He entered the laboratory and grinned hello to his colleagues as he weaved to his desk and a thought surfaced, a possible solution. He didn't know much about Halina's background or her family, but then he had never asked. Maybe she had a mother or a sibling, somebody who could help her emotionally, perhaps even physically. He resolved to ask her when he called at the hospital later.

Marek wheeled his chair back to sit, inadvertently knocking a colleague who was passing and the small tray he was carrying clattered to the floor. Rob yelled, his eyes burning with fear, transparent droplets glistening on his face. "That was a TTX vial. It's smashed. I think some went in my mouth." He wiped his face, scraping at the poison that could kill him.

Marek pressed the alarm button by his desk and, alongside the other lab assistants, donned protective headgear to avoid breathing any deadly droplets that may be in the air. He snatched the phone, asking the receptionist to call an ambulance due to an Emergency Code 10 in Lab 4.13.

Nearby, Rose had poured a plastic cup of water from the dispenser and was encouraging the petrified man to swill his mouth out repeatedly. "It's okay, Rob, we've got an ambulance coming, you'll be fine."

He spat the latest mouthful of water onto the floor. "I know, it was only a drop anyway. At least I'll get the day off work."

Three adrenaline pumped scientists, now wearing protective gloves as well as the headgear, smirked at his stab of humour, relieved he was in good spirits. They all knew the effects of the poison, its deadliness had been drilled into them time and again. And it was the first time any of them had seen it ingested. However, with urgent treatment, he had a good chance of surviving.

Marek helped Rob to his feet, guiding him to a seat. "It's okay, I'm fine. There's no tingling or numbness so I reckon I got it out before it did any damage."

"That's good, but you know you still need to go…" Marek's mind whirred as a he tried to remember his training instructions, "I know Hillingdon's the closest hospital, but I seem to recall we'd be taken to Boxton Park if there was a Code 10 because of their large toxicology department."

Rose nodded. "You remember rightly."

"Look, I feel a bit guilty, it was me who knocked him flying. I'll go with him to the hospital and make sure he's okay." Perfect. Now he could spend some time with Halina as well.

"Skiver!" Rose laughed and Marek winked in reply.

Halina seethed as she lay on the hard hospital bed, angry that Marek hadn't bothered to call her. How could he love her if he wasn't concerned about her and the baby? A nurse strode over with a smile. "The porter's just coming to take you for a scan, is your bladder full?"

Halina raised the empty plastic jug from her over-bed table, tipping it in demonstration. "A whole litre. It's as full as it'll ever be. Nurse, I'm scared."

She put a hand on Halina's arm. "I'm sure everything will be fine. Is this your first pregnancy?"

Halina explained about Karol, the difficult pregnancy and his sudden death. "When he was born it was such a relief that he was okay, and then that happened. I felt like I was being punished."

"That's terrible. Did they ever tell you what caused his death?"

"Yes, that's why..." She stopped, chastising herself for losing control. "Hole in the heart, that's what it was."

"Oh, I thought that's what scans were for, to pick up things like that."

Halina wished the nurse – she scanned her badge for her name – would leave, she was asking too many questions. "Deborah, things aren't the same in Poland as they are here. We have a health service but it's not as good. Most people go private, but I couldn't afford to. Maybe if I'd had more money my Karol would still be alive."

Deborah was uncomfortable with the bitterness that ebbed from the depressed woman and she forced a smile as she backed away. "Yes, lack of money is always a pain. Anyway, like I said, the porter will be here soon."

As the nurse left the room, both Marek and the porter, pushing a wheelchair, passed her and Halina smiled. He did love her after all. She pushed the covers back and slipped her feet over the side of the bed, and Marek planted a gentle kiss on her forehead. "How are you? The baby?"

She dropped from the bed, her hand clasping the small of her back and waddled to the wheelchair, grimacing as she sat. "We're just going for the scan now. Thank you for being here, I'm so relieved. I'm so scared something bad's going to happen, or has already happened."

As the porter wheeled Halina through the doorway, Marek clasped her hand, trotting to keep up. "Just keep calm. Getting stressed out won't do you any good. Did you sleep well?"

She had slept through, surprising herself. "I was tossing and turning all night, I've been so worried. And I was missing you like crazy."

He squeezed her hand reassuringly while they waited for the lift to arrive and soon they were on the ground floor, heading for the radiology department on the other side of Accident and Emergency. Rob waved as they passed, calling, "Marek. Please stay with me."

He had hoped his colleague would be with a doctor by now, but the waiting room was heaving with people. Marek stopped and tagged the porter's arm. "Can you just wait a minute?"

The porter shrugged and Halina frowned. "Who's he?"

"Just a colleague from work, I came in with him earlier."

Halina crossed her arms, indignant. "I see. You didn't come in to see me, you were with him. You don't bloody love me at all. Well, go to your stupid friend, I don't need you there and I don't want you there." She glanced at the porter. "Can we go, please?"

He began to wheel her away and Marek was torn. His girlfriend needed his support, but if Rob told anyone he had not waited with him, he would be in trouble. A rock and a hard place. "Halina." It was pained and imploring.

"It's taking effect, Marek, I've got pins and needles in my mouth and tongue and now my face has gone numb." The fear showed in Rob's eyes and Marek wished he could split himself in two to be with them both. Or just disappear in a puff of smoke so all his problems would go away.

The porter rounded the corner and Halina was out of sight. Marek made his decision, knowing he would regret it later, and he traipsed over to Rob, reassuring him that all would be fine.

The anger from the previous night had re-erupted and Halina was fuming that Marek wasn't by her side. Borys would never have left her to face such a situation alone. Or would he? The truth was that when she had needed him the most he'd not been there. When Karol had died on the hospital trolley, his tiny body surrounded by medics, Borys had dragged her away, not letting her near. She had been the child's mother; surely the best place for him as his life ebbed was in her loving and protective arms. No, Borys had been a bastard and it seemed that Marek was the same.

Halina lay, as directed, on the couch and lifted her pyjama top up as the sonographer pushed the waistband of the bottoms down to expose her abdomen, tucking a paper towel into them and squirting some jelly on her skin. Halina winced at the coldness, as icy as her heart as she debated whether she should leave Marek once she was released from hospital. After all, if the baby was dead, what would be the point of them being together any more?

The sonographer moved the scanner back and forth, low and high. "How far along did you say you were?"

Halina knew that a five week embryo was unlikely to show on the screen and realised the truth had to come out. "I thought I was twelve weeks, but thinking it through I might not be that far gone."

"No problem, we'll try a transvaginal scan, that'll give us a clearer picture of what's going on." She placed some absorbent towels on Halina's belly, wiping the transparent gel away. "Clean yourself up and wait outside, I'll call you in half an hour or so. And wee as much as possible, we need your bladder to be empty for this one."

Halina smiled weakly. "Thank you."

Marek and Rob were still in the waiting room, two hours of tedium watching a soundless television high on the wall, and

Marek was increasingly concerned about his colleague. "I feel a bit dizzy now, it's all a bit strange."

"I'll go and see how long they'll be." Glad to have something to do, Marek spoke to the receptionist at the front desk. "The thing is, the drug he's ingested, tetrodotoxin, is extremely dangerous, in fact it's banned in this country. Can't somebody see him quickly?"

She looked at him wryly over the top of her glasses. "If it's illegal, what was he doing playing with it?"

Marek was astounded at the insinuation that Rob was a junkie. "Have you not put it in the notes that this is a Code 10 from Randall's Biotech? The company has an arrangement with Boxton Park for the immediate treatment of any company member who comes in contact with TTX. That should have been flagged up when the ambulance brought us in."

The receptionist preened her short hair, adjusting her glasses as she flicked through the files on the screen before her. "Oh. Yes. I see now. I'll alert a doctor immediately. Sorry about that, nobody made us aware."

Within minutes, Rob's name was called and he staggered into a cubicle with Marek following him. A nurse helped Rob onto the trolley and he lay on his back, eyes vacant and staring. "Will the doctor be long? It's just he's showing definite signs of poisoning. We weren't sure if he'd actually got any in his system, but looking at him now…"

She wheeled a high table closer to the trolley and took a cannula from its packaging. "He'll be here in a minute, he knows the urgency. I'll just pop this in his hand first."

Another nurse joined them, pushing an obs machine. "Hey, Sarah, doc told me to get these done. He's on his way."

There may have been an initial delay through lack of communication, but Marek was impressed now with their efficiency. He could not deny that, realistically, the accident should never have happened if the correct procedure for moving the deadly vials had been adhered to. Under no circumstance should Rob have been carrying them on a tray. They should have been in a custom-made holder and transported on a sturdy, metal, wheeled table.

Rob, for whatever reason, had put himself and the rest of the technicians in danger.

A bearded man, oddly authoritarian despite his casual attire, slid past the curtain and spoke softly. "Is this the TTX poisoning? Curious. Rob," he waved his hand over Rob's face but the man made no response, "Rob, can you hear me?" He turned to Justin. "Obs?"

"Blood pressure one sixty-seven over one-eighteen, pulse one-twelve, respiration twenty and temp thirty-seven point two."

"Has blood been sent for analysis?"

Sarah was peeling the protective paper layer from the cannula plaster, having secured it in the back of Rob's wrist. "I'm just about to take some. Urgent, I'm guessing?"

"Yes. We may have to do haemodialysis, all the same. How long has he been like this?" He waved his hand over Rob's face again.

"That's the weird thing, he walked in here unsupported, but as I helped him on the trolley he went droopy and his eyes glazed over. He's been unresponsive since."

Now the doctor addressed Marek. "You were there when the accident happened?"

Nodding, "He shouldn't have been carrying it, we have safety rules in place."

"And it was a small amount that he ingested?"

"Yes, he said it was just a drop and he swilled his mouth out several times. I'm surprised it's affected him at all. The only reason we called an ambulance was because of procedure. He seemed fine."

"And how long is it since it happened?"

Marek glanced at his watch. "Just over two hours, we had to wait for ages in reception just to get seen, it was only because..."

The doctor had the information he needed and turned to Sarah, who was withdrawing the last of Rob's blood samples for testing. "We need a urine sample if possible. Find a space in intensive care for him, he needs to be closely monitored."

Halina had taken a bus home after the scan and her inkling of hope that Marek would be there waiting for her was dashed as she entered the chilly, empty house. She scooped up the letters from the doormat and turned the heating on, and traipsed to the kitchen, setting the kettle to boil. Her mobile began to ring and she saw it was the agency calling. "I know you're halfway through a temp position, but we were wondering if you're available for work for a few hours today. Four until twelve. We're desperate."

Halina debated whether she was up to it and surmised she may as well go in; they needed the money and Marek clearly had no time or attention for her. "Yes, I've just come from hospital after a scare with the baby – I'm pregnant, you see – but everything's okay."

"Are you sure?"

"Yes, what hospital this time?"

"The Padway, Ward 14."

Oxford was thirty miles away, but the journey was relatively easy by train. After the Nellie Gleeson fiasco she had been unsure if the hospital would want to use her services again and she was relieved. "I'll do my best to be there for four."

Halina, her fingers frozen from the journey, hastily prepared a mug of cocoa and wrapped her hands around it to warm them, sipping at the steaming drink. She toyed with her mobile, considering whether to call Marek to let him know, but her anger at his desertion was raw. Why had he not wanted to see their baby in the womb?

Through the frosty windows the sky was stark, a moody grey of heavy clouds, and Halina shivered as she watched a robin on the windowsill, pecking at the bacon rinds and crumbled bread Marek had left for the birds. Her hand drifted to her belly and she had never felt so alone. Destined to be lonely, ousted from a family who only cared for themselves, and lost forever to Karol and Borys. She had dared to hope that Marek would fill the void in her life, but where was he now when she needed him?

Halina noticed the clock and finished her drink. If she had an hour or so sleep she could catch the 14:05 train to Oxford. So what if she wasn't there when Marek returned from work, or the hospital, or wherever he was that wasn't with her. Maybe she should make that a permanent arrangement.

Once Marek had ensured Rob was settled on the unit, he went to the ward to find Halina, but was told she had been discharged. He decided to go straight home; there would be no point returning to work by the time he had navigated the complicated public transport route from the hospital. He called Rose to update her on Rob's condition. "It's like he's not there. His heart is beating, he's breathing deeply, but he's in some kind of a trance. They closed his eyes for him to stop the dust getting in. I'm going to talk to the bosses about the safety procedure here, because this should never have happened."

"Trouble is, we have a comprehensive one already and Rob ignored it. What can you do if people refuse to play by the rules?"

"True. Anyway, the hospital wanted to know if we have the name and address of his next of kin. He really needs some family there, or a girlfriend. Someone."

"I've got his parents' details." Marek chuckled and she immediately became defensive. "I was at uni with him, we were on the same course, so you can put your dirty thoughts back in the box. I'll give them a call, shall I?"

The bus stopped close to his house and Marek jumped off. He was dreading facing his girlfriend and her mood swings, but was sure she would understand his dilemma when he explained what had happened to Rob. However, when he opened the door with trepidation, waiting for the tirade to start, nothing came and he stepped inside, worried now. He checked the living room and kitchen and plodded up the stairs, checking their bedroom and the bathroom. Maybe she had left a note.

Marek returned to the kitchen, searching while he boiled the kettle and dropped some bread into the toaster, and on the table he found 'gone out' scribbled on the back of an envelope. Annoyed, both at the brusque note and that she wasn't resting when she had only just returned from the short stay in hospital, he dialled her number but, as expected, it went to voicemail. "It's me, where the hell are you? Call me when you get a moment. I'm not angry, but we need to talk."

Halina had been in the restaurant at the Padway Hospital for a while by the time she listened to the message, and she re-locked her phone, placing it back in her bag. Marek was going to have to stew for a while, see where he was going wrong. She would see him after midnight when her shift ended.

She had a couple of black, sweet teas, ate a healthy salad and eavesdropped on several conversations and, eventually, when the wall clock showed three-thirty, she headed for the ward she had worked on once before.

Graham Calderbank smiled. "We've got you back, have we?"

"Is that a problem?" Halina felt her cheeks prickling and hoped she wouldn't blush. Had she done something wrong in the past?

"Of course not, at least you know your way around. Fancy a cup of tea while we wait for the handover? If we stay here they'll get us working early."

She followed him to the staff kitchen, too cluttered to be as sterile as Health and Safety would have liked and overly warm from the permanently hot urn, and she sat on a plastic chair while he prepared the drinks. They chatted idly about the news and weather, Halina mentioning her night in Boxton Park Hospital. "Anyway, less of that, has anything happened since I was last here, you know, gossip."

"Not that I can think of, just the same old same old. They go home, we get new ones in, all the usual problems – bottoms and prostate for the men, down-below and gall bladders for the women." Halina snorted at his accurate summary of their regular duties. "Oh, you might remember Wayne West, nasty syphilis guy? I'm sure he was in last time you did a shift here. Anyway, he's back in."

Halina's stomach lurched, her face paling. "I thought he was on death's door last time?"

"No, he had a bad spell but after a couple of days he was fine again."

"I see." She remembered the odious man as if she had seen him yesterday. Wayne had been infected with the syphilis bacteria roughly eight years previously, a testament to his sexuality and lifestyle, and had not helped himself or others by continuing with his wayward encounters. Whereas syphilis is easily treatable with a simple course of antibiotics, Wayne had never been concerned about his health, sexual or otherwise, so when the untreated disease had become symptom-free in a latent period lasting several years, he continued to procure conquests via the internet, plying them with alcohol and sometimes hallucinatory, illegal drugs prior to bedding them, and he had caustically refused to use condoms to protect the women and men.

His presence had left chaos for many of his sexual partners, most more responsible than he by ensuring they received treatment in the early stages of their own infections, but when the brave had attempted to warn him that he might be a fellow sufferer, he had ignored them with scorn. Wayne had never been one to believe in karma and the irony that his mind was now reducing to mush as a consequence of the disease, the burgeoning dementia that would eventually render him bed-bound and infantile, did not register with him. If anybody deserved such a cruel and undignified ending, Wayne West was that man. "You know he came on to me last time I was here, don't you?"

"He comes on to me, Halina, and I'm a bloke. It's nothing you can't handle."

"I don't want to get upset, what with the threatened miscarriage and everything."

"Halina, he's harmless, let it go."

Every bed on the ward was occupied and, due to understaffing, time passed swiftly. Halina was grateful, although she was uncomfortable knowing that Wayne West was nearby. An hour into her shift, she managed to find a couple of spare minutes to make herself a mug of tea and she wearily walked to the kitchen, turning her head away as she passed the bay Wayne occupied with five other patients. "I remember you."

His menacing voice was unmistakeable and Halina felt sweat prickle on her back, her forehead, chest. She darted through the door and closed it behind, breathing heavily.

The Intensive Care Unit had never experienced a tetrodotoxin poisoning before, but Randall's Biotech had worked with the hospital in the early days of their research into the poison and submitted a comprehensive guide of how to care for a victim should one of their employees be affected. When Rob Sanders had been brought to his room they had sedated and intubated him immediately to make breathing easier, and they had littered his young body with sensors to monitor his blood pressure and flow, pulse and heart rate, his oxygen levels, temperature and central venous pressure. He also had a catheter so they could check his urine output.

With no antidote available for tetrodotoxin poisoning the only treatment they could give was an intravenous drip to feed saline solution into his bloodstream, and close supervision. If he was still alive twenty-four hours after he had ingested the poison, there was a strong chance he would not only survive, but be able to put whatever experience was happening inside his head in the past and live a long and happy life. He had managed six hours but his condition was critical.

The machine started to wail and a nurse rushed over, hoping it was merely a malfunction. "He's crashing."

A swarm of medics swooped around the patient, each helping in their own way to restart Rob's heart, but despite defibrillation, working for a full five minutes on the man who had barely started his adult life, they had no choice but to accept he was not about to recover. "Time of death, sixteen hundred hours."

While the resuscitation team dribbled away, the patient to be forgotten by the time they had their breakfast the next morning, a nurse carefully draped the sheet over Rob's head. A sound behind stopped her and she turned to see a middle-aged couple, the woman sobbing uncontrollably. "We're his parents. We're too late."

"Mr and Mrs Sanders?" She strode to the pair, her face pained. "I'm so sorry."

"What exactly happened here? We got a call this afternoon from the company he works for telling us he was in hospital.

They said it was nothing to worry about. We would have made it here earlier if we had known his life was in danger."

"Didn't someone from the hospital call?"

"If you did, we weren't there to take it."

Mrs Sanders cleared her throat with a cough. "We left soon after we heard the news. My husband said it wasn't an emergency but I was worried." As an afterthought she added, "Rob was our only child."

"We've come from Portsmouth, we would have taken an express train if we'd known he was seriously ill."

The nurse had as much detail as she could wish for of the background leading to Rob's stay on the unit, but something about Mr Sanders' tone told her to be careful with what she said. "He was poisoned at work, a substance called tetrodotoxin. We've not had a case before."

"You didn't know how to treat him? I'll find out exactly what's happened to my son and I'll throw the book at you. Somebody here has screwed up and I'll work out the truth, so help me God. I'll be suing your arses off."

Mr Sanders spun on his heel, preparing for a grand exit, but his wife grasped his hand. "I need to see him. I can't just leave him alone on the bed, he needs me."

"He's gone, Martha, there's nothing you can do."

Her tears restarted and the nurse could feel her pain. Slowly she followed her husband from the room, her whole life and future in tatters. Nothing would ever be the same again.

Chapter 12
Unnecessary Drama

Marek stepped off the bus and strode the short distance to Randall's Biotech, all the while pondering his relationship with Halina. She had crept into their bed at some time overnight, not waking him, and had been fast asleep when the alarm woke him. He hadn't bothered to wake her, unable to contemplate bickering while he worried for his colleague.

He entered the building, climbing the familiar stairs and treading the usual corridors. The truth was he didn't even know if Halina was still carrying their child, the chasm between them had opened so wide, and the two-word note she had left was deliberately taunting. Then again, perhaps she had lost the baby and was running away, unable to tell him. He decided to try her mobile again once he reached his bench.

"Marek."

He took a few steps backwards and craned his head around the door of the kitchen. Rose, eyes red and skin blotchy, was preparing a tray of drinks. "Have you been crying?"

It was all she could do to get the words out. "Rob died." A fresh torrent of tears coursed down her cheeks.

Marek slumped against the fridge, eyes to the floor, mouth gaping. "Fuck. When?"

"Yesterday afternoon. They've called us all for an emergency meeting, that's why I'm making teas. Do you want one, by the way?"

"Black, three sugars, thanks." He put a comforting arm around her shoulder. "I'll help you."

The training room, the largest room on the fifth floor, was teeming with laboratory staff. Presently, three suited men entered, sombre and commanding, and the room hushed. Two of the men sat at the top table, the other stood in the middle. "I'm sure the terrible news has reached everybody's ears by now, but just in case there's anyone who pays no heed to gossip, I am sorry to inform you that one of our valued and talented laboratory assistants, Robert Sanders, died of tetrodotoxin

119

poisoning yesterday. It was a nasty accident that would never have taken place had the safety rules and regulations been adhered to."

The man to his right strutted to the projector screen behind. "This is Sanjeev Patel, he will be going through the safety procedure with you all."

Marek was stunned by the news, although he berated himself for being so. He had seen how ill Rob was when he'd left the hospital, why was this such a surprise? Perhaps he should have stayed. Then he remembered how angry Halina had been at him for not attending the scan. It was clear he could not have done right for doing wrong the previous day, because however good his intentions had been to Rob and Halina, he would never have been able to please them both.

Maybe it would help settle the argument between the two of them, though. When he told Halina how serious his colleague's condition had become, perhaps she would be rational and understand he'd not really had a choice.

Of course he could always try to get on her good side, sneak out of the room, tell them he needed the loo and nip to Uxbridge town centre to find a decent engagement ring. She couldn't possibly be angry with him after receiving a diamond solitaire. But no, he'd only had one payday since he had started at the company and he wanted to save the money towards a deposit on a new tenancy. Or maybe they could stay where they were and he could buy the ring.

Fed up with mulling the same choices for far too long, he resolved to call the number he had found for Halina's mother two days before. After all, he'd intended to phone her the previous night but Halina's disappearance had scuppered every plan he'd had. Marek snapped back to reality and the emergency training, all of which he had learnt only five weeks before. It was going to be a long day.

Pete arrived at the Coroner's Court as the caretaker was unlocking the door and he lurked in the empty waiting area until a receptionist had checked her make-up and hair. "Can I help you?" Her voice had a Monday morning drabness.

120

"An inquest was held here on Friday regarding Mrs Nellie Gleeson, are there any notes available for viewing yet?"

"Oh, they won't be ready yet, it'll be at least a few days."

"Specifically I need the name of one of the nurses who testified."

"No can do, sorry."

Pete tried for a while longer, using every ounce of charm he possessed, but the woman refused to entertain him and as he came down the steps he realised that, despite her crush on him, he would need to speak to Angela again. He dialled her mobile number and waited. "Angela, it's Pete Benson. I'm still looking for the other nurse who was working with you the night Nellie Gleeson died, Halina. Have you remembered her surname yet?"

"I wasn't aware I was supposed to." It was her first morning back at the Padway after her leave and she was annoyed at the world. "She's working at Kendrick Hospital at the moment, the SHDU on Ward 34. She works days so she'll be there now."

Pete glanced to the sky and said a quick thanks to God; he would have no reason to contact Angela again now. Kendrick Hospital was twenty miles from Oxford, but interviewing the woman he had heard so many dodgy things about was worth the distance. He drove into the steady stream of traffic and headed east through the maze of rush-hour roads towards the M40.

It took Pete an hour to reach the hospital and he found the ward easily. He approached the nurses' station confidently. Sister Kennedy nudged her glasses down her nose slightly to regard him. "I'm looking for a nurse named Halina who's working on the SHDU."

"I'm her superior. Can I ask what you want her for on work's time?"

As he commonly did with a high success rate, he flashed his card. "Detective Benson, it's confidential."

"That wasn't a policeman's badge." She had crossed her arms now.

"You noticed. I, er, I left it at home by accident. Can I see her?"

"Her lunch begins at two, you can do what you like with her for that hour."

He intended to loiter for a while but Kennedy wasn't having it and eventually she marched him from the ward. "Two o'clock, I told you. Don't come back before then."

So far from Oxford, all Pete could do was waste the next couple of hours in the canteen and he ordered some food and a pot of tea, taking them to a vacant table. A regular stream of people, staff and the public, came and went and soon a bunch of medics sat by the table next to him, joking and chatting. In his subconscious he heard someone mention Halina and his fork stopped en-route to his mouth, listening intently.

"I heard she'd gone to an inquest on Friday."

"Did she tell you that?"

"No, I overheard her telling Sister Kennedy she needed some time off to attend."

"So what happened there? First two nurses are arrested, then they find that the morphine's been switched with insulin, and then Halina's a witness at an inquest. All sounds a bit funny to me."

Pete set his cutlery down and turned to the voice, a young trainee not long out of college. "Excuse me, I couldn't help but hear you mention two nurses had been arrested. What's that all about?"

Aware she had said too much, too loud, the girl blushed and shrank. Her friend beside her was protective. "Who are you? The press?"

"No, the police." He mentally crossed his fingers as he flashed the deceptive business card in his wallet again, "Detective Benson. I'm waiting here to interview Halina about an unrelated matter, but I just wondered why you mentioned her together with two nurses being arrested and drugs being switched. Come and sit here."

Impressed and helpful, the two young women took their plates to his table and seated themselves. "We were just chatting, really. There's no link that I know of. Halina's been working on the SHDU and since she's been there two men have been poisoned with insulin. One died. Two nurses were arrested, but she wasn't one of them."

"She wasn't? Do you think she should have been?"

"Don't know really. All I know is she's only been working here two weeks – this is her third week – and all these things have happened."

"How were the men poisoned?"

"Somebody put insulin in... Hold on a minute, shouldn't you know that if you're a copper?"

"As I said, I'm here about an unrelated matter, but what you're saying could have a bearing on that."

"There was insulin in the morphine bottle. They were both drugged by one of the nurses who was arrested, Rebecca Burke, but she didn't mean to, I don't think. The police have let her go so she must be innocent."

Pete checked his watch; it was nearly two and time he was making his way back to the ward. He made his way to the fourth floor and waited by the doors for a few minutes, and presently a nurse left the ward. "Halina?"

The nurse checked behind her. "No, she's just on her way. The one with the scruffy hair."

Halina approached, catching the door before it closed. "Are you looking for me? Who are you?"

"I'm here about Nellie Gleeson's inquest, I wondered if you could give me five minutes."

"Only over a cigarette, I'm desperate." He followed her down the stairs and through the corridors to a doorway adorned with 'no smoking' stickers on the outside, and joined her in the cold. Shielding the flame from the gusting wind, she inhaled deeply, holding her breath as the nicotine swamped her body. "What do you want?"

"I've been speaking to the patient who was in the bed next to Mrs Gleeson on the night she died. She says you injected something into Mrs Gleeson shortly before she died. Can you tell me about that?" It was a lie but he was fishing.

"I'm qualified to administer whatever medication a doctor has prescribed. If Mrs Gleeson had medicine, it was my job to give it to her. And if she died shortly after that, and I'm not so sure she did, then it was a coincidence."

"Do you remember that night clearly?"

"Of course I don't, it was weeks ago. We see different people every single day, it's impossible to remember them all, especially the fine detail."

"What about the ward you're working on now, I believe there's been an incident where one drug was swapped for another?"

Halina's brow furrowed. "Who are you? Are you a policeman? We've been questioned about this."

"No, I'm a private detective employed by one of Mrs Gleeson's sons to try and prove his brother killed their mother."

"I thought all that shameful money grabbing was dealt with at the inquest."

"It was, but he still wants to pay me to prove himself right anyway. Who am I to object if he wants to throw his money away?"

She chuckled and Pete was amazed how much her face changed. Almost pretty, but not quite. "Mrs Gleeson died of an unexplained air embolism in the heart and her death has been recorded as natural. She was elderly and old bodies do odd things. They always have, but more post-mortems are done nowadays so these things get chucked up occasionally. I wasn't concerned then and I'm not now. If I were you I'd find another case to work on as you'll get no result from this one."

"Do you remember the brother who's being accused? His name is Nicholas Gleeson."

Halina took a long drag on her cigarette, dropping the butt to the floor and treading it out. "I vaguely remember him, but only because I saw him at the inquest. If it hadn't been for that I doubt I'd have recalled him."

"But you saw her after he visited and she seemed fine?"

"I did her observations at ten and there was nothing remarkable. If he'd injected air into her she would have been showing signs of distress by then. Like the ruling at the inquest said, she died of natural causes."

"Is that Hugh Smythe?"

"Yes, can I help you?"

"You sent my secretary an email at the weekend, my name's Ismail Berker. Doctor."

"Thanks for calling me so promptly and I hope you don't mind me contacting you. I wanted to ask you about the results of a post-mortem you carried out on a Mrs Gleeson."

"Yes, the inquest was held on Friday, death was recorded as of natural causes."

"I know, but the thing is, I've recently completed a PM on another elderly woman and found she'd died of a massive air-embolism in the heart. She was eighty."

"Post-surgical?"

"No, my case is almost an exact replica of yours, the only real difference the ten year age gap of the deceased."

"Where are you going with this?"

"Have you heard about the troubles Kendrick Hospital is currently having?"

"I heard that two nurses had been arrested and released over the death of a patient."

"Can we meet, Ismail? I can drive to Oxford after I finish work at five."

"Can't we just talk now?"

"That's just it, suddenly I feel very uncomfortable talking on the phone."

Ismail sighed deeply. "Meet me at the Grouse in Wallingford at seven."

"Well, Mr West, I don't think we'll need to keep you here much longer. Stay another night and if everything goes smoothly you can go home tomorrow."

"I look forward to it. At least nobody tries killing me at home."

The consultant was unsure of how to reply. Was he joking? Wayne West was a hideous man inside and out and he would be glad to see him off the ward. "Yes, yes." He moved to the next patient, leaving a nurse with Wayne.

"What's the name of that nurse who was on last night?" Wayne scrutinised the nurse with lecherous eyes, leaving her feeling violated.

"I'm not sure who was on last night. Have you got somebody at home to help you?"

"My ex-wife and two boys will help out if I need them. She had dark hair, bit grey at the edges and really pale blue eyes. Cold eyes."

"What about getting home, will you be able to arrange transport?"

"You must have a register or something, can't you take a look?"

"Wayne, we can't go giving out our staff details, that's not how it works."

"What nights does she work? Is she on tonight?"

"If you need transport home let me know before my shift ends after dinner." She brusquely left the bay, annoyed at the revolting man and his lust for whichever nurse had been working the previous night.

"Fancy that one from last night, do you?"

Wayne turned to the bed beside him, eyeing the old man with no teeth or hair. "I've never been that desperate, mate."

"I was gonna say. Ugly old cow if you ask me." He coughed and spat green mucous into a tissue. "Her name was Halina, I saw it on her name tag when she was changing my drip last night. I thought the name was too pretty for the face."

Wayne swung his feet from the bed and hurriedly scribbled inside the front cover of the children's book he had nearly finished.

It occurred to Hugh as he walked into the Grouse that he had no idea what Ismail Berker looked like, but as he scanned the busy room a man at a table waved at him, smiling. He went over. "Dr Berker?"

"You must be Hugh. Take a seat while I get you a drink."

"Thanks, I'll just have a coke." Hugh sat on the maroon velvet, unsure how to spark up what would sound like a crazy conversation. A minute later, Ismail was back and he threw two bags of crisps on the table, handing Hugh his drink. "What exactly do you know about what's been happening at Kendrick Hospital?"

"I don't know anything, I've just heard rumours that two nurses were arrested over the death of a patient. I also heard they've been released now."

"They were. My friend was telling me about the inquest last week, where you testified."

"You could at least let me know me the truth behind the gossip." Ismail sipped his red wine.

"I'll get to that. Like I told you on the phone, the reason I'm curious is because I had a similar death to Nellie Gleeson's a couple of weeks ago, an eighty year old female who died of a massive air embolism in the heart. I also referred it to the coroner and this was before I'd heard about Mrs Gleeson."

"How did you hear about her?"

"Angela Crabtree, one of the nurses who found her dead, is a good friend and she told me."

"So why contact me? I'm supposing you think something suspicious is happening."

"It's an unusual cause of death, yes. The thing is, I wouldn't have been so interested but then the nurses were arrested, oh, and I nearly forgot, there was another really weird case. I was doing a PM on a young guy, who toxicology later reported had died of paracetamol overdose, and I found a note in his oesophagus." He opened his wallet and pulled out the photocopy of the original. Ismail read it and frowned.

"Hallucinations, maybe?"

"Probably, or delusions, but with everything else that's been happening it stirred my interest."

"Did you refer him to the coroner too?"

"I did after the PM, but once I'd received the tox report I would have had to anyway."

"Have you told the police about any of this?"

"Yes, but as far as I know all charges against the nurses have been dropped and the hospital's doing an internal investigation."

"So let them. Tell them what you know and let them do their jobs. If there's anything untoward about it they'll find out and appropriate action will be taken."

"Does it not worry you that there may be someone corrupt working for the hospital?"

"Your hospital. There's nothing corrupt about the Padway and, anyway, the inquest ruled that Nellie Gleeson died of natural causes. Reporting to the coroner was standard procedure."

Hugh was embarrassed now, put in his place by the older doctor. He felt foolish, especially having sounded so dramatic on the phone. He wanted to skulk away unnoticed, but Ismail was staring at him, intense, waiting for a response. Hugh could guess which one he wanted – to forget everything and stop being silly – but he wasn't about to do that. "Would you at least look into all your deaths in the past, say, three months with a fresh eye, just to see if there's anything suspicious at all."

"I'm a busy man, Hugh, I haven't got time. And, being honest, even if I had the time I wouldn't do it. If those nurses at Kendrick have done anything wrong the investigation will find out. Now," he gulped the last of his wine and stood, "I've got a busy night so I'm off home. If there's anything else you have my email." Ismail shook Hugh's hand, firm and authoritative. "Nice to meet you."

Hugh watched Ismail leave the pub, not up to the journey home just yet; he had some thinking to do. He went to the bar and ordered another coke, despite a sudden yearning for a beer since he had been humiliated. He sat at the table with his back to the bar for privacy and opened one of the bags of crisps Ismail had bought but not eaten. Was he seeing something that wasn't there? Should he trust the hospital to not cover up any misdemeanours? He couldn't put his finger on what felt wrong, why the whole bunch of recent deaths seemed darker than usual, why they were affecting him and his credibility.

He briefly thought of Angela, realising Oxford, where she lived, wasn't far from Wallingford, but any thoughts of visiting her were scuppered when he remembered she was moonlighting at the Kendrick again on weekday nights. Feeling more stupid than he ever had, he finished his drink and left.

Chapter 13
Fox Amongst Hounds

Although they had been in impromptu training all day, leaving an hour earlier than usual, it had been a tiring day at work and the atmosphere had been dour after the news of Rob's death. Marek opened the door and settled a carrier bag of food on the table, all the ingredients for the meal he would prepare for Halina to try and smooth their blustery relationship. And the ring. A glorious emerald set with five diamonds, chosen from an antique shop he had found a few doors from the convenience store. The truth was, he didn't even know if she was still expecting his baby and he felt ashamed. Perhaps he should have called her as he had planned before hearing the devastating news about Rob. Marek took the steak, frozen chips and peas – a British favourite – from the bag and busied himself at the stove, slicing mushrooms he found in the fridge into a frying pan.

He garnished the plates with salad and prepared everything he needed to, and he sat by the table. There was no point heating the food yet, Halina wouldn't be back from work for another hour. He dragged her address book across the table, re-finding the number for the woman he assumed to be her mother. Steeling himself, he picked up the handset and dialled. "Is that Gabryjela Bakalar?" he asked in Polish.

"Who wants to know?" The woman's voice was harsh, as if she had smoked forty a day since birth.

"My name's Marek Stanislaw, I'm dating your daughter and I…"

"My daughter is five years old so I doubt that very much."

Marek laughed, embarrassed. "I found you in Halina's address book and just assumed you were her mother. I'm sorry." He waited a while, wondering why the woman hadn't seen the funny side of his mistake. "Hello?"

"Look, whoever you are, if you're anything to do with Halina then I don't want to know."

"I'm her fiancé, well, I will be…" The dial tone buzzed and he realised she had put the phone down. Or maybe he was being paranoid and it was a bad line. He dialled again and waited. "Gabryjela?"

"This is Gabryjela's husband. We want nothing to do with you or Halina. Leave us alone. Don't call again."

"Please don't put the phone down, I need to know why? Has she done something wrong?"

"Halina Lewinski is a dangerous woman and we want nothing to do with her." The dial tone buzzed again and Marek stared at the handset, puzzled. Once more, he dialled but this time there was no answer. The man had called her Lewinski, yet he had seen her passport and her surname was definitely Kostuch. A few moments before he had been about to ask her mother for permission to marry her and now, well, was she even who she said she was? And what had she done to make these people despise her so much? Marek took the box from his pocket and pushed it open, watching the light coruscate from the cut of the precious gems. He wouldn't ask her tonight, in fact he wouldn't propose until he knew the story behind the odd exchange that had just taken place.

The following fifty minutes took forever to pass. The food was ready to go, leaving him with nothing to do but contemplate the million questions that floated through his mind. Finally, he heard footsteps along the path and the door opened, Halina shaking the rain from her coat. He re-boiled the kettle and made the drink he had already prepared, unsure which question to begin with. "I've made some tea. How are you?" He started softly, not wanting another argument.

She nodded, dragging her coat off and hanging it, dripping, from the back of a chair, but she didn't speak so he tried again. "How was the scan?"

"The baby is fine, I haven't miscarried."

"I didn't think you'd have been to work if you had." Marek tried to put his arms around her but she shrugged him away. "That's good news, though. Why don't you want a cuddle?" He could feel the ring-box in his pocket and he wavered on whether to soften her by proposing, but Gabryjela and her husband's harsh voices rang in his mind: *Halina Lewinski is a dangerous woman.*

"I just don't. I'm still angry that you didn't wait to see the baby on the scan."

Marek pushed her gently until she was seated on a chair and sat beside her, holding both her hands in his. "My colleague was seriously ill. He died yesterday."

Suddenly Halina wasn't remote any more, she scanned his face with interest. "My God, what happened?"

"It's the drug we're working on, it can be lethal if you come into contact with it. There was a spillage and Rob ingested a drop. He was in a coma after two hours and died a few hours later."

"You've barely told me about the work you do. I know it's lab work, but I didn't realise you were testing dangerous drugs. What is it? What are you testing it for?"

"Tetrodotoxin. We're working on a new type of anaesthetic that utilises its power to put people into a trance-like state. Rob didn't follow the procedure for moving it and he paid with his life."

"That's amazing. I've never heard of it before." Amazing? Marek could think of more appropriate words to describe the drug. "Where does it come from?"

"It's found in several sea-creatures, although our source is solely the Takifugu Rubripes, a type of puffer fish, and it's roughly twelve hundred times more toxic to humans than cyanide. As Rob found out."

"So one tiny drop of this stuff kills? My God. How have I not heard of this?"

Marek's brow furrowed and he let Halina's hands go. "Why on earth would you have?"

Halina sipped her sweet, black tea. "What does it look like?"

"Why do you care?"

"I work in a hospital and I need to know everything about what can harm people. I mean, what did they do for him at Boxton Park, your friend Rob? Did he die because they hadn't heard of it or is there no antidote?"

"The hospital has a code of practice for anybody poisoned at Randall's, although I do think that if they'd got round to

132

treating him earlier he may have stood a better chance. A and E was pretty lame yesterday."

"So if I'd known about the drug and had been working there, he would have stood a better chance?"

Marek was bored of the subject and confused by her interest and he moved to the deep fat fryer, switching it on, before lighting the gas under the frying pan. "I don't know. Maybe, maybe not. Tetrodotoxin is banned in the UK, Randall's have a special research license so I doubt there are many cases a year. I don't think they even check for it on the tox screens during a post-mortem, well, unless they know the person has had it."

"I can't imagine there are many people who would have it, unless they're suicidal." She chuckled, finishing the dregs of her drink.

"That's the weird thing, there are restaurants in Japan that serve puffer fish. Apparently they have specially trained and licensed chefs who know how to prepare the fish in a way that makes it safe to eat. It's called fugu and it gives the diner a bit of a high. A buzz."

"I so want to try that stuff."

Marek couldn't understand why his girlfriend was so fascinated by a mind-numbing experience. He had barely seen her drink, let alone take illegal substances, and she had given up smoking. Or so he had been led to believe. For the second time that day he wondered if he knew her at all. "Well, I don't see any chance of us going to Japan in the near future, so it'll have to stay on your wish list." Marek lowered the chips into the oil and placed two pieces of rib-eye in the frying pan, the melted, peppered butter spitting. "Halina, are you happy with us?"

"Of course I am, why do you ask?"

"Sometimes you're so distant, I feel like I've annoyed you all the time. It's like you never let me in."

"I'm pregnant with your child. Isn't that the biggest commitment a person can make?"

He knew he shouldn't, the possibility of an argument heightened every time he tried to find out more about her.

"You've committed yourself to raising a child, not to being with me."

"But we share a room. You said you were going to find us a place of our own for when the baby's born. How is that not showing commitment?"

It was the wrong thing to do, he didn't know her well enough to make such a sweeping gesture, but it was too late. The box was out of his pocket, the ring displayed beautifully against a backdrop of holly-green velvet, and he was on bended knee. "Marry me?"

Marek had never seen Halina so utterly shocked before, her mouth hanging open, eyes wide and staring. He hoped she would say no. "You don't think I'd be seen as unfaithful to Borys?"`

"Does it matter what other people think? What do you think your family would think, do you think they'd like me?"

She waved her hand, dismissive. "They wouldn't care."

Marek's knee, against cheap linoleum stretched thinly over concrete, was cold and sore and he shuffled a little, unsure what do. Maybe once they were married she would feel more secure and would open up to him. Lewinski, though? What was that about? Please say no. "Will you?"

Halina leant across and kissed his cheek, holding the sides of his head in her hands. "When I have seen tetrodotoxin with my own eyes and eaten fugu in a restaurant, I will marry you like a shot."

"What?" He could imagine a billion ways so say either yes or no, but her answer stunned him. "You're not serious."

"Yes I am."

"Then if you're going to put stipulations in place, so am I. I'll find somewhere that will serve you fugu, even if we have to fly abroad to eat it, but only after the baby is born. In return I want an open and honest discussion about your family and past."

"I've told you everything about them, Borys and Karol, how they died..."

"No, you've told me they died and how that made you feel, you didn't say how, where. You've never told me about your family, whether you have sisters or brothers. I barely know anything about your past."

"I think the steak may be burning, it's a bit smoky in here."

"Shit!" Marek scrabbled up, his knee aching and leg asleep, and he lifted the chips and turned the cooker off. "So much for a celebratory meal. So much for a celebration," he glared at her, "seeing as we're at stalemate."

Halina stood and grasped her coat, still dripping from the rain. "Not to worry, I've got to go out for a while anyway, I'll bring a take-away home with me. I'm not sure how long I'll be."

Marek ran his hand through his hair, frustrated. "For God's sake, I've just asked you to marry me and you're going to leave. Just like that."

"I won't be too long, so what's the problem?"

"Who is Gabryjela and why did she call you Halina Lewinski?" She glared at him with a coldness he had not seen before and closed the door behind her, leaving him flummoxed.

Angela had spent all day at the Padway doing her day job, eight solid hours of walking the ward and tending to patients. She had nipped home to change from one hospital uniform to another and driven to Kendrick Hospital ready for the next twelve-hour shift. She was exhausted, unable to imagine how she would possibly make it through the night without some sleep, especially as she had to return to Oxford the next morning and do it all over again.

She took the lift to the fourth floor and was surprised to see Hugh waiting. "I'm glad I caught you. Can I have a quick word?"

"You're not in my good books, actually." She didn't mean to be snappy but she was tired.

"Why? I haven't done anything wrong."

"Dr Berker – Ismail Berker – came to see me at work today."

"So?"

"He was angry, said you'd instigated a meeting about the possibility of some dodgy dealings going on here. He told me I shouldn't have said anything to you about Nellie Gleeson's inquest."

"Why not? It was a public inquiry."

135

"He said tittle-tattle like that could be scandalous for a hospital and he didn't like the way you were trying to include the Padway in your suspicions."

"Hell, I only wanted to know if he'd had any other unexplained deaths. It was a reasonable question."

"Fair enough, do what you want, but next time don't use my name if it's something I've told you. He suggested that my career would pay if he heard of anything else like that."

Hugh found the overreaction of his counterpart strange, it had been a simple conversation with no bias. It made him more suspicious than ever. "I'm sorry. You're right, I should have said my source was anonymous."

Angela hadn't expected an apology and the conversation ceased, neither knowing what to say. Finally she managed, "Why did you want to see me, anyway?"

"You'll bite my head off."

"No I won't."

He sighed, steeling himself. "I think there's something in it all, I think there's malpractice, maybe even murder going on. I wanted to know how you felt about it, whether you're suspicious too. Or if I'm just being an idiot."

"Off the record?"

"Strictly."

"The morphine didn't switch itself with insulin and I don't trust Rebecca and Theresa. However, that cop you know has looked into it and if he's not investigating, it's a waste of time to be worrying about it. I'm sure that if something else odd happens he'll be on to it like a shot."

"So you're happy to wait for somebody else to die?"

"There's nothing I can do. I'll keep my eyes and ears open while I'm on the SHDU, and obviously if anything happens I'll do something then. I've got to go." She pressed the button for entry onto the ward.

"Angela, phone me, won't you? If anything does happen. Doesn't matter what time of night. I think I'm in this too deep."

"Then swim back to the surface and get a grip. And stop reading thrillers."

Hugh drove home and found the flat empty. He had no idea what shift Marcus was working and nor did he care. He pottered around the kitchen and living room, trying to find something that would take his mind off his troubles, but eventually switched the television and stereo off, discarded his book and shut the computer down. He found a number on his mobile and pressed the call button. "Thirsk, it's Hugh."

"What have you got for me?"

"I just wondered how the investigation into the hospital was going."

"It's not, there is no investigation. You know that."

"I sent the PM results of another death to the coroner the other day. Mrs Peters, I told you about it."

"I looked at those myself and didn't see anything to be bothered about, it'll just be a natural death. Anyway, she didn't go anywhere near the SHDU."

"No, but there was an inquest on Friday into a similar death, a ninety year old woman, the cause of death also an air embolism in the heart."

"There's probably a case in every hospital over the country."

"Yes, if deep-sea diving is their hobby, or they've recently had surgery. But an eighty year old and a ninety year old without those factors? It's almost unheard of."

"I'm going to be frank with you, Hugh. I do suspect that something's going on at the hospital and the fact they're doing an internal investigation smacks of a cover-up to me, but my superior has made it crystal clear that if I don't drop the bone my job is on the line. I told you I had no problem with your friend – what's her name?"

"Angela Crabtree."

"Well, is she still spying on the ward?"

"Yes."

"Tell her that if she sees anything to tell you or to call me, but officially there is nothing happening. I'll tell you what, though, I'll go to the coroner's office when I'm in the area and look up the details of that inquest."

"It was held in Oxford because she died at the Padway. It wasn't me who did the PM."

"For god's sake! Then it's a bloody coincidence."

Hugh was a quiet man, barely anybody had seen his temper rise since he was a toddler when it was expected of him, but he was frustrated with the constant brick walls he was encountering. "It's not a coincidence. This is happening and people are dying, why the fuck am I the only person who cares? Get the results of the inquest tomorrow, Thirsk, and start looking at this seriously. Plus, the inquests into Tobias Sutherland and Mrs Peters' deaths are both on Thursday. I'm attending both and I bloody well expect you to as well. Please."

Thirsk was silent for a while and Hugh wondered whether he had gone too far. Eventually, "I respect you, Hugh, you're a damned good pathologist. Don't make me change my opinion of you."

"But you said yourself you think something's going on."

"I'm paid to see the worst in people. You're not." The line went dead and Hugh held his phone out, wanting to throw it across the room but aware of how childish that would be. He slammed it on the table and took a can of lager from the fridge; not his usual drink but it would do.

He was on his third when Marcus came in, hair mussed and eyes darkened with tiredness. "You could have told me you were drinking my booze, I would have picked up another box if I'd known." He took a can for himself from the shelf in the fridge door and sat at the table with his friend. "All hell broke loose in the SHDU tonight, Angela told me that a box of tramadol hydrochloride vials has gone missing."

"No way! Surely Rebecca and Theresa wouldn't have been that stupid to do it on their own shift."

"They contacted Sister Kennedy and she called the daytime team, but Angela doesn't know what the result of that was."

"What about the police? Have they been called?"

"Don't be daft, drugs go missing in hospitals all the time. You're still convinced there's a murderer on the loose, aren't you? From what Angela says they're more concerned that one of the nurses has a little addiction."

Hugh grasped his mobile and ran through his contact list. "I'll call her now, see what's going on."

"Oh, don't. She specifically told me to tell you not to call."

"Is she still pissed off with me?"

"She said it was just an in-house problem, that you weren't to start looking at it laterally. And she said you've got to stop reading detective novels. I think I agree with her."

Wayne had managed to get through the monotony of the day and was pleased he would be returning home tomorrow. Syphilis was a bugger of a disease once it got to grips and he hated that it made him sickly at such a relatively young age. He had so much more to do with his life and so many people still to screw before he succumbed to being bed bound. The nurse had left the bay and a few visitors sat with the other patients. Wayne, however, was alone, as he always was. He'd not had a visitor in the five days he'd been in, but he found being close to others annoying anyway. Who would want friends that talk behind your back and judge you?

He pulled the screen that hung like a War of the Worlds Martian over the bed and plugged the earphones in, flicking through the channels to find something half-decent to watch. The choice was limited to soap operas and he settled on Eastenders, watching the characters he vaguely recognised from the few times he had seen it. It had been on for ten minutes when he became aware of company and he turned to see a face he recognised glaring from the bottom of his bed. Immediately, he felt uncomfortable and tugged the earphones out. "What are you doing here?"

The woman pulled the curtain up one side of the bed and around the corner, bringing the second curtain to meet it. "I heard you had syphilis. Did it not occur to you to tell me?"

"Clare, I shagged you what, three, four times? That's hardly a relationship where I'd tell you all my dark secrets, is it?"

"I've been to the clinic. I've caught it from you."

"They told me that if I'd discovered it earlier than I did it would have been completely treatable with antibiotics, so what's all the fuss about?"

"I'm on antibiotics now, but I lost a baby a while ago and the clinic said that the syphilis could have been the reason."

"The kid wouldn't have had a father anyway, so it's no loss."

"What?"

"Well, I'm not sticking around with anyone to bring up an unwanted brat, am I? I'm not stupid."

She was flabbergasted. "You egotistical prick. It wasn't your baby, it was my fiancé's. I'd rather die than have a child of yours."

The curtain wobbled behind Clare and another female peeped around. "Is it okay to come in?" Clare moved aside and Sharon stood next to her. "Didn't you think it was important to tell me you had syphilis before you slept with me?"

"You too?" Clare regarded Sharon with a new camaraderie, all girls together, and Sharon nodded. Presently, three more women had joined the hunt, pointing fingers at Wayne for their health problems and shame.

When Fiona drew the curtain aside and shot daggers at him, Wayne had had enough. "What the fuck is this? How come everybody knows about the syphilis suddenly? I've had it eight years and it's never been a problem before."

"If you don't want people to know things, don't advertise them on Facebook. Twat."

"I haven't posted anything on Facebook. Well, except that the nurses here are hot."

Sharon scrolled through her Facebook wall on her Galaxy and found the comment. "See. Last night: 'If you've ever slept with me you need to get yourself tested for syphilis. I'm in the Padway Hospital if you want to talk about it.'"

"I'll guess by your reputation that the STI clinic must be bursting at the seams by now," Clare chipped in.

"I was fraped." Wayne had his phone in his hand, searching his account for the message. It was at the top of the page. "I didn't post that. I'd never post something like that."

"Then we need to thank whoever did, because without them we'd never have known we were infected." The girls all mumbled in agreement and Wayne felt like a fox amongst hounds.

Chapter 14
A Yearning for Fugu

Pete had managed to find Nicholas Gleeson's address, not a difficult task due to his prominence in the local newspapers, and when he answered the call from the man's brother, he explained he was still investigating but didn't give any detail. He didn't want John to know he intended to visit Nicholas. Playing them against each other would be far more fun.

He drove to the address, a suburban avenue lined with beech trees, and once he had located the house he parked nearby, a vantage point to watch for the best time to pay a visit. For two hours nothing happened, except a woman who he assumed to be Nicholas's wife collecting a bottle of milk from the front step, but finally a man who resembled his brother, albeit a smarter, friendlier version, came outside and climbed into his car. Now was the time and Pete waited for Nicholas to drive away before edging his car to the house. He smoothed his boiler suit, collected some tools and headed for the door.

Presently the woman answered, a quick double take at his youthful looks and impish grin. "I've come to work on the garden, should I just go through?"

"I haven't asked anybody." Adele crossed her arms, leaning against the doorframe.

Pete dragged a crumpled piece of paper from his chest pocket and unfolded it. "Mr and Mrs Gleeson, five Granary Avenue? Mr Gleeson called me last Friday, I said Tuesday was the soonest I could be here. Of course, if it's a problem..."

"No, no. Of course it's not a problem. He must have told me and I forgot, that's all. Some days I'd forget my own name, it's an age thing. Come on in. Can I get you a tea? Coffee?"

He followed her along the tasteful hallway, through the kitchen to the back door. "A tea would be lovely, please. White, no sugar -I'm sweet enough already."

Adele watched him through the window as the kettle boiled. She knew she hadn't forgotten anything, she and Nicholas hadn't discussed getting anybody in to do the garden, but he had probably forgotten to tell her. It was no big deal. Until this year, she had always kept on top of the weeding and planting, but nowadays her aging body had started to complain more than usual. She was glad to have help, especially from someone so easy on the eye.

She arranged a few biscuits on a plate, placing it on a tray with the pot of tea and two china cups with saucers. Outside, the weather had slightly improved from the previous few days, the smidgeon of sun peeping through the clouds casting a happier hue over the pleasant garden. She set the tray on the edge of the decking and called, "I'm sorry, I don't know your name but your tea's ready."

This was what Pete had been waiting for, a chance for a chat, and he was pleased to see she had brought two cups. He stopped stabbing at a flowerbed with his trowel and strolled over. "Thanks, that'll oil my cogs. My name's Pete, by the way."

Adele poured the tea, the quality aroma of Lapsang Souchong hitting Pete's nose and making his mouth twist. "Just black, or do you want a slice of lemon?"

"Milk, no sugar." He could have sworn he'd said that already, and anyway, black tea? It shouldn't be allowed.

Adele cringed with distaste, collecting a small jug of milk from the kitchen, and she sat on the edge of the decking alongside Pete. They made small talk for a few minutes, Pete unsuccessfully trying to steer the conversation to Nicholas, and some noises from the house turned out to be another woman, overweight and badly maintained. "Ah, Pete, meet my sister-in-law, Fran. She's staying with us for a while."

Pete deduced she must be John's wife and he was curious as to why she wasnot at home with her husband. He also realised he would have to be more careful about what he said as John had specifically told him not to let his wife know about his investigation. He shook her hand, wiping the clamminess on his overalls afterwards. "A holiday?"

"No, I've, um, argued with my husband. Quite seriously."

John hadn't mentioned his wife had left him and Pete was intrigued. "Oh, what caused that?"

"He's got this stupid bee in his bonnet that Adele here's husband killed their mother. It's ridiculous. I mean, he's the loveliest man you could meet."

"So you're recently bereaved, I'm sorry to hear that." Goal! They were finally on the right subject and Fran was a talker, one of those who nattered relentlessly about themselves without regard for their privacy or dignity.

"Just over six weeks, but she was ninety so she had a good innings."

"How did she die?"

"It was a heart attack in the end, although she'd been sick for a while before."

"So why does your husband think she was murdered?"

"The thing is, Nellie was about to change her will." Adele coughed loudly, stopping Fran mid flow. "And..."

"Fran, a quick word inside please."

Confused and shrugging, Fran followed her sister-in-law to the kitchen and Pete punched the railing, irritated that the details that had been about to spill had been stunted.

"I've never seen him before and you're about to tell him we've just come into a million pounds. He could be – what do they say – casing the joint for all we know."

"I'm sorry, Adele, I never thought. Anyway, I thought he was your gardener."

"Nicholas called him, but that's not to say he's decent. There are a lot of people out there who'd burgle a place for far less than that."

"I've never had nice things so I've never had to worry about stuff like that. I'll be careful of what I say. Sorry."

The two women returned and sat once more with Pete. "You were saying," he said hopefully.

Fran took a deep breath, carefully choosing her words. "Nellie's death was reported to the coroner because she had an air-embolical or something..."

"Embolism," corrected Adele.

"Apparently that kind of thing only happens in deep-sea divers..."

144

Again, Adele interrupted, "There are other causes, but none that our Nellie would be susceptible to."

Pete felt the need to speed things up. "So John thinks that Nicholas injected air into her vein."

Adele stopped sipping her tea, eyes fixed on their visitor, and Fran wrinkled her chubby face into a puzzled expression. "We never told you the names of our husbands. Who exactly are you?"

"Shit. I never was any good at lying." Pete looked from one woman to the next, searching for sympathy, a forlorn puppy. But they were standing now, looming over him with their arms crossed and heads tipped to the side. "Okay, okay, you've got me. I'm a private detective. John hired me to prove that Nicholas killed Nellie."

"The conniving bastard." Fran was indignant as she realised the only way her husband had of paying the man was their hard-come-by savings.

"And have you found any proof?" Adele was severe.

"Of course not, the man's as innocent as a two year old. But I do think she was murdered."

"So why come around here telling fibs about being a gardener?"

"I just wanted," he wasn't sure what, it wasn't as if he could be honest and tell them he intended Nicholas to counter-employ him, "to put a face to the name."

"Rubbish and you know it. If you believed Nellie had been unlawfully killed you would have – should have – gone to the police."

"They wouldn't have believed me, in fact I bet neither of you do either, especially after the ruling at the Coroner's Court."

Adele and Fran looked at each other, the latter fuming that her life savings were being wasted on the hapless man. "Have you found anything solid to back your claim up?"

"Nothing that I can take to the police. I had my suspicions about one of the nurses who was working the ward that night, but I've met her and can't imagine she'd be capable. I need to look into it further."

Fran finally found her voice. "Using my bloody money. You're off the case, mister whatever-your-name-is. Tell me how much John owes you and I'll arrange for it to be sorted. And while I'm there I'll bloody kill him."

Lydia Davenport wrapped her silk neck scarf across her mouth and entered the examination room, balking at the sight of the body Ismail was working on, the chest organs on display through the Y-cut. She remained by the door, loath to get any closer to the dead man and his smell. "Is that him?"

"It's a him, but I don't know if it's the him you're looking for."

"Pardon? Is that Wayne West that you're working on?"

"Oh, right. No, his name is," Ismail glanced at the hospital identity band, "Franklin Smith."

Lydia strode to a trolley by the wall. "What does one have to do round here to get something done? I left a note," she picked a post-it note from the sheet covering the body, "Here it is: 'Please do this PM as soon as you get in. Suspicious death.'"

"I'm sorry about that, Mrs Davenport, I didn't notice. Do you want me to leave Mr Smith and get started now?"

She rolled her eyes, annoyed. "How long will it take to finish that one?"

"Not long. Anyway, give me a head start, why is his death suspicious?"

"He was due to go home today. He was being treated for syphilis, he'd had it eight years and it had grossly affected his health, but he wasn't about to die. Shortly after ten last night he began having seizures, then he was sick repeatedly, full-on bilious vomiting. They hooked him to a monitor but his condition worsened over the next couple of hours. They noted the whites of his eyes had yellowed and fitted him with a catheter to monitor his urine output, deducing he had liver and possibly kidney failure. At two-thirty this morning he had another seizure and arrested. They weren't able to bring him back and they called me straight away."

"So you need me to pay particular attention to what? His brain for the seizures, his stomach for the sickness, or his liver..."

"All of the above, and make sure that samples are sent to toxicology as soon as possible." She dropped the memo and smoothed her hands on her skirt, eager to wipe the room from her skin. "He had loads of visitors last night, apparently. Maybe one of them didn't like him much. The nurses tell me he wasn't the most pleasant of men."

"Okay. I'll get started as soon as I've finished Mr Smith." Ismail tried not to, but he couldn't help the fleeting thought of Hugh Smythe and his warning.

The previous night, crowded by Wayne's bedside with the gaggle of other disgruntled women, Clare and Sharon had arranged to meet for lunch, both confident they had more in common than a slag of an ex-boyfriend. They sat at the table, a dark oak to match the beams, and perused the mouth-watering menu. "I'll have the spaghetti carbonara please, but no garlic bread."

Sharon clicked her menu shut and handed it to the waiter. "I'll have the same, thanks, and I'll have her garlic bread as well as mine." The two women smiled at each other as the man headed for the kitchen. "I'm one of those annoying people who can eat what they like and not put on weight. It drives my friends crazy."

"I wish I was, I just have to look at a cream cake and I put on three pounds. How did you meet Wayne?"

Sharon was coy. "I hate to admit it, but on an internet dating site. I always swore I'd never use one, then one of my friends met a lovely guy and I thought I'd give it a try."

"Don't worry, you're in good company, that's how I met him too."

"I tell you, they should have exposé pages, or buttons, or whatever. Somewhere a girl can relate her experience if it's a bad one."

"Good idea, that. Sift through the bastards without going to the trouble of meeting them." The conversation ceased and both women struggled to fill the uncomfortable silence. Finally, Clare managed, "What did he do to you?"

"Never called after I let him in my bed. I was gutted because I'd been single five years after my marriage failed and I was looking for something serious, not someone who'd fuck me and chuck me." The po-faced couple at the next table glanced over.

"You poor thing. He saw me for a couple of weeks after we first, you know. I thought we had something, then he stopped contacting me. Who do you think it was that put the message on Facebook?"

"Probably an ex who he'd treated badly. After seeing how many women turned up last night I think there'd be plenty to choose from. As soon as I saw it I got myself down to the Churchill and they gave me antibiotics straight away, as well as doing an internal. Filthy bastard, I should have guessed he was riddled with STIs."

The young couple at the next table were staring again and Clare squirmed, putting her finger to her lips to quieten Sharon. Once the pair had returned to their meal, faces puckered with distaste, she uttered, "Same, but I'm not sure this is the place to talk about it, we're getting some funny looks."

"Oh, sod them, nosy bastards. Did you ever do anything to get revenge?" It appeared Sharon was incapable of speaking quietly and Clare began to wonder why she had believed they could be friends.

"No, I'm not that kind of person. I didn't even delete him from Facebook, although I was tempted."

"I did, but I re-added him a couple of weeks later. Glad I did now or I'd never have found out about the syphilis." Once more the couple were engrossed in their should-be private conversation and Clare wished Sharon would shut up. She didn't. "I've got my revenge now, though. You're going to love this." Sharon fished inside her large handbag, placing used tissues, her Samsung Galaxy, an address book and diary and some grimy cosmetics on the table. Eventually she found the Blackberry and set it in front of Clare, dragging the other items back into the tardis bag. "I nicked his phone."

148

"Shit, Sharon, what are you going to do with it?"

"I don't know yet. Maybe a few posts here and there. He'll guess it was me, he knows what I'm like, and I'm sure he'll be in touch in the next few days to beg for it back." She pressed the Facebook icon with her finger. "Easy, he left it logged on. What do you fancy putting? It's got to be something even more embarrassing than..."

"Shush!" Clare had her finger to her lips, eyes wide and chastising.

Sharon glanced at the couple and grinned. "If they don't like what they're hearing they shouldn't be bloody listening." Her attention returned to the phone, contemplating what to write as his status, but suddenly she paled and dropped it on the table.

"What?"

Sharon shoved the mobile towards Clare. "I don't know if that's a frape or if it's serious."

Clare read and gasped. "This is not a joke. Went to see Wayne this morning about his recent post, only to be told he died in the early hours." She pushed the Blackberry across the table with her fingertips as if it were a steaming dog-log. "If I were you I'd get down to the hospital pronto and give his mobile back, you don't want to be caught up in this."

As soon as Ismail uncovered Wayne West's body he could see the yellowing of the skin, an ochre pallor, and he checked the whites of the eyes that confirmed there had been liver problems prior to death. He checked his medical notes and could not see anything to suggest prevailing hepatic failure. He opened the body up and the enlarged liver with its unhealthy greyish tinge and signs of necrosis confirmed his suspicions. Immediately, Ismail took blood and tissue samples and addressed them to the toxicology department, labelling them urgent in red pen and suggesting drugs to test for based on the man's hospital notes.

The telephone on his desk began to ring and Ismail had a policy not to answer if he was elbow deep in a corpse, but when it clicked to answerphone and he heard Hugh Smythe's voice, he stopped to listen. "I know you thought what I had to say was rubbish, but please do one thing for me: if you have a sudden, unexpected death in the next couple of weeks, please test for tramadol hydrochloride. Humour me. Thanks."

Ismail scanned the internal organs in front of him, Hugh's words echoing in his mind and he hastily added the painkiller to the list of substances to test. He underlined the 'urgent' twice in red.

Sister Kennedy was too busy for the extra work the drugs theft had presented and her mood was worse than usual. She barked at Halina, who swiftly adjusted the drip of the patient she was with and followed the shorter woman. They sat in the side bay, the only empty room available, Halina on the chair and Kennedy perched on the side of the bed. "I guess you'll have heard that a box of tramadol has gone missing."

"I think everybody has."

Kennedy stood and wheeled a metal table towards Halina, unwrapping a syringe and a testing kit. "I'm taking blood samples from each staff member to test for drugs, first and foremost tramadol but also for illegal substances." She deftly prepared the equipment and turned to Halina, syringe in hand. "Well, roll your sleeve up."

"Sister Kennedy, I'm pregnant, I'm hardly going to be an addict with a growing baby inside me."

"Pregnant? Why haven't you told us this?"

"The assignment is for four weeks, it didn't seem relevant."

"How far gone are you?"

"Six weeks."

"Roll your sleeve up. There's always been something odd about you and drugs would explain that."

"Are you accusing me?"

"Nothing of the sort. Anyway, if you've nothing to hide you've nothing to worry about." Kennedy pushed Halina's sleeve up and clicked a tourniquet around her upper arm. "I want you to keep your eyes and ears to the ground this week and if you hear or see anything suspicious, you must let me know immediately, no matter how small or insignificant. Something is going on in SHDU and I want to know about it."

150

"I wasn't going to say anything, but seeing as I'm under suspicion now I suppose I'd better. I heard a patient complaining about Theresa yesterday." Kennedy drew blood into a test tube but didn't speak. "She said she wouldn't let her have the commode, leaving her to soil herself."

Kennedy withdrew the syringe, her finger pressed firmly on a cotton ball to stem the blood. "Which patient?"

"Bed two, I forget her name but she's not there today."

"Margaret Collins, she's a bit of a drama queen but I'll look into it." She had heard rumours before about Rebecca and Theresa 'playing' with patients, making them mess themselves, but had put it down as tittle-tattle. She sent Halina back to the SHDU and trotted to bay ten, where Margaret had been given a bed after her release from the high dependency unit. Kennedy scanned through the notes for anything unusual but nothing stood out. "How are you, Margaret?"

"I'm in ever so much pain, nurse, I feel like I'm going to die."

Kennedy's teeth gritted. Melodrama was common, especially amongst the older patients and she had no time for it. "How are your bowel movements?"

"Under control now I'm allowed the commode, those cows in there wouldn't let me have it. They knew I was busting but they just laughed at me, then called me a filthy cow when I pooed myself."

"I'm sure it was just a misunderstanding."

"What, to wait until I've just started to go and tell me that someone else needs the commode? They took it away and I couldn't hold it in. There must be more than one commode available. I was so embarrassed."

"I'm sorry to hear that, Margaret, I'll have a word with the girls and make sure nothing like that happens again."

Kennedy left the woman seething indignantly and headed for the SHDU. She'd had enough of the scandal on her ward and was beginning to think that the only solution would be to stop Theresa and Rebecca from working together, which seemed a shame as they had been close colleagues for nearly five years and their teamwork was impressive. But there was every chance that

Margaret would consult a solicitor in the burgeoning blame culture and bring unwanted attention to the hospital. It was her job to ensure that did not happen. Halina Kostuch and Angela Crabtree were currently employed to monitor the department and she would wait until she had seen their reports before she cemented her decision.

Marek hated that his job had become sordid since Rob's death and the atmosphere in the lab was subdued enough for him to be concerned that his colleagues blamed him for the accident. If he hadn't moved his chair back when he did, Rob may well still be alive. He knew it wasn't his fault, Rob should have adhered to the safety rules, but he couldn't help the guilt that taunted him.

He was also uneasy about the brief conversation with Gabryjela and her husband the night before. Suddenly his world seemed to have turned upside down. One minute he was in a relationship with a woman he adored, a proud father-to-be with an excellent future, and now he had a man's death at his door and his love life was shattering before his eyes. He glanced at Rose and thankfully she smiled, relieving him partly of his burden. "Have you ever eaten this stuff?"

"Do I look stupid? No, don't answer that," she sniggered and he laughed alongside, drawing glares from the other technicians. "Sorry guys, I know Rob's dead and all, but Marek wanted to know if I'd eaten fugu. I'm sure you can understand why I found it funny."

"I've had it." Haruto seemed embarrassed by his admission and his co-workers were shocked. "My parents took me to Fuguyoshi in Tokyo the last time I was over. It was actually very nice, both the taste and experience."

"Are there any restaurants over here that serve it?"

"You're not seriously thinking of…"

Marek hushed Rose. "It's not for me, it's my girlfriend. She says she really wants to try it. I don't think I do personally, but if it makes her happy."

"You'd risk your girlfriend's life to make her happy?"

"She wants to risk it, not me."

"She's an idiot then. Anyway, no, fugu is banned in the UK. In fact, it's banned most places."

Haruto jumped in, "There are a few places in America that do it, but you'll not find anywhere in the European Union."

"Take her to a sushi restaurant instead, it's far safer."

Chapter 15
Mrs Peters and Tobias

Hugh scanned the foyer of Kendrick County Court Offices for the hundredth time but there was still no sign of Thirsk, which annoyed him. He had asked – ordered – the detective to attend the inquest into Mrs Peters' death but had been ignored. The inquest had resulted, as he'd suspected it would, in her death being recorded as of natural causes, but the uncomfortable sense that everybody was missing something ate away at him. The main door opened and Thirsk stepped through, dripping from the downpour that showed no signs of abating. Hugh rushed over. "Where were you this morning?"

"I'm here now, aren't I?" Thirsk shed his coat and hung it over the back of an empty seat. "What was the outcome? Natural?" Hugh nodded, a scolded child sulking. "How's your search for an angel of death going?"

"Don't ridicule me, Thirsk."

"I'm not, I think you're on to something." He leaned closer to the shocked man and lowered his voice. "A fellow detective who's based in Oxford told me this morning that a suspicious death was reported by the Padway this morning. I'd put out feelers, you see."

"It's probably too early for the toxicology tests, but I'll bet it's something to do with tramadol hydrochloride."

Thirsk sat upright, stunned. "How do you know?"

"A box of it went missing from the SHDU sometime between Sunday and Monday, nobody's sure exactly when."

"Why the hell wasn't I told about this?" Hugh gave the detective a wry stare. "You're right, the pathologist suspected a tramadol overdose and requested urgent testing and the results were positive. They got the police involved because the patient hadn't been prescribed tramadol and there was no residue in his stomach contents, leading them to believe it was injected intravenously."

"How much of a priority are they giving the investigation?"

"My friend thinks it's an open and shut case. The guy had been hospitalised due to complications caused by syphilis, not a nice character by all accounts, and some joker told everybody on a social site about it. Seems on Monday night he had a dozen or so disgruntled exes turn up baying for blood. I hear the STI clinic's been booming this week."

Hugh caught Thirsk's eye and held the stare. "Find out what nurses were on." Uncomfortable with the intensity, Thirsk glanced away. "Or do I have to get Angela to do that as well?"

"Has she discovered anything untoward yet?"

"You're a patronising bastard, Thirsk."

"I'm serious, I need to know because I told my friend what had been going on here and we're meeting up tomorrow to discuss it. I can't just tell him the pathologist was in a huff and decided not to play ball."

"Hell, I'd hug you if I didn't hate you so much. Can I come to the meeting?"

"No."

"Why not? Surely if you're talking about medical matters it would be helpful to have a medical man present?"

"I only said no because I wanted to hear you beg."

A clerk opened the door to the courtroom. "All parties interested in the inquest into Mr Tobias Benjamin Sutherland's death please enter."

The two men were amazed how many people were joining the growing queue and they moved to the end, behind Kate Sutherland and her mother, who were following Rebecca Burke and Theresa Heinrich. They edged slowly towards the court. "Are you a witness?" Rhea directed the question at Thirsk.

"Yes, but not one of much help to your cause if you're looking for a murderer. We closed the case due to lack of evidence."

"I heard." She turned her back haughtily and Thirsk shrugged at Hugh.

The preliminaries took minutes to complete and Hugh was the first to be called to the front. He swore on the Bible regardless that he, as a scientist, had no regard for the book's God, nor any other god, and the Coroner, Timothy Bartlett, once a high-powered criminal lawyer, began. "Dr Smythe, after completing the post-mortem on Mr Sutherland's body, you referred his death to my office and also to the police. Could you tell me why?"

Hugh detailed the moments when his suspicions became aroused, of the note, of the man's condition and how quickly he had deteriorated. He explained how tissue and blood samples had been sent to toxicology and that they were found to contain a large quantity of paracetamol indicating the probable cause of death. "Paracetamol had been prescribed for him, which would explain its presence."

"He was prescribed enough paracetamol to kill him?" Bartlett was astounded, albeit sarcastically.

"Not according to his notes, no, but his stature was slight and it's possible that a regular safe dose over a period of time may have resulted in an overdose."

"But you did feel it was necessary to share your concerns with the police?"

"I already had, I called them as soon as I found the note in his oesophagus. The tox report came back a couple of weeks afterwards."

Theresa was the next witness called and she stood facing the press-heavy crowd, head held high and shoulders back. She told the court that Tobias had been transferred to the SHDU because he was showing signs of liver failure whilst on the ward. They had monitored him closely and during the night he'd become anxious, confused and paranoid. "Every time we came near, myself and the other nurse on duty, he would thrash about and swear."

"The note he wrote and swallowed, did you know about that?"

"Of course not, I wouldn't have even believed he was capable of writing at that stage. He was very ill."

"I trust you're not suggesting he was forced to swallow it?" Tittering rang through to room leading Bartlett to hush the audience.

"No. I don't know why he wrote the note or why he swallowed it. I also don't understand the content as nobody had made any suggestions or threats to his life."

"Could his anxiety have risen from the treatment he was having or the condition he was in?"

"Absolutely. We were recording hypoxemia and..."

"We're not all medically trained, Mrs Heinrich."

"Low oxygen levels in his blood. His behaviour was typical of somebody with oxygen depravation."

"The cause of Mr Sutherland's death has been recorded as an overdose of paracetamol and I understand this drug was prescribed for him."

"Yes, we were giving him the standard dosage of one gram intravenously every six hours. When the police were called we checked his notes and were satisfied he hadn't been given extra by mistake."

"Very thorough indeed." Timothy Bartlett's acerbic belittling was well known in the courthouse but Theresa was resilient. "Thank you, Mrs Heinrich, you may step down. I'll now call Rebecca Burke. For the benefit of those present, she was the other nurse who was on duty the night Mr Sutherland died."

Rebecca's account of Tobias and his final night was almost verbatim to Theresa's and gave interested parties no further insight, or qualification, of how or why a healthy man had suddenly died. Eventually it was Thirsk's turn to address the court. "Dr Smythe was concerned during the post-mortem and called me unofficially regarding the note. I placed it in an evidence bag and spoke with my superior who agreed a case should be opened tentatively. We didn't actively start an inquiry at that point as the results from toxicology weren't available."

"But when you did receive the results you closed the case. That seems somewhat odd."

"We were satisfied that it was not a criminal matter."

"That's not consistent with what," Bartlett scanned his notes, "Miss Burke said about your intrusion onto the SHDU on the night another patient died, the night you arrested both her and Mrs Heinrich."

Thirsk took a deep breath, finding words from the jumble inside his head. "My superior…"

"Who is?"

"Superintendent Fitzpatrick, sir. He had spoken to members of the hospital's board and they'd assured him that an internal investigation was taking place. Contrary to your belief, we didn't close the investigation, but left it open pending further evidence on the assurance that anything irregular would be reported to us."

"Did you agree with this?"

"It's not my place to question my superiors' decisions, sir."

"Maybe not, but did you agree with it?"

His questioning was like a knife, slicing and direct, and Thirsk knew he would have hell to pay when Fitzpatrick found out. "No, sir, I didn't. From the few enquiries I've made, I am convinced that there is more to this situation than the facts so far have suggested."

"You think Mr Sutherland was killed unlawfully?"

"Yes, I do."

"You may sit, Mr Thirsk. There is little point continuing with the inquest at this stage as I don't believe we are in full receipt of the facts. I adjourn the inquest for a total of four weeks pending a full police investigation into the death of Mr Sutherland and any further deaths that may be relevant to the inquiry."

It was late afternoon by the time Thirsk arrived at the station and he went straight to Fitzpatrick's office to update him on the result of the inquest. "Right, thanks for letting me know. I take it you told them an investigation would be futile."

Here we go, thought Thirsk, death by fury. "No, I didn't."

Fitzpatrick sighed, his shoulders slumping. "Thanks. Thanks a lot."

The reaction had not been as violent as he was expecting and Thirsk let his breath go. "Don't take it personally, sir, I just think there's more to it and surely the public have a right to protection."

"Nurses are trained to care, of course there's not something going on."

"The law of average says that there are going to be bad ones as well as good. I could state the obvious and remind you of Allitt, then there's Benjamin Green in the early two thousands right next door in Oxfordshire, not to mention Rebecca Leighton, Barbara Salisbury and Dorothea Waddingham. And what about the doctors with the same duty of care? Harold Shipman, John Bodkin-Adams..."

"Oh, shut up, Thirsk, have you swallowed the internet or something? I get it: you think there's foul play going on. Well, before we start anything I'll need to speak to my friend on the hospital board."

"Which hospital though?"

"What do you mean?"

"It's possible there has been a murder in the Padway." Fitzpatrick was silenced. He stood and began to pace, eventually stopping at the window and sightlessly staring into the bleakness outside. "I've got a meeting lined up with an inspector I know in Oxford tomorrow."

"Then I want to be there."

"No. I'm sorry, sir, but it's informal and only for us to discuss what's been going on. Your presence would make it official and neither of us are ready for that yet."

Fitzpatrick sat, flummoxed by the revelations and the media circus that was bound to happen. "Just go away. I'll let you know what's going on when I've spoken to my friend."

Thirsk left, and Fitzpatrick picked up the phone, dialling. "Snippy, it's Fitz."

"I thought you'd be calling soon and I'm glad you have. I take it you've heard about the inquest? Can we meet tomorrow?"

"I'll clear my diary to suit you."

Angela had been exhausted all week, somehow managing her regular ten 'til six shift at the Padway alongside the eight 'til eight night shifts at Kendrick, and not once had she fallen asleep on the job, but it was approaching midnight and she couldn't stay awake a moment longer. Head on the desk, the patients comfortable and undemanding, she relented. Theresa nudged Rebecca and put her finger to her lips. "The Gestapo's asleep. You know, Fred in bed four hasn't used the loo today."

"I'm not sure, Theresa."

"That's not like you. Come on, I think he needs a bit of help."

The two women walked the length of the room, past the sleeping patients in beds one, two and three. Fred was awake but sleepy. "Have you emptied your bowels today, Fred?"

"I haven't managed yet, it's getting quite uncomfortable."

Theresa grinned. "We can give you something for that. Rebecca, get two Bisacodyl suppositories. Not to worry, Fred, we'll have you cleared out in no time."

Rebecca returned to the desk, briefly checking on Angela, and unlocked the top drawer. She rummaged through the medication and withdrew a packet, popping two suppositories from the bubble pack, and relocked it away. When she reached bed four, Theresa had prepared the patient, rolled to the side with his knees up and bum exposed. With a gloved finger she inserted the medication. "Just let us know when you need to go, Fred, we'll bring the commode in."

They headed back to the desk and sat, each toying with paperwork, and after twenty minutes Fred began to groan, his body tossing and turning. Theresa nodded to Rebecca and they strolled over. "How's it going there, Fred, you look a little uncomfortable?"

"My belly's cramping, it really hurts."

"That's just the suppositories working, I'll go and get the commode." She left the room and when she returned with the portable loo he had clambered from the bed, bent double. She left the chair by the door and went to him. "You shouldn't be out of bed, you silly man, you're tying your wires in knots."

"I need to go."

"Get back in bed."

"I need the commode."

"Get back in bed and I'll get it for you."

"Just bring it over, I'll only have to get out of bed again if I get in."

He wailed, distraught, and a foul odour crept from the floor. Theresa saw the mess splattered by the bed and slapped his head. "You revolting man, you did that deliberately. You disgust me."

"I couldn't help it."

"Now we have to clear it all up." Theresa glanced back to see Rebecca on her way over, a syringe in her hand. "Good idea, Rebecca, let's get him back on the bed and sedate him before he causes more damage. Filthy bastard."

They manhandled the protesting man onto the bed, his diarrhoea smearing on the sheets, and Rebecca adjusted the multitude of tubes and wires on his body before returning with Theresa to the head of the room. She arranged for a cleaner and they continued with their paperwork, smirking every time they made eye contact. Angela snuffled a little and quietened, deeply asleep.

Over the course of the night, Fred soiled himself countless more times and his emotions went from embarrassed to ashamed, to angry, scared and finally timid. The angels ridiculed him, berated him, teased him, shouted, reprimanded. All night he lay on the same messed sheet, the smell pervading, the faeces stinging his tender, aging skin.

Angela awoke at six and immediately realised she had missed most of the shift, and poured her apologies to the two nurses, but they assured her there wasn't a problem. "Has much happened tonight?"

"Beds one, two and three have been fine, but Fred in bed four has been difficult. Nothing we couldn't handle though."

"I'll go and take a look at him, give you two a break."

Fred lay, his genitals exposed, on a large pool of fetid diarrhoea, and his cheeks were stained with dried tears. His eyes watered once more as the nurse he did not recognise approached. As soon as she saw the condition he was in, she held his hand and soothed him. "Fred, it's okay, these things happen." She pulled his gown over his privates for some dignity and stroked his wispy hair. "Don't let it get you down, we deal with far worse every day. I'll arrange for clean sheets in a minute, we'll get you all tidied up and comfortable."

"But I'm disgusting. Filthy. Revolting."

Angela chuckled gently, "No you're not, it's just one of those things. I don't think any worse of you for it. In fact, I feel bad myself because I shouldn't have let you get yourself into such a state."

"I wish you'd been my nurse overnight."

Something about the way he said it made the hairs on the nape of her neck stand on end. "Fred, has something bad happened?"

"They'll kill me if I say anything."

Angela snatched a look behind and saw Rebecca and Theresa approaching. She squeezed his hand tightly. "Fred, there are two hours left of this shift. I won't let them do anything to you. When they go home, I want you to tell me exactly what happened to you overnight." She brightened her voice and spoke loudly. "Fred here needs his sheets changing, can you help me with that please, Rebecca?"

"I'll go and get some clean bedding."

Chapter 16
Must Try Harder

Hugh hadn't been sure whether to tell the truth or lie about the reason he needed to take the afternoon off and he had chosen the latter when faced with Erika's sour face, telling her he had an emergency appointment with the dentist. He picked Thirsk up from Castle Street Police Station on his way, happy to provide transport so the older man could have a drink. "Something happened last night that I think you should know."

Thirsk stared at Hugh as he navigated his way into the heavy traffic on the M40. "If it's anything to do with your private life, I'm not interested."

"Angela called this morning and told me something quite horrific about Rebecca and Theresa."

Thirsk quit the flippant mood and listened as the pathologist detailed what Fred had told Angela about his treatment during the night. "I'll speak to the Super about it when I get back. He's got a golf buddy on the hospital board and doesn't want to tread on his toes. Is Angela staying at yours still?"

"She won't be now until Monday, that's if she decides to come back to the job at Kendrick. She's been working double shifts between here and Oxford all week and she's knackered."

"You're kidding. Is that even legal?"

"It's lucky she is or that poor old man would have had nobody to tell. I feel so sorry for him."

"This is the thing, they have a duty of care and a sick person has no choice but to trust in them. It's a lottery."

"Most of us medics are good guys, I can assure you."

Thirsk turned to the view on his left, a fresh spring palette of greens growing on the Chilterns under a glimpse of sunlight that peeped shyly through the clouds, and he thought about the case he was dreading being involved in. When Hugh had called him regarding Tobias Sutherland's bizarre note he had done some late-night, beer-fuelled research on medical murderers and the thing that had stood out the most was how difficult their employers had been during the investigations, creating vast walls of silence as they protected their killers. It all boiled down to money, as with everything. If a hospital is found to have homed a murderer it brings bad press. Bad press brings fewer patients. Fewer patients mean less income. Less income means... hospital closure. Why put yourself out of a job for one bad seed?

"Penny for them?" Hugh had reached the junction for the A40 and slowed as he reached the slip road. "Beer for them?"

"You'll be buying me one of those anyway."

"You know, now that something's happened at the Padway we can't be sure it's all down to Rebecca and Theresa any more. They can't physically have done it."

"Angela could, she's working both." Hugh laughed until tears ran down his cheeks and Thirsk eyed him, humourless. "Well, she could."

"You're serious, aren't you?" He wiped his eyes with his sleeve.

"Just because you've got the hots for her doesn't mean she can't be bad."

"She's the sweetest, loveliest girl ever."

"You're biased. Then there's that other nurse who works days on the SHDU, she's a supply nurse so could technically work at any hospital."

"I've not met her but Marcus says she's okay now he's met her a couple of times."

Thirsk exhaled loudly, demonstrating his weariness. "Do you think serial killers come with a badge attached to their lapel? Hi, look at me, I kill for fun. Every killer is a relatively normal person, every single one has neighbours and friends, even family saying they'd never have thought him or her capable. The essence of a serial killer is to keep that part of their world strictly private."

"When you call it serial killing is gets ten times more scary."

"It does, but there's also the possibility that there's a reasonable explanation to everything. The suspected murder in the Padway is probably completely isolated from the events in Kendrick. That's what I'm here for, to investigate and find out the truth."

"Yeah, but you're a detective and they have gut feelings, and you've told me you've got one about this."

"I've got a bad feeling about Theresa. Rebecca's just a prop, a silly lapdog. She's too stupid to be the instigator, but Theresa is clever and devious." Thirsk took his mobile out and found Toni in his contacts. "It's me. I want you to tail Theresa Heinrich, her details are in a folder on my desk."

The SatNav announced that they had reached their destination on the left and Hugh braked to navigate the small entrance to the car park. The inn was old, the honey Cotswold stone thick and weathered under a thatched roof that probably supped much of the profits. They went inside, ducking to avoid hitting the low doorframe, and Krein waved from the bar. "You got here at last."

Thirsk shook his friend's hand warmly. "The traffic was a nightmare." Hugh shook his head at the lie that had slipped out so easily. "Hugh, this is Detective Inspector... You are still..."

"Yes," it was a question he had clearly been asked too often, "still a DI. Pleased to meet you, Hugh, I hear you've been playing detective yourself."

"Not so much me but my friend, Angela. All I did was alert the police on a dodgy PM."

"The note, yes. That was strange." Krein ordered a pint of Brakspear's for Thirsk and orange juice with lemonade for Hugh, adding an extra half to top up his own pint, and they sat at an old oak table. "Where do we start?"

"Tell me about the man who died."

"Wayne West. Sounds like he was a bit of a prick, from everything I've heard."

"Which is?"

"He'd been hospitalised for five days with complications from advanced – tertiary, they called it – syphilis, but his condition had improved and they were ready to send him home the next day. Anyway, on Monday a herd of women turned up to visit causing some commotion on the ward. It seems that somebody had written about his condition on his Facebook wall and these women were furious because he'd knowingly put them at risk of infection."

"Have you found out who did that?"

"We've interviewed most of the women – haven't traced a couple of them yet – and the most likely candidate is Sharon Wells. As revenge – her words, not mine – she took his phone that night, then the next day, when she heard he had died, she brought it straight to the station. She swears she didn't post the original message, but she's certainly capable."

"Why admit to taking the phone but not the message, that's inconsistent."

Krein shrugged. "I haven't got anything better."

"So we'll assume she didn't post the original message. Whoever did was deliberately trying to stir things up. So, this poor guy…"

"No, he wasn't. He deserved everything he got, from what I hear."

"Okay, this arsehole is lying there feebly on his hospital bed when, how many? Five, six women?"

"We've identified eight and each has said there were between ten and twelve."

"So these women descend on him and give him hell because he's given them syphilis, or at least put them at risk."

"All the women that we've interviewed are undergoing treatment."

"Don't give me their numbers then," Thirsk quipped.

Hugh watched the two men, their friendship clearly an old one, and he was amazed at how comfortable Thirsk was beside Krein. In the few years he had known Thirsk, he'd always seen a grumpy, unhappy, unfulfilled grouch who had no friends or family, and to see him animated and laughing was surreal. He wished he could bring out that side of him occasionally.

"Anyway, later that night he started having fits and ultimately a fatal heart attack. They took his body to pathology for an immediate PM, the pathologist ordered tox tests to be done, again immediately, and as soon as they got the results, they called us in. The hospital can't have been more efficient."

"The opposite to the Kendrick. Sorry, Hugh."

"I agree with you." He'd been wondering if they had forgotten his presence and was reassured.

"So Wayne has been given an overdose of tramadol and you think it was by one of the disgruntled exes who turned up at his bedside?"

"Perhaps, but bar Sharon Wells, who's a little cocky for my liking, not one of the women I've identified so far."

"An overdose of tramadol given intravenously?"

"A nurse or care worker, it can't be too hard to get your hands on a liquid infusion."

"Or somebody who'd stolen it from a hospital. A box of thirty vials has been missing from Kendrick since Sunday or Monday."

Krein remained silent as the reality of the situation engulfed him and when the shock had worn off he downed half his beer. "I should stop trying to identify the missing girls, shouldn't I?"

"No, find them by all means, but don't hang and quarter them based on what would seem like the obvious. Has it ever occurred to you that the person who killed him may be the one who posted that message on Wayne's Facebook page? It would be a brilliant plan, don't you think? Put the message up knowing that lord knows how many irate females would turn up to come under our suspicion."

"If that were the case then we're looking for somebody who either works for, or has unquestioned access to both hospitals. The first step is to get the names of the nurses working when Wayne was killed, and to contact the employment agencies who supply the bank nurses." Krein could feel the case being taken from his shoulders and he felt perturbed at the intrusion. "I'll get someone to contact the ones in Oxfordshire if you like?"

"Yes, thanks."

"You've known about this for a few weeks and I know you well; who's your suspect?"

"Theresa Heinrich is one, without a doubt." Thirsk related her behaviour right from the start, her snarky comments and arrogance, ending with the atrocious alleged behaviour towards an elderly man the night before. "I just haven't worked out how she can be in two places at a time. The thing is though, her sidekick, Rebecca Burke, is like a pathetic lapdog, obeying her every whim, so I wouldn't put it past her to be covering for her."

"Then why did you need to meet me? You've got a suspect, a means, so why involve me?" Krein was feeling truly left out now and Thirsk punched him on the arm playfully. "Really though, you could have told me all of this on the phone."

"I'm kind of wondering the same thing, I was expecting a bit of brainstorming." Hugh thought of the trouble he'd had getting the time off work and grimaced.

"I'm about to be banging my head against a brick wall of hospital conspiracy and I need all the help I can get. It's not just them being obstructive, it's my own boss too. He's already threatened my job security over this."

"So you want us to sit on the sidelines looking pretty until you need a pat on the back?"

"Dave, I can't believe you just said that. You know me better than that. I want you to head the investigation in Oxford, but under my direction. Bloody hell man, I thought I'd be doing you a favour."

"And what about me?" Hugh may as well have blended into the textured wallpaper.

"There's no way that the bigwigs at Kendrick will allow any plain-clothes into the hospital so we need eyes and ears. Both you and Angela are perfect for that."

"Unpaid, no doubt?"

"Where's your public spirit, Hugh?"

Fitzpatrick dragged his set of golf clubs from the boot, a quick glance at the sky to check it wasn't about to rain, and he made his way into the clubhouse to meet the old friend he had associated with during their days at Eton College. They shook hands and patted each other on the back as soon as they met, jovial and comfortable. "Snippy, it's good to see you."

"Could have been under better circumstances, of course, but that's neither down to you nor me." Barnabas 'Snippy' Snippleton led his friend through the bar to the green, dragging his plush leather bag behind him. "This really is such a pain. It's going to do the hospital no good, mark my words."

"Yes, but we have no choice, you understand that?"

Snippy muttered under his breath at the words, reluctantly nodding.

"So how do you see the investigation progressing, what would suit you?"

"Not at all would suit me. I just can't believe we have a rogue member of staff; our interview processes are impeccable. I certainly don't want the press involved."

"They are already. I think Tobias Sutherland's family have caused a bit of a hoo-hah and by all accounts there were several reporters at the inquest."

"Bastards."

"I've not seen anything in the papers yet, though. We'll do our best to keep them off your back all the same. Snippy, I'm going to put one of my best detectives on the case and I'll make sure he doesn't get in the way."

"Not that idiot who bulldozed in and arrested those two nurses, I credit? You must have some fast-track officer somewhere who could do the job with a sympathetic view to mine."

"Thirsk is one of our top men, he gets results through brainwork, not bully-boy tactics."

"Etonian, was he? Harrow?"

Fitzpatrick shifted his feet, nervous. "No."

"Fitz, he's the idiot, isn't he? Come on, he's got the manners of a cuckoo. I cannot allow this."

"I'll make it clear to him that he's to behave, you'll get no trouble. He's the best man and I trust he'll find who's responsible for this hodgepodge with the least disturbance."

Snippy placed his ball on the tee and got into position, gently swinging the club back and forth to warm up. He walloped the ball and it flew through the clear sky, only traceable by the sun glinting from it, leaving Fitzpatrick in no doubt of his anger. "We're not going to make this easy for you, I can assure you, Fitz."

The atmosphere in Laboratory 4.13 had not improved over the course of the week, the news of Rob's death still reverberating from the walls and casting a shadow over every person and every moment that they worked with the dangerous drug. Marek took a fresh vial from the transporting table, carefully securing it into a holder and injecting a syringe to withdraw a minute drop. As he injected it into some acetic acid and began his latest test, his thoughts wandered to his girlfriend. *Halina Lewinski*. Or was she really Kostuch? They had barely seen each other all week, her long hours at the Kendrick combined with pregnancy had left her going to bed early every night, often just after dinner.

He reflected that it may be a good thing, the distance between them, to give them both time to consider the future, be it together or their separate ways. He was no longer sure which he would prefer. He loved her, but there was something dark and mysterious about her past that she insisted on keeping buried. Was it wise to marry a woman he couldn't trust? Of course it wasn't. As Marek put the test tube into the centrifuge, he had almost convinced himself to have the argument that had been on hold all week. But he might lose her. She might run away, hide from him, and he wasn't sure he could bear that. It was such a dilemma.

Marek thought back to the accidental, badly-timed proposal he had made. She had asked him to agree to two conditions before she would accept: to eat fugu and to see tetrodotoxin. Both silly. And dangerous. The only reason she would stipulate such bizarre requests would be to ask him for the impossible, things he would never be able to do and therefore a canny, diplomatic refusal. Had she made a fool of him and he'd not realised. He stared at the sturdy pyramid-shaped bottle on the table, innocuous and innocent.

Then there was the baby. He had always wanted a child, in fact he believed himself to have been born to be a father, but it wasn't something they had considered, let alone discussed. She had assured him she was on the pill and he had believed her, yet he hadn't been angry when they'd discovered she was expecting because they were both ecstatic. Plus he had considered it might be helpful in enabling her to forget the past. At that stage Marek would have done anything to make Halina happy. But she wasn't happy, not that she had said in so many words, he could just sense it.

And the rash proposal, something he'd decided against after the odd phone call to Poland, but had gone ahead with on the spur of the moment. The ring lay in its box, hidden in his bedside drawer when it should be displayed to the world on her finger. Marek winced at the thought of his bank balance and the amount of overtime he would have to work to repay the overdraft. Maybe she hated it; that could explain her reticence to accept it as her own. Or perhaps it was the proposal itself, unromantic in both setting and style. On reflection he should have arranged for a waiter in a posh restaurant – a fugu restaurant, he thought with irony – to bring a bunch of roses over with the ring propped in a bud, or carved the question into the sand on a remote beach. Or arranged for a plane with a trailer.

Marek stopped the centrifuge and took the test tube from its cavity, placing it in a secure holder. He had so many things he wanted to say and hear, things that would click the pieces of the jigsaw that was Halina into place. Her past in Poland, the whole story of Borys and their child, their deaths and the reasons behind.

He reflected how his heart felt physical pain when he caught her thinking, reminiscing, her eyes and mind distant with an expression so helpless he wished he could reach inside her and pull out the badness, the sadness. And he reasoned that she would never admit it, but she relied on him. He would have to be the strong one, the man who protected her from the world. The further she pulled away, the more he was going to love and cherish her, give her the security she needed.

Marek resolved to try harder.

Chapter 17
Missing, Presumed Guilty

Halina's shift was nearly over, her last of the week, and she was looking forward to spending time with the man she cared for, assuming that he hadn't accepted another weekend of overtime. Fred had been playing up all day, his emotions all over the place after the traumatic night before and by mid afternoon a doctor had prescribed a more powerful sedative that should help him to settle. He was due for his early evening dose and Halina noticed the medicine wasn't on the drugs trolley. After the tramadol had been discovered missing, Sister Kennedy had kept the keys to the medical cabinet on her person and Halina approached her at the desk. "I need to get some more Diazepam out, can you unlock the cupboard for me please?"

Kennedy huffed as she walked across, overworked and underpaid. She opened the lid and searched the vials and packets, then again with more care. "Kerry, did you pick up that order from the pharmacy earlier?"

The youngster nodded, "I went on my way back from lunch."

"So what did you do with it?"

"Put it on your desk. I did tell you. You were busy though. It was in a paper bag, a white one."

With growing panic Kennedy rifled through the messy desk, begging God to give her reprieve from the nightmare that seemed to go on and on. "I can't find it, are you sure you didn't put it somewhere else?"

"No, you were sitting right there," she indicated the desk, "you even acknowledged me when I spoke."

At the end of her tether with her staff, incompetent at best and dishonest at worst, Kennedy exploded. "Nobody is to leave this room until this matter is resolved. I'm calling Erika Gomez and I'm going to ask her to go through everybody's personal belongings and lockers."

An hour later Erika was on the phone to her superior. "Mr Snippleton, I'm sorry to call you during your game."

"What?"

"Some Diazepam has gone missing from the SHDU. I've searched the staff and their belongings but no one has it. Sister Kennedy wants to call the police but I said not until I've spoken to you."

Snippy turned his back to Fitzpatrick, who was about to take a shot, and checked his watch. He lowered his voice. "Keep everybody in the room and I'll be back as soon as I can. I'm on the eighteenth hole now so it won't be long." He ended the call and strode across the soft lawn, the grass healthy and springy. "I won't be able to dine with you Fitz, something has come up at work and I need to get back."

Fitzpatrick was smiling, having chipped the ball close to the hole and watched it roll in. "I understand. Nothing too major, I hope."

"Not at all, not at all."

Angela was determined not to fall asleep on the job two nights running, but wasn't sure how. Working twenty hours a day all week had exhausted her. On Tuesday she had resorted to using the bus rather than driving to enable her to doze during the journey, and every toilet break had been extended with a power nap, but even so, her eyelids needed stitching open. She opened the door to the SHDU and was shocked to see the day staff lounging on chairs and three suited men she didn't recognise standing in a huddle. Erika Gomez she remembered from her interview. She sidled up to Kennedy, whose eyes were reddened and swollen. "What's going on?"

"Some Diazepam has gone missing and it's my fault. If I'd put them away as soon as Kerry got them…"

Angela went to hug her shoulders but hesitated, not willing to provoke more tears. She dropped her arm and nodded towards the men. "Who are they?"

"Top dogs, that's who. I'm going to get fired for this, I know it."

"Has nobody called the police?"

"I wanted to, but Mr Snippleton, he's on the hospital board, about as high as you can go, he's insisting we keep it in-house."

"I see. What should I do?"

Kennedy wiped her eyes and nose with a tissue and coughed to clear her throat. "Mr Snippleton, the night staff have started to arrive and it's our end of shift in five minutes, what shall we do?"

"I haven't decided, but I don't want anybody in the room who wasn't on duty when the medication went missing."

"I'll go to the canteen then if that's okay, wait for you to call me. Shall I get you all some drinks before I go?"

Kennedy shook her head. She was thirsty but sure that Snippleton would go ballistic if she submitted to such luxury.

Angela was pleased of the reprieve and although she knew Kennedy would call her at some stage, she hoped she would get some sleep beforehand. First, she had to make a call. "Hugh, it's me and before you say anything, if I get my words wrong it's because I'm just about dead from lack of sleep." She could hear a tinny voice and realised she had gone through to his voicemail. Huffing, she waited for the message to end and the following beep. "Hugh, more drugs have gone missing but they haven't called the police. I suggest you talk to your copper friend."

Hugh had agreed to work late when he'd wheedled time off to attend the meeting with Thirsk and Krein, waste of time that it had been, and he was about to go home when he noticed a voicemail from Angela on his mobile. He raced to the SHDU to see her but she was nowhere to be found. With barely any details, he phoned Thirsk and told him about the message. "Why haven't they called us, they know they're under investigation?"

Hugh had no answers, merely the message boy, but he agreed to wait for Thirsk to arrive. His journey didn't take long, the station only a couple of miles from the hospital, and he met Hugh by the main entrance. "Have you found Angela yet?"

"No, I've searched the canteen, the staff room, the ward. No sign."

"Well, have you called her?"

Hugh slapped his forehead, embarrassed. "I didn't even think of that. That's what comes of too much hard work." He pressed a button and waited. "Angela, I've been trying to find you for ages, where are you."

"In the bogs having a sleep, you woke me up." She yawned loudly. "Wassup?"

"I'm in the foyer with Thirsk and he wants to ask you some questions about that message you left for me."

A few moments passed as she tried to remember what had been going on and as soon as the memories flooded back she was wide awake. "Be right there." She ended the call and searched her phone to see if Sister Kennedy had called but there was nothing, and a quick glance at her watch showed it was nearing ten in the evening. Surely the management hadn't been holding her colleagues for so long? She tapped out a text to Hugh and raced down the corridor to the SHDU, peeping through the doorway. Bar the patients, the room was empty. "Shit."

On the ground floor, Hugh sighed as he read the text and informed Thirsk that they would have to meet Angela in the SHDU. "Those lifts had better be working."

"Trust me, Thirsk, you need the exercise."

"Cheeky git, it's middle-age spread."

When they arrived, Angela was alone and having difficulty changing the sheet underneath Fred, engulfed in the stench of his stools. Hugh darted over to help her. "You'll do your back in trying to do that alone. Where is everybody?"

"I have no idea. Sister Kennedy never called me to come back, unless my mobile's playing up. There were three suits in here and all the day staff when I called you, then I got back here just now and... Fred, you don't happen to know what's going on, do you?"

"There's been some angst in here, love. I thought one of the geezers in suits was going to explode, his face was so purple. Never seen nothing like it!"

"When did they all leave?"

"After you turned up earlier, those two cows from last night came in, then there was some to-ing and fro-ing and everybody just went."

"That's probably about an hour and a half then. They can't just leave a high dependency unit unmanned for that length of time. Has everyone been okay?"

"Lady in the bed next to me was shouting earlier but I think she's asleep now."

Hugh and Angela finished his bed and Thirsk sauntered over, sniffing tentatively. "Get rid of those stinking sheets, will you. Is this the guy who Rebecca and Theresa gave a hard time to last night?"

"That's right." Angela stuffed the odorous cotton into a laundry crate and wheeled it outside the door.

"Tell him an officer will need to take a statement from him later."

Angela stared at him, dumfounded by his ignorance. "Tell him yourself, he's right next to you."

Thirsk glanced from Angela to Hugh, grimacing. "I can't, he's… sick."

She marched back over, squirting some antibacterial fluid onto her hands and rubbing. "Fred, this man is a policeman, and Pete Benson was right, he's an exceptionally cowardly one. As you probably heard he'll need to talk to you soon. Is that okay?"

"He can talk to me now."

Thirsk, shocked at hearing his old colleague's name, shuddered and made his way to the desk, making a mental note to get Toni to interview the patients to save him being contaminated. Hugh laughed and followed him, leaving Angela embarrassed. "Fred, I'm so sorry about that, I'd heard he was a pain but I didn't expect him to be so rude. You do still remember what happened last night, don't you?" He nodded and she strode across the room to join the men. "I take it tact isn't in your dictionary."

"How do you know Pete Benson?"

"Why?"

"Are you dating him?"

She thought back to her fleeting interest in the man and how he had balked at the suggestion of a romance. "Don't be daft, I wouldn't touch him with a bargepole."

"Keep it that way, he's a loser. If you're not with him, how do you know him?"

"He was employed by one of Nellie Gleeson's sons to try and find the other one guilty of her death."

"Employed? In what capacity?"

"He's a private detective."

"Detective, my arse. Too bloody incompetent to tie his shoelaces, that one. I'd bet a million pounds he didn't find anything."

"I wouldn't know, I only met up with him once."

"Give me his number, I'll call him later." Angela rooted in her handbag for the card Pete had given her, glad to see the back of it. "So what's going on here, then? Hugh tells me some more drugs have gone missing."

"I don't know much about it. Sister Kennedy said she hadn't put some Diazepam away and it went missing. The hospital wanted to keep it in-house, so I assume it was Hugh who called you and not them."

"So where is everybody? I thought you worked alongside Theresa and Rebecca?"

"I do and I have no idea." Thirsk was ignorant that he had made an enemy so easily, but Angela had no time for wimps and she treated them with sarcasm every time. "I'll leave the unit unmanned and go and look for them, shall I?"

"Yes, good idea. I'll wait here." He sat in the chair, ankle on knee, and drummed on the desk with his fingertips.

Angela grabbed Hugh's hand and dragged him through the doors. "Is he for bloody real?" Hugh, who had burst into laughter as soon as the door had closed, nodded, tears brimming. "And he's banging heads with the hospital big boys to get to the bottom of things? All I can say is good luck to the patients."

The two medics soon found the night sister, who was concerned to hear that the SHDU had been left unattended. She directed them to a side room, explaining the group had moved because they'd been disturbing the patients and that, as far as she knew, they were still in there. Angela knocked on the door to be met with silence and she opened the door a crack, but apart from a woman in the bed the room was empty. "I'm sorry, I must have the wrong... Hold on a minute, it's Halina, isn't it?" Angela and Hugh slipped inside.

"Yes, you're Angela, we share a job."

"I heard about what happened earlier and was told you had all gone to this room. What's going on? Why are you in bed?"

"I'm pregnant and all the stress made me anxious. I started to bleed and Sister Kennedy told me to lie in here, stay here for the night."

"I'm so sorry. How are you feeling?"

"I'm still bleeding so I'm keeping very still."

"Has anyone told your... Have you got a partner?" Halina nodded. "Has someone let him know?"

"I texted him and he's on his way."

"So what happened to everybody else?"

"After I started bleeding that Snippleton guy said everyone could go home. He said he was launching a full inquiry in the morning."

"So the Diazepam was never found?"

"No, and I don't think it was even taken. I think Kerry forgot to pick it up and then tried to cover her own back by lying, then it all got out of hand. I'll bet anything it's still waiting to be picked up from the pharmacy." Halina noticed the door opening. "Who are you?"

"Detective Chief Inspector Thirsk." Hugh and Angela turned to the doorway. "One of the ill people is trying to get out of bed so I got out of there as quickly as possible." Angela groaned and trotted back towards the SHDU, and Thirsk moved to the bedside. "I overheard you saying you think this drug business is all a misunderstanding. Who are you?"

She shifted up the bed slightly. "Halina Kostuch, I work days on the SHDU."

"You're the temp, aren't you?"

"Supply nurse, yes. I've got one week left here."

Hugh remembered her from the inquest and he nudged Thirsk in the ribs. "She's also worked in the Padway, she was one of the nurses on duty when Mrs Gleeson died."

"Is that so? Interesting. Why are you in bed?"

"She's pregnant and bleeding, in here for bed rest. Thirsk, let's go outside a minute, leave her be." Hugh edged the large man through the door and closed it firmly. "I didn't realise she was the other nurse involved in the unit's review and it does sound oh-so suspicious, but not right now, not if she's threatening miscarriage. I don't like the management but I love my job, so I don't want the hospital coming under another lawsuit."

"You're right, of course. However," Thirsk shoved the door open and stormed to the bed, Halina's jaw dropping, "I want to know exactly what dates you've worked and who for over the past two months, and don't even think about lying because I'm going to triple check everything you say."

Marek arrived on Ward 34 and headed for the nurses' station, explaining who he was and the night sister directed him to the side room, but when he opened the door the bed, although crumpled, was empty. He perched on the chair, assuming Halina had gone to the toilet, but she hadn't returned after ten minutes and he wandered outside to find a member of staff. "Is Halina in the ladies? I can't find her."

She checked both bathrooms but they were unoccupied. "She's due for her obs, so tell her to go back to bed when you find her. She's probably sneaked out for a fag."

"No, she doesn't smoke."

"Yes she does, I've been out with her for one myself when I've been working days."

Yet again Marek realised he didn't know the woman he had asked to marry him and his heart sank. He tried ringing her mobile but there was no answer, and now he didn't know whether to worry or walk away. He kicked the chair, wishing he hadn't as his toe throbbed, and strutted back to the lift, angry. The doors opened and he stepped inside, noticing a huge man leaving the ward. "Hold the lift for me." Thirsk ran the few yards, puffing, and Marek pressed the button for the ground floor. "Do you work in this godforsaken place?"

Marek shook his head. "I was supposed to be visiting my girlfriend but she's disappeared."

Thirsk had no intention of getting involved with a marital and he hoped they would reach their destination soon, but when Marek spoke again, telling him about the hospital's neglect to keep a pregnant patient on the ward, his stomach filled with butterflies. "Is your girlfriend's name Halina Kostuch?"

When Marek agreed, Thirsk flashed his badge and soon he was driving towards Slough with the Polish man beside him. "Do you think she'll have gone home?"

"I don't know. I'm not sure her name's even Kostuch any more, if it ever was." He told Thirsk about the phone call to Poland – *Halina Lewinski is a dangerous woman* – about Borys and Karol, and her reluctance to discuss her past. "Why are you so interested in her, anyway? Has she done something wrong?"

"She's a suspect in a murder case."

Marek was speechless, yet unable to object where he once would have defended her to the end of the world. He pointed to the terrace they shared with two other Polish deserters and Thirsk squeezed into a tight parking space nearby. Marek let them in. "Halina?" No answer came as he checked the kitchen, the living room and finally, going upstairs, the bedroom and bathroom. "Halina?"

"Shut up, we're trying to sleep in here."

"Sorry, but have you seen her. She was supposed to be staying the night in hospital but she's not there."

Jozef opened the door to his room, unkempt and bleary-eyed and he snuffled, wiping his sleeve over his nose. "She was here when we went to bed. I think she was packing you some sandwiches for lunch because she had your workbag. I haven't heard her go out, but then again I was asleep."

Marek paled visibly, horrified, and he dashed down the stairs, searching for his bag. The kitchen. Living room. Hallway. He raced back up the stairs and searched the bathroom and bedroom, shovelling piles of clothes aside recklessly. "Are you going to tell me what's going on?" Thirsk hovered in the doorway, hands in pockets. "Why is your bag so precious to you?"

Marek flipped the pillows aside, avoiding eye contact. "I think she's used it to put her things in. I think she's gone. Did she know you suspected her of murder?"

"I can't imagine I left her with any doubt that I did."

"Then I think she's gone, who knows where."

"Check her personal things, see if anything's missing." Thirsk was finding a number on his phone. "Toiletries, clothes, important documents. Find her passport; if that's gone we're in trouble."

Marek opened her bedside drawer and rummaged through the paperwork inside. "Her passport isn't here." Crouching, arms on knees and head burrowed into them, he began to whimper. "She's pregnant with my baby. What if we never find her?"

"Guv, it's Thirsk. It's a long story but I need all hands on deck back at the station... I know it's nearly midnight, I wouldn't call if it wasn't urgent... Just give me the okay to do what I want and I won't disturb you again." He cut the call, angry. "Wanker." He pressed a button and put the phone to his ear again. "Toni, I'm picking you up in five minutes, be ready... Stop whingeing and do as you're told."

Chapter 18
Lainz Angels of Death: 1983 to 1989

An evening rush-hour road accident on the A4 had left the emergency department in Boxton Park Hospital teeming with injured drivers and passengers requiring beds, and past midnight they still had a backlog, with patients on trolleys lining the corridors. Vincent Rogers' injuries were too serious for them to discharge him, yet not serious enough for him to be tolerant and he complained to anybody who would listen. "You been here long, love?"

"Not really."

"I've been here six hours and they still ain't got a bed for me. What's your name?"

"Grace."

"I'm Vince. Was you in the accident and all?"

"No, was it bad?"

"Bleeding horrendous, there was about fifty cars all piled up, bodies everywhere, limbs, severed heads, you name it."

A nurse had arrived to check on him and she put a cuff around his arm, a thermometer in his ear and a pulse clip on his finger. "Vince, stop exaggerating, will you. Mind you, it was bad enough, but luckily Hillingdon and Wycombe General have agreed to take some of the more seriously injured so we should have a bed for you soon. Do you two know each other?"

"No. I guess it's been all hands on deck, a serious incident like that."

"Yep, I've never met half the nurses here, we've got that many from the bank tonight. But don't you be worrying yourself about that, everybody will get a bed in the end."

"Nurse, would I be able to go outside for a cigarette? I'll come straight back."

"Good idea, Grace, I'll join you."

The nurse, a smoker herself, understood their need and although she didn't agree in as many words, she said she would turn a blind eye as long as they were quick. Grace, clutching her stomach, and Vince, bloodstained and wobbly, made their way to the exit, moving to the side underneath one of the many 'No Smoking' signs. She offered him one of her black-market cheapies and he offered her a light. They both leant against the wall, enjoying the nicotine rush. "First one in hours, this is. My bleeding head's spinning. You don't say much, do you?"

She took another drag, savouring the smoke as she slowly let it through her lips to join the cold spring air. "What do you want me to say?"

"I don't know, tell me a bit about yourself. Might as well, it's going to be a long night. Where do you live?"

"I'm just staying with friends at the moment so I don't really live anywhere."

"In Slough?"

"Yeah, I work here, just started a job on the trading estate. I figured it wouldn't be too hard to find a flat or something." She dropped the butt of the cigarette on the floor, immediately lighting another from Vince's lighter and she offered him the packet. "Have another, they won't miss us for another five minutes."

"My mate's got a flat to let. It's quite nice, you know, modern and all that, but it's in Cippenham."

"As if that's a bad thing. Cippenham's alright, it can't be as bad as the last place I was at."

"Give us your number and I'll pass it on to him."

Grace felt her pockets and splayed her hands. "Can't, I haven't got my mobile on me." She didn't want to give him a number where he could hassle her and she had no intention of renting a flat from his mate. He was an annoying man and she just wanted to be alone. She wished she hadn't given him another cigarette.

"I can take you out sometime if you'd like, when we're all patched up and out of here."

Grace chucked the second fag on the floor, too tired to be chatted up by a blood-soaked stranger who didn't know when to shut up. She made her way through the overflowing waiting room to the trolley she had left before, clambering on and lying down. "Just in time, Grace, we've found you a bed. Can you walk there? We need as many trolleys as possible down here."

"Yeah, just get me out of here before that bloody letch gets back."

Grace walked to the ward with a porter and settled herself on the bed, starchy, white and unaccustomed to fabric softener. Within moments she was asleep.

Toni had flung a tracksuit on without the slightest idea where she was going or why, and when Thirsk picked her up he filled her in with some basic details about Halina and why he suspected her. He started the car, but before he pulled away he passed her the business card Angela had given him. "His name's Pete Benson, tell him you're calling on my behalf. Ask him what he found out when he was – hah, investigating is too strong a word for a prat like him – playing coppers over Nellie Gleeson's death. And put it on loudspeaker."

Toni obeyed reluctantly, angry at being woken at such an hour when she was due to run a half-marathon the next afternoon. Pete was sleepy when he answered and she apologised, but when she mentioned on whose behalf she was calling he swore. "Tell him I don't work for him any more."

"You never worked when you did work for me, you useless cockwomble."

"Is that you, Thirsk? You've got a fucking cheek calling me at this hour."

"What did you get on the Nellie Gleeson case? Obviously not the son, I take it. Mind you, you're such a shit detective you probably did find it was him."

"Piss off, Thirsk. I didn't, as it happens. But I do think she was murdered. It's all in the past now, anyway, I'm off the case. I tried to do the dirty and got rumbled."

"Some things never change. When are you going to learn you're not clever enough to pull stunts?" They had reached the police station and Thirsk pulled into the car park. "Did you suspect anybody?"

"None of your business."

Toni had had enough of the childishness and she clicked the phone off loudspeaker, putting it to her ear. "Pete, it's Toni again. Look, you and the guv obviously have a history but right now I need you to forget it. There's a nurse out there who we believe has been killing her patients and now she's on the run. We need to know everything you know."

Pete was silent for a moment but, an honest person, he didn't want a patient's death on his hands. "I thought at first that it was a supply nurse, her name is Halina Kostuch, but I've met her and she's okay."

Unfortunately for Toni, Pete had a loud voice and Thirsk could still hear him. "And that's why you were sacked, always seeing the bloody good in everybody."

"They didn't sack me, I was retired on medical grounds."

Toni ceased the bickering again by interrupting. "Can you come in and make a statement as soon as possible?" With no plans for the weekend, as usual, he agreed to come in the next morning and she ended the call.

Toni and Thirsk got out of the car and he threw the keys at her, ordering her to lock it, and stormed to the building. For the first time Toni noticed there was a passenger in the back. She opened the door to let him out. "Does he know you're in here?"

Marek dragged himself out and walked towards the station beside her. "Yes, I'm Halina's, well, I was her boyfriend. Detective Thirsk asked me to come in voluntarily in case I can help find her. I've no idea where she'd be though."

"No relatives in England, friends?"

"Not that I know of, but it seems our entire relationship was based on lies so your guess is as good as mine."

They reached the incident room to find Thirsk already preparing a whiteboard whilst he briefed the officers on duty. "Everybody, this is Marek Stanislaw, he's the spurned lover. Marek, come with me, I want you to tell me everything about Halina, even down to her bra size."

"What about me? You woke me up in the middle of the night and you haven't given me anything to do."

"Compile a list of all possible victims with as much detail as you can. We'll get a proper team together tomorrow."

"Today," Toni reminded Thirsk and he growled at her, too tired for cheek, and headed to his office with Marek.

Angela had manned the ward single-handedly since Hugh had left at one, having helped her as much as his tiredness would allow. His parting comment – I'm not used to them talking back – had kept her in good spirits all night; she liked him more than she wanted to admit. However, by the time the weekend day staff arrived she was frazzled. She gave them the history of what had happened the previous night, pointing out that the police were involved. As she explained, Erika Gomez entered the room and Angela fell silent. "I'm sorry to tell you all that this unit is being closed until further notice. I'm afraid we can't offer work to any of you this weekend as it's such short notice, but we'll endeavour to have you all working again on other departments come this time next week."

"What about the patients?"

"That's for us to worry about. And please listen very carefully, the police are probably going to want to talk to everybody who has worked on this ward recently. If they contact you, although I'd never suggest dishonesty, I want you to think about the possible damage to this hospital when you answer their questions. Obviously we can't continue to employ anybody who isn't loyal to the workplace."

"Do you want me to stay until you've moved the patients?" Angela hoped not, surmising she could sleep for England.

"No, I have everything in hand."

Angela took the bus to Hugh and Marcus's flat, intending to pick her car up and travel home to Oxford, but when she arrived she wasn't sure she was even capable of starting the car, let alone driving twenty miles. Marcus was in the living room, clad in pyjamas and dressing gown. "Hey you, is Hugh in?"

"No idea, I haven't seen him. You look knackered." She followed him to the kitchen and sat at the breakfast bar, leaning her head against her arms on the counter. "I'm guessing you want tea."

"I suppose so. Look, do you mind if I go to his room to see if he's in, it's important I see him as soon as possible."

"Doesn't bother me."

When she opened the door she saw a bump under the covers and she whispered his name, receiving no response.

186

Wearily, she traipsed to the bed and tapped his shoulder, but he was soundly asleep. Faced with a bed after almost twenty-four hours with scant sleep, Angela moved the cover back and climbed in and within seconds was snoring alongside him.

Pete had woken early, too excited to get back to sleep once he remembered the late-night tiff with his former boss, and he drove straight to Kendrick as soon as he was dressed and breakfasted. The desk sergeant had been told to expect him and a community support officer took him upstairs, introducing him to Steadman, who had just come on duty. "Look who just crawled out of the woodwork. Peter Benson, I didn't think I'd see you again."

"Alright, Diane, old mate. The tubby tosser's expecting me."

She glanced through the window of Thirsk's office. "He's asleep."

Toni had been watching and she patted a seat nearby. "I'll take him, Diane, I know what it's about." Steadman and Toni had been colleagues for the best part of three years and the older woman still hated the hold Toni had over the man she adored. Rumours of a relationship between Thirsk and Toni, despite the vast age difference, were commonplace due to their closeness, but none had ever been proven. Bristling, Steadman returned to the hastily prepared brief she had been given as soon as she walked in, and Pete sat beside Toni. "Nice to put a face to the name. What's the story behind you and Thirsk then?

Pete was sheepish, unwilling to go into detail. "It's a long story." He took a folder from a carrier bag and opened it, stacks of haphazardly arranged paperwork flitting across the desk. "I brought my notes with me, I thought they might help. Is it you who'll be taking my statement then? It's just you're pretty young."

"I'll probably be there to mediate if last night's phone call is anything to go by, but no, I think the guv wants to see you himself. You know, we don't know a lot at all…"

"Never admit that." Toni looked at him, quizzical. "I used to work with Thirsk in Oxford, I'm an ex-cop. Don't ever say you don't know anything, always act as if you do; it unarms people and makes them talk."

"Oh, okay. Right, we know everything there is to know about the woman we're looking for and what she's done, so we don't really need anything from you but you may as well tell us anyway seeing as you're here."

"That's my girl."

A commotion by the door made everyone in the room turn and Fitzpatrick stormed through, heading straight for Thirsk's office. He shoved the door aside and barked, "Thirsk, wake up now. What the hell is going on?" The detective groaned as he raised his head, supporting it on one hand. "Who's that?" Fitzpatrick pointed to Marek, sleeping soundly on the guest chair.

"He's my suspect's other half, I asked him to come in on the off chance he could work out where she's gone."

"Theresa's at home, I spoke to her last night after Snippleton called me. He filled me in with the latest drug theft and I interviewed her. Snippleton has decided to temporarily close the SHDU due to this hullabaloo and Theresa's been suspended. So has the other woman."

"I'm not saying Heinrich is clean, but she's not who I'm looking for right now. I have a strong suspicion that the woman who's been harming patients is a temp nurse named Halina Kostuch and she's disappeared." Fitzpatrick was silenced, his thread lost and Thirsk continued, "She was there when Nellie Gleeson died and she's been temping at the Kendrick, on the SHDU."

"Are you sure about this?"

"Of course I'm not, but right now she's my prime suspect."

"We have witnesses who say Theresa and the other one mistreated them. She denies it, of course, but Snippleton has decided on precautionary methods all the same. So where does this Halina person fit in with her?"

"I can't work that one out, and both Theresa and Rebecca swear they haven't met her before her stint on the SHDU." Thirsk flicked through the scant paperwork he had on Heinrich and mused for a while. "Do you know where Heinrich is from? I mean, her name's not British, is it?"

"I assumed she was English, we're a multi-national country. All the same, Heinrich sounds German to me."

"Maybe she's Polish, maybe they're in cahoots. For all we know there could be a ring of nurses, hell bent on abusing their power."

"Don't be so ridiculous, I can tolerate there may be one bad apple, but a group of them working together? Tosh."

"What about the Lainz Angels of Death in Austria, there were four of them?"

"The who?"

Thirsk pulled himself up, wearily walking to the door and opening it. "Steadman, I want Theresa Heinrich and Rebecca Burke brought in. Now."

"What am I charging them with, guv?"

"Try and get them in voluntarily for now, but arrest them for having a bent spoon or whatever if they won't play ball."

Fitzpatrick shook his head, puzzled. "What now?"

"The Lainz Angels. That's it, the three of them are in it together. I don't know how, but I promise you I'll find out."

Vincent Rogers lay in his bed unable to move, his head glued to the pillow, his limbs a hundredweight each. He could hear perfectly, every movement or sentence booming in his ears, but he couldn't open his eyelids. He felt his arm lifted and a cuff put in place, a clip attached to his finger and a thermometer shoved in his ear, but when the nurse had finished taking his observations his arm dropped on the bed like a rock. He wanted to scream at her, tell her he was trapped in his own body, but his mouth wouldn't work. All he could do was listen to the comings and goings of the ward and smell the toast that was being served. A cup of tea? Yes, he would love a nice cuppa, he thought miserably, his mouth dry as the Sahara.

Across the mixed ward Grace also felt unwell and she retched into a cardboard tray, not bringing anything up. "Are you okay?" The kindly nurse held a clean tray out for her, the other splattered with saliva.

Grace looked up sadly, her skin pale and glistening with sweat from the heaving. "It's the smell of the toast, it's setting me off. Is he okay over there?"

The nurse followed Grace's eyes to Vincent, static under the covers. "You know him?"

"We met on A and E last night. He was very chatty. Is he okay?"

"Yes, just sleeping the shock of the accident off, I imagine."

"I heard it was a big one. I'll bet it was on the Sainsbury's roundabout."

"You guessed right. We're always getting emergencies from there, it's an accident hotspot."

Behind the nurse's back Grace could see the covers on Vincent's bed begin to jerk erratically and she pushed herself up the bed. "Are you sure he's okay? He looks like he's having a seizure."

Seconds later, Vincent's bed was surrounded by medics, all talking at the same time, the machines that had been urgently strapped to him beeping and wailing. Eventually, an auxiliary closed the curtain around his bed and all Grace could do was hope. She climbed from the bed and shuffled from the room to the toilet, wheeling her drip with her.

Chapter 19
The Upper Hand

"Marek, you said that you called a number in Poland the other day, have you got it with you?"

"Yes, I thought you might need it so I brought her address book with me."

Thirsk dialled the number and presently a woman's voice came through. "Cześć"

"Do you speak English?" Thirsk hadn't been expecting an answer in Polish, which seemed bizarre in retrospect.

"A little. Who are you?"

"I'm a detective chief inspector – a policeman – from England, I need to speak to Gabryjela."

"I am Gabryjela, what is this about?"

"I need to ask you some questions about Halina Kostuch."

"Kostuch! So she got rid of him all then. How do you say it? Is it fook? Fack? No, that is not right," an indistinct male voice rang out in the background, "that is right. Fuck you."

The line went dead and Thirsk rolled his eyes dramatically. "That's me told then, she cut me off."

"I got the same treatment when I tried calling her."

"I'll have to get a statement from her somehow, what she knows about Halina could help us find her, it could even help solve the case. You might be able to answer this, though: when I said her name, Gabryjela said something about getting rid of him all, any idea what that's about?"

Marek shook his head. "I'm beginning to think I don't know anything about her, anything at all."

"Do you have details of where and when she's worked over the past few months?"

"Not really, she works all over the place and doesn't keep a diary. That I know of, anyway."

"Wage slips? I presume agency workers get them."

"Maybe. She's pretty organised so if she does keep them I'll be able to find them."

"What about friends, or does she have family over here?"

Marek was about to answer when Toni knocked on the door and entered without invitation, bringing some stapled sheets of paper over. "I've compiled a list of all the possible victims that we know of. I'll go through them with you."

"No you won't, I trust you. I want you to take them out there and do a presentation, get everybody up to speed."

"You've got to be joking. I've never spoken publicly before."

"For god's sake woman, all you need to do is say what you were going to say to me. Anyway, there's a first time for everything. Get out there now, that's an order, but don't start until Fitzpatrick gets here. I'll call him in a minute."

"What about me?" Thirsk had forgotten Marek was in the room.

"Have you got a photo of Halina I could borrow?"

Marek withdrew his wallet and pulled a tiny booth photo from the front, her features softened by an enigmatic smile. "I don't want it back. Burn it."

Toni arranged for a support officer to take Marek home and soon Thirsk had settled the team of officers in the incident room. Toni, shaking lightly and feeling nauseous, stood at the front. "I'll be giving you all a copy of this report," she waved the stapled pages, "once I've photocopied it. It details our known victims…"

"Who I'll stress could be unrelated to our investigation."

Toni glared at Thirsk, her flow thwarted. "Thanks, guv. Where was I?" She stared at her notes, the words jumbling before her eyes. "Our first known victim was twenty-eight year old Tobias Sutherland who died of a paracetamol overdose. He was incapacitated in the SHDU at Kendrick Hospital, which is situated within Ward 34, without access to drugs apart from the prescribed medication he was being given intravenously, so the overdose had to have been administered by someone else. The hospital suggests that the dose he was on could have caused liver failure as he was a small man."

"He was five foot six and weighed nine stone seven. The dosage he'd been prescribed should not have caused him harm."

192

"Do you want to take over, guv?" Toni now had her arms crossed, indignant, but she had all but forgotten the crowd before her.

"No thanks. Carry on."

"The result of Tobias's inquest is pending our investigation. Although she has only recently been linked to our investigation, chronologically the next vic was a ninety year old woman named Nellie Gleeson who died in the Padway Hospital in Oxford, Ward 29, on the eleventh of February and her case has been to inquest where the ruling was that she died of natural causes. Nellie had an air embolism in her heart, which led to a fatal cardiac arrest. Regardless of the inquest and because of our investigations, we suspect that somebody may have injected a large quantity of air into her vein.

"Eighty year old Thelma Peters died on the twentieth of February in Kendrick Hospital, Ward 34, also of a heart attack caused by an air embolism. An inquest also recorded death by natural causes but, again, we suspect an injection of air."

"Now, James Cameron, aged fifty-five, had had his appendix removed the day before his death and had been transferred to the SHDU in Kendrick Hospital because he had low oxygen levels. Nothing life threatening. He was given an injection, supposedly of morphine, which later transpired to be insulin. Somebody had replaced the morphine in the bottle with insulin. Another patient, Jacob Middleton, was injected from the same bottle whilst Thirsk and I were there and went into cardiac arrest. Luckily he survived.

"The last victim we have linked to this case is that of Wayne West, aged forty-five, who died in the early hours of Tuesday morning on Ward 14 of the Padway. Toxicology found a large quantity of tramadol hydrochloride in his blood and tissue samples, however he had not been prescribed this drug. A box of thirty tramadol vials went missing from the SHDU in Kendrick Hospital the day before."

Thirsk stepped to the front and Toni relaxed her shoulders, relieved her ordeal was over. In the absence of photographs he scribbled a rudimentary face with a few wrinkles on a page of A4 and pinned it to the whiteboard, writing Nellie Gleeson above.

"The nurses who were caring for Nellie in the Padway at the time of her death were Angela Crabtree and Halina Kostuch."

He drew another cartoon face, complete with age lines and pinned it up. "Thelma Peters was on Ward 34 in Kendrick. The SHDU is on that ward. Theresa Heinrich and Rebecca Burke were working in the SHDU that night, and for those who don't already know, we have witnesses who are willing to testify that these two women have been treating some of their patients abhorrently. Steadman is bringing them in as we speak."

"James Cameron was being treated after his surgery on the SHDU, as was Jacob Middleton, and the injection that led to his death was given by Rebecca Burke, who swears she had no idea the morphine had been switched with insulin. We have not been able to establish when the drug was switched, but Lydia Kennedy, Kerry Absolom and Halina Kostuch had been on duty during the day, and Theresa Heinrich, Rebecca Burke and Angela Crabtree were working when he died."

Thirsk sat and murmuring trickled through the room until Sergeant Feldman posed the query they all wanted to ask. "You've missed off Tobias and Wayne from your list."

"The trouble is I can't find a link. Tobias died on the SHDU in Kendrick, but the two nurses on weekend duty have solid alibis for all the other deaths."

"Could his medication have been switched too?"

"No, there was nothing remarkable on the tox report except paracetamol. He'd been given the right drug and we can't say a hundred percent that he was given too much. The reason he's on our list is because of the odd note found in his gullet during the post-mortem; you've all seen a copy."

"What about Wayne?"

"Yes, this one is where it all becomes more sinister and, again, at this stage we can't directly link it to the case, but there was an odd message on Facebook that he claimed he didn't write, which led to a dozen or so ex-girlfriends turning up at his bedside the night he died. Our boys in Oxford initially thought it was one of these disgruntled ladies who administered the tramadol, but I suspect our killer or killers were trying to throw us off the scent. I believe the killer put the message on Facebook to put other people in the frame for his murder."

"Who was working the night he died?"

Thirsk scanned his notes. "Graham Calderbank, Beverley Aldrich and Tavis Hunter and we need to interview them to rule them out." He pointed to an officer, "Perhaps you can sort that out, have an all expenses paid day out to the Cotswolds. The Oxford boys have located all but two of the ex-girlfriends, but have no suspicions on any of them at this point as none work in the medical profession, and somebody would need some kind of medical knowledge to have administered the tramadol intravenously."

"So you're linking him because of the tramadol theft?"

"Yes."

Feldman waited for the murmuring to cease. "So what next?"

"We already have Theresa and Rebecca coming in so we'll hopefully know more about them later. Angela Crabtree has been reporting anything odd that has happened on the SHDU to me for the past couple of weeks via her friend, who is a pathologist we know."

"Hold on a minute," Fitzpatrick crossed his arms and sat back, eyeing Thirsk sourly, "you mean you've had someone spying on the ward despite me telling you to leave them alone?"

"In all fairness, sir, it's lucky I did. However, Angela is still a suspect, along with Halina who has, on hearing my suspicions, mysteriously disappeared. We need to find her, that's our priority at the moment."

Pete had been sitting in the corner the whole time, relishing the thrill of investigation that he missed dearly. "Am I part of this? Like, on a consultancy basis or something."

"Oh, bloody hell, I'd forgotten you were there. No you're bloody not. Come into my office and I'll take your statement now, then you can get the hell out of here."

"Do you treat all your witnesses like that?" Fitzpatrick was astounded.

"Only the dickheads."

The police had taken Marek home as soon as they'd taken a statement, assured he knew as little about Halina's whereabouts as they did, although they had taken the precaution of asking him to stay nearby. He was a man lost in the world, unable to make any sense of the crazy things happening to and around him. The shocking things he had been told about his ex-girlfriend had pummelled into him that he had not known her at all. The Halina he thought he had known was a figment of his imagination. Lies. The whole six weeks they had been dating, plus the year they had been friends, all based on deceit.

But she was carrying his child. He would never be able to be with her now, not after the disgusting nightmare he was caught up in, but they were having a child and he would have to be there for him or her. Maybe she would go to prison and he could bring up the baby without her menacing and untrustworthy influence. One way or the other he was not going to shirk his responsibilities.

He sat at the kitchen table idly stirring a cold mug of black tea, unable to consider doing anything except mope. He needed time to grieve. He had been there, still and morose, for an hour when Jozef came downstairs, filling the kettle and switching it on. "Hey Marek, you look like someone's died."

"Halina's dead to me."

Jozef spooned coffee and sugar into two mugs. "It's not like you two to argue."

"You came over from Poland with her, didn't you?"

"No, she came here with Julita a few weeks before I did, then Julita and I got together and I moved in. I didn't know her in Poland."

"Is Julita upstairs?"

"Still in bed. I'm just making her coffee to wake her up a bit, you know what she's like in the mornings."

"I need to speak to her, do you think she'd mind if I brought my," he sipped the cold tea and grimaced, "drink up. I mean, she's covered up, isn't she?"

Jozef chuckled, thinking of his girlfriend in her winter pyjamas and housecoat with curlers in her hair and bed socks. "She's covered up alright. I'm sure she won't mind." The two made their way upstairs and Jozef checked his fiancée was happy to have company before inviting Marek in. He opened the curtains and indicated the desk chair for Marek to sit.

"Halina's in trouble and she left the hospital last night. Nobody knows where she is. You haven't heard from her, have you?"

Julita moved to the centre of the bed to allow Jozef to sit, pulling herself upright against the pillows. She checked her mobile for texts and missed calls. "No. What hasshe done?" He furnished them with the few details he knew and they stared at him, bewildered. "She wouldn't be involved, not with something like that."

"So why run away?"

"She must be scared. Maybe her documents aren't up to date and she's worried about deportation."

"You knew her in Poland, did you know Borys and Karol?"

"No, I met her after they died, just before we moved here. She's never really talked about what happened, but I know she's still hurting."

"Do you know Gabryjela Bakalar?"

"I know the name, hold on," Julita squeezed her eyes shut, reaching into her memory, "she's her sister, but I've never met her. They don't get on, I know that much."

"Do you know why? The thing is, I phoned her – Gabryjela – I assumed she was her mother and was going to ask her and her husband for Halina's hand in marriage. Gabryjela called her Halina Lewinski and said she was a dangerous woman."

"Lewinski? She's been Kostuch for as long as I've known her. Maybe Lewinski was her maiden name and she took Borys's name when they married. I'm sure there's a simple explanation."

"But why say she's a dangerous woman?"

"If they hate each other she's hardly going to say nice things, is she?"

"Do you know why they don't get on?"

"She never said, she's always been really quiet about her private life."

"I thought girls told each other everything." Jozef's attempt at joviality failed to clear the atmosphere.

Marek raised his eyebrows. "I thought fiancés told each other everything. Do you think she'll have gone back to Poland?"

"No way, she hated it there. Something bad happened and I've never known what, but she's always been adamant she'd never return home. She probably needs some space to clear her head. I bet she'll be back before the weekend is over."

Pete spent an hour with Thirsk, although half of the time was wasted with their petty bickering. He passed on all the details of the work he had done for John Gleeson, explaining that he had known from the start there was nothing in it. Thirsk, however, had an uncommon respect for Pete's early suspicion that Nellie had been murdered nonetheless, but pride wouldn't let him admit that. He probed Pete about his conversation outside the hospital with Halina. "I ruled her out. She was nice enough and I guessed I was on the wrong track. Money's tight though, so I thought I would play the brothers off each other for a while, have them both paying me. When they realised what I was up to I had to stop."

"You were sacked again. Story of your life."

"I wasn't sacked, John paid me for the work I'd done."

"So you left it there, no more playing cops and murderers?"

"I had no choice, I had to find paid work."

"Have you?"

Pete lowered his eyes, teeth gritted. "Not yet."

"You're as useless as a choc ice in a sauna. Leave your notes here, I'll get someone to decipher through the scrawl. I doubt there's anything worth tuppence in there, but you never know. Go home, Pete. I hope I never see you again."

"There is one thing before I go."

"Trying to make yourself look important again, are you? Just bugger off under whatever stone you crawled from."

Pete had had enough and his happy-go-lucky temperament was stretched to the limit. He moved inches from his ex-guv'nor and held his eye. "While I was waiting for you, Toni let me read the transcript of Nellie Gleeson's inquest, but you're doing a fine job here so you'll already be aware of Pat Bond, who wasn't there."

198

Thirsk was ruffled but didn't let it show. "Of course we know about him."

"Which indicates you don't, seeing as she's female. She was the patient in the bed next to Nellie and was awake when the old bird died. One of the things she said about Halina stood out."

"I'll admit you've got the upper hand here, but don't prolong it."

"At the inquest Halina said she last saw Nellie when she did the drugs round at ten. However, Pat insists that she came back later, shortly after Nellie began fitting. The statement I took from her is in my notes and I'm certain she's a credible witness. But, of course, you don't need my help, do you?"

Pete stormed from the room with his dignity intact and Steadman put her head around the door. "Theresa is in room one, Rebecca in two. Are you going in or shall I?"

"You do Rebecca, take Sally in with you, and I'll do Theresa with Toni. Oh, and get Andy to speak to Detective Inspector Krein from Oxford branch to see if he can send us the statements he took from the exes who visited Wayne West. And to ask him if he's found the unidentified two. Ask him specifically if any witnessed a nurse attending to Wayne during their time there. And..."

"Guv, my brain's a sieve at the best of times, if you want anybody to do anything else then ask them yourself." She tagged a young constable on the shoulder. "Come on, Sal, we're off to interview a deadly angel."

Thirsk came from his room, his energy waning from the long night, and he stretched, long and wide. "Toni, you're with me."

She grabbed a pad and pen and joined him in the corridor where he was waiting for the lift to arrive. "Oh no you don't, you lazy git. You've put on loads of weight recently so you need some exercise. Stairs."

Thirsk shamefully rubbed his oversized belly and had to concede the wicked taskmaster was right, and he followed her down the stairs, puffing. By the time they reached the first floor he had to stop to catch his breath and he watched her smirking without being able to admonish her. Through the window he could see Theresa's harsh features and his shoulders sagged, not relishing the fact he was about to lock horns with her for a second time. They went in and sat, Thirsk dictating to the tape his and Toni's names, and that of their suspect. "You know why you're in?"

"Yes, but I've done nothing wrong."

"We have witnesses to you abusing patients."

"My word against theirs."

"Didn't you want a solicitor?"

"I've decided I don't need one this time. The last one took hours to arrive and I figure I'll get home earlier without one because I've done nothing wrong."

Thirsk sighed audibly and leant his head on his hand. "Theresa, we can either stay here all day – all night if need be – wasting time, or you can just tell us what you know. You're going down anyway, you may as well be honest from the start."

"I've done nothing wrong."

"Fred McDonald gave a statement yesterday saying that he was given medication the clear his bowels, but when he needed the commode you refused to bring it over."

"He gave no indication that he was ready to go. Had I known, I would have brought it straight over."

"He said he'd climbed from the bed and was bent double but you insisted he get back into bed."

"Then he's either confused or lying. He's an old man and old people's memories aren't so good."

Thirsk skimmed through the statement. "Fred said that when he soiled himself on the floor as a result of you not bringing the commode, you slapped and berated him. He said this happened numerous times overnight as he had no control of his bowel. He told us that it was only when Angela Crabtree tended to him that he was treated with respect."

"Angela Crabtree was totally unprofessional that night, she slept for most of her shift."

"That makes no difference to the accusations that have been made about you. And then there's Margaret Collins, who also gave a statement yesterday. She had also been given a laxative and claims that she was actually on the commode when you said you wanted it."

"When was this?"

"Last Tuesday."

Theresa searched for some recognition to the name. "I remember, she'd been sitting there for ages and another patient needed it. She told me she'd finished."

"She also says that when she soiled the bed she was scorned and sworn at."

"Mr Thirsk, have you ever worked on a ward? No, of course you haven't. Well let me tell you that it's no bed of roses. We have to clean up spillages from every orifice yet we're understaffed and working sixty hours plus a week. We try to keep cheerful, really we do, but everybody has a breaking point."

"So you admit that you mistreated Mrs Collins."

"No I don't, you're twisting my words. I wasn't happy that she'd crapped the bed and I was tutting and perhaps curt, but I didn't mistreat her."

"Both of these people are willing to swear in a court of law that you did."

"And I'm willing to swear in the same court of law that I didn't and I know that Rebecca will be saying the same."

"Your fingerprints were on the morphine bottle that was later found to contain insulin."

"Of course they were, I have to administer morphine to patients all the time."

"Do you know Halina Kostuch?"

"I know a Halina but not her surname. If she's the lady who has been working days in the same capacity as Crabtree then yes, I know of her."

"Did you know her before she started this temporary position?"

"I said I know of her, I don't know her personally. I've seen her at handover but that's all."

"Where were you born, Theresa?" Toni was as nonplussed as the nurse at the sudden change of direction and she eyed Thirsk quizzically. "Well?"

"Burton on Trent, not that I can see how that can possibly be relevant."

"Second generation? Third?"

"What?"

Toni nudged her boss on the arm and whispered, "Guv, it's her married name." Thirsk stood, attempting to hide his embarrassment from the women and he nodded towards the door before leaving. Toni followed him, stating to the camcorder that the interview was suspended. "What happened there?"

"She's lying through her teeth but how can we prove it? Who's going to believe two ancient crinklies against her, with her twenty-seven years of professional service? We need to find some more people who've been abused by either her or Rebecca. Get in touch with Kendrick Hospital and tell them you need the names of every patient who's been on the SHDU for the past, what, six months. No, make that three, we can always extend it."

"Aren't we going back in?"

"I'm not going to get anything out of her just yet. Do you know if she came in voluntarily, or if she was charged?"

"Don't you read any of the memos I give you?"

"Oh, is that what all those pages of smiley faces in my inbox are. Stop smothering me with emoticons and I might just take you seriously."

"Sounds like that computer course was useful after all, guv. Yes, she refused to come in so Steadman charged her with, um, it was obstructing an investigation, I think."

Thirsk looked at his watch and checked the time Theresa was brought in. "We've got twenty-two hours to get something out of her. Get her in the cells, I'll drag her out at three in the morning and give her hell. You can be there if you want, I don't care either way."

Chapter 20
Playing on Wet Roads

"I'm calling from Kendrick Hospital. Can I speak to Halina Kostuch please?"

"She's not here." Marek was about to put the phone down but curiosity won. "I'm her fiancé, can I help?"

"I'm just calling to tell her that the test was negative."

"What test?"

"The pregnancy test. We've tested both her blood and urine and she hasn't had a miscarriage because she wasn't pregnant. It must have been a phantom pregnancy, love." The nurse ended the call but Marek remained still, trying to understand why Halina would lie to him about something so important. A few days before he would have assumed it was a mistake, but now he knew her to be a liar and a bitch, she had to have had an ulterior motive.

It was the last straw and Marek intended to do anything he could to help the investigation as long as it didn't interfere with his employment, and the first to address was her wage slips. Halina was an organised person. Untidy, maybe, but when it came to important documents her system was impeccable and he found them in minutes. Each one detailed the date she had worked and at which hospital. It seemed a waste of time to write the details down so he put the file in a carrier bag and phoned the station to let Thirsk know he could pick them up any time.

Marek sat on the bed, lost and lonely, and he stroked Halina's pillow as he remembered the good times, eventually bringing it to his face to smell her scent. *Halina Lewinski is a dangerous woman.* He shoved it back on the bed, following with a punch, and another, over and over until his anger was spent.

Enwrapped in a chasm of sadness, his heart a void, he opened her bedside drawer. In all the time they had shared a room he had respected her privacy, but she was a charlatan and he wanted to know the extent of her deceit. He rummaged through, throwing the contents either back inside or on the floor, not caring if they were damaged in the process. One by one he went through every cupboard and drawer containing her belongings and was burrowing inside her wardrobe when a tapping on the door stopped him.

"Marek, I made you some dinner, I didn't think you'd bother to cook for yourself."

"That's kind of you."

Julita laid the tray on the desk and hovered in the doorway. "You've made a right mess in here, are you taking your temper out on her belongings?"

"No," he scanned the havoc he had wreaked, "well, a bit. I was trying to find out something about her, something that might explain why all this is happening."

"Marek, you've got to forget her, she's just not worth your time and effort. You're a good-looking guy, Miss Right will be just around the corner."

"Look, I didn't tell you everything earlier. The police think she may be involved with some deaths in the hospital, I had to give a statement first thing this morning."

"You're kidding!" She leant through the doorway and shouted, "Jozef," but on second thoughts picked up the meal she had prepared and trotted down the stairs, "Marek, come and eat with us, tell us all about it."

They finished their food whilst Marek explained the fewdetails he knew and he found their company helpful, a chance to get things off his chest.When Jozef suggested breaking a bottle of wine open he agreed. They languished on the sofa, glasses in hand. "She wasn't pregnant. I had a call from the hospital."

"So she did have a miscarriage."

"No, they said it must have been a phantom pregnancy."

Jozef had been disgusted by Marek's account and had never trusted his fiancée's friend. "Or a lie to keep you by her side."

"That would be the worst form of manipulation. I'd never do something like that." Julita sipped her wine, aghast. "You know, the weirdest thing is that I can't say she'd never do that. Most people you know wouldn't be capable, but with Halina, well, it seems possible. Do you think we should try that Gabryjela again?"

"I've tried twice more but all she does is put the phone down. I can't get her words out of my head and I can't help but be suspicious about her using a different surname. Maybe Kostuch is her married name, but then again, maybe it isn't. I have no idea what the truth is when it comes to Halina. I wish I'd never met her."

"Maybe she killed Borys and Karol and that's why she never talks about them. Maybe she's wanted in Poland and that's why she swears she'll never return." Marek and Jozef stared at Julita, astounded.

Over the course of the day, Thirsk and his team had interviewed no end of people, including the Gleeson brothers and their wives, Pat Bond and Angela Crabtree, but they could only tell them things they already knew. DI Krein had emailed the statements his officers in Oxford had taken from Wayne West's ex-girlfriends, all of whom appeared to be innocent of everything other than hatred for a man who had put their health at risk. It was the early hours of the morning, and Thirsk had been asleep at his desk for hours when Toni crept in, unsure whether waking him was wise. She tentatively stepped towards him and patted his shoulder. "Boss."

"What? Who… Shit, I fell asleep. What time is it?"

"It's nearly three, you said you wanted to interview Theresa at three."

"Did I? I'm a bloody fool. Do me a favour, get me a coffee. One you can stand a spoon in, I need the caffeine." She followed orders and he called after her, "What are you doing here at this ridiculous hour, anyway?"

"You said I could be at the interview if I wanted. Well, I do want."

"You could at least be a little less cheerful, people like you do my head in."

Quarter of an hour later they were waiting in the interview room and Theresa, dishevelled and puffy, was brought in. "I didn't realise torture was still legal."

"Are you still claiming you don't want a solicitor present?"

"I've done nothing wrong."

"We're back to that, are we? Theresa, the hospital is giving us details of every patient who has been in your care for the past three months and we're going to interview them all. We already have a solid case against you and your Girl Friday and I have no doubt that these interviews will provide us with more tales of mistreatment. Isn't it about time you accepted how much trouble you're in and started coming clean?"

"I won't admit to things I haven't done. People who are ill have one thing to focus on and that's their health, and often they see things that aren't there."

"Or you're using their illnesses as an excuse to cover up your malpractice. How long have you known Halina Kostuch?"

"Only since she started temping on my unit."

"I suspect that you've known her longer. I think you, Rebecca and Halina have been working as a team, getting some sick enjoyment out of watching helpless people suffer."

"I'm not part of any team and I haven't done anything wrong. Anyway, this is a bit of pot calling kettle black, don't you think? Dragging me out here at stupid o'clock in the morning just to go over the same rubbish you've been over before."

"You think Tobias Sutherland's death from an overdose of paracetamol is rubbish? Think back, Theresa. Who, exactly, gave him too much?"

"His liver was failing before he was brought to our unit, which makes it likely it was somebody on Ward 34. That's if there was any negligence in the first place, which is doubtful."

Her point was valid and Thirsk felt lost in a quagmire of what-ifs and how-comes. He was drained. However, a trooper, he continued, "Then there's Thelma Peters, she was on Ward 34 and..."

"My point exactly. Ward 34 is where you should be looking for the murderous nurse you're determined to find, not my unit. Rebecca and I are professionals and we've been working together – without complaint, I must add – for five years. I can't say about the foreigner, I haven't worked with her so I wouldn't know what she gets up to."

"Did you put insulin in the morphine bottle?"

"Of course I didn't. And nor did Rebecca. The immigrant was working the day he was injected though, try her."

"She's disappeared. Do you have any idea where she may have gone?"

Theresa glared at Thirsk, her rat-like eyes boring into him through thick lenses. "Then that's about as much an admission of guilt as you can get, isn't it."

"She wasn't there for some of the events we're investigating. Personally, I'm certain she's in this mess somewhere, but she can't be operating alone. I have witnesses to your mistreatment and I believe you know Halina better than you're admitting to."

"You can believe what you like, but I'll say again – yet again – that I won't admit to something I haven't done. I work hard and I care for my patients' needs. Both Fred McDonald and Margaret Collins were confused and poorly and the mind plays tricks when you're ill. I treated them with exactly the same level of care I do all my patients."

Toni nudged Thirsk and leaned over, whispering, "Now the shock of losing Toby has passed, Kate Sutherland clearly remembers everything about the day before he died. Do you want me to interview her formally tomorrow – well, later today?"

He nodded and turned to Theresa. "Do you recall Tobias's wife, Kate?"

"Vaguely, why?"

"My colleague here interviewed her today and she is also willing to testify against you regarding your mistreatment of her late husband."

Theresa paled, her body shrinking in the chair, eyes wide and frightened. "I didn't know she'd seen anything." She paused, thoughts and recollections dashing through her mind. "I'd like to use my right to have a solicitor present."

Snippleton loved Sundays and had been enjoying an afternoon of drinks with old friends at the country club he was pleased to call his local, but the mood was broken when Fitzpatrick arrived with a hostile expression. "Your daughter told me you'd be here, Snippy. Can we talk for a minute?" They headed to a table and sat, Snippleton waving to the bar manager to order his friend a drink. "Theresa Heinrich has admitted everything and she's implicated Rebecca Burke too."

Snippleton rested back against the seat, hands clasped over his belly. "What has she said?"

"The two of them have been using unprescribed drugs on their patients for the past two years."

"Obviously they're fired now, I shall arrange that formally tomorrow. Does that mean this investigation is over and we can go back to normal?"

Fitzpatrick was uncomfortable. "No."

"Then on your head be it when patients start dying because the SHDU remains closed. You're a fool, Fitzpatrick."

"Theresa has sworn that she had nothing to do with Tobias's overdose and my inspector believes her."

"Why?"

"She admitted in detail to using laxative suppositories and intravenous diuretics to make numerous patients mess themselves, which then gave her reason to admonish them. She couldn't remember all of them, but has supplied the names of over thirty."

"So she got bored and moved on to something more powerful: paracetamol."

"My inspector said…"

"Here we go," Snippleton took a sip of his red wine, "you're still using that Thirsk character, aren't you? The overweight oaf."

"He's a good detective."

"But he believes a woman capable of such atrocities over clear facts. She won't admit to the lad that died because she'll be looking at a murder charge instead of what? GBH, or something similar that means nothing?"

"Either that or ABH. Snippy, I trust Thirsk. He told me that once Theresa realised she was in trouble no matter what, she was completely cooperative in answering questions and giving her statement."

"And of course she'll deny murder. Come on, pal, what will she get for grievous or actual bodily harm, eh? Two, three years, maybe even suspended. If she admits to murder she may be looking at a life sentence."

"We've currently linked five suspicious deaths, two of which happened in the Padway, and Theresa couldn't have physically been there as she was working in Kendrick with Rebecca."

"Five deaths? How did that happen? There was only Sutherland a minute ago."

"His death was just the start and for all we know there could be many before him."

Snippleton grumbled to himself, muttering expletives and playing with his glass. "I know about Sutherland but you said there were two more deaths at Kendrick, what happened? Why are they suspicious?"

"An eighty year old, Mrs Peters..."

"Been to inquest and they ruled natural causes. Next?"

"James Cameron, he was the man injected..."

"With insulin from a morphine bottle, I remember. Well, she obviously switched the drug, her or Burke." He slid his chair back and stood, taking his drink. "If that's all you've got, I refuse to cooperate with any further investigation into the hospital. You have your women and they are no longer employed by us, so as far as I'm concerned that's the end of it all. Good day, Fitz."

"Then I'll contact the Care Quality Commission." It was the worst threat he could give the man whose working life had been devoted to running Kendrick Hospital. "You'll have no choice but to comply."

"That will destroy my hospital."

Fitzpatrick now stood, angry that his long time friend was being such an arse. "Then stop trying to bury your staffs' failings and let my officers do their jobs without hindrance."

Kate answered the door and was shocked to see Toni and Thirsk waiting, dripping from the latest downpour. Since Tobias's death she had been through a personal hell, of questioning with no answers, loneliness with no hope of redress and anger that the course of her life had been irrevocably altered. Only recently, now that he was buried, had she begun to wash

209

and dress in the mornings instead of vegetating on the sofa wishing she could die and join the love of her life. "What's going on?" Over her shoulder she yelled, "Mum, the police are here."

Toni reached out and patted her arm. "Don't worry, Kate, we just need a quick chat."

"Is it because I kept phoning you? I'm sorry about that, I don't know what I was thinking."

Thirsk had had enough of the pussyfooting around. "We have arrested two people on suspicion of malpractice and have re-opened your husband's file. I need to take a formal statement from you."

"Richard, I didn't expect to see you again." Rhea had come from the kitchen, wiping her hands on a tea towel.

He nodded to her and made his way into the living room without being asked, and Rhea was embarrassed, she thought they had shared an attraction after Tobias had died. Toni noticed. "Sorry about him, he barely had any sleep last night."

"Oh, I didn't realise you two were…"

"No!" She had shouted involuntarily. "No, we were up most of the night interviewing one of the suspects. Come on, let's go and sit down."

Kate curled into her favourite part of the sofa that had seen far too much of her the past few weeks and her mother sat upright on an armchair, indicating the empty seats to their visitors. Toni sat but Thirsk remained standing. "You've told us before that Tobias had been told he was to be discharged on the Friday, but in the early hours of the morning his condition deteriorated. Were you there?"

"No, I got a call from the hospital asking me to come in."

"I drove her; she can't drive."

"Thank you, Mrs Parkins, but I'd like Kate to answer."

"Oh," Rhea could tell a cold shoulder and she was embarrassed once more, "I'll go and make some tea then."

She hurried from the room and Kate continued, "Mum took me straight there, we got to the SHDU at about five in the morning."

"Think back to the day before, how did Tobias seems to you."

"He was happy, in fact he was excited about coming home."

"And when you left him?"

Kate was flustered and unable to see where the questioning was heading. "The same, he was fine. That's why it was such a shock when the hospital called, that's why I asked mum to take me in rather than get a taxi."

"When you arrived, how was he?"

"He looked terrible. He was barely awake and his skin was all yellow. He was going on about the bitch hounds and I was really worried."

"Think clearly now, was it bitch hound or hounds. It's important."

Kate fidgeted with her buttons, her neckline, her fingertips. "I don't know. Both, I'm sure he said both. The nurse came over and she said he was delirious and gave him an injection."

"Of what?"

"I think it was a sedative. He went straight to sleep."

"Do you remember what the nurse looked like or, better still, her name?"

"I don't know. Why? Why all these questions? I was out of my brains with worry, I was concentrating on Toby."

"Her name was Rebecca, she was the kinder of the two. I didn't like the other one." Rhea was in the doorway wiping her hands once more.

"Had you seen Rebecca or the other nurse on the ward before he was transferred to the SHDU?"

"Not that I recall."

"Had any of the staff given him an injection that wasn't explained to you?"

Kate began to cry, the whole distressing period forced from her memory again. "I don't know. He was still on a drip and having antibiotics so nurses were in and out, and he'd also become incontinent so they'd cleaned him up a couple of times."

Thirsk took a photo from his shirt pocket. "Have you seen this woman before?"

Kate wiped her eyes, willing away the next crop of tears that threatened. "Vaguely, I think she was one of the nurses on

Ward 34.Yes, I remember now, she injected him through his cannula, it stuck in my mind because all the others had just fitted a new bag on the drip stand, but she used a syringe."

"And it was definitely this woman?"

"Well, I can't be one hundred percent, the nurse I saw wasn't smiling for a start, she was really distant and didn't say a word."

"You didn't see a name badge or anything like that?"

"No. Who is she? Was it that injection that made Toby ill? I should have stopped her, it was my fault."

Rhea had prepared a tray of tea and biscuits and she set it on the table, swiftly comforting her daughter again, wrapping her arms tightly around her head and holding her to her bosom protectively. "Well, was it the injection that made him deteriorate?"

Toni had seen enough of Thirsk's lack of compassion and she jumped in to soften the blow. "It's just one of a few things we need to speak to the hospital about, but nothing to concern yourselves with at this stage."

Kate wriggled free of the imprisoning cuddle. "He was murdered, wasn't he? I've always thought that and everyone told me to stop being stupid. I knew he'd never have left me without a fight."

This time Toni couldn't stop him. "I believe he was, yes." They said their goodbyes and as soon as they had climbed in the car, Thirsk glared at Toni. "What was that about earlier, apologising for me?"

"What?"

"Don't ever do that again. Or leap into my line of questioning. You're a bloody upstart, has anyone ever told you that?"

"I have no idea what you're on about." She started the car and reversed from the narrow dirt-track onto the empty country lane that served it.

"You need to get a grip of your behaviour. I may tolerate it, but that doesn't mean every superior you have will."

Toni slammed the car into first and put her foot down, continuing to accelerate through a sharp bend and Thirsk

212

grasped his seat with both hands. "And I think you should get a grip of your behaviour too. You're the most arrogant, pig-headed man I've ever met. And you're abominably rude."

The silence between them was palpable, he clinging to the seat for dear life, while she used the road as a racetrack and she hurtled alarmingly along the lane. A bend approached and she slowed slightly, the brakes screeching, but not enough. He felt the car lurch as she swung into the corner and they were in the air and upside down, the branches of a tree directly ahead. A sickening crunch boomed in his ears, coupled with terrified screaming and intense pain. A moment of blurry confusion and everything went black.

Chapter 21
Wheeler Dealer Pete

"Richard, can you hear me?" Thirsk opened his eyes to a fuzziness that made no sense, hazy colours in a fog of brightness. He could hear people around him, feeling the gentle breeze of their movements, but he could not move or speak. He tried to nod but nothing moved. "You've been in an accident and you've been brought to Boxton Park Hospital. You're going to be fine, you're in good hands."

He could feel no pain. He could feel nothing, and his consciousness wavered in and out, a dreamlike state, suspended from reality. He tried to remember what had happened but nothing was clear. "We've got you a bed now, the porter's on his way."

The voices surrounding him were haunting as they floated in and out of his psyche, nothing made sense but the lights that flashed above him. He tried to concentrate, to remember what had happened, but his memory was a mist of snapshots. They were in the car. Who? Who was he with? He wasn't driving so he knew he couldn't have been alone. A noise. The squealing of rubber on wet tarmac. The thunderous crunching of metal. Screaming. Who was screaming?

The porter edged the trolley into the space beside a bed and helped two nurses to transfer him, struggling with his weight. One nurse checked his wrist with her finger. "His pulse is fast, I think he's in pain. Has he had a sedative?"

The other nurse scanned the haphazardly scrawled notes that had come from accident and emergency with him. "Just morphine, it says here."

"I'll get the doctor."

"They said he was on his way. Shall I give him some for now?" Thirsk had no pain, but he could feel his heart going crazy. Why? Why was he upset? Why could he remember nothing?

"No, we'll have to wait for the doctor."

He tried to speak again but his lips and tongue wouldn't move. The flashing recollection of the accident replayed in his head and he wanted to drown it out, the consuming fear and hideous sounds. Moments later his consciousness waned and blackness took over again.

As soon as the control room heard that Thirsk and Toni had been involved in an accident they called Fitzpatrick at home. He instructed them to send a couple of officers to Toni's parents' house to take them to see her and he grabbed his car keys, dinner forgotten. The journey from his home in Buckinghamshire to the hospital was over twenty miles but traffic was minimal, being a Sunday, and he was there in half an hour. He found Ward 1B, the trauma unit, and was shown to Thirsk's bed.

Fitzpatrick carried a chair across and sat by the bed, unsure what to do. His best detective appeared to be sleeping and the machine he was attached to monitored his vital outputs with a rhythmic purring. A nurse entered the room and he called her over. "Is he okay?"

"He's got no broken bones or internal injuries, the only concern is that he hit his head and has moderate traumatic brain injury to the temporal lobe. The next twenty-four hours will tell us more."

"You mean he's brain-damaged?"

"It's not too serious, most patients recover well from a concussion."

"What about the girl? There was another officer in the car with him, Toni Fowler. How is she?"

"I'm sorry but she's not come to this ward, you'll have to ask at A and E, or try reception."

"Can he hear me?"

"I'm not sure. He's had a large dose of morphine so he could be asleep, but that doesn't mean you shouldn't try talking to him, he may respond to your voice."

Fitzpatrick said a few encouraging words but felt like a lemon, the unresponsive body heaving up and down with each breath, the closed eyes and occasional twitching off-putting.

215

Eventually, he gave up and phoned Castle Street Police Station. "Do you know which ward Toni Fowler's been taken to?"

Presently he strutted back through the corridors, through A and E to the Emergency Department Decision Unit and asked a nurse, who directed him to a seated area. "That couple there are her parents, they'll be able to tell you what's going on."

Abandoned and disconcerted, Fitzpatrick watched the nurse walk away and was reticent to approach the two distraught parents, the mother sobbing heavily on her husband's shoulder. Surely if Toni was okay she wouldn't be making such a scene. With trepidation and a heavy dose of confidence he traipsed over, concerned about disturbing them and their sorrow. "I'm sorry to barge in but I'm Superintendent Fitzpatrick, Toni works for me. How is she?"

Dan Fowler was engulfed in sadness, desperate not to cry for want of being strong. "They've taken her for surgery. She has internal injuries, but we don't know to what extent until she comes out."

"She looked a mess. Her face." Carol's words were difficult to decipher, her sobbing so extreme.

"Do you know what happened? Your officers must have reported back to you."

Fitzpatrick swallowed, uncomfortable. "We know that Toni was driving and at the moment we're assuming she lost control of the car. The wet roads and all that."

"It was Toni's fault?" Carol sobbed, wretched. "Are you sure?"

"She was in the driver's seat when they pulled her from the wreckage and her colleague was unconscious in the passenger seat."

"There was someone else in the car?" And now Carol was overwhelmed with guilt on her daughter's behalf, on top of the raw fear that she would die.

Quick to notice her pain, Fitzpatrick added, "Don't worry, he has a concussion but nothing he won't recover from."

"What's his name?"

"Thirsk."

216

Carol took a sharp breath and her husband stood back, watching her reaction, tempered with jealousy at the man he had only recently discovered had had an affair with his wife years before. She noticed and bowed her head. "Oh. Well I'm glad he's okay."

Thirsk was drifting in and out of consciousness, caught on a wave of weirdness that seemed normal in his mind; he couldn't remember any other way of life. Occasionally he opened his eyes but the scene before him was blurred and unreal, indistinct figures coming and going, voices floating into his psyche, ethereal and fleeting. He could vaguely remember his home, his bed, but nothing more, and with no concept of who he was or what he did. Or why. Unaware that the doctor and his team surrounded his bed discussing his condition and treatment.

"Has he been lucid at all?" Dr Harbecker scanned the notes on his new patient.

"Not completely, but he has had extra morphine so it's no surprise."

"What do you mean?"

"I told her to wait for you but she did it anyway. Quite a big dose too. I stopped her as soon as I noticed what she was doing."

"Who? What did she do?"

"One of the bank nurses gave him morphine when he arrived on the ward. I said you were on your way but she didn't listen. She said she was used to working with trauma injuries and it was better not to leave him waiting in pain."

Harbecker sighed. Time was an issue and he needed to move on to the next patient. "It's what I would have prescribed so it's no matter, but make sure she doesn't do it again. I want you to keep him sedated with morphine for now, but no more after midnight so I get a clear picture of how he is tomorrow morning. Oh, and keep up the hourly obs, please. Who have we next?"

The floating noises dissipated and Thirsk was in an envelope of calm, a greyness where nothing mattered. He wasn't aware of Fitzpatrick's return, of him sitting by the bed hopelessly willing him to recover, considering whether to pat him in concern or hold his hand, despite it seeming unmanly. He was saved by a monotonous ring-tone. He opened the cupboard beside the bed and silenced Thirsk's mobile, noting from the display that the call was from DI Krein, whom he knew from several years before.

Having a chat about work didn't seem appropriate on the ward and he scribbled the number on an old receipt to return the call once he got to Castle Street. The crushing reality that he would have to take control of the job that Thirsk and Toni were now incapable of doing was daunting and he realised he knew next to nothing about the investigation. "By God, I wish you were awake Thirsk. I don't even know where to start." Without thinking, he slipped the mobile into his pocket for safekeeping, adding the wallet that was also in the cupboard.

"I asked where Richard was at reception." Fitzpatrick jumped, returning to the present instantly. "Sorry, I didn't mean to scare you."

"Mrs Fowler, I didn't expect to see you here. How's Toni?"

"She's out of surgery and conscious, they say she's going to be fine. One of her ribs had punctured her lung but they've fixed everything and say she'll be out of here in a week or so. No work for a while, though. Sorry."

"Of course I don't expect her back in, she can take as much time as she needs. I'm just relieved she's going to recover."

Carol cast her eyes over the bed, the mountain caused by the once slim man. "He could do with losing some weight." Fitzpatrick was taken aback. "Oh, it's okay, I know him… used to know him. I met him when he was investigating the Baby Jane case twelve years ago. That's why Toni became a policewoman, she was the one who found the baby's body."

Fitzpatrick rested against the back of the chair, smiling. "That's right, I remember Thirsk telling me now. That'll explain why they're so close."

Carol blushed, recalling how close she had been to Thirsk herself. "How is he, anyway?"

"Okay, I think. He'll be off work for a while too, I imagine."

"Carol. We need to talk." Now it was she who jumped, guilty eyes meeting her husband's as she hastily moved from the bedside and joined Dan. "I followed you. I suspected you'd go and see him and I was right."

"I just wanted to make sure..."

"You still have feelings for him." Dan was agitated, Carol mortified and Fitzpatrick wished he wasn't there.

A nurse came over, stern. "You're disturbing the patients, please leave." Dan grabbed Carol's arm roughly and dragged her through the door leaving Fitzpatrick intrigued by his detective's personal history. The nurse checked Thirsk's chart, scrabbling in a box to prepare his medicine, and fed a syringe into his cannula. "You may as well go too, he'll not wake for a while after this."

Fitzpatrick glanced at the nurse, efficient and businesslike, wiry hair with greying edges tied back in a roughshod bun. "He will be alright, won't he?" She smiled and hurried away and, resigned, Fitzpatrick decided to go to the station to absorb the notes on the case he was now heading.

DI Krein had worked on the infamous Kopycat Killer case seven years before and had never shaken off the repulsive horrors he had witnessed. For a long time after, he had intended to quit the force and patch up the marriage that had broken as a result of the harrowing investigation, but it had been too little, too late for Linda and he'd been left with nothing except the job he had come to abhor.

He lost his enthusiasm that year, his zest for society and work, becoming a shell of the man who'd once had so much to anticipate, and the only things that had saved his sanity were his daughter and his friends on the force. Thirsk had been there for him many a time, a drinking buddy and distant colleague who refused to let him wallow in self-pity. With nothing to look forward to but the job, working weekends had become the norm and as it was Thirsk's case he was working on, he had no qualms. The phone on his desk rang and he answered, surprised to hear Thirsk's superior. "Superintendent Fitzpatrick, what a surprise. I haven't heard from you for a long time."

"I'm at Thirsk's desk, trying to grasp the ropes of this dreadful business at Kendrick and the Padway hospitals, and your name's popped up a few times. I was at the hospital when you called Thirsk. Have you heard about the accident?" Krein hadn't but was soon updated, much to his shock. "Anyway, I've taken over the investigation and thought I'd better see if you'd called for anything important."

"I had a guy come to see me, Peter Benson. He said that Thirsk had asked him to act as a consultant on the case."

"If he did, I know nothing about it. Highly irregular, but you never know with Thirsk. What did he want you for?"

On his desk, Krein opened the incriminating children's book that Pete had passed him. "He's been to see Wayne West's ex-wife and she gave him a book that had something odd written inside the front cover. He wrote these words: *It was nurse Halina that tried to kill me – big fail – bitch.*"

Fitzpatrick was silent for a while, stunned. "Email me a copy. In fact, I don't suppose you'd be able to bring it over? You could tell me everything you know and get me up to speed." It was a Sunday and the only thing Krein had to go home to was an empty, soulless bed-sit. The decision was easy. "Good, thanks. Look," Fitzpatrick had been flicking through some notes and was surprised to see a name he recognised, "did you say the bloke's name was Peter Benson?"

"Yes, he was a mine of information."

"Bring him in too, if you can."

Angela and Hugh had barely got out of bed since she'd slid under the covers to join him the morning before. Her reason had been practical, in fact the only thing on her mind had been sleep, but when they had woken, arms entwined, it seemed like the most natural thing in the world. They both realised it was love, and although she was scared of committing, the calm togetherness overruled her fears. Hugh dragged himself from the bed, kissing her repeatedly, unwilling to break away. "I'll make us some tea."

She groaned, half-asleep. "What time is it?"

He picked up her mobile to check. "Half seven, nearly bedtime," he said, winking. "You've got a missed call here."

"No message?"

"Yes, from a person named Pete Benson."

He chucked the phone at her and she threw it to one side, noting the glimpse of hurt on his face. "He's the private detective who Nellie Gleeson's son was using. I'll take a look later.'"

"Why would he call you? I thought all that rubbish had been sorted out."

"So did I." Reluctantly, she opened the message. "It just says 'call me, urgent'." She pressed a button to return the call. "Pete, it's Angela, you wanted me." His reply was indistinguishable and Angela frowned. "I don't understand a word you're saying."

A frothy whisper came through, "Can't talk now. Will call you ASAP." Pete ended the call and realised Krein and Fitzpatrick were standing behind him, and he grinned shamefacedly. "My wife. Never stops calling me. It's a pain in the bum."

"I know your face. Thirsk interviewed you yesterday. You aren't contracted, you're a witness." Fitzpatrick remembered the altercation between the two men and understood why Thirsk had been so rude. "What are you doing, messing with our enquiry?"

"I was present for the whole brief yesterday and could see that you lot were clutching at straws. I was a detective sergeant on the Thames Valley force until I was retired on medical grounds. Thirsk is an old mate and he asked for my help."

"From the way he was talking to you, he didn't appear to value you much."

"That's what he's like with his friends, I'm used to it."

"So you're doing this work as a favour?"

"I'm a busy man, my work doesn't come for free, but I did give him a discount. He was paying me at the subsidised rate of two hundred pounds per day."

"Very irregular, but that's Thirsk for you. So what do you know on the case?"

"I collected a vast amount of information when Thirsk first had suspicions that something was amiss. I gave my notes to him yesterday."

Fitzpatrick rummaged through the stacks of paperwork on Thirsk's desk and pulled out a lurid-pink cardboard folder. "Is this it?"

"Yes, and since then I've been to see Wayne West's ex-wife and revisited a woman named Pat Bond for clarification that Halina definitely returned to Nellie Gleeson just before she died. I've also visited Sharon Wells, one of Wayne's ex-girlfriends, who was at his bedside the night he died."

Krein remembered the brassy brunette with distaste. "I interviewed her; as good as useless."

"Maybe she is, but she witnessed a murder." He paused long enough for the two officers to digest his revelation. "She clearly recalls a nurse injecting Wayne through his arm needle thing."

"Why didn't she tell me that when I saw her? And anyway, how do we know it wasn't a kosher prescription medicine?"

Pete was relishing his moment of glory, a chance to prove he would have been a fine officer if they hadn't made it impossible for him to remain on the force. "First of all, Sharon was there a long time, she was the second to get there and stayed to the end of visiting time. It was only in retrospect, after she had spoken to you, that she remembered from visiting a relation at the hospital that they don't do a drugs round within visiting hours."

"Then why didn't she call me and tell me?"

"Because I got there first, I expect."

"Did she give a description of the nurse?"

"It was Halina, all right. No doubt about it. There's just one thing though, I called my friend Lorna, she works in the admin department for the Padway, and she said that although Halina had been working on that ward the night before, she wasn't on the night he died. She'd also worked on that ward a few weeks before, shortly before Wayne became inexplicably very ill."

Following the conversation was problematic, too many details in such a short time, and Fitzpatrick was confused. "So did she pose as one of the disgruntled girlfriends?"

"No, she was dressed in uniform. I think she came back after realising that her first attempt on Wayne's life had failed, the one he'd recorded in his book. She came back to finish him off, but made sure there were plenty of other people there who would undoubtedly be suspects after his death. All with a motive."

"So we finally have proof that Halina is involved and an explanation to one of the murders that Theresa and Rebecca couldn't physically have done. I'm guessing that's the easy part, because it doesn't bring us any closer to finding her." Krein was despondent, knowing they had dreadful odds of locating her soon with Thirsk and his computer of a memory incapacitated.

Fitzpatrick jumped, his pocket vibrating, and he remembered he had taken Thirsk's mobile. He noted the name Marek on the display and answered, clueless, explaining his officer would not be working for the near future. "Oh, it's just he was supposed to pick up my ex-girlfriend's wage slips yesterday afternoon, he reckoned they'd help him establish where and when she'd worked. If he doesn't get them soon I'm going to burn them, I don't want any trace of her left in the house."

"Who is your ex-girlfriend?"

"Halina Kostuch."

"Give me your address, I'll be there as soon as possible."

Pete's exciting day as part of the investigation was over and he was proud of how he had blagged his way onto the team with a tiny lie here and there. It had been worth a try and for once it had worked. He realised that as soon as Thirsk was back on the scene his contracting days would be over, but hopefully he would get at least one wage packet in the meantime. Now he didn't have Krein nearby and could speak freely, he redialled Angela, pompously telling her once she answered about his sudden thrust into the limelight. She was unimpressed. "So why tell me?"

"I want to interview you about Halina."

"There isn't anything I could tell you even if I wanted to. The night that Nellie Gleeson died is all documented and I haven't worked directly with her since. Anyway, Thirsk's head of the investigation and he's happy that I've given all I can."

He was enthusiastic with his superior knowledge, bragging, "Not any more. He's in hospital following a car accident. Him and that pretty bird he takes around with him."

"Oh my god, are they okay?"

Pete saw no harm in exaggerating a little. "They'll both survive, they reckon, but it was touch and go for a while."

Angela cut the call and pulled from Hugh's loving cuddle. "Thirsk's in hospital. There's been an accident."

He sat straight, astonished. "Not Kendrick, I hope."

"Shit, I didn't even think to ask which hospital, it was such a shock. I'll call him back."

When she heard that Thirsk and Toni had been taken to Boxton Park she relaxed with relief, reassuring Hugh, but he worried still. "There's nothing to say that Halina isn't working there now. I mean, she's missing, isn't she?"

"Do you know anyone who works there?"

"No, not that I can think of. The police have probably got somebody guarding him, I'm sure. Did Pete say anything?"

"No. Do you think we should visit him?"

Hugh snuggled his head to her bare chest, basking in comfortable love. "Thirsk's got a good team behind him. Nobody's going to let anything happen to him."

224

Chapter 22
In Good Hands?

Laila Talpur and her assistant, Melanie, sipped their coffees as they reviewed the notes of the patients who had died during the weekend. Laila glossed over one file after another. "Old age, old age, old age," she scanned the notes of the latest file with interest, "I think we'll do this one first."

"We? You usually work alone."

"I'm here to teach you and this case isn't typical, so it's in your interests to do it. Fetch me another coffee while I read the notes properly." Melanie soon returned and Laila began her summary. "This man was involved in a car accident on Friday and his injuries, although requiring a stay in hospital for observation, were deemed to be non-life-threatening; mild concussion, some lacerations to his face and extremities and minor whiplash injuries. His initial observations were unremarkable and continued to be so for most of the night. However, when his obs were taken at six in the morning his blood pressure, heart and respiratory rate were elevated and he was unresponsive. An hour later he had a seizure and, despite intervention, didn't recover. Death was called at," she skimmed to the bottom, "seven thirty-one. I want you to perform the PM, I'll observe."

Melanie was unsure whether to be pleased or not. It was wonderful to be trusted to work on such an intriguing death, but she wasn't keen on the notoriously stringent Laila watching over her shoulder. She dragged the sheet from the body of Vincent Rogers, aged forty-one, and held a scalpel to his chest. "No, no! Check the body for unaccounted injury before you cut."

Melanie followed orders, her confidence zapped that little bit more with each bark she received, and reminded herself continuously that she was lucky to be working with Laila; her reputation was solid and her by-the-book methodology made her a great instructor. But she loved to nit-pick, unaware that this made her annual students shudder for fear of making a mistake. "Any clues to what I'm looking for?"

"A seizure, plus the accident would suggest brain trauma, but you'll need to open him up first. Just perform it as you would with any other PM and take tissue and blood samples for toxicology as you go." She regarded the younger woman for a moment, having seen her uneasy expression in many of her students over the years. "You don't like me watching, do you?" Melanie shook her head. "I've been told I'm a bit of a control freak. I'll get on with another body and leave you be, but if there's anything unusual you must let me know."

The door opened and a porter pushed a sheeted trolley through. "From Ward 1B, Dr Harbecker asked if you could take a look as soon as."

"Any reason other than impatience?"

"You'll have to ask him that."

And the porter was gone, leaving Laila to mutter under her breath as she found the doctor's number and dialled. "You've just sent a body down for a PM and the porter tells me it's urgent."

"Falak Ghadi? Yes, she died suddenly and as far as I can see for no reason. She'd been admitted after a fall, just a slight bang on the head, and the only reason we kept her in was because we felt she needed home assistance. We did a precautionary MRI, which showed nothing untoward and her output was within normal limits. Obs taken at six this morning showed hypertension and tachycardia, hyperventilation and hypoxia. She was unresponsive. At six-thirty she had a seizure and we couldn't resuscitate her."

The feeling of déjà vu was overwhelming and Laila stared at Melanie as she placed Vincent's heart in a dish. "I think we may have a super-bug on the loose. I'll get samples sent to microbiology and toxicology as quickly as I can and," she waved her hand to get Melanie's attention, holding her hand over the mouthpiece, "What ward was your body on?"

The student flicked the file open with her elbow. "Twelve."

"Oh. You're not on twelve, are you?"

"No, same as I've always been: 1B."

"It's just we have another one, exactly the same symptoms. He was on twelve. Can you let management and ward twelve know that you need to put the necessary strategies in place."

He chuckled sardonically. "They're in place constantly, Laila, the super-bugs are bigger than us nowadays. No matter, I'll raise the alarm."

Now that Fitzpatrick had a record of where and when Halina had worked, he found the victims all fitted, bar Wayne West, to her work pattern like the final pieces of a jigsaw. He had not bothered to go home, a favourite trick of Thirsk's, and had called Steadman shortly after six to ask her to come in early to help him catch up. In any other circumstance he would have placed the case in her care, she was a competent and dedicated detective, but he felt a certain amount of guilt that he had been the one who had pushed Thirsk, which made the case personal. He passed his hand-scrawled summary of Halina's recent employment dates, which he'd tallied to the known murders, to Steadman. "I think that Halina has been working alone."

"But Theresa's confessed to mistreating her patients."

"Nothing more than a coincidence in my eyes. Yes, let's get them convicted for what they've done, but with no charge further than ABH. The worrying thing is that Halina worked in numerous hospitals within a thirty-forty mile radius of her home in Slough, and her boyfriend told me last night that she always kept her uniforms. Uniforms that she's taken with her, wherever she's gone."

"You think there may be more?" Steadman's stomach heaved, the extent of the horror sickening.

"Have you met the boyfriend before?" She shook her head. "He was everso helpful last night, answering every question, dotting the i's and crossing the t's."

"He knows more than he's letting on, then."

"I think so, but what, I don't know."

"I'll go and see him if you want. The other thing we must do is contact the other hospitals she's worked for, see if any suspicious deaths have occurred while, or shortly after, she worked for them."

"Yes, perhaps distribute a photo of her, if you have one."

227

Steadman nimbly leafed through the paperwork and pulled out Halina's file. "I can't find one in here. I'll see if the boyfriend has one when I visit."

Fitzpatrick scanned the array of post-it notes stuck randomly across the desk, murmuring when he found it. "Here we are," he placed the memo before Steadman, "any idea about this."

"*Bitch*," she withheld a chuckle at Thirsk's boorishness, "*Gabryjela Bakalar, Halina's sister. Hangs upon mention of Halina.*"

"I take it he didn't like her?"

"She wasn't cooperative, told him to fack off." His puzzled face made her want to laugh, but this wasn't foul-mouthed Thirsk who tolerated backchat, it was Mr Big. "She's from Poland and I think her English is limited. Anyway, she clearly had no time for Halina, said she was a dangerous woman."

"Hmmm, interesting. As soon as the day starts properly, get onto Interpol and ask them to get her local force to interview her."

"Aren't they open twenty-four hours a day?"

"Contact them sooner then."

"Count it done, sir."

"Do you know where Thirsk and Toni had been on Sunday before the accident? I mean, it was work related, wasn't it?"

It better be, she thought, but said, "No, you know what he's like for running off on a tangent."

"The accident happened near Astbury, does that give you a clue?"

"Actually yes, that's where the first victim lived, maybe they went to see his wife."

"Call her, see if you can validate that." He turned several pages over, scanning the notes. "*Tob blood test before/after death – ask hosp.* Any idea?"

"No, but it sounds as if he was going to see if the hospital had a blood trail leading up to Tobias's death. That's what I would have done and our minds work in similar ways. It may pinpoint when Tobias was given the overdose."

"Get on to that too."

Although his condition was stable, Thirsk remained sleeping most of the time, and when he wasn't, he was unable to open his eyes, never fully compos mentis. His world was a sea of indistinct sounds, waves of recollection passing vividly sometimes, moments of horrifying screams and sights disturbing his peace, making him twitch and moan. He wasn't there, but he was no longer in and out of consciousness. Apart from the flashbacks, something else was bothering him yet he couldn't make sense of anything.

A voice close by was familiar. "I'm just going to take your blood pressure, Mr Thirsk." He felt his arm raise and a clip on his finger. A thermometer was poked in his ear. He couldn't bear it but his body wouldn't move to object.

"How's he doing?" Another voice he recognised, male this time.

The nurse showed Dr Harbecker the observation chart. "He's stable."

The doctor pulled Thirsk's eyelids up and the blue irises followed his face. "He's definitely conscious, but with a mild concussion he should be up and about by now, it's been nearly twenty-four hours since he came in. Do we have the results of the MRI yet?"

A medical student beside him whisked efficiently through the paperwork in her hand and squirmed at the bollocking she suspected she was about to get. "It's not been done yet. Nurse, why's it not been done yet?"

"They haven't got an available gap until tomorrow."

"I want it done now. See to it. And," he hushed his voice, not wanting the patients to overhear, "there's a possibility we have another super-bug on the loose, so take swabs and blood tests. And get urine and stool samples too."

"Is that what killed Mrs Ghadi this morning?"

Harbecker gave her an admonishing glare. "Keep your voice down, we don't want to alarm the patients. Keep your eye on him and I want him back on hourly obs. And see if there's an isolation room available."

"What about medication? Shall I continue with the morphine?"

229

He looked at her, quizzical. "I said not to give him any after midnight so I could see his true condition this morning."

Flustered, she leafed through the notes in her hand and was relieved she had not been imagining the entry. "There it is, clear as day. Morphine, twenty milligrams per hour."

He snatched the file, annoyed. "Who prescribed this?"

"Probably the night staff."

"No more unless I prescribe it. He doesn't need it, it's keeping him sedated. If his obs change at all, let me know and I'll write it up again. I'm going to put him on a couple of wide spectrum antibiotics and I want them started right away."

Carol had had a humdinger of a weekend beginning with the dreadful news of Toni's accident and ending with the possible breakdown of her fragile marriage. The one saving grace was that she worked for her husband's business and was able to take compassionate leave without difficulty. Dan, however, in their final argument before he had packed his bags and gone to a cheap hotel, had vowed to only see their eldest daughter when he was certain Carol wasn't there. She had taken the bus that morning after packing their youngest off to school, else she would have nothing better to do all day than mope. When she saw Toni sitting in the bed with her trademark smile, she knew that the new week had at least brought some good news. "You're looking so much better."

"Thanks, I feel it too."

"Have they... Have they told you what happened?"

"Yes, how's my guv?"

Carol swallowed. "I only saw him briefly on Sunday and he seemed fine then. He was asleep but I don't think there was too much concern from what I could gather."

"Thank god for that, I'd never have been able to live with myself if something had happened to him. Where's dad?" Carol dragged a chair over and sat down, hoping the time it took would make her daughter forget the question but, "How did you get here if dad didn't drive you?"

"I took the bus, your dad's really busy at work. I'm sure he'll be in to see you tonight. Do you know when you'll be home yet?"

"As soon as I can escape, I hate hospitals." Carol was still waiting for an answer. "I'm pretty sure not tomorrow, but they said maybe Wednesday, as long as everything's healing well and there's no sign of infection."

"You won't be able to manage at home so come and stay with us. I'm off work until I'm happy you've recovered, so I can be at your beck and call."

Although a mum of three, Carol had never relished being a mother – a simple word that translated to slavery – and Toni now realised something was wrong. "You hate people being dependent on you, you thrashed that out of us years ago, so something's up. Have you and dad been arguing?"

"No, of course not."

"You're lying. Is it because of the accident? Am I causing problems? If so I…"

"No. Your dad's gone. He's staying in a hotel because I went to see how Richard was. He reckons I've still got feelings for him but I haven't, Toni, it was over years ago and I thought your father had forgiven me."

"Shit. The old bugger's in a hospital bed and he still manages to cause problems. I'll have a word with dad tonight, make him see sense."

"Thanks love, he always listens to you."

"Do you fancy a walk to go and see my guv now? I've been out of bed to go to the loo a few times so I can hobble okay."

"Your dad…"

Toni tapped her nose. "He'll never know. I want to see him but I can't go alone." She dragged the covers back and lifted her legs across, wincing from the stitched wound underneath her rib cage. "Come on." Towing her drip alongside, Toni waddled uncomfortably towards the doorway, headstrong as always, and Carol had no choice but to follow.

Steadman had briefed the team that Fitzpatrick was now leading the investigation, and that she was the go-to guy, issuing a limited summary of the accident and assuring that both officers were expected to recover. The more information Kendrick and the Padway hospitals supplied, the more people there were to interview, and whilst Krein's Oxfordshire team were responsible for the ex-patients of the Padway, the many who had been treated in Kendrick were enough to keep Steadman's team busy for the rest of the week. The groundwork was tedious yet necessary, but the number one priority was to find Halina.

Steadman found the number for the National Central Bureau, the middleman between the police force and Interpol, and dialled, and she outlined the reason for her call, explaining that Thirsk's notes were incomplete. "Her name is Gabryjela Bakalar but we don't have her address, just a phone number."

"No problem, we can find her locality from the dialling code and go from there. What exactly do you need from her?"

"Absolutely everything she can tell us about her sister, Halina Kostuch, and…"

"We can also see what the official records in Poland can tell us about Ms Kostuch, if that helps."

"Yes, it really would. In that case, her sister called her by the name Lewinski so you may find something under that too. We also believe she was married to a man named Borys – we have no surname or dates – and they had a child named Karol. We've been led to understand they are both deceased."

"Thank you, we'll do what we can and be in touch."

"Before you go, I must stress that we have no knowledge of Ms Kostuch's whereabouts and she is a major suspect in a murder investigation, so I'd appreciate if you could deal with this urgently."

Steadman ended the call and immediately dialled the direct line she had been given to liaise with Kendrick Hospital. Erika Gomez answered and agreed to have someone check the labs to see if they had any of Tobias's blood from before his death. Steadman put the receiver down and was about to call Tobias's wife but, needing fresh air, she decided to visit her before Marek as it was on the way to Slough.

Astbury originated from a small Roman settlement that had barely grown over the years, despite new housing estates having overwhelmed most of the villages on the outskirts of Kendrick, and the surrounding view of farmland set amongst rolling hills was breathtaking. Steadman enjoyed the pleasant journey along winding country lanes until she reached the corner where her boss and colleague had skidded out of control and crashed head-on into a tree. Without thinking, she slowed and parked in a muddy entrance to a field. The tree that had taken the brunt of the collision was damaged and the undergrowth flattened, but there were no other signs that the accident had happened.

In her mid thirties, her attractive looks slipping and her ring finger remaining unclaimed, Steadman had been keen on Thirsk for as long as she could remember. She had joined the police force after finishing university and had become a constable on the Major Investigation Team soon after, before training to become a detective. This had been the first time she'd worked for Thirsk, then quite a catch with his greying temples and well-toned physique. As the grey had whitened and spread and his figure filled out, her crush had developed while they worked as partners.

When he had been promoted to Chief Inspector, he transferred to the Child Abuse Investigation Unit and she followed him, although they no longer worked directly together, and when he'd decided the job was unsuitable due to his notorious dislike of youngsters, she had followed again. She knew he didn't feel for her the way she did for him, that he never had, but it didn't stop her caring.

She climbed back into the car, resolving to visit him in hospital after she had seen Kate. She soon arrived, soaking in the beauty and charm of the row of terraced cottages, all constructed from stone and smothered in ivy, with weather-beaten woodwork and tiny, panelled windows. She parked in a lay-by and breathed in the freshness of the country air as she walked towards them, searching the house numbers. "Have you come to see me?"

Steadman turned to the open door, a young woman dressed in dungarees and slippers. "Kate Sutherland?"

"Yes. I heard about the accident down the road, are they okay?"

Steadman followed Kate into her home. "Yes, they'll be fine, thanks for asking. That's kind of why I'm here, it's just," Thirsk's habit of storing information in his head was annoying, but she wasn't about to discredit him and prepared a white lie, "I've been placed in charge of the investigation and unfortunately Thirsk's notes were destroyed in the accident. We know that he visited you on Sunday, but we don't know why."

"He showed me a photo of a woman and told me that she'd killed Toby. He asked me all sorts of questions about her injecting him."

"What did she look like?"

"I don't know, dark hair tied back and she was going a bit grey. Pale blue eyes, quite cold. She was sort of half-smiling. Not very pretty but not hideous either. Her face was unusual, quite severe looking."

"Did he say anything else during his time with you?"

"No, they were only here a few minutes. He just asked about the injections. If they'd stayed long enough for the tea mum had made... Well, they may never have had the crash."

Steadman didn't gain much from the ten minutes she spent with Kate but the photo she had described couldn't have been Rebecca or Theresa, so he must have reached the same conclusion as she had: that Halina was definitely involved. She waved goodbye and drove straight to Boxton Park Hospital, eager to see Thirsk, yet nervous of his condition. She was directed to Ward 1B and navigated the corridors, asking a nurse for his whereabouts when she reached the nursing station.

Seeing him in the bed, she gasped. She had assumed he would be sitting up, scowling at the world and berating anybody who came near him, but instead he looked so small, despite the vast belly, a mountain under the blanket. Six-foot four and too chunky to be healthy, he towered over most at the station, an intimidating presence and disagreeable manner that had his team and the criminals he interrogated cowering. Yet here he was, feeble and broken.

Steadman pulled a plastic chair to the bed and sat, taking his hand. "Are you awake, guv?" His body remained still, bar the laboured breathing. Steadman felt for a pulse and his heart was rocketing, so she took the notes from the end of the bed and made as much sense as she could from them. The last entry had been taken at eleven, an hour before. She dropped them on the foot of the bed and found a nurse outside the bay. "I've just taken his pulse and it's way higher than it was when you last did your rounds, can you check on him?"

"He's on hourly obs so I was about to anyway." She tapped a syringe, holding it to the light. "Just got to give him this first." The nurse attached the end to the cannula in Thirsk's arm and dispensed the fluid, and collected an observation machine from the corridor, wheeling it into the bay. She placed the cuff on his arm, the heart monitor clip on his finger and the thermometer in his ear. When the machine beeped she wheeled it outside again, but not before Steadman had seen the display and, trained in first aid, she was concerned.

Moments later a doctor was by his side, checking his condition. "Are you a relative?"

"I'm a colleague. What's happening?"

Dr Harbecker turned to the nurse. "Have the results of the tests I ordered come back yet?"

"I'll go and take a look." The nurse trotted out and the doctor followed her, leaving Steadman worried, and she grasped Thirsk's hand, clutching his fingers tightly. "Don't you dare die on me, guv. Whether you like it or not, people care about you, me probably the most of all." His body began to twitch, head arching backwards against the pillow as a seizure took hold and Steadman shouted for help.

She stood to the side as a team of medics rushed in, and watched helplessly as they held him steady for the duration of the fit, two nurses fixing electrodes to his body to monitor him continuously. Without time to digest the seriousness of what had just happened she followed them as they took him, in the bed, along the corridor to the exit. "What are you doing? Where are you going?"

The nurse she had spoken to previously stepped over to her, resting a hand on her arm. "Don't worry, they're taking him to intensive care where they can keep a constant eye on him. It's probably a reaction to the antibiotics."

"Antibiotics? He's here because he was in a road accident."

"The doctor suspected he may have contracted an infection and prescribed them as a precaution. Don't worry, he's in good hands."

"Can I go with him?"

"Later, once he's stabilised, just give the doctors a chance to get him comfortable." An intermittent buzz started and the nurse headed for the door. "I have to see another patient. Would you be able to check his cabinet, make sure there isn't anything left behind? That would help me greatly."

Steadman couldn't imagine what Thirsk may have brought with him in the state he was in, but she searched anyway and was pleased she had as the bottom drawer contained some clothing. She pulled out some trousers, socks and shoes, but the other drawers were empty and she guessed they must have cut the clothes from his top half and discarded them. All she could do was take them home with her in the hope that one day he would be well enough to wear them again.

Chapter 23
The Missing Link

Nobody had a clue why they had been brought together in the training room again and rumours were rampant as they waited to see what happened next. Soon, the managing director, a man unfamiliar to them all, breezed in, confident and commanding. His presence alone silenced the room and they awaited an explanation. "It has been reported to me that during Friday night's pharmaceutical audit, a vial of tetrodotoxin was unaccounted for. We double-checked our records this morning and are confident that there are no errors in the paperwork. We believe the vial has been stolen."

Marek squirmed, certain his face was reddened enough to be conspicuous, and waited for hefty hands on his shoulders to guide him from the room and give him hell. But the man at the podium continued to speak, hammering in the disastrous effects of the dangerous drug and how, in the wrong hands, it could cause havoc. It had happened in the blink of an eye. One minute the vial was before him, tempting him to snatch it to appease his girlfriend into the marriage he wasn't sure he wanted, the next it was in his bag and he was shuffling through security, willing the guilt from his face.

How could he have known that Halina had been admitted to hospital with another miscarriage scare for the baby she had never been expecting, leading him to drop his bag and race over to see her? That while he was seeking her, she had returned to the house and emptied his workbag of everything but the clearly-labelled drug, filling it with her spare uniforms. He had kept schtum about the drug, aware that he would be unceremoniously fired for its possession, hoping all the while that what the police were saying about her – that she may be a murderer – was unfounded.

"I want you all to think hard about what you did last week, and we're giving you the rest of the day to consider this, but if the vial isn't accounted for by four p.m. we will have no choice but to inform the police."

Marek followed the crowd from the room and traipsed back to the lab, despondent and scared. Maybe in his anger and recklessness he had missed the vial and it would be there when he returned home, but he had no way of checking. An easy solution would be to inject a drop of water in another vial to look as if it were tetrodotoxin, but the bottles were an irregular shape, sturdy glass pyramids that were far from the usual design, and none were spare. All this kerfuffle for a woman he now detested.

Should he be brave and admit he was a thief, a low-life scum who had put the world at risk by allowing a murderer to have the perfect poison. If he did, he would lose his job and credibility, on top of a custodial sentence. If he didn't, it was their word against his, if they ever singled him from the masses who worked for the company in the first place. If he kept his head down this problem would go away. It had to.

He whiled away the hours, helping his colleagues to search their lab for any trace of the missing substance, agreeing with their collective baying that the perpetrator was an idiot. He knew he was an idiot. This wasn't down to bad luck, or fate, or destiny, it was he who had cut his life cord. The minutes ticked by dauntingly and at four, all employees were instructed to return to the meeting room.

The managing director took to the stand again and announced regretfully that, as the drug had not been returned, they had contacted Uxbridge Police Station.

Steadman visited Marek's home and his housemate informed her that he was at work. She stayed for a coffee with the young woman to glean as much information as she could about Halina, on the off chance it may give a clue of her whereabouts, and agreed to come back after six when he should have returned. She headed back to the station, picking up a sandwich on the way, and found her desk covered in post-it notes regarding phone calls she had missed in her absence. The most urgent was from Interpol and she dialled the scribbled number immediately, asking for Marlene.

238

"The Polish policja are very pleased you've found Halina Lewinski, it seems they've been searching for her for several years."

"We haven't found her, she's on the run."

"Yes, but we now have more idea of where she is than before. There's a huge amount of history, far too much for a phone call. Would you like me to email all the documentation across?"

"What sort of thing? I mean, we're busy trying to find her, it would be much easier to give me an idea on the phone. Of course we'll need the paperwork for our case against her, but right now, could you simplify it for me?"

"In a nutshell, Halina was a nurse in Poland and after her husband and son died she was investigated for their possible murders, along with that of her niece, which opened a can of worms. Seems she's suspected of nine other deaths that occurred in three hospitals. When she got wind that she was under suspicion, she did a runner and your contact is the first they've heard of her since."

"My god, this is insane. Look, thanks for your help, Marlene. Can you email me the files and I'll step up our enquiries to red alert." She dropped the phone and headed straight for Thirsk's Office, where Fitzpatrick sat, buried in files, at the desk. "Sir."

"Ah, Diane, I heard from Erika Gomez earlier, regarding the blood you wanted testing."

"Sir, I..."

"It proves that Tobias Sutherland was given a substantial dose of paracetamol on Ward 34, before he was moved to the SHDU. We also now know that Halina was temping on Ward 33 that day, which is across the central corridor."

"So he was murdered. I went to see Kate this morning and apparently Thirsk showed her a picture that couldn't have been Rebecca or Theresa, and Kate had identified that woman, who I assume to be Halina, to have administered a syringe of a clear liquid to Tobias whilst she was there."

"Halina's either brave or stupid, that's for sure. Did you find a picture of her so we have a clearer idea of who we're looking for?"

"Marek was at work and his housemate didn't have one."

"We need to get one as soon as possible. Try Marek again, and maybe the agencies keep photos of their temps."

"Sir, there's more." She explained what Marlene had told her of Halina's history and Fitzpatrick melted into his seat, speechless. "We need to get a description to every hospital in the area to alert them. This has to be done immediately."

"Then a photo is imperative."

"Yes, I'm sure there'll be one coming with all the documentation Interpol are sending." Steadman recalled the clothing she had taken from Thirsk's bedside. "In fact, I've got Rich... Thirsk's trousers in the car, I'll check the pockets for the one he showed Kate."

Fitzpatrick didn't stop to consider why she had his clothes in her possession, burgeoning from the office and commanding attention of the team, reporting the latest shocking news. "We need to circulate her photo, and we need all hands on deck. I want everybody, regardless of their shifts, working on this now."

Thirsk had been in pain for some time now they had restricted the morphine but he was unable to ask for help. Inside he was bubbling with frustration thathis mind had no control of his body and he tried to blink, to move a finger, to nod. Nothing worked. He recalled everything now, every single moment in the prelude to the accident, of the urgency to find Halina and the spat with Toni. Poor Toni, where was she? Was she dead? He tried to scream the scenario away but made no sound.

He also knew what had been bothering him, the sense of fear that had made his heart race so badly and sweat glands pour. The voice he had recognised now had an image as his eyesight had cleared, and the woman he knew to be a murderer had been tending to him, injecting him, her cold eyes callous and full of hatred. She must have done something to make him lose his body and he wanted to tell them, tell his carers, tell them he was in the process of being murdered. Was this how Tobias had felt?

240

At least he had been able to move his fingers, to scribble and swallow a note.

He felt a presence by the bed, but his eyes wouldn't move to see who was visiting. His arm was lifted, held in the air and he heard a quiet clicking. She was back. His killer was back. Please, God, I've never believed in you but I'll change, I promise I'll change. I promise.

"Nurse! What are you doing?"

Doctor Harbecker's voice, he was sure. "I'm just giving him some morphine." And Halina's.

"What are you doing in intensive care, you work in 1B?"

"I'm sorry, I was just trying to help."

Thirsk tried to move his eyes, to raise his eyebrows, to indicate his fear somehow. Anyhow. Nothing. The brightness faded and his mind clouded, sounds dissipating to silence. The world went black.

Steadman didn't waste time in running back to the incident room to alert Fitzpatrick and the team; Thirsk's life could depend on her. Instead, she slammed her car into first and the wheels squealed with complaint as she accelerated, slamming a blue light on the bonnet and setting the siren wailing. Dodging through traffic as fast as she could, she took a glance at the photo she had found in Thirsk's trousers. The woman in the picture was the one who was nursing him now. The one who had injected him, maybe even killed him – who knew? Somehow during the treacherous journey she managed to put her mobile on loudspeaker and call Thirsk's office phone, and with few words she conveyed her suspicions and destination to her superior.

Leaving the car in an ambulance bay, she raced to the Intensive Care Unit, praying that Thirsk hadn't been moved again, and the first thing she did was to check his breathing. Puffing with a mixture of fear and exertion, she laid her hand on his chest and the relief that came as it rose and fell was indescribable. She snuggled to his chest, holding him close, never wanting to let go. "Thank god."

Dr Harbecker was rarely stumped but, try as he might, he could not work out why his patient's condition was deteriorating. The MRI scan had shown minimal physical injury to the head and no broken bones, so there seemed to be no reason for him to be in a near-comatose state. He suspected that the erroneous nurse had administered some morphine, but she had barely deployed the syringe when he snatched it from her. However, even if she'd given him the full shot it shouldn't have left him unconscious.

Coupled with that was his racing heart rate, his laboured breathing and the seizure, none of which made sense. He dialled the pathology lab and waited until Laila finally answered. "Have you got any results back from the tox and microbiology samples of Falak Ghadi and the other one you suspected of having a super-bug?"

"We only sent them this morning, they can take weeks to come back."

"No, that's not good enough. I have a patient who is deteriorating rapidly and if you can isolate what caused their deaths I may be able to treat him in time."

"Of course, you told me all of this when I spoke to you this morning. Not. Am I supposed to be telepathic now? I suggest you call them directly." The dial tone buzzed and Harbecker replaced the phone. He searched the desk for a telephone list and was about to call the lab when a commotion outside his office drew his attention. He opened the door to see several people crowding his inexplicably ill patient. "You must leave, please, he needs quiet."

Fitzpatrick displayed his badge and explained why they were there, and Steadman stopped hugging Thirsk's chest for long enough to pass him the photo of their suspect. He paled. "I caught her injecting him a short while ago. I still have the syringe. Could whatever's in it be the reason his condition is worsening?"

"Have any patients died suspiciously since Friday night?"

"Actually yes, two that I know of. I only know the name of one, FalakGhadi, she died earlier... That nurse was on duty yesterday... Do you think...?"

"Is she still on the premises? The nurse."

242

"I don't know, I last saw her about half an hour ago."

Fitzpatrick ran into Harbecker's office and snatched the phone, pressing the zero button repeatedly until he got an answer. "My name is Superintendent Fitzpatrick. We need security to search for a woman posing as a nurse. Immediately. She's Polish, speaks good English, about five-foot six with wiry, greying black hair and a stern face... I know that could be anybody. Better still, stop everybody leaving the hospital."

He slammed the phone down and passed the small photo to a colleague. "Get as good a copy of this as you can and circulate it straight away."

"Back at the station?"

"No, here. Get at least one image for every ward and department. If she's still here there may be someone who'll recognise her. Email a copy to the station too, let them know what it is. And get back-up. As many officers as possible."

"My secretary will help." Harbecker indicated the ward office. "Have you any idea of what she's given him that has caused him to relapse? His condition is quite worrying."

"We were hoping you'd be able to tell us that. This woman has so far used paracetamol, tramadol, insulin and air. That we know of."

"It would have to be a hefty dosage, but insulin could possibly have caused his symptoms. I'll get a blood sample taken straight away, and I was about to phone the lab to ask them to speed up the results of the tox tests on the other two people who died."

"I'll do it." Fitzpatrick picked up the receiver and pressed zero.

In the background, Sally, adrenaline pumping from the frightful urgency, had other things on her mind. "Has anyone thought to check Toni?"

One of the greatest abilities Pete had was to look at situations laterally and he figured that the man who had been intimate with Halina would have the best knowledge, whether he knew it or not, of pinpointing him in the right direction in his search for Halina. He had seen Marek in the police station the day before and asked Toni who he was, and while she had been delivering her summary of the victims, he had discreetly peeped in Halina's file to memorise some details. It was five o'clock and Pete was waiting by the front door of Randall's Biotech. As soon as he saw Marek come through the doors he approached, introducing himself as Detective Benson.

Marek paled, his body beginning to tremble. The company obviously knew more than they had admitted and had somehow found their thief already. "I was going to bring it back, I just wanted to show her."

Pete had no idea what he was talking about but he could spot a guilty man when he saw one. "I'll need to take a statement."

"I already gave one to you guys yesterday." Marek's knees had joined in with his body and his clothes shook lightly as he shuddered.

Now Pete was clutching at straws. It was clear that the man was hiding something, but as he was clueless to what, his questions would have to be generalised. "Not about this, you didn't. Where can we talk? I'd rather not go to the station."

Marek's whole body was quivering, a terrified expression and watering eyes. "This is my dream job. I'll never get another one after this."

So the guilt was work related. "Look, I can see you didn't mean to and I'll go easy on you, but in return I need the whole story from you, every last bit. Go and get in my car, you can't miss it," he pointed to a lime-green Citroen 2CV, a classic car that resembled a rusty Mr Man shoe, "it's the green one over there." He handed the keys over. "I'll be with you in a second, and don't think of doing a runner because there are police cars surrounding the building."

Keeping one eye on Marek as he stumbled across the car park, Pete grasped a young woman by the arm. "What's happened here, I'm worried for my girlfriend; she works here."

"A vial of TTX has been stolen."

"TTX?"

"Tetrodotoxin. Don't you and your girlfriend speak?"

Anything with toxin in the word had to be bad and he adjusted his expression suitably. "She never talks about work. How bad is it?"

"It's bloody dangerous, the tiniest drop can kill and some bloody idiot thought it would be a good idea to take it home. Knob." She marched off, leaving Pete with no doubt about the cause of Marek's anxiety, though why he would want to steal something so deadly was an enigma. He strolled over to his car to accompany the man.

"Where do you want to talk? A pub? Café?"

"Home. Just take me home. My housemates will be there. It's about time they hear I'm just as bad as Halina. Have you found her yet?"

Pete turned the engine for the fourth time and it finally grumbled into life. "No, still on the run as far as I know. Do you have any idea...?"

"No, I've told you guys a zillion times, everything she ever told me was a lie."

"Why did you take the TTX?"

"I've felt so guilty about that ever since I found out she's been killing people. She told me she wanted to see it, told me that she'd marry me if she saw it and ate it."

"Ate it? Why would somebody want to eat a deadly poison? Was she suicidal?"

"Prepared correctly it's apparently a good experience. I didn't even want to marry her in the end, I'd stopped trusting her, but then the vial was on my desk and nobody was looking, and I... I don't know why, I just slipped it in my bag. Of course I regret that moment now, I will do forever."

"Did you give it to Halina then?"

"No, it's a long story, but she found it in my bag and took it, the drug, the bag, everything."

"Everything?"

"Well, she packed a few things and the uniforms she uses for work. She was gone by the time I got home."

"So there's a killer loose with a catastrophic drug and she can pose as a nurse at any hospital round here. Can she? Where's she worked? Which one is she most likely to go to?"

245

"God knows, she's worked at them all."

The revelation was staggering and Pete had two choices. He could either take the information straight to the police to let them know what they were dealing with, or he could try and be the hero, drive round the hospitals and catch her in the act. With a credit like that to his name he could even be re-instated on the police force, a wish he thought would never come to fruition. However, he knew right from wrong and parked by the police station minutes later. "I thought you said you didn't want to take me to the station?"

"I changed my mind. Come with me."

Half an hour later, on Fitzpatrick's orders, Pete and Marek were in a patrol car being escorted to Boxton Park Hospital.

Chapter 24
A Monster in Her Vulgar Little World

Fitzpatrick rushed from Harbecker's hijacked office, now an impromptu incident room, and grasped the doctor's arm. "What do you know about tetrodotoxin?"

The doctor explained he had only heard of the poison just over a week previously when a patient had been brought in suffering the effects. He'd had to lean heavily on the manual supplied by the company the man had worked for to treat him. "His name was Robert Sanders, if I remember rightly, and he died."

Fitzpatrick leaned through the doorway and glanced at Marek, whose head was bowed. "Robert Sanders?"

"We were colleagues, he died a week last Sunday."

Fitzpatrick re-addressed the doctor. "Is it routinely tested for, you know, in blood tests, or post-mortem tests?"

"Not at all. In Robert's case we knew it was tetrodotoxin because he was a code ten from Randall's Biotech. When they started working with the drug, they supplied the hospital with a manual of how to treat their staff if they were subjected to it. All I know is what's in the manual."

"New evidence has come to light and we think Thirsk has been poisoned with it. Is it as simple as administering an antidote? Can you do that?"

"No, there is no antidote, but I'll arrange for him to be intubated and sedated, and increase the saline. Then it's a matter of time will tell."

Fitzpatrick laid his head against the doorframe, eyes closed, teeth gritted. "This Robert, how long, you know, before he died?"

"About six hours and he only ingested a tiny amount. You don't know how much, if any, your officer has had." Harbecker leaned into his office. "Who's the person who worked with the poison?"

Marek lamely raised his hand.

"I seem to recall that TTX is a solid, what do you use as a base?"

"Acetic acid is what we're currently using."

"Which wouldn't be remarkable in a blood test. Rachel," the overloaded woman skidded to a stop beside him, withholding a stressed sigh. "Bed one, I want you to intubate..."

"Oh, no you don't," Fitzpatrick stood tall, "no delegating our officer any more. I want you, and you only, caring for Thirsk."

Harbecker, overworked himself, relented with grace and understanding. "Rachel, phone the tox lab and get them to test Mrs Ghadi's blood sample for tetrodotoxin." He nodded to Fitzpatrick and made his way to his patient, leaving the tense atmosphere.

Seconds later, a metallic clanging broke the silence and all eyes moved to the doorway. Toni, in pyjamas and slippers and wheeling a drip stand, and Sally Ross stood, worried. "She insisted on coming down, I couldn't stop her."

"Sal said he's been poisoned by Halina. What's going on?"

"Are you okay? You look, well... tired."

"I'll be fine, sir, but I'm concerned about the guv."

"Sadly, Fowler, we all are." He scanned the expectant officers, all anxious and concerned, all waiting for him to take control. "Look, all of us gathered here in Harbecker's office isn't going to help anything. Just get out of here and start searching the hospital to see if you can find her. Diane, stop by the ward office, Harbecker's secretary may have some likenesses copied by now for you to start circulating." Toni blinked, scared of missing out, and Fitzpatrick rolled his eyes. "Get her in a wheelchair, Sally, take her with you."

In the past, killing had been easy. Careful planning and well-timed execution had ensured that the deaths of the victims were rarely found to be suspicious, but Tobias and his damned note coupled with the eagle-eyed pathologist at the Padway, who had reported Nellie's death to the coroner, had started the police ball rolling and her murderous career was now threatened. This time capture had been too close and she'd had no choice but to leave without knowing if Thirsk had succumbed to the tetrodotoxin or not.

It had been easy to filter into the system at Boxton Park. She had arrived in accident and emergency on the Friday night under the moniker Grace Bakalar, the name of the niece she had helped to die years before, complaining of a threatened miscarriage. Of course, she wasn't pregnant, she hadn't been since she'd had Karol, but she had needed a rope to drag Marek alongside and a possible child seemed the most effective. Such a waste of time now she had left him. It was out of her control though, the police were on her back.

She had described the right symptoms to be given a bed for the night and Vincent Rogers had been so tempting: lecherous and crude, much like the despicable Wayne West.Both deserved their fates, as had all the idiots she had chosen. Lying in her bed, she had imagined using the newly acquired drug to force his life away and the hospital had made it easy when they'd found him a bed opposite hers. It was her trial for the drug she had been told was potent enough to only need a miniscule amount to secure a victim.

On discharge she had taken Marek's workbag to the toilets and changed into the correct uniform for the hospital, and the recent road accident ensured her face was only one of the many bank nurses who had been brought in to cover the extra patients. She chose Ward 1B for its proximity to the main doors should escape be necessary, and used Falak Ghadi as the next guinea pig.

When Thirsk had been brought in on Sunday she knew he was a gift from God. The man who suspected her, threatened to upend her life and reveal her deepest secret, the man who could stop her obsession with death; he lay helpless on a bed and she intended him to stay that way. Morphine had been a start, a way of subduing him for the moment she was preparing for: a clear window to administer the poison. But it hadn't worked, and when she tried for the second time, Harbecker yelled at her, a foreboding tone of mistrust in his voice. She had realised there was no time to wait and see if he would die. She had to move on.

There was enough tetrodotoxin left to kill countless people, but if she assumed an alias she would have no paperwork, and if she didn't they would find her. The option of not killing again was redundant, she enjoyed it too much, the power over life and death. And why not? If somebody was rude, or inconsiderate, arrogant, if they were racist or sexist, surely she was doing the world a favour by extinguishing their foul existences.

She had seen that Thirsk was in a trance, although Dr Harbecker hadn't realised without the benefit of knowledge she had of his condition, and she suspected his vast frame and bulk were the reason he had not died from the first dose. She could only hope her work would be successful, as her presence was no longer possible. She had seen the police cars arriving as she walked through the main gates of the hospital grounds and realised her escape had been on a knife-edge. With her head down and walking fast, she made her way to Slough Railway Station, without a clue where she was heading. Fate would direct her in the end.

Inspektor Sikorski knocked on the aging wooden door and presently Patryk opened it, immediately crossing his arms, defensive. "I'm looking for Gabryjela Bakalar."

"I'm her husband. What do you want?"

"I need to speak to her." He pushed his way past, with no hindrance from the disgruntled man. "Gabryjela".

A young girl bounced up to the officer with a tentative, toothless grin. "That's my mama. She's called that."

Hearing her daughter's involvement, Gabryjela stepped from behind the curtain, her hopes of avoiding him dashed. "I'm Gabryjela Bakalar. I'm guessing this is about my sister."

"Yes, she's up to her old tricks in the UK and we need to ask you some questions."

"I'll be no help to you, I haven't seen her since the day she killed my daughter."

"You know her as a person which is more than we, or the British Police, do."

"She isn't a person. A monster. A vicious psychopath. She took my child."

Gabryjela sat on the sofa and Patryk joined her, a protective arm over her shoulders, and Sikorski followed their direction to sit.

"Interpol contacted me. I was one of the officers involved with the investigation into Halina's crimes six years ago."

"But I don't recall you or your name."

"No, I've been promoted since. The inspector you dealt with has retired now. Do you have any idea where Halina is? Have you heard from her?"

"No, but we knew something was going on because several people have contacted us recently asking after her."

"The British Police are hopeful they have almost found her, but they want to know – in their words – all about her past. Is she older than you?"

"No, two years younger, the baby of the family. This has destroyed my mother. She was devoted to Halina right from the start, babied her well into her teens. She's been a shell since the bitch went on the run. Speaks to no one, may as well be dead. God forbid."

"Tell me about Halina when you were growing up."

Gabryjela was resigned. "She was very selfish and always different. Quiet, like a dormouse. Mama worried about her constantly, if she had a cold or she'd scratched herself, if she'd taken a tumble, it was always a dramatic occasion, whisking her to the doctor or hospital for reassurance. Tata would tell her not to worry so, that she needn't make such a fuss, but mama seemed to thrive from her visits to the hospital, as if she were looking for someone to tell her it was okay, that she was doing just fine as a mother."

"How many of you are there?"

"I had three older brothers, two have died, one in service in Afghanistan, the other in a motorcycle accident. I'm the fourth, then Halina. Mama had a difficult pregnancy and birth with her and they did a hysterectomy alongside the caesarean section. Mama still won't accept that Halina has done anything wrong, despite the mountain of proof."

"What was she like as a child, growing up?"

251

"She was a devious little cow, knew just how to play mama and tata against each other. She'd run to one or the other and bat her bloody eyelids to get whatever she wanted, and she invariably got it. She killed our cousin when she was six."

Inspektor Sikorski was surprised, such a statement hadn't been in the substantial notes. "Why do you say that?"

"I was there. Rafal was just a baby, my aunt had left him outside in the pram – said the sunlight was good for newborns – while she stayed in the kitchen with mama and tata. There were some concrete steps out the back leading down to the garden and Halina said she was taking the baby for a walk amongst the roses my tata loved so much. He's a keen gardener, always was. My brothers told her not to, I remember them begging, and Andrzej was going to tell mama.

"Well, the threat to Halina was a red rag to a bull, she seemed to delight in being centre of attention, and she instantly wheeled the pram to the steps. It happened so quickly. The pram jerked forward, then spun over and baby Rafal was thrown out. He landed on his head and we watched, dumfounded, as his blood spilled over the path, sickly red and glistening. It was like we were trapped in our own bodies, none of us could move, then all hell broke loose as the adults all crowded out, my aunt and uncle rushing to their baby, screaming, crying. Halina told my parents it was Andrzej who'd done it and they wouldn't listen to us defending him. They wouldn't know the truth, they couldn't conceive their precious baby was capable of such an act. I think she realised then that she could literally get away with murder."

"That wasn't mentioned in our paperwork."

"I was living with mama and tata during the investigation, my own baby had just been killed and I went through a dreadful time. If I'd said anything I swear my parents would have disowned me, they wanted complete loyalty to Halina despite her being accused of killing my Grace. They said I was wrong, that Grace's death had been natural. Luckily the police didn't believe them and I understand she's still on your records as being one of Halina's victims, but none of it will ever bring my daughter back."

"You weren't close sisters then, at any stage?"

"No, I think she truly thought her brothers and I were the enemy, that now she'd been born, her rights to our parents eclipsed ours and we were now surplus to requirements. She treated us all like shit, getting us into trouble for her own pleasure, conniving and plotting in her vulgar little world. She thought she was – in fact, as far as our parents were concerned, she was – the centre of the universe. She could do no wrong, she was their angel. She's an angel of death."

"So when she left school, what happened then?"

"Obviously, there was no way she was going to leave home. Tata gave her money when she wanted, gave her everything she asked for, and mama doted on her, cooking her meals, doing her laundry, tidying after her. I didn't think she would bother to find work so it was a surprise when they said she was training to be a nurse. I was horrified. Something felt wrong, someone so caustic and demanding being a person responsible for the care of vulnerable people. Maybe I knew her better than I thought."

"Had she qualified when she first killed in the hospital?"

"I have no idea when she first killed. You were investigating nine at the hospitals, it wouldn't surprise me if there were many more."

Sikorski glanced up from the notes he was taking, debating her words. "There are now, the English have linked at least five more to her. Tell me about Borys, her husband."

"Husband! A hand puppet, more like. She was the boss, she told him what to do and when, and when he did as he was told they were fine. If he took even a step out of line she'd scream and yell at him, a temper like a tornado. He did whatever she wanted just to keep the peace. It was me he came to when he thought she'd killed their child. Nobody else was suspicious, the officials said Karol's was a natural death. But Borys had seen her shaking him before when he wouldn't stop crying. He didn't go to the police, he was too scared of her, but when they started investigating her after some suspicious deaths at the hospital they reopened Karol's case and came to the same conclusion as he had, and he gave a full statement then. He died soon after and they said she'd killed him by injecting air into his veins while he was asleep. He was the last victim that we know of before she disappeared."

"When, in all of this, did your daughter die?"

"After Karol's death. She'd come round to my house, crying and wailing that she'd lost her baby, and she'd hug Grace – she was two months older – as if she were her own child. I thought nothing of it, thought it was all part of the grieving process, and although we didn't get on, I felt sorry for her. Felt sorry for her." Her face twisted and she spat on the floor with vitriolic disgust.

"What happened to Grace?"

"The bitch suffocated her. She used *my* pillow to kill my child, held it over her face so hard it dislocated her jaw – they found that when they exhumed her body to do a second post-mortem. I was the one who found my baby, dead – God, I screamed so hard – and I knew it had to have been something to do with Halina. I have never seen her since that day and I never want to see her again. Until the investigation started, I was told that it was a cot death, but I knew it was her."

Sikorski watched the child in the corner playing innocently with her dolls, the toothless smile appealing and nonsensical jabbering cute. "She's beautiful, how old is she?"

"Five, nearly six. I was newly pregnant when Grace died. It was a blessing and the only thing that kept me going. She looks like Grace, just older now."

"So, after your child died…"

"Was murdered." There was a steeliness in Gabryjela's eyes that emphasised her inner strength and bravery.

"You haven't seen Halina since? Did you know she'd moved to England?"

"No, and I wouldn't have cared anyway. She's nothing to me. In fact, I wish her dead, I hate her so."

Sikorski stood and leaned over the wronged woman, rubbing her shoulder gently. "I know it's been hard for you to relive such a terrible time, but thank you for doing so, I hope that understanding how Halina ticks will bring the British one step closer to finding her."

"If they do, will they send her back here?"

"I don't know, that's the truth."
"She can rot in hell for all I care."

Chapter 25
Those Who Judge Will Pay

Halina had taken a train to London and braved the underground rush hour to Kings Cross and, from there, she had boarded the express, destination Edinburgh. Meanwhile, at Boxton Park Hospital, hundreds of copies of her image were floating around like confetti. A couple of tentative sightings had been reported, but from hours before, and a press statement had been arranged for later that evening, which pained Fitzpatrick, knowing that the public and media involvement would make everything so much messier. However, it was a necessity as Halina had no intention of making things easy for them.

Fitzpatrick stood, his officers reassembled from their search. "There's no point us being here. And you, young lady," he pointed to Toni, clearly weakened by her jaunt, "need some rest."

Steadman could think of nothing else. "What about Thirsk?"

Fitzpatrick looked to Harbecker for help. "Is it worth us staying?"

"I've read the manual from cover to cover and there's nothing more anybody can do but wait. I see no point in you being here, not if you can be more effective in finding the woman from the police station."

"You heard the man, let's get back."

"He's crashing." A flat tone rang out to blend with the nurse's warning and Harbecker shoved through the crowd in his office, rushing to Thirsk's bedside as the crash cart arrived, and the officers trickled out behind him, frowning and worried.

"Epinephrine, one milligram. Thank you," Harbecker fed the adrenaline through the dying man's cannula, "paddles, two hundred joules." Thirsk's body jerked forward, but the monotonous tone continued and Steadman began to cry.

The sun was setting on the horizon, throwing a rainbow of orange and red across the sky, silhouettes of pink tipped clouds scattered randomly, and Halina gazed sightlessly through the window of the train as it traversed the Bedfordshire countryside. Having nothing to do but think during the five hour journey was frustrating, because the cacophony of her dire situation repressed all other thought, leaving her in an agitated state of panic. It was too late to turn back, to go home and pretend nothing had happened. It had happened and life as she had known it had ceased. No more Marek, no commuting across the home counties to a selection of hospitals to pick her victims with ease. What she would do when she reached Edinburgh, she didn't know.

The police would be on her tail by now, of that she was sure. They would have tracked the expenditure on her bankcard, having used it to purchase the ticket. They would know she was on her way to Scotland. Would they be waiting for her, the station surrounded by squad cars, to arrest her and lock her away? Would she disappear into the crowd and forge a new life, a new start? Perhaps she should disembark early, but they could have officers waiting at every stop on the way. Maybe she should jump from the train.

Halina shook her head, willing her brain to shut up. The answer would come if she stopped fretting long enough to let it be heard. She closed her eyes, the jolting and rumbling of the train comforting. Why had her life taken this turn, a life with the power to choose another's death, to send them to a better place without the horrors of the civilised human?

Her first adult in Poland had been an accident. She had misread the dosage and administered too much diacetylmorphine, but her gift of the gab had laid the blame squarely on another nurse's shoulders. Relieving the patient of his tawdry existence, coupled with comeuppance for the nurse she hated had felt amazing.

So the next one was planned. The sensation of adrenaline pumping through her body, the fear of being caught tinged with the most incredible excitement, the decision to take a life or give it. It was unbeatable. Addictive.

Halina reached into Marek's workbag and brought out the glass pyramid with a circular rubber bung, a vial that held enough

257

poison to kill everybody on the train and more. To an outsider it would seem innocent, a bottle of sweet-smelling perfume or cologne. But without the opportunity to use it, it was worthless. She slowly scanned the carriage from her aisle seat, the man to her right snoring and snuffling, the skanky woman with too many children that she couldn't control, the prim and proper stink-under-the-nose who appeared to be a successful businesswoman, but was probably a high-class prostitute. They all deserved to die.

People disgusted her, revolted her. From her weak-willed parents who had inanely believed every word she said, to her bullying brothers and envious sister who had ganged up on her at every opportunity. Neighbours sticking their noses into other people's business, people on the street judging on looks alone. Parliamentarians who controlled the lives of the masses, doctors who chose if and when somebody should die. Vile creatures, all of them, with their fake smiles and bitter minds.

She pushed the bottle back into the bag and remembered the uniforms she had brought with her. She would have to dispose of them; not only were they bulky, but working in another hospital would be impossible for a while. She glanced around again to ensure nobody was watching, that the pig beside her was still asleep, and fed the dresses under her seat one by one, until only a jumper, some toiletries and the poison remained in the bag.

It would be past eleven by the time she reached Edinburgh and what she would do then, she had no idea. She would have to wing it. Halina closed her eyes and let the moving train, with its whispering and rhythmic rocking, lull her to sleep.

Harbecker had been told that the toxicology department had no means of testing for tetrodotoxin, so Steadman had arranged for Randall's Biotech to do the work. They had raised no objection, and the three samples – blood from Thirsk, Falak Ghadi and Vincent Rogers – had all tested positive.

Steadman had also informed them of Marek's involvement and subsequent arrest. A P45 was arranged for him in minutes.

The panic had died down at the hospital once Thirsk's heart had been restarted, and although the beats were few and far between, a complication that Harbecker had read about in the manual, he was still alive. Steadman sat by his bed, her head on his chest, listening to the periodic thud that showed on the monitor screen, willing him to recover with every bone in her body.

At Castle Street Police Station the atmosphere was turbulent, the fact that two officers were down increasing productivity in their determination to find the errant suspect. Many were working overtime and prepared to work for no pay if need be. Whether they knew it or not, Thirsk was highly respected and Toni was popular, her sunny disposition a source of joy.

Fitzpatrick scanned the room, a hopelessness about him that had luckily not transferred to his colleagues, and his eyes settled on Pete Benson, somehow still with them and helping the team by bringing endless coffee and biscuits to keep them functioning. He called him across. "Come into the office a minute."

Pete would have wagged his tail if he could, the day swimming with memories of how much he had enjoyed his time on the force, and he followed the superintendent into Thirsk's room. "What's up?"

Fitzpatrick sat heavily on the chair and sagged. "Imagine you're Halina... No, imagine you've murdered, say, ten people and the cops are after you. What would you do?"

"I'd run away, but this isn't about me, it's her mind you need to figure out."

"What can she do now? Both her married and maiden names are known and soon the media will ensure that everyone in the country knows her face. She can't go back to Poland as they'd pick her up at the airport. If she was part of one of those foreign communities that litter every city and town there's a possibility she could acquire fake documentation, but her face is unusual, her features unique. Somebody somewhere would recognise her. So what's she doing? Where has she gone?"

"As far away as possible, I imagine. Abroad, maybe?"

"Unlikely, her photo's been circulated at passport control, the airports and docks are aware of her."

259

"She's going to lie low then, find somewhere to hide away while the heat is on."

The door opened and Sally stuck her head through. "It's nearly eight o'clock, the press release is about to start."

Pete followed Fitzpatrick from the room and they joined the officers crowded around the television, counting down the seconds. "There's Commander Nilson, I've not seen that old bastard for a long time." Various shushes echoed, silencing Pete.

Nilson had a two minute slot and he was situated to the right of the screen, the rest filled with Halina's image, and subtitles ran along the bottom to clarify his speech. He gave brief details of Halina's appearance and recent crimes, repeating the helpline number thrice and stressing the urgency.

Hugh sat on the sofa with his arm around Angela's shoulder, Marcus on his chair, engrossed in the television. Likewise in Nicholas and Adele's lounge, watching alongside Fran, who had outstayed her welcome within days, eating them out of house and home and creating a mess wherever she went. John watched alone from the barstool of his local, supping the pint that would turn into eight before he wove his way home to bed.

On the train, Halina and her fellow passengers were unaware. Until Miss Prim-and-Proper, who had been keeping up with trending news on her Smartphone, stared at the fugitive with realisation and paled. Leaving her case under the table, and attempting not to appear alarmed, she slid from her seat and squeezed along the aisle, snatching glances at Halina as she headed towards the front of the train. As the automatic doors at the end of the carriage closed behind her, she relaxed against the metal wall, catching her breath, her heart rocketing. A quick glance back to check she hadn't been tailed and she continued through the carriages.

The driver's door was locked and a guard hurried behind her, having spotted her trying to gain entry. "You can't go in there, ma'am."

"We need to contact the police, there's a murderer on the train. Carriage D. I've just seen her photo on the internet. She's wanted. There's been a press release." Her breathing was laboured, adrenaline pumping through her system. At first he assumed she was playing a prank, but the fear in her eyes soon had him contacting his superiors for advice and instruction.

Within half an hour, the driver had been ordered to slow the train, but not stop, and police cars swarmed the area, two helicopters circling overhead. On the agreed signal, the driver brought the train to a standstill and police officers clambered into the carriages. One detective met with the frightened, yet excited, lady who had raised the alarm. "You said she was in carriage D?"

"Yes, she was on the other side facing me. I was in seat 44."

"There's nobody of our suspect's description there, or anywhere else on the train, for that matter."

"She was there, I swear she was. Maybe she went to the loo."

"We've checked them all."

"Then she must be somewhere, I wasn't imagining things. Ask the other passengers on the carriage, they'll tell you I'm not making it up."

"We're taking statements now."

Halina knew she needed medical attention because, although her jump had been broken by undergrowth, she had twisted her ankle and it was swollen and throbbing. To turn up at a hospital or walk-in centre would be suicide if she wanted her liberty, plus the walk to find one would be excruciating, but it wasn't the kind of injury that would heal itself without firm support. She had seen Miss Prim-and-Proper staring, the tell of horror that briefly swept her face, and realised her image must have been released. A disguise was what she needed, but how?

Struggling up, she scoured the countryside that surrounded her, the Pennines barren and stark, eerie in the cold moonlight. There were no signs of life anywhere near, the flickering lights of a small settlement ahead, but clearly miles away. Too far to walk with an unsupported sprained ankle. She wished forlornly that she hadn't ditched the spare uniforms, she could have torn them to use as a bandage.

If she were to tear the jumper she was now wearing, the icy wind would ensure hypothermia followed swiftly, but if she didn't she had no choice but to find a sheltered place to sleep in the hope that her ankle would begin to heal overnight. She took a step and howled with the pain. Without a second thought, she tugged her anorak off, followed by the jumper. Using the small scissors she kept in the breast pocket of the Boxton Park uniform she still wore, she cut the sleeve and bound her ankle securely. She pulled the one-sleeved jumper back over her dress and replaced the coat. Shrugging against the chilly air, she limped towards the lights.

Halina filled her mind to obscure the agony, thoughts of her childhood, of Borys, of her beloved Karol. Her mother and father, brothers, sister. Marek. Work…Murder.

The most formative memories she had were centred in hospital, nurses and doctors, her distressed, flustered mama, everybody fussing and smiling, with her poorly, sad face demanding sympathy. She had worked it for as long as she could remember, even though half the time she had felt fine, her mother mentioning symptoms she didn't think she had. She had loved it and continued the dramatics into her teens.

Rafal was her first death and it had not been planned. All she had wanted was to take the baby for a stroll, let him see the colours and beauty of the abundant roses her father had tended and relished. It never crossed her mind that the pram might be too heavy on the steps. It happened in an instant, the weight of the handrail, snatching her arms high until she'd had to let go, and everything had gone into slow motion, the baby flying through the air, his alarmed eyes wide and confused, the delicious crack as his head met with the concrete. The blood, seeping his life away.

Andrzej had tried to stop her, the big bully of a brother who lived a life of jealousy for the attention she got, and her revenge was to tell the grown-ups that he had been the one to move Rafal. They believed her, they always did, but her siblings had seen the truth. They had seen the smile that involuntarily spread across her face when the baby lay, unmoving, on the ground. They knew what she was, and at that moment she had realised the same. Killing, and the fuss it created, had given her the biggest buzz she had ever experienced.

There had been two more before she left school. Aged ten, she and a group of friends had been playing on a building site. They had known it was naughty, in fact possibly dangerous, but that added to the thrill. One lad, a red-headed loudmouth whom she detested, had fallen from a half-built wall and banged himself on the stray bricks below. Blood oozed from a large wound on his forehead, his body stilled. She told the others to run for help, and once she was alone with him, she took a broken brick and slammed it into his head. The cracking sound had been wonderful, his body melting into the brick dust, and she had sat back to watch him die.

The second time, she had been fourteen and on a hiking trip as part of her school's curriculum. One of her contemporaries shared a kiss with the boy they both admired and Halina was engulfed with envy. She suggested they both sneak from the campsite that night, have a few cigarettes, and some booze if they could manage to steal it from the supply tent. Marcelina, a rebel to the end, had been excited.

They had procured two bottles of beer, opening them against the rocks on the riverside, and Halina had stolen two cigarettes from their form teacher's pack, along with a box of matches. They sat by the bank, sharing each cigarette to make them last longer, supping their ale and giggling. After an hour, Halina persuaded Marcelina to follow her onto the rickety footbridge, eager to see the moonlit view across the stunning countryside. All it took was a light push, such a simple act to remove the girl who had what she wanted: Borys's affections.

Tittle-tattles suggested that Halina had been with Marcelina that night, but she denied involvement, using her greatest acting skills, and eventually Marcelina's death was recorded as misadventure. The whole event, from the idea, to the midnight outing, to the execution of the plan – hearing the splashing water and the crack of her skull against the rocks resound across the valley – had been magnificent. She knew then that killing was her weakness. Or strength.

With her vast knowledge of hospitals, gained over years of her mother's misplaced hypochondria – or was it Munchausen's by proxy – nursing had been the obvious vocation, a calling from God to both nurture and destroy as she saw fit. She snared Borys easily, offering a friendly shoulder to cry on as he rebounded from Marcelina, using her sexual wiles to keep him in place, and they married aged twenty, setting up a comfortable, if small, home of their own. Her own hypochondria continued throughout the years, losing work through the countless incarcerations in hospital, yet although the doctors had stabbed at irritable bowel syndrome and myalgic encephalopathy, chronic fatigue syndrome and even a possible autoimmune disease, there had never been a formal diagnosis. Of course there hadn't; she had been inventing her symptoms.

For years, she withheld her lust to kill, too scared of repercussions to take the risk, but one patient, an elderly lady whom Nellie Gleeson had reminded her of, with her bitching and moaning, complaints and prejudice, provoked her too far. There was no planning, it was a spur of the moment decision. She pulled back the plunger of a large syringe and attached it to the patient's cannula, expelling the air into her veins. Once empty, she repeated the act and continued her rounds until the woman squirmed and gurgled, dying minutes later. She told her superiors she had tried to resuscitate the woman, although the efforts she'd made had been purely for the benefit of the witnessing patients; the shallow massage would never have restarteda heart. Miraculously, there was no suspicion, the body interred without a post-mortem. It was a further sign that this was what Halina had been born to do.

Killing had been so easy, Halina hadn't seen a reason quell the urge, and six months later she repeated the performance on a lecherous old man who had repeatedly groped her bottom. He died in similar agony, but this time the authorities were suspicious and although ultimately she was deemed innocent, the investigation was intense and harrowing. From then she had curbed the temptation.

Shortly after turning twenty-five, Halina had fallen pregnant. She and Borys had yearned for a child to complete their union, and both had privately suspected the other of a fertility problem. But months later, their cute, perfect bundle of joy arrived and they doted on him from the start, their cherubic miracle.

Motherhood had not come easily to Halina, she found the whole debacle exhausting and never-ending; if she didn't have the baby hanging from her bosom she would be changing his nappy or trying to pacify him as he wailed with colic. But she had loved Karol, she never meant to harm him. As a result of their extreme fatigue, Halina and Borys became unhappy, arguing at the slightest disgruntlement, and eventually she suspected he was collecting what he couldn't get at home from another woman. She needed to grasp his attention and the only way seemed to be through their child.

On the fateful day, she dropped Karol deliberately, using the bruising that swiftly appeared as an excuse to take him to hospital, and she summonsed Borys in tears. He was wonderful, such a support, but when Halina saw the doctors crowd around her baby, shouting and commanding, her heart seized. He had only received a bruise, why were they trying to resuscitate him?

A week later, Karol's tiny, vulnerable body was laid to rest in the starkness of the cemetery, with only a small, wooden coffin – the white veneer signalling his tender age – to protect him from the acrid, freezing earth. From that day, Borys became unattainable, blaming himself, or so she believed, for not protecting his child. Halina became increasingly jealous of Gabryjela, whose daughter, Grace, was so close to her own son's age. The child she should have in her arms to love forever. It was consuming and one day it reached a dizzy height where she could contain herself no longer. On the pretence of visiting the toilet, Halina smothered the sleeping baby, forcing the pillow over her face with a strength she hadn't realised she had.

Halina had thrown herself into work, replacing her lost child by working longer and longer hours. The demanding patients increasingly exposed her to the shallowness and idiocy of those who walk on every street in every country, tempting her to

265

silence their acerbic statements, their judgements, their intolerance. Her murderous spree had begun and the more she killed, the greater the thrill.

One night, after she had been interviewed by the police about a death at the hospital, she discovered that Borys had given a statement to the police saying he had suspected her of killing Karol from the start. The betrayal was excruciating, especially when she discovered he had discussed his concerns with her sister after Grace's death. She felt she had no choice but to kill the man she loved and she took a large syringe, stolen from her workplace, and injected him with air while he slept. After, she insisted that he had been complaining of heart pain for months. That he had refused to see a doctor. That he'd never recovered from the death of their son. But suspicion hung over her like a dark cloud and she knew the time had come to move on.

And here she was again, only in another country with fresh victims. After six years of periodic killing, she now had to vanish from society, try and find somewhere, somehow, to start afresh.

Her ankle throbbed with intense pain and Halina stopped to look around. Losing herself in her memories had bitten a substantial chunk of the journey and she found herself close to the boundary of Danby Wiske. Bumping into somebody would be too risky, but she needed to find a doorway or some public toilets, somewhere she could sleep with protection from the elements.

Chapter 26
Deadly Spree

Halina woke, uncomfortable from the night spent on a wooden bench under a remote bus shelter on the outskirts of Danby Wiske. Her head thudded – she assumed she must have bumped it during the fall from the train – and her body ached from the hard slats that had bruised her bones. Worse, her ankle was twice its normal size. If she found a doctor, she would be sent to hospital for examination and x-ray, and the more people around her, the higher the likelihood of being recognised. The temptation to find a newsagent and scan the headlines was great, but the danger was the same. Perhaps she was being paranoid, maybe Miss Prim-and-Proper had simply gone to the toilet, but she couldn't take the risk.

Halina opened Marek's workbag and delved inside, bringing out the pyramid bottle for reassurance. There was plenty of the innocuous fluid inside and a brief longing swept over her, wishing she could find somewhere to use it. She could kill a roomful of people and more so easily if the conditions were right.

She watched as a young man came from the first garden leading into the village and he turned her way. She shrank to the corner and pulled the hood of her anorak over her head. Snatching a glance every now and then, she realised he was heading for the bus stop and she kept her head down, willing him to disappear, but soon he joined her under the shelter, nodding a greeting before sitting on the other end of the bench. He was a handsome young chap, with fashionably scruffy hair that must have taken an hour to tease into shape. Halina wanted to kill him, and she had the means, but not the opportunity.

"I hope you don't mind me asking, but do I know you?"

Halina's chin rested on her chest, hiding her face in the only way possible. "No, I don't think so. I'm not from round here."

She shoved her hands in her pockets, hiding every patch of bare skin that may jolt the memory of whatever medium he had seen her likeness on, but he persevered. "Were you in the pub last night?"

That would do it. "Yes, that must be where you've seen me before."

She hoped he would leave her be but, "Your ankle looks sore, lass, you should get that looked at."

She nodded, obscuring her face with her hood. "I fell off my stilettos last night, gave it a twist. It'll be fine."

A few minutes later, the bus arrived. He stepped aside, waiting for Halina to embark, but she remained seated. "Aren't you getting on?"

She shook her head, her hand holding the side of her hood across her face to avoid being spotted by the passengers. The bus chugged from the shelter, dark clouds of stench belching from the exhaust, and Brandon took a seat, curious of the woman he had encountered.

Once more, Fitzpatrick had copied Thirsk's habit of sleeping on the camp bed in the detective's office, in situ should any news of either Thirsk's condition or Halina's whereabouts surface. Even though he had been practically asleep on his feet by the time he had collapsed under the cover, he was surprised to notice it was gone nine in the morning. He shoved the blanket back and stood, stretching, before dialling Harbecker to see how the patient was. "He's still alive, if that helps."

"It's a start. Has there been any change in his condition?"

"No, his heart is alarmingly slow and he's shown no sign of consciousness, but he's not had any more seizures, which is hopeful."

"Keep me informed." Fitzpatrick ended the call, running his hands through his mussed hair and wiping the sleep from his eyes, and he sauntered to the incident room as he fixed his tie in place. Steadman was at her desk. "Any news, Diane?"

"They worked out that when Pippy Stinkleberger saw Halina on the train…"

"Are we sure it was Halina, though?"

"Her spare uniforms were found under seat 58, exactly where Pippy said she'd been sitting. It was definitely her."

268

He sighed, "Go on."

"The train was travelling north after a stop of about five minutes at Northallerton when Pippy looked up from the news site she'd been reading and noticed Halina. She immediately went to find a guard. It took roughly thirty minutes before police boarded the train, shortly before they were due to reach Durham. That's a distance of forty miles and Halina could have jumped from the train – she had to have jumped – at any stage throughout. Obviously Durham Constabulary and the North Yorkshire Police have every officer available searching for her, but she's still the proverbial needle in a haystack."

"I see. Surely if she leapt from a train moving at what, a hundred miles per hour, she'll have hurt, if not killed, herself."

"They thought of that and have had officers check the line on both sides for any evidence. There was nothing, though. As a precaution all hospitals in North Yorkshire and County Durham have been given her details," she grasped an A4 flyer from the desk, which showed Halina's face and statistics, "with instructions to contact us immediately if she's seen. Also all local newspapers, TV and radio stations in that area have been asked for their help."

"Good, that's pretty much every base covered." He paused, debating whether to ask or not. "When did you leave the hospital?"

She blushed, the evidence of her unrequited love having been displayed openly the day before. "Nothing's ever happened between me and Thirsk, sir."

"Then I hope for your sake that he'll get better and return your affections, you're the salt to his pepper. Bad analogy, but you know what I mean. I've just spoken to the hospital and there's no change, which I see as a good sign."

"Yes, at least he's not getting worse." The phone rang on Steadman's desk and she reached across to answer. As she listened, a grin spread across her face. She caught her boss's eye, holding a finger up to signal she had news. Fitzpatrick watched her intently and eventually the call ended. "That was the North Yorkshire force, they've had a call from a man who says he saw

Halina at a bus stop just outside a place called Danby Wiske. They've sent every car available to search the area."

"Have they taken a statement?" This was the best news Fitzpatrick had heard for a while and he couldn't help smiling.

"He was calling from his mobile on his way to work, they're meeting him when he gets there. Seems he was chatting to her and knew he'd seen her face, but didn't twig where until he boarded the bus. Said she'd been trying to pull her hood across to obscure her face, so she must know we've alerted the public. Anyway, the haystack just got significantly smaller."

After Brandon had departed, Halina limped to the dwelling she had seen him leave. He was only a youngster, probably late-teens, twenty at most, so the likelihood was that he still lived with parents, and they were probably still at home, but her ankle was agony and she couldn't hobble any further without proper support. The absence of a car in the driveway was promising and she slid through the gate to the side of the dormer bungalow, clinging to the wall as she peeped through the first window she reached. Inside she could see a woman on a sofa, the television flickering, and she crept across to the back door, trying the handle. It was unlocked and she peered inside, checking for any signs of life. The room was empty, a decent sized kitchen with oak units and a slate floor. Quietly, she slipped inside.

Beside the kettle on the counter was a teapot, a flowery cosy keeping it warm. Fingering inside Marek's bag as she watched the two doors, one she knew to be to the living room, the other she assumed to the hall, she grasped the pyramid bottle and one of the syringes, feeding it through the cork and suctioning a tiny amount. With barely a sound, she lifted the cosy and squirted a drop into the pot. It was enough to kill several. However, the lazy waste-of-space watching the goggle-box deserved it, lying about all day, no doubt living on taxpayers' money.

A noise came from the lounge and she darted through the door to the hallway, sliding into the cloakroom beside the front door. She locked it and held her breath, heart hammering wildly.

Half an hour had passed by the time she heard a crash and she hoped it was the woman succumbing to the poison. She unlocked the door and took a couple of tentative steps across the hall. A gurgling came from the living room and Halina opened the second door to the through room. The woman was slumped on the floor, dressing gown over her nightclothes, slippers hooked over the top of her shaking feet. Her body shuddered violently for an age and finally she gasped, eyes open but unseeing, and Halina knew her work was almost done.

She limped up the stairs, no longer concerned of making a noise, and located the bathroom, searching the wall cabinet for a bandage to support her injured ankle. Next, she found the woman's bedroom, pink and fluffy with not a man in sight. She searched the drawers, the wardrobe, picking outfits that may fit and throwing them on the bed. The final part of the insufficient disguise was make-up. Halina rarely put a face on yet she knew it transformed her features from severe to acceptable, enhancing her small eyes and puckering her lips. If anyone saw her briefly, they wouldn't – shouldn't – associate her with whatever image had been bandied nationwide.

On her descent, Halina checked her latest victim, sprawled across the floor, ungainly and cumbersome, repulsive fat hanging from her sides in mounds. She was still breathing. Just. But Halina was confidant she wouldn't be soon and wished the woman enough time to enjoy the reported euphoria as the toxin messed with her brain, before her heart stopped bothering to beat.

Halina now had a refuge, a place to stay until the fuss died down and the public's fickle memories forgot. However, twenty minutes later, whilst eating a welcome sandwich in the kitchen, the doorbell chimed.

When Bev received no response, she banged on the door, calling out, "Rosie, love, it's the district nurse. Can you let me in?" The house appeared to be empty. Through the net curtains Halina could see her, the uniform belying her job. She knew the nurse's responsibility to her patient would ensure she gained entry somehow, if not through an open door then with the police in tow, and she swore bitterly. Her eyes darted across the room,

271

seeking somewhere safe to hide should a constable decide to search. Or perhaps she should leave? She wiggled her burning foot and winced. Maybe not.

Halina crawled up the stairs on hands and knees for a better view of the road and from the woman's bedroom could see police cars further up the lane. The caller trotted to a constable and struck up a conversation, and Halina realised her time had run out.

Faced with the thought of the rest of her life in prison, slopping out and bearing the tedium – existing, not living – Halina knew the only eventual option was to poison herself, leave the planet on a cloud of hallucination, vibrant and colourful as the drug took effect. But she was damned if she was going to go alone. There was enough tetrodotoxin for dozens more and she intended to share. Glancing through the window again to check they were still chatting, Halina tolerated the pain from her ankle and hobbled down the stairs, unlocking the back door and stumbling to the end of the garden.

She scrambled over the fence, landing in an expansive field, and limped heavily along, eagerly seeking a suitable hiding place. Ahead she could hear voices, an engine running, and she followed the sound until it could be seen. A truck was parked by an open cellar, two steel casks of beer on the yard, just over a Yorkstone wall. Under cover of the low branches of a mature oak, Halina glanced this way and that, checking for onlookers. She clambered over the wall and climbed onto the trailer, squeezing behind the heavy containers and crouching.

Ten minutes later the lorry was moving and she allowed herself a breath of relief.

Rosie could hear a fuss around her but was powerless to open her eyes and see the commotion. Her lips and tongue were swollen, with an irritating pinprick sensation. She was lying on the floor, her head lolled to one side, and she listened to the voices, feeling her body being moved. Onto the sofa, legs up on the cushions, flat on her back now with her head in a more comfortable position. "Her breathing is shallow and heart racing, temp slightly high but not feverish. What were you visiting for?"

The district nurse scratched her head, dragging a few wisps from the clip that held her hair back. "She's got cancer. They removed a tumour and part of her bowel last week and I come every day to change the dressing. Is this something to do with that?"

The paramedic shook his head. "Her temperature would be higher if she had an infection. I don't know what's going on, to be honest."

His colleague lifted Rosie's eyelids, her dilated pupils staring straight ahead. "I'm just going to pop back to the ambulance. I was given a memo just before we left and didn't really read it, but I'm sure there was something about poisoning on it."

Brian ran his hands over Rosie's jaw line, probing the lymph glands underneath. "No swelling and no signs of having been sick." He smelt her breath to be sure. "A little sulphuric but she's probably just not brushed her teeth this morning." Brian squirted antibacterial cleanser on his palm and rubbed it in, and he lifted the dressing from her surgery wound. "Seems to be healing nicely," he palpated her abdomen, "no distension or fullness, so I assume she's not bleeding internally. What's wrong with you, Rosie?"

She lay paralysed, unable to move her mouth to say 'I don't know'. Colin came rushing through brandishing a sheet of paper. "It's this, I swear it's this. Temperature?"

"Pretty much normal, you said."

"Tachycardia, breathing laboured. Is she clammy?"

Brian felt her forehead, her palms. "A little. What is it?"

Colin, aghast, showed the flyer to Brian and Bev. "Something called tetrodotoxin, or TTX. Believe it or not this woman," he stabbed at the picture of Halina, the light smile not reaching her cold eyes, "has killed several people with it over the past few days. We saw as we arrived that the village is teeming with coppers. Bri, we need to let them know. I'll radio the Friarage and let them know we're bringing her in, you go and speak to one of the bobbies."

Ever practical, Bev asked, "What can I do to help."

"Does she have a husband or family?"

"No husband, but she's got a teenage son who lives with her. His name's Brandon. Nice lad."

Colin nodded to a mobile on the coffee table, noting a bowl that had traces of milk-soaked Weetabix around the edges. "Get him on the phone and find out what she ate this morning, although I doubt very much she had home prepared," he squinted at the leaflet through hyperopic eyes, "fugu, whatever that is, for breakfast."

Bev pressed a few buttons, swearing. "I can't work these bloody things. Oh, here we are." She waited and presently a male voice greeted her. "Is that Brandon?"

Fitzpatrick was more frustrated than ever, stuck in Castle Street Station over two hundred miles from where the action was happening. He wanted to trust the northern forces but had never dealt with them before. What if they were stereotypically too laid back to give the search the urgency it required? Steadman had told him minutes before that a suspected tetrodotoxin poisoning had been brought to hospital, so Halina seemed to have no intention of stopping her deadly spree any time soon. He glanced at Steadman, her mind on other matters. "Go and see him, Diane. Let us know how he is, will you? And can you check on Toni too?"

Steadman bristled on hearing the name of her nemesis. "Thanks, sir. I will."

Fitzpatrick pressed the intercom. "Sally, bring me a strong coffee, please. Have you heard anything?"

"You've told them to contact you direct, sir, why would I have?"

The phone rang on the desk, leaving Fitzpatrick no time to reprimand her insolence, and he snatched the receiver, struggling to understand the broad Yorkshire accent, with its dropped letters and merged words. "We've nearly finished the house to house and have no sightings yet. How do you want us to proceed?"

"What about the helicopters?"

"Nothing, sir, just a couple of false alarms."

"Have you set up the roadblocks as I requested?"

"We're in the process of doing so."

Fitzpatrick sighed, helpless. "It'll probably be too late now, anyway. Just keep looking, make sure the helicopters are watching the surrounding countryside."

Every time the lorry drove over a bump, or one of the many potholes in the frost-damaged tarmac, the rattling seared through Halina's throbbing ankle, up her legs and along her spine. Surely they would have to stop soon. But she was clueless to what would happen when they did. Would they be back at the brewery? She doubted it, the casks in the truck were full so they must be delivering still. Berating herself for not having thought of it before, she investigated the neck of the only cask that wasn't stacked, noting the plastic safety cap. The pubs probably wouldn't use a cask if the seal was broken, but it was worth a try. She took the syringe from the bag, which still contained a few drops of poison, broke the plastic and, with force, pushed the needle through the cork.

She smiled, considering there could be few better ways to die than with a glass of cold beer in the hand. She re-fitted the plastic cap, attempting to disguise the fact it had been broken, and ducked back to her hiding place amongst the casks.

Just in time. The lorry slowed around a tight bend and stopped. The engine cut out and her heart thudded with anticipation, not knowing if she was about to get caught, or manage to escape once more. It was a tremendous sensation, the danger, the fear.

Halina could hear voices outside, but not what they were saying. She listened intently and felt safer when laughter rang out; they wouldn't be amused if they knew of her presence.

The roller door clanked up and the truck wobbled as the driver stepped inside, grasping the cask she had poisoned. Once more she smiled. The process was repeated twice more, replacing the full casks with empties, and soon the lorry was moving again. Two casks were now un-stacked and she siphoned all the poison but a drop from the pyramid, saving the final dregs in the bottle for herself when the inevitable time came.

In the cab, unheard by the stowaway, Steve heard a warning call on his CB radio. "All truckers, news is that the fuzz are setting up roadblocks on the main roads throughout North Yorkshire and some parts of South Teeside. Stop if you see one, they're handing out photos of that nurse who's been killing her patients. If you see her, she is armed and dangerous so don't approach, but call the boys in blue immediately."

Steve grinned, certain some goon was playing a prank, but he recalled the copious police presence when he had delivered to The Olde Oak in Danby Wiske. He felt for the Swiss army knife in the pocket of the door, flicking open a blade; maybe he was overcautious, but he wasn't prepared to take a risk. Hopefully he would reach a roadblock soon.

Twenty minutes later, he had reached his final drop-off in Barningham without seeing a single patrol car and he disarmed the knife, placing it back in the door-pocket. "Daft buggers, always playing them damned tricks and I'm chuffing stupid enough to fall for it."

It was now or never and she was going to have to act fast. She waited for the door to lift, heart speeding and syringe at the ready should she be apprehended, and could hear and feel two people mount the truck. With relief she heard two casks scraping the floor and the trailer bounced up as each man stepped onto the tail lift. Peeping from her hiding place behind the empties, she waited until they had entered the cellar. Halina limped to the opening and searched the surroundings, the remote inn close to a village, but not overseen by any buildings.

She jumped down, a bolt of pain shooting from her ankle, and hobbled to the nearest boundary wall, pushing herself over and ducking from sight. Faint from the pain and danger, she waited, and soon she heard the engine chug to life, accelerating away and leaving her free. Halina limped across the muddy field to a tree that overhung the first shoots of a wheat crop. Breathing as deeply – as slowly – as possible, she sat in the shade, the spring sun beaming down from an unusually clear sky, and thanked her God that she'd not been spotted.

Chapter 27
Escaping to Hell

For the first time in days Thirsk could feel his lips and tongue, dry and uncomfortable, the numbness gone. His toes and fingers tingled, prickling, and although they didn't move when he tried to wiggle them, he knew it was a good sign. He'd had the most bizarre adventure, a land full of colours and bright lights, of floating sounds and waves of visions, not that he understood any of it.

A droning noise drifted to his ears and echoed away. "Nurse, I think he's waking up."

The nurse lifted his eyelids and checked his output but saw no change. "Why?"

Steadman was excitable. "I swear his finger moved." And on cue, the left hand shuddered slightly. "See, it moved again."

"I'll get the doctor."

Steadman leant over the boss she adored and whispered, "Richard, can you hear me?" No response came and she repeated herself. This time, his fingers moved again and she smiled widely, gratefully. "Thank god." She leant over again, whispering, "I love you, you old fart." His fingers remained still and she realised how foolish she had been; such a statement would cause endless trouble at work if he had heard. She knew he wasn't attracted to her.

Although despondent, Steadman was relieved he was coming round. Even if her love was unreturned, she would never wish him harm. But now he was safe she remembered she had agreed to check on Toni – cute, nice, bouncy, perfect Toni who wouldn't leave her man alone – and she resolved to wait with Thirsk while the doctor, who was approaching, attended him. If there would be no change for a while she would suffer ten minutes with the irritating man-snatcher.

Harbecker reached the bed and Steadman told him of the movement. "Richard, move your fingers if you can hear me." The hand stretched weakly. "My name is Doctor Harbecker,

277

you're in Boxton Park Hospital. You've been in an accident. Do you understand me?"

Again, the hand moved briefly on the covers. His hearing was improving and he had been horrified to hear Steadman's declaration. She was a nice enough woman but not his type by any stretch of the imagination and he was going to have to make sure he didn't encourage her in any way. Lord knows what she saw in him with his excess fat and abundant wrinkles.

Harbecker continued to talk and he responded in the only way he could, for whenever he tried to speak he could feel something pressing on his tongue.

Steadman was alarmed by the rattling from Thirsk's throat, but Harbecker assured her it was normal with a ventilator in place. Concerned, but aware he had to try, he carefully removed the endotracheal tube and mentally crossed his fingers that Thirsk would breathe unaided. He did.

Elated, Steadman punched a concise text into her phone and sent it to Fitzpatrick, and when she heard Thirsk's first word for three days – dizzy – she'd never felt such relief.

Halina had fallen asleep almost instantly when she had settled under the tree, her body responding to the intense pain in the best way it could, and when she awoke the sun had disappeared, replaced by a dark and cloudy, threatening sky. Dribbling rain spat over the field with a light pattering that was as comforting as it was a prelude to the oncoming storm that could be heard in the distance. With hospital treatment out of the question, the only way her ankle would recover was with ample rest, but she couldn't stay in the middle of nowhere exposed to the elements. She needed somewhere covered and comfortable.

Bites pockmarked her neck and cheek from where she had been lying and she scratched furiously, annoyed at the bugs for their hunger, and her foot and lower leg were massive and mottled from the injury. She untied the supporting bandage, checking the purple and blue bruising as best she could in the moonlight, and for the first time she considered she may have broken bones. Regardless, she had to find somewhere to stay, and she tightened the dressing.

Each step Halina took on her journey to find shelter was agony, spears of fire shooting up her leg and along her backbone, radiating an uncomfortable warmth throughout her body, andshe felt like she had hobbled miles. She was tired, thirsty and hungry, not having eaten since being in the good-for-nothing woman's house that morning. During her travels the sun had risen, filling the sky with a vibrant orangey-red, but now the clouds had blanketed, threatening another downpour.

Almost at the point of exhaustion, tempted to lay where she stood and die, a blackened barn came into view and at last she had somewhere to head for. With the newly found hope and purpose, the journey took less time than she had anticipated and she was thrilled to see the structure looked as if it had been abandoned, the stone walls charcoaled from a fire. Luck was on her side.

She traipsed around and found an entrance, a yawning gap with no door, and she entered the clamminess inside. Mounds of damp, foul-smelling hay were scattered sparsely and she gathered a pile in the far corner, some for a bed and the rest to obscure her from view should anyone enter. Stacking a little more to raise her leg as she slept, Halina fell onto the scratchy mattress and closed her eyes, drained.

The landlord of the Red Lion in Barningham was furious. He had taken delivery of four casks of ale that day, yet two had broken seals. Rather than risk serving a bad pint, he had set the barrels aside, ready to complain bitterly to the brewery the next morning.

In nearby Melsonby, the affable and cheery landlady of The Rising Sun hadn't been so cautious. The pub was as empty as usual on a Wednesday night, with a mere few regulars supping their pints at the bar, homes to go to but wives they were avoiding. The five men chatted with Bernice, telling her things they had regaled umpteen times before. Jack mentioned that his tongue and lips felt weird and the others agreed in unison. "Not enough beer, I say," Bernice chuckled, pouring Jack another pint. "Get this down you, flower."

Jack handed over the money, extortionate at half the price, and grumbled that his fingertips had needles and pins too. He downed his fifth drink and staggered to the door, bidding his friends goodnight. His farmhouse was conveniently located a short walk away and he hurried to get home, not feeling right, but knowing he would get no sympathy from his wife.

By the time he unlocked the door and stepped into the kitchen, his head was muzzy, a worrying cloud of fog descending. Using all his strength, he made his way up the stairs, clutching the handrail for support and he made it to the bathroom just in time, vomiting repeatedly, his stomach purging the alcohol.

When the nausea and retching finally abated he slid into bed, resolving to call Bernice in the morning and moan about the beer being off.

Unknown to Jack, his four drinking partners had been feeling the same in differing degrees. Not a single one thought to seek medical advice.

Joan woke to the regular early alarm, a crescendo of strings belting out Beethoven's Violin Concerto in D major on the radio and, as she always did, she tugged her housecoat over her ample bosom and trotted down the stairs to feed the dogs, wagging their tails and begging with their eyes. She filled the kettle and slid it onto the Aga, chucking handfuls of crunchies into the dogs' bowls.

The morning paper rustled through the letterbox and she collected it to read over her mug of tea. Halina's Mona Lisa smile covered the front page, leaving only enough room for one paragraph of text, and Joan tutted at the state of the world; what were things coming to when the fairer sex were capable of such atrocities. However, ready for the gossips at the market, she digested every word.

When she finally returned to the bedroom with a steaming mug of tea for her husband, she was surprised to see him still asleep. He never slept in. Tentatively she wobbled his shoulder, calling his name. With disbelief – he was fit as a fiddle despite his age – she realised he wasn't breathing. His colour was wrong. No pulse. Ice cold. "Jack." Panic. "Wake up."

Moments later she was on the phone, pleading for the ambulance to get there quickly. "I think he's dead."

Thirsk sat in bed, greedily demolishing a meagre, unappetising breakfast of cereal and cardboard toast. During his gradual recovery from the powerful drug the day before, Steadman had explained what had been happening, of Halina's escape and his own miracle recovery. In return he had described the final moments before his car had crashed into the tree, obliterating his memory and consciousness.

Harbecker had told him that his unhealthy size had probably been the reason he'd not died and he felt he'd the last laugh over everybody who had been nagging him to lose weight.

Today, he was eager to return to work, but Fitzpatrick thought differently. "Absolutely not. You've been at death's door, worrying the bloody lot of us. You can't return to work just like that. Be patient for once."

"At least talk to me about the case if nothing else, my brain's still functioning. It's boring as hell in here. What's the latest?"

Fitzpatrick growled, resigned. "We nearly had her but she's managed to escape and now we haven't the foggiest where she is. She's killed seven that we know of, with a further woman in hospital in a critical condition. She's not expected to survive, but bear in mind they were saying that about you yesterday morning." His mobile sounded and he answered.

Eventually, his face drawn and sorrowful, he spoke, his voice crackling. "Thank you. I'll be back as quickly as I can." He hung up and nodded to Steadman, who was walking towards the bed with a vending-machine coffee. "One man has died and a further four are in hospital, all suspected TTX poisoning."

"Fuck! Where?"

"All in a village south west of Darlington. Either Halina's sneaking into people's houses or there's a common denominator where they've all been."

"What, like the workplace, or something?"

281

"Yes. You know, I can't sit around here for another day hearing non-stop bad news. I think I'm going to drive up. Well, get someone to drive me."

"I'll do it." Thirsk and Steadman had spoken in unison and Fitzpatrick scorned at the former.

Thirsk leant across the bed and pressed the alarm to summon a nurse and she responded promptly. "Can you get me whatever I have to sign to discharge myself? Pronto."

"Oh no you don't." Fitzpatrick was stern.

"Yes, I bloody well do. I'm coming with you. I'll concede to Steadman driving, but I'm not staying here to vegetate while all the excitement happens around me."

Amongst the copious research Harbecker had studied the previous couple of days, he had read that once the patient was over the critical period, he or she would make a quick and complete recovery, and he felt that Thirsk of all people deserved the right to apprehend the woman who had tried to kill him. He released him with a caution and his blessing.

They travelled along the M1 for mile after mile, the complex and becoming scenery reminding them of the beauty of their modest island. It was hard to believe that somewhere amongst the wilderness was a killer, intent on taking as many lives with her as possible. During one of their many conversations, the three had concluded the likelihood that Halina would poison herself before resigning to a life behind bars, but this was mere assumption. Thirsk was determined she wouldn't get off that lightly if he were to get hold of her. It was only just that she should suffer for her wrongdoings.

An incident room in Darlington Police Station had been dragged together by the few officers who weren't out and about seeking the killer, and the southerners arrived at three in the afternoon to bad news from DCI Denton; three of the hospitalised men had died from confirmed TTX poisoning. "All of the latest poison victims had frequented The Rising Sun pub in Melsonby yesterday. Cropton Brewery, who supplied the pub, has also reported that the safety seals of two of the casks delivered to the Red Lion in Barningham had been tampered with, and the contents are currently being tested." Steadman was engrossed with his Geordie accent, so much tamer than the widely recognised voice of Big Brother. "There have been no sightings.It's as if she's disappeared into thin air."

"Very poetic but hardly rational. She's out there alright and heaven knows how much poison she has left. What are you doing to find her?"

"We've got men out..."

"Waste of time, you don't have a clue where she's gone," Thirsk snapped, dismissing the officer with irritation, "you may as well put monkeys on the streets."

Denton issued a withering glare. "We have come to an *educated* conclusion that she was on Cropton Brewery's delivery truck, which delivered to a pub in Danby Wiske – where Rosie Roberts was poisoned – around the time our men were flooding the area. The next delivery was the Rising Sun in Melsonby, and the final stop-off was the Red Lion in Barningham. Ring any bells?" His tone was patronising; Thirsk had already made himself an enemy.

But the detective had never been a wilting flower. "So she either alighted at Barningham or wherever the brewery is based. Where are you searching? The Outer Hebrides, no doubt."

Denton's hatred of southerners was impacted and he seemed set to explode. "The driver was adamant that nobody was on the trailer on his return to the brewery in Pickering so our search is in and around Barningham. We currently have twenty officers deployed there..."

"Twenty! What is this, Operation Mickey Mouse?"

Denton's voice was caustic. "Barningham only has roughly sixty houses, what's your problem, officer?"

"Bloody hell, that's a cul-de-sac in the Home Counties." Thirsk was weary, the lengthy trip tiring after his hospital stay and he sighed, shunning the battle. "She won't have gone to a house, not after nearly being caught in the cancer woman's bungalow. She'll be in the countryside somewhere. Have you had birds up?"

"Birds, officer?"

"Helicopters," Fitzpatrick found the relentless and pointless bickering tiresome, "they have had two in operation at any given time. It's in your notes, Thirsk."

"Then why haven't they found her? Is a heat-seeking device," Thirsk couldn't help himself and he directed the question at Denton, "too modern for you?"

Halina woke to the sound of voices coming from outside the barn and she rolled off the makeshift bed, cowering behind the hay. She checked her watch. It was just after four and as it was light outside, it had to be the afternoon. She waited, the voices nearing.

"It's burnt out inside too. Let's just go."

"No, Gareth, just look around, it's massive. Imagine this area covered in glass with patio doors set inside. Look at the sun shining through, it would be beautiful."

"Freezing in winter, it's that remote."

The bites were itching and driving Halina mad. She sank her nails into her skin.

"That's what you wanted, secluded with no neighbours for miles, you said. And look, this corner here's perfect for a kitchen. Imagine it running... What was that?"

"Probably a rat. Forget it."

Halina was still, holding her breath, doing her best to ignore the intolerable itching. "No it wasn't." Rustling footsteps approached Halina and she gritted her teeth. Seconds later the hay was whisked aside and she was face to face with a suited and stilettoed woman, who gasped. Fight or flight. A split second decision. Halina leapt on the woman, nails and teeth sinking into her skin, knees kicking, using her sturdy body to throw the woman on the floor.

Gareth raced over, yelling at her to stop, trying to drag her from his wife but Halina was a vixen, growling menacingly as she flailed around, punching in all directions and booting anything that appeared before her. Gareth, usually placid unless provoked, managed to overwhelm her and he sat on her abdomen, panting and sweating. "What shall I do, Gareth?" Felicity had unwarranted tears streaming over her cheeks from the shock of the attack.

"Get the police. And there's some rope in the boot, get it so I can tie the mad fucking cow up."

Denton answered the call from the control room and was instantly on his feet and dragging his parka over his arms. Oblivious to the cause but noting the urgency, Thirsk, Fitzpatrick and Steadman followed suit, along with two uniforms. "A man and woman have been attacked by, their words, a wild woman at a disused barn near Newsham." They bundled through the door and ran down the stairs. "She meets the suspect's description." He grasped a young constable's shoulder. "Put a call out for all nearby officers to attend as soon as possible, but not to approach until I'm there. Ensure they know she's dangerous."

They were in Denton's car with the sirens wailing, overtaking slower vehicles and dodging through traffic jams, the Thursday night rush hour in central Darlington beginning to form. "What happened?"

"All I listened to was what I told you. We'll see when we get there."

Now on the open roads, the three southerners clutched their seats to steady themselves, Thirsk's stomach clenching as snippets of the accident flashed before his eyes.

Gareth was a large man, over six foot and bulky from the gym, but Halina continued to struggle, her feet kicking at the back of his head and her trapped arms pulling against the restraint of his legs. Felicity had collected the rope and placed it beside him, but he was sure that if he relaxed his grip, she would be on her feet and running in a flash. He'd not noticed her injury in the scuffle.

Halina's survival instincts were intense, even if it was only to give her the chance to kill herself, but the poison was in the workbag she had used as a pillow, maybe six feet away. She recalled placing the empty syringe in the pocket of her anorak and that was closer.

285

"I'm not sure if this is the right time to tell you, Gareth, but I think she's that wanted woman we saw on the news last night."

"Don't you think I fucking know that? She's right in front of me. Can't you sit on her fucking legs, or something?"

Dodging the kicks, her heels sinking in the muddy straw, Felicity stood astride Halina, forcing her legs to the floor, and she sat, pushing down heavily. Gareth's concentration had lapsed during the exchange and Halina had worked her arm free. She grasped for the jacket, into the pocket, and brandished the syringe. "This contains enough tetrodotoxin to kill you both. Get off me or I'm injecting you."

"Gareth, get off her, she's about to kill you." Felicity had already jumped up and she tried to hold Halina's hand back as she struggled to stab him with the syringe. "Give it to me, you bitch."

Felicity caught herself on the needle and she paled, jaw dropping. "Oh my God. She got me. Gareth, she got me." Halina's bluff had worked.

He crawled from her thrashing body and swiftly moved aside, and Halina dashed to Marek's bag, scooping it up and grasping for the almost empty pyramid. Again, she had a choice: run on her injury even though she knew the police were on their way, or inject the final drop now. The desire to die on her own terms raged and she backed out of the barn, eyes fixed on the terrified couple.

Agony flooded her body despite the rest, but Halina was mentally stronger than she had realised and gritted her teeth, wincing and yelping with every step she took.

The air became full with a cacophony of sirens and she could see flashing lights approaching on the road from both directions. Gareth and Felicity still clutched one another in the barn, and Halina took her chance for escape. She turned and limped as fast as possible towards a barbed-wire topped fence that led to a field, a herd of cattle in the distance.

Glancing over her shoulder, she noticed two police cars had stopped by the barn, the officers standing lamely, not approaching, but more cars were on their way. She took a foothold on the fence and pushed herself up, the barbs tearing her clothes and drawing blood, although the pain from the wounds was negated by that of her ankle. She forced herself over, struggling to unhook herself, and dropped, landing on her damaged foot. Excruciating shards of intense fire shot up her leg and through her body, rendering her useless and unwanted tears coursed down her cheeks. She lay, helplessly clutching her leg to her chest.

Gareth and Felicity stood hugging each other as one patrol car after another screeched to a halt on the weedy verge outside the barn. Rather than follow the precedent of the cars that had arrived, Denton drove around the barn, the car creaking and complaining with every bump, and he leant through the window. "Where is she?"

Gareth pointed. "In that field. Just climbed over the fence. I didn't see her running away."

Denton revved the engine, skidding in the mud before hurtling forward. They reached the fence and the four officers leapt from the car, dashing to the boundary. "She's down. I think she's injured. Let's get her out." Steadman scrabbled up the fence, trying to avoid the barbs that snagged her clothes.

Halina knew the time had come and she withdrew the pyramid, still clutching the syringe in her hand. Willing the pain away to give her the final strength she needed to take her own life, her shaking hands affecting her coordination, she stabbed repeatedly towards the cork. From nowhere, a kick knocked the syringe flying, and she angrily grabbed the foot, tipping Steadman to the ground.

"Steadman, grab her, for god's sake."

Halina followed the voice and to her surprise saw Thirsk's massive frame inelegantly clambering over the fence.She gasped. "How the fuck are you still alive?" She scrabbled in the grass for the syringe.

Thirsk could see that the fall had disabled his colleague;the battle was now between him and Halina. "Wage a war with me, you bitch, and I'm always going to win."

"Don't be so fucking sure." The final drop of poison glistened at the bottom of the pyramid, tempting yet inaccessible,

287

and she pushed at the tiny cork with her fingernail, trying to dislodge it. It stood firm and her agitation increased.

And now Thirsk was beside Halina, his sausage fingers clenched around her wrist. "You okay, Steadman?"

"Fine guv, just winded. You got her?"

"You lot need to get out of there, those cows are on the move."

Thirsk looked up and rolled his eyes. "For fuck's sake." He dropped Halina's arm and scooped Steadman from the grass, hoisting her awkwardly over his shoulder, and pushed her to Fitzpatrick and Denton's waiting arms.

Halina, aware it was her final chance, grabbed a twig and hammered at the cork, pushing until the useless wood snapped. She crashed the bottle against the ground but the soil was too soggy to offer resistance. Desperate now, she threw herself onto the grass, hands groping.Finally she noticed the syringe a couple of feet away and scrabbled towards it on her hands and knees. She stabbed through the cork, angling the bottle so the dregs pooled in a corner, suctioningthem up.

"I'll take this before I let you get any closer." Challenging, she glared in Thirsk's direction, expecting him to gallantly attempt to save her.In utter shock, she realised he had climbed back over the fence.

"You'd better get a move on, Halina, those cows are looking frisky."

She dropped the bottle, retaining the syringe, and crawled swiftly towards the fence. "You need to help me."

"You need to help her." Fitzpatrick was aghast. He whipped his jacket off and leaned over, reaching for her outstretched hand as she reached the boundary, and Denton followed suit.

"I don't need to help anybody." Thirsk stood, nonchalant, his arms crossed.

The sound of hooves on soil was thundering and Halina's eyes widened, terrified. "They're going to crush me. Get me out of here." Fitzpatrick vainly tried for her hand but the barbs tore into his chest and he backed away. Denton bravely continued. "Please. Help me."

A shot rang out and time slipped into slow motion as the cows, startled and confused, stopped charging and changed direction. Fitzpatrick reached further and Halina caught his hand, dragging herself up as he and Denton hauled her over the barbs, ripping into their flesh and hers. The three slumped down, muddy and bloody, and suddenly Thirsk was on top, wrestling with Halina as she growled and spat, the other two easing their way out of the fight, unable to comprehend what was happening.

As quickly as the scuffle had begun, it was over. Halina lay, stilled, on the soil. Beside her, Thirsk panted breathlessly, dragging himself to sit. Denton glanced at Fitzpatrick, who shrugged, and they both looked to Steadman, who was open-mouthed. "Guv?"

"She tried to inject you." Thirsk was panting.

"Who? What just happened? Is she okay?"

"She was about to inject you, sir. I stopped her." The four officers stared at Halina, prostrate and unmoving. "I don't know why she's lying there. All I did was stop her from getting you."

Steadman broke the spell, dropping to her knees and checking Halina's pulse and breathing. "She's alive."

"I don't know what just happened. Who fired a shot?"

"I didn't ask for armed response." Denton sat beside Fitzpatrick, shivering.

"Has she been shot?" Thirsk nodded to Halina, but no blood, bar from the superficial wounds caused by the barbed wire, was apparent. He reached for her hand and took the syringe from her limp fingers, holding it to the light. It was empty and he gasped. "I think she got herself in the end."

In their confusion none of the four had noticed the officers approaching and they were each helped to their feet, bombarded with questions for their welfare, assisted to the waiting cars. Two paramedics took charge of Halina as she lay, senseless.

Denton was too shaken to drive and he was taken, alongside Fitzpatrick, in a car back to the station. Another car took Steadman and Thirsk, and Halina, handcuffed to a uniformed officer, was taken by ambulance to hospital. Within half an hour nobody could have known of the drama that had recently unfolded at the serene location.

They assembled in Denton's office, each with a mug of tea supplied by worried colleagues, trying to ascertain what exactly had occurred during the skirmish. Denton put the phone down, sighing deeply. "The shot was fired by a man named Gareth Jones. He was the one who alerted us to Halina's whereabouts. He insists he has a licence, which they're checking now."

"He saved Halina's life. Those cows would have crushed her to death."

"Should have left them to it. Bloody psychopathic bitch."

"But she injected herself in the end, it seems." Fitzpatrick took a sip of his tea. "Any word from the hospital?"

DI Garner, bringing a few packaged sandwiches through, answered, "She's fine. Swearing a lot, they said, but should be ready for the cells by tomorrow."

"Fine? How can she be fine? What about the tetrodotoxin? She should be..." Thirsk jumped up, shaking Fitzpatrick by the shoulders. "Sir?"

"Get off me, you idiot."

"Oh my god." Thirsk and Fitzpatrick's eyes followed Steadman's to Denton, whose head had lolled to one side, a fine trail of dribble seeping from his mouth. "Someone get an ambulance."

The End

290

Biography

Ricki Thomas is the best-selling author of seven crime-thrillers and a keen scriptwriter for film, television, radio and stage. Her adaptation of Rod Glenn's thriller, Sinema, is set to be the biggest independent feature film made in northern England to date. She also writes articles and short stories.

From Oxford, Ricki is well-travelled and lives with her two sons and four cats in Yorkshire. She also fosters kittens for Cats Protection.

Her biggest interests are serial killers, criminal psychology, DIY and comedies.

www.rickithomas.com

9 781907 954443